THE
FACTS
OF
DEATH

Also by Raymond Benson

The James Bond Bedside Companion

Zero Minus Ten

Tomorrow Never Dies
(based upon the screenplay by Bruce Feirstein)

THE
FACTS
OF
DEATH

Raymond Benson

G. P. PUTNAM'S SONS / New York

G. P. Putnam's Sons
Publishers Since 1838
a member of
Penguin Putnam Inc.
200 Madison Avenue
New York, NY 10016

Library of Congress Cataloging-in-Publication Data

Benson, Raymond, date.
    The facts of death / Raymond Benson.
      p.   cm.
    ISBN 0-399-14405-6 (alk. paper)
    1. Bond, James (Fictitious character)—Fiction.
2. Secret service—Great Britain—Fiction.   I. Title.
PS3552.E547666F3   1998   97-52926 CIP
813'.54—dc21

Printed in the United States of America

10 9 8 7 6 5 4 3 2 1

This book is printed on acid-free paper. ∞

Book design by Gretchen Achilles

Acknowledgments

The author wishes to thank the following individuals and organizations for their help in the writing of this book.

In the U.S. and Canada—Robert Coats; Susan Elder and Invacare; Dr. Ed Fugger and Fairfax CryoBank; James Goodner; Kathleen Hamilton and Jaguar Cars; Dan Harvey; Ambassador Namik Korhan; Stephen McKelvain and Interarms; James McMahon; Page Nordstrom and Chuy's Restaurant; Charles Plante; Doug Redenius; David A. Reinhardt; Moana Re Robertson; Gary Rosenfeld; Thomas J. Savvides and National Travel Service, Inc.; Dan Workman; and my wonderful wife, Randi

In the U.K.—Carolyn Caughey; Peter Janson-Smith; Lucy Oliver; Fergus Pollock (for the Jaguar design); Corinne B. Turner; Elaine Wiltshire; and the heirs of the late Ian Lancaster Fleming

In Greece—Casino Au Mont Parnes; C. Dino Vondjidis and the Hotel Grande Bretagne

In Cyprus—Zehra Basaran; Ambassador Kenneth Brill; Louis Travel Service; Valerie Mawdsley; Christina Mita; Ashley Spencer, Captain Sean Tully and the Sovereign Base Areas Administration

A very special thanks to Panos Sambrakos, my guide in Greece, for the initial Inspiration.

CONTENTS

PROLOGUE

It was supposed to have been routine.

In early October, Carl Williams, a fifty-eight-year-old African-American, had gallbladder surgery at Veterans Hospital in Los Angeles. He needed a blood transfusion to make up for what he had lost during the procedure. He was type A, and there was plenty of that in supply. The operation was a complete success, and he spent an hour in the recovery room before being wheeled back to his bed.

Several hours later, as his wife sat by his side reading, Williams began to choke. At first, Mrs. Williams thought some juice he was sipping had gone down Carl's windpipe. She slapped his back, but it didn't seem to work. Carl's eyes started to bulge and he panicked. Mrs. Williams screamed for the nurse.

A code blue was declared. A doctor rushed in and attempted to save the patient, who went into cardiac arrest just as they were fitting an oxygen mask over his face.

Carl Williams died fifteen minutes after the onset of the symptoms. His wife was hysterical. The hospital staff were shocked and bewildered. The doctor ordered that a postmortem examination be performed.

The next morning, Mrs. Williams was sitting in her kitchen in Van Nuys, trying to make sense of what had happened to her husband. It must have been the hospital's fault. She was going to speak to a lawyer that very day.

As she stood up to pour some more coffee, she inexplicably felt her throat close. Gasping for air, she lunged for the telephone to dial 911. She managed to get through, but could barely speak into the receiver to tell them where to send the ambulance.

When the paramedics arrived, she was dead.

Halfway across the metropolis of Los Angeles, in Culver City, the nurse who had first attended to Carl Williams's emergency also died of respiratory failure and cardiac arrest as she was unloading groceries from the back of her car. Fifteen minutes later, in Pasadena, the doctor who had rushed into the room to help the nurse collapsed of the same ailment. He had been on the fourth hole of his favorite golf course.

By the end of the day, eight more people who had come into contact with Carl Williams were dead.

The next day there were several more.

By the third week of October, health officials realized they had a crisis on their hands. Although they tried to keep the mysterious epidemic a secret, news leaked out and was reported in the *Los Angeles Times*. A small story ran in the *Times*, but few people in London paid much attention to it.

By the end of October, thirty-three people had died. Health officials were stumped and scared.

Halfway around the world, in Tokyo, Hiroshi Nagawa received his October injection. It was his monthly shot of blood to help combat the leukemia that he had contracted five months ago. Doctors were hopeful that the transfusions would prolong his life at least another six months. Hiroshi was optimistic, for he felt much better every time he got a shot.

Hiroshi went from the doctor's office to his job as a computer programmer. The day went well, but he began to feel a little dizzy as he got on the underground train to go home. In the middle of the packed train, Hiroshi suddenly felt as if his esophagus had been clamped with a vise. Thankfully, the train was just pulling into a station. Choking horribly, he pushed his way through the crowd of people to the opening doors. He stumbled out onto the platform and collapsed a few feet away from the train.

Everyone in the subway car with Hiroshi that afternoon was concerned, but they went about their business and let the medics handle the situation. Little did they know that in twenty-four hours, they too would be in the morgue.

►1.
THE SMELL OF DEATH

The tableau of pain and suffering might have been a freeze-frame from a macabre dance of death.

The twelve men—three corporals and nine privates—were sprawled about in various positions in the barracks room. They were fully dressed. One man was half on, half off a cot. Three were piled together, clutching one another in a final embrace. All of them had vomited and bled from the nose and mouth. They had clearly experienced a horrible death.

The team of four investigators dressed in protective clothing made a thorough search of the premises. Each wore a Willson AR 1700 full-face gas mask with respirator and "in-cheek" filters, airtight goggles, a hood, an impermeable butyl rubber suit, eighteen-gauge rubber gloves and boots. Every inch of skin was covered. The investigators were thankful that the gas masks blocked out the stench of death. They were sweating profusely beneath the suits, for in late October, it was still hot in southern Cyprus.

James Bond peered through the eyepieces of his gas mask, taking in every detail. Twelve soldiers had been killed by an as yet unknown chemical agent, possibly administered through the air ducts. It seemed the only possible explanation. Equally disturbing was the number "3" painted in red on the wall of the room. Beneath the number, on the floor, was a six-inch-high alabaster statuette of the ancient Greek god Poseidon.

Bond watched the two British SAS investigators do their work and then followed them outside into the sun. One investigator, the sole Greek in the team, remained inside to finish making notes and to take photographs.

The men removed their gas masks and hoods. The temperature was already eighty-five degrees. It would have been a good day for a swim.

The British Sovereign Base Areas in the Republic of Cyprus cover approximately three percent of the island's land area. The Western Sovereign Base Area, which consists of the Episkopi Garrison buildings and the Akrotiri RAF airfield, and the Eastern Sovereign Base Area—the garrison at Dhekelia—remained under British jurisdiction when the Treaty of Establishment created the independent Republic of Cyprus in 1960. Prior to that time, Cyprus had been a British crown colony.

Bond had been dispatched to Cyprus shortly after midnight and had been shuttled to Akrotiri by a Royal Navy aircraft. He had been met by Captain Sean Tully and taken directly to Episkopi, the area which housed the Sovereign Base Areas Administration and the headquarters of the British Forces Cyprus. James Bond always thought the island was a lovely place, with its beautiful beaches, its rolling hills in the north, its near-perfect climate, and its quaint and colorful cities. It was unfortunate that Cyprus had such a turbulent recent history.

It was an unnamed British officer who had drawn a line with a green marker across the map in 1963, when tensions between the Greek and Turkish Cypriots culminated in violence. The United Nations moved in shortly thereafter in an attempt to keep the peace along the aptly named Green Line. Eleven years later, as a result of an attempted coup by the Greek government and the Turkish invasion of the northern part of the island in reaction to that attempt, the island was divided not just by a symbolic Green Line, but by a physical and political one. Today, Her Majesty's Government, along with the UN, recognizes only the government of the Republic of Cyprus, which administers the southern two thirds of the island. The so-called Turkish Republic of Northern Cyprus, which illegally occupies the northeast third of the island, is not recognized by any nation other than Turkey. The situation has been a source of tension, mistrust, and conflict for over twenty years.

The current disaster had struck in a barracks near the Episkopi helicopter landing site. Bond had been joined by two SAS forensic identification specialists from London and, at the last minute, by a member of the Greek Secret Service. He was a bit puzzled by the presence of the Greek agent, who was still inside the barracks taking notes. M had advised him that a Greek agent would be contacting him in Episkopi, but this was obviously a British matter, as it involved British military personnel and occurred on territory governed by neither the Republic of Cyprus nor Greece.

Winninger, one of the London investigators, wiped the sweat from his brow and asked, "Commander Bond, do you have any preliminary impressions?"

"It was some kind of aerosol agent, I would imagine," Bond said. "The number on the wall and the little statue are some kind of signature that the killer or killers left behind. I understand there was something similar at Dhekelia two days ago."

"Right," the second man, Ashcraft, said. "A small squad of men was killed by a nerve toxin called sarin. The same stuff that was used in a Japanese underground train recently by a religious fanatic."

Winninger added, "And then there was poor Whitten two days before that."

Bond nodded. He had been briefed. Christopher Whitten had been an MI6 operative in Athens. His body had been found by the Greek police sprawled on the steps of the Temple of Hephaisteion in the Ancient Agora near the Acropolis. He had died by an as yet unidentified poison, but Forensic Toxicology believed the cause of death to have been ricin, a deadly chemical derived from the simple castor bean plant.

In all three cases, the perpetrators had left a number painted near the body or bodies. The number "1" had been scrawled on a rock by Whitten's head. The number "2" had been painted on the wall of the Dhekelia barracks where the small squad of soldiers died the other day. A similarity to the Episkopi incident was that another small statuette of a Greek god was left at the Dhekelia scene.

Ashcraft said, "And now we have the third attack in four days. Looks like we've got a serial terrorist or something. . . . One complete section and half of another from the platoon were killed. That's three corporals and nine privates—three fire teams. It happened late last night after they had come in from drill. What do you make of the condition of the bodies, Ray?"

Winninger rubbed his chin. "From the amount of bleeding the victims experienced—from nearly every orifice of their bodies—it appears to be Tricotheneces. Wouldn't you agree?"

"Yes," Ashcraft said. "We'll have to get the lab to verify, of course.

Terrible way to go." He turned to Bond. "Tricotheneces is a poison that causes radical bleeding from the eyes, ears, and mouth, internal bleeding, burns, convulsion and death—all within half an hour."

Bond was familiar with the various types of chemicals used in terrorist attacks and in warfare.

"Is it my imagination, or can I smell their bodies from out here?" Winninger asked.

The Greek agent emerged from the barracks, still wearing the gas mask and protective hood. Now out in the fresh air, the gas mask and coverings were quickly removed, revealing a head of long, black hair. She had Mediterranean features—tan skin, thick eyebrows, brown eyes, full lips, a large but not unattractive nose, and a long neck. She was unusually tall—nearly six feet. Bond and the other two men were surprised. They hadn't realized the agent was a woman when she walked into the barracks after them. She hadn't spoken and the protective uniform covered any hint of female shape.

"Are you from the NIS? You're Mirakos?" Winninger asked.

"That's right," she said. "Niki Mirakos of the Greek National Intelligence Service." She pronounced her first name "Nee-kee."

"What are you doing here, exactly?" Ashcraft asked. "If you don't mind my asking."

"I'm investigating these terrorist attacks, just as you are," she said with a look of disdain. "Your man Whitten was found in a public area of Athens—in a national park that was a holy place for the ancient Greeks, no less. These attacks are not random. There is a purpose behind them. My government has an interest in what has happened."

"Maybe you can fill us in on your hypothesis, then?" Ashcraft said.

"Later," she said. "I want to get out of these hot clothes and take a shower." She turned to Bond. "You're 007, aren't you?"

Bond held out his hand. "Bond," he said. "James Bond."

"We're supposed to have a little talk," she said. She glanced at the two other officers and added, "Alone."

Bond nodded. He led her away from the other two toward the building in the barracks that had been assigned to them as temporary quarters. As they walked, she unzipped her coveralls, revealing a white T-shirt soaked in sweat. Her full breasts were perfectly molded into the shirt. Bond couldn't help stealing a glance or two as they walked. She wasn't "beautiful" in the cover girl sense, but she exhibited an air of sensuality that made her extremely attractive.

"We believe this to be the work of terrorists specializing in chemical and biological weaponry," she said. "The targets thus far have been British, but we believe there is something behind the attacks which will ultimately involve Greece." She had a fairly thick accent, but her English was very good. Although most people under the age of forty in Greece have learned English, very few practice it on a daily basis.

"Do you have any idea who these people are?"

"No, and that's part of the problem. We're still investigating the death of your man Whitten, with the cooperation of your government, of course."

"Is there a significance in the site where the body was dumped?" he asked.

"Perhaps. The Ancient Agora was the Athenian marketplace. You know about the coin?"

Bond nodded. "Whitten had an ancient Greek coin in his mouth."

Niki continued, "That's right. The ancient Greeks believed that the dead should have a coin handy to give to Charon, the boatman on the River Styx, so that he could ferry them across the river to Hades. A dead person was usually buried with a coin in their mouth to use as fare."

"So the body placement, the coin, the number . . . are all symbolic," Bond said.

"Of what?" she said. "If we can find the connection between that murder and the incidents here on Cyprus, it would be a big help."

"The statuettes could be a substitute for the temple," Bond said. "Ideally, maybe the killers wanted to send some sort of message linking the deaths to ancient Greece. That's why Whitten's body was dropped where it was. Since they couldn't do that here on Cyprus, maybe the statuettes are supposed to symbolize the equivalent. Whatever that is."

"That's an interesting point, Mr. Bond," Niki said. "The statuette at Dhekelia was that of Hera, the queen of the gods. This one was Poseidon. I wonder if that means anything."

"I'm no ancient Greek scholar," Bond said, "but I do know that Hera was a vengeful, jealous god."

"What do you make of the numbers?"

Bond shrugged. "It's a definite indication that these three acts were committed by the same group . . . and that there will probably be more."

They had now reached two three-story white buildings of brick and plaster, some two hundred meters from the Helicopter Landing Site. The orange wind sock could be clearly seen blowing in the wind. The sound of an approaching Westland Wessex Mark II search-and-rescue helicopter was growing louder. They glanced up toward the sun and saw it descending from the sky, its silhouette resembling a humpback whale.

"I'm going to take a shower," Niki said. She looked at her watch. It was just after noon. "Let's meet in the mess at one? We can compare notes before we meet the base personnel at two. They will want answers."

"Fine," Bond said. "I'll take a shower too. Perhaps we can go for a swim after the debriefing? And then maybe dinner?"

"You work fast, Mr. Bond," she said with a slight smile.

He shrugged. "I leave in the morning."

"We'll see," she said as they separated. Bond went up to the second floor of one building, normally occupied by a platoon. As he passed the showers, he noticed a sign on the door proclaiming that the plumbing was out of order. Bond turned and shouted to Niki, who was entering the barracks across the road.

"I need to use one of your showers! Mine are out!"

Niki waved and gestured for him to come over.

Bond had been assigned a room that was currently vacant, although bits of the kit of three soldiers were still there. The rooms were all alike—sparsely furnished with three cots, three cupboards, a sink, a ceiling fan, two strips of fluorescent lights, and a dozen posters on the walls of various popular pinup celebrities. He grabbed his open carry-on bag and made his way across the road to Niki's barracks. Bare-shouldered, she stuck her head out of her door as he passed by, and said, "You can use the next room. The showers are a few doors down. You go first, I can wait."

"Why not join me? We could do our part in conserving Cyprus's precious water supply."

The door shut in his face.

Bond entered the room, removed his clothes, and threw his bag on one of the cots. He hadn't brought much with him, as he knew that he would be on a plane back to London in the morning. As an afterthought, he had thrown in his swimming trunks and a diving utility belt that Q Branch supplied to agents normally working near water. Perhaps there really would be some time for that swim with the lovely Niki Mirakos. . . .

Bond wrapped a towel around his waist and walked out of the room to the showers.

There were five shower stalls, two bathtubs and toilets. No one else was around. Bond dropped the towel and stepped into one of the stalls. He twisted the knob and turned on the hot water. It got warm very quickly and he felt the spray begin to wash away the sweat. As he reached for the soap the water suddenly turned cold. He ducked back and held his hand under the spray. Suddenly, the water cut off. In a few seconds, warm water burst out of the spigot. Bond chalked it up to poor plumbing on a military base and moved under the spray once again. When the water turned cold a second time, he became suspicious and stepped out of the stall. Immediately the smell of ammonia enveloped the room. Smoke funneled out of the stall as some kind of abrasive chemical poured onto the tiles on the floor.

Bond ran out of the room naked. He ducked into his temporary quarters, taking a few seconds to grab his swimming trunks and slip them on. He grasped the utility belt, which also held his new Walther P99 in a waterproof holster, and ran back outside. Niki, a towel wrapped around her shapely body, stepped out of her room in time to see him leap over the railing and gracefully land on the grass below in his bare feet. A couple of perplexed privates in uniform were standing beside a jeep watching him.

Paying no attention to them, Bond ran around the building in time to see a figure dressed in camouflage fatigues running away from the barracks toward the helicopter landing site. The Wessex that had landed earlier was still there, its rotor blades spinning. Bond took off after the running figure, who was wearing a gas mask and protective hood.

The figure made it to the Wessex and climbed into the open door. The helicopter immediately began to rise just as Bond made it to the HLS. He leaped forward and just managed to grab hold of the trooping step, the metal attachment used as an extra step to assist soldiers entering or leaving the aircraft. The Wessex continued to rise, with Bond hanging on for dear life. Within moments, they were flying over the base toward the Mediterranean.

The door was still open, and Bond could see two camouflaged figures from his position. One was holding a gun to the pilot's head. The aircraft had been hijacked!

The gas-masked figure he had seen earlier leaned out of the door and saw Bond hanging on to the trooping step. He pulled a large knife from a sheath, then squatted down closer to the floor of the aircraft. Holding on to the inside of the cabin with one hand, the figure leaned out with the knife in the other. He swung the knife across Bond's knuckles, slicing the skin. Bond winced with pain but forced himself to hang on. The helicopter was a good two hundred feet above the ground. He would surely fall to his death if he let go. The assassin leaned out again, but this time Bond was ready. As the knife swung, Bond lifted one hand off the trooping step and grasped the piece of metal beneath the step that fastened onto the helicopter. It wasn't as good a handhold as the step itself, but it was shielded from the assassin's knife. He then inched out onto the wheel axle and wrapped his legs around it. The killer would have to venture out of the aircraft to get him now.

As the helicopter flew over the RAF airfield at Akrotiri, the pilot was ordered to maneuver the vehicle wildly in an attempt to throw Bond off. The pain was almost unbearable, and the blood from the cuts dripped onto his face. But he hung on tightly. If only he could manage to keep hold until they got over the water . . .

The figure leaned out of the door again, this time holding an automatic pistol—a Daewoo, Bond thought. Bond swung his body up under the helicopter as the assassin fired at him. The bullets whizzed past him as he swung back and forth. Fortunately, the jerking movement of the helicopter spoiled the man's aim and he shouted angrily back at the pilot.

The helicopter was now over the Mediterranean, flying south. The water below was choppy and rough.

The assassin did what Bond was afraid he might do: he crawled out onto the trooping step. Now that the chopper was flying level, Bond could be shot at point-blank range. He couldn't see the assassin's face behind the gas mask, but he knew the man was smiling in triumph. The assassin raised the pistol and pointed it at Bond's head.

Bond used all of his strength to swing back underneath the trooping step and used the momentum to push himself away from the helicopter. In midair, he somersaulted so that his body ended up in the diving position. He heard the shot ring out above him as he soared down to the sea. The impact might have killed an ordinary man, but Bond's graceful Olympic-style dive smoothly cut through the surface of the water.

He swam up for air and saw the Wessex continuing its trek southward. He looked at the shore, which was at least a mile away. Could he swim back? The water was very rough. It would be a challenge for even the strongest of swimmers. It was lucky that he had thought to take the utility belt.

While treading water, Bond unzipped the belt and removed two coiled rubber items which, when shaken, opened out to their proper size. They were portable flippers. He quickly placed them on his feet. Next, Bond removed a small can the size of a shaving cream container. Two long elastic bands allowed him to strap the can onto his back. A flexible tube uncoiled from the top of the can, and he stuck the end in his mouth. The can was a ten-minute version of an aqualung, which would be helpful in swimming through the choppy water. He hoped that the current wasn't so strong that he couldn't make headway toward shore.

Bond began the slow crawl toward land, thankful that he had brushed up on his diving skills a couple of weeks ago. He was also grateful that Major Boothroyd was indeed a genius.

He fought the sea as best he could, but it was a case of two steps forward, one step back. Still, he was an expert swimmer and extremely fit. An ordinary man might have drowned by now. Five minutes later, Bond estimated that he was about half a mile from shore. The air would last him another five minutes and then he would have to depend on short, deep breaths stolen from the choppy surface.

The sound of another helicopter grew nearer and its shadow

blocked out the sun. Bond stopped swimming and treaded water. A Gazelle was directly above him, and a rope ladder was being lowered to him. He took hold of it and swiftly climbed up into the small, round helicopter. To his surprise, it was piloted by none other than Niki Mirakos. An RAF airman had manned the ladder.

"What kept you?" Bond asked.

"You said you wanted to go swimming!" Niki shouted over the noise. "I wanted to make sure you had a little time to enjoy yourself."

The Gazelle pulled away toward the shore and back to Episkopi, passing two more Wessex helicopters heading out to sea in pursuit of the hijacked aircraft.

Back at the base, Bond and Niki learned that whoever it was wearing the gas mask had managed to attach a tank of cyanogen chloride to the water line. The chemical was classified as a "blood agent" because it attacked blood cells and spread quickly throughout the body. If it had made contact with Bond's skin, he would have been a dead man. Investigators believed that this same assassin was responsible for the attack on the fire teams. More disturbing was that it was a blatant attempt on Niki Mirakos's life.

That evening, the search-and-rescue personnel made their reports. The hijacked Wessex was found abandoned, floating in the sea about a hundred miles south of Cyprus. The saltwater flotation cans had been activated, allowing the helicopter to land on the water safely. The pilot's body was found on board. He had been shot in the back of the head. It was surmised that the killer and his accomplice had somehow hijacked the craft and forced the pilot to fly them in and out of the base. It must have been met by a boat or a seaplane, for there was no trace of them.

After the briefing, Bond and Niki rode in her rented Honda Civic into town. They found a loud, festive restaurant, but managed to be seated at a small table for two in the back, away from the noise.

"How do you feel?" she asked. The candle on the table cast a glow across her bronze face.

"That fight with the sea today exhausted me, but otherwise I couldn't be better," Bond said. "I'm hungry, how about you?"

"Famished."

They shared a Cypriot mixed grill—ham, sausage, and beef burgers—and *halloumi,* a chewy cheese, all grilled over charcoal. The house wine was Ambelida, a dry, light wine made from the Xynistri white grape.

"Why is it that Cypriot cuisine normally consists of an enormous amount of meat?" Bond asked.

Niki laughed. "I don't know. We eat a lot of meat in Greece too, but not this much. Maybe it's the reason for the high level of testosterone on this island."

"Why do you think someone tried to kill you in the shower, Niki? That dirty trick was meant for you," he said.

"I don't have a clue. Someone obviously knew I would come to investigate. I've been on this case since they found your man Whitten. Maybe whoever's responsible knew that. Don't worry, I can take care of myself."

"I'm sure you can. When do you go back?"

"Tomorrow morning, same as you," she said.

Bond settled the bill, even though she wanted to pay for her own meal. In the car on the way back to the base, he asked her if they would see each other again. She nodded.

"My middle name is Cassandra," she said. "Believe it or not, I think I've always had the ability to see into people's hearts, and sometimes into the future."

"Oh, really?" Bond asked, smiling. "And what does the future hold for us?"

"We'll see each other again at least once," she said as they pulled into the front gate of the base.

After saying goodnight, he returned to his barracks room and slipped under the blanket of one of the cots. He was about to drift off to sleep when a knock at the door jarred him awake. "Come in," he said.

Niki Mirakos, still wearing civilian clothes, stepped into the dark room. "I told you we'd see each other at least one more time. Besides, I wanted to make sure you were all right. You must be very sore after that fall into the sea."

She moved closer to him. He sat up in the bed, about to protest, but she gently pushed him back down. She turned him onto his stomach and began to massage his broad shoulders.

"This will work out all the . . . uhm, how do you say in English . . . kinkies?" she asked.

Bond turned over onto his back and pulled her down on top of him. "The word is 'kinks,' " he said, chuckling. "But I'll be happy to show you what 'kinky' means. . . ."

With that, his mouth met hers and she moaned aloud.

▶2.
A DAY IN THE CITY

The beginning of November brought a bone-chilling rain to London, and it looked as if winter would come very early this year. Gray days always made James Bond feel a little melancholy himself. He stood at the bay window of the sitting room in his flat off the King's Road in Chelsea, looking out at the square of plane trees that occupied the center of his street. The trees had lost their leaves, which made the scene even more dreary. If he hadn't been on call, Bond would have flown to Jamaica to spend a few days at Shamelady, his recently purchased holiday home on the north shore of the island. After returning from Cyprus, however, M had given him strict orders to remain on call. The business of the terrorist attacks was far from over.

"Yer watchin' the time—sir?" came the familiar mother hen voice behind him. May, his elderly Scottish housekeeper, was his cook, maid, and alarm clock. The way she pronounced "sir" came out as "suh." Apart from Bond, she would never call anyone else "sir" except for royalty and men of the cloth.

"Yes, May," Bond said. "I won't be late. I'm not expected for another hour or so."

May gave her obligatory "Tsk . . . tsk . . . tsk . . ." and said, "I don't like to see you this way—sir. Yer hardly touched your breakfast. 'Tisn't like you."

She was right. Bond felt the malaise that never failed to plague him when he was "on call" or between assignments. He always became restless and bored.

Bond sighed heavily and moved away from the window. He sat down at the ornate Empire desk and stared at the room around him. The white and gold Cole wallpaper was terribly out of date, but he didn't care. He hadn't changed a single thing in his converted Regency flat since he moved in many years ago. He disliked change, which was one of the main reasons he had remained a widower since the death of his only bride.

Bond managed a smile when he reflected back to an evening he'd had a few weeks ago at his favorite club, Blades. He'd been having drinks with Sir James Molony, the Service's staff neurologist, who jokingly accused Bond of being so obsessive about details and set in his ways that he walked a thin line between sanity and sociopathy.

"Look at you, James!" Molony had said. "You were *painfully* specific about how you wanted that martini made. *No one* does that except someone who's obsessed with minutiae. You don't want just any martini, you want *your* martini! A Bic lighter won't do for you! It's got to be a Ronson lighter and nothing else! You've got to have your tobacco made specially for you, because you have to smoke *your* cigarettes! I wouldn't be surprised if you're wearing the same kind of underwear you wore as a boy."

"As a matter of fact, Sir James, I am," Bond replied. "And if you get any more personal than that, I'll have to ask you to step outside."

Molony chuckled and shook his head. "It's all right, James." He finished his drink and said, "Given the life you've led and the work you do for our good government . . . it's a small wonder you're not already in the madhouse. Whatever it takes to keep you on this side of the line, then so be it."

Bond was brought back to the present when May entered the room with a cup of *his* favorite strong coffee from De Bry in New Oxford Street. "I brought you somethin' to perk you up—sir," she said.

"Thank you, May, you're a dear," he said. He took the cup and set it down in front of him. He liked *his* coffee black, with no sugar.

Bond stared at the pile of mail he needed to go through. It was one of his least favored activities. May stood at the doorway watching him with concern. Bond looked up at her. "What is it?"

"Tsk . . . tsk . . . tsk . . ." was all she said; then she turned and left the room.

Bond took a sip of the coffee and felt it warm him up a little. The piece of correspondence now on the top of the pile had somehow got buried under other papers when it arrived. It was an invitation to a dinner party at the home of Sir Miles Messervy, the former M. The party was that night, to be held at Quarterdeck, his home near Windsor Great Park. Bond supposed he would go, although it would be full of people he really didn't want to meet. There would be the usual crowd of Sir Miles's parliamentary friends, retired Royal Navy officers and their wives, and colleagues from SIS whom he saw every day anyway, but he did enjoy seeing his old boss from time to time. Since Sir Miles's retirement as M, he and Bond had developed even more of a mentor-pupil relationship than they had had when the old man was in charge. A more apt description was perhaps that of a father-son relationship, and it had lasted.

Bond picked up the phone and called Quarterdeck. He spoke to Davison, Sir Miles's butler and manservant, and said he hoped he could still RSVP. Davison replied that Sir Miles would be very happy to hear that Bond was coming.

An hour later, Bond drove his ageing but reliable Bentley Turbo R onto the Embankment, then to the gaudy building by the Thames that housed SIS headquarters. Stepping out of the lift onto the fourth floor, he was greeted by Helena Marksbury, his attractive personal assistant. Her warm smile and sparkling large green eyes never failed to cheer him up, even when he was in the darkest of moods. She had recently cut her silky brown hair in a pageboy style that some of the newer fashion models seemed to favor. Bond also found her to be highly intelligent, a hard worker, and easygoing—all of which made her that much more desirable.

"Good afternoon, James," she said.

"Helena, you're looking lovely," he said with a nod.

"James, if you smiled when you said that, I might believe you."

Bond managed to form his normally cruel mouth into a grin. "I never lie to women, Helena, you should know that by now."

"Of *course* you don't, James . . ." She quickly changed the subject. "There's a new file on your desk concerning the incidents in Cyprus, and M would like to see you in an hour."

Bond smiled, nodded, then turned and walked toward his private office.

The file on his desk contained a number of reports—the forensic findings from the murder sites in Cyprus and Athens, analyses of the chemical weapons used in the attacks, and various other documents.

Bond sat down and studied each report, losing himself in the work so that he might climb out of the dark hole he was in.

For lack of a better term, the reports now referred to the perpetrators as the "Number Killer" because of the numerals left at the sites. The Number Killer was believed to be several individuals—a team of terrorists—although evidence seemed to indicate that only one person was involved in the actual attacks. Because no communication from the perpetrators had been received, the motives were still unclear. At present, there was no connection between the victims except that two were groups of military personnel on Cyprus. Since three different chemical weapons were used in the attacks, investigators speculated that the terrorists were receiving their supplies from a separate and sophisticated source. In other words, it was unlikely that a Middle Eastern or Mediterranean terrorist group would have the means to manufacture so many different types of chemical weapons. Bond doubted the reasoning behind that report. He believed that there were groups entirely capable of creating such deadly materials. Recipes were widely available in books sold in alternative bookstores and even on the Internet.

Another document listed known terrorist groups around the world and their bases of operation. Among these were the ones already in the headlines, such as the Islamic militant groups working out of the Middle East, the Aryan Nation factions in the northwestern United States, the IRA, and the Weathermen. Some of the names Bond wasn't familiar with, such as the Suppliers, an American outfit working out of the southwestern U.S. Bond made a point to study the lists of lesser-known groups, especially those working out of Europe.

The biggest question was—what were these people after?

"I assume you've read all the relevant reports, 007?" M asked, swiveling around in her chair to face him.

"Yes, ma'am. I can't say they've added to what I already knew."

M made a gesture with her eyebrows as if to say, "Right, of course not." Since she took over as the head of SIS, James Bond's relationship with his boss had not always been comfortable. The woman had respect for the man who some said was her top agent, but he always felt she saw him as a loose cannon. She was also more vocal than her predecessor had been in criticizing Bond's womanizing and sometimes unorthodox methods of working. Still, 007 had proved his worth to her more than once, and she had learned quickly that she had to put up with his lifestyle if she wanted to keep him.

"All right, then," she said. "What's your guess about the terrorists?"

"There's not a lot to go on, really," he replied. "Without knowing their motives, it's difficult to analyze what it's all about. I'll admit I'm baffled by the whole affair."

"We're having some professional profiles drawn up based on the crime scene evidence. There's something you don't know about our man Whitten. He was working on something top-secret."

"Oh?"

"As you know, he was a field agent temporarily working out of Station G. About six months ago, the Athens police confiscated two suitcases full of chemical weapons at the airport. They were unclaimed, and they were never traced to their rightful owners. You'll never guess what the toxins were smuggled in."

"Tell me."

"Sperm," she said with a straight face. "Frozen sperm. Vials of frozen sperm. They were in refrigerated cartons—very sophisticated, with timers and locks. Acting on a tip, Whitten had learned of some sort of pipeline of chemicals being shipped to Athens from London. This one, supposedly a second shipment, was confiscated, and Whitten was about to pin down exactly where it had come from. He believed the shipments did not originate in London. That was on the day before his death."

"Then Whitten's murder may have been nothing more than an act to silence him."

"Correct. Perhaps he learned more than our terrorist friends wanted him to know. His office and files have been thoroughly searched. So far nothing has turned up."

"Any more news on the Cyprus incidents?"

"Only that there was hell to pay in their security areas. How the assassin and the accomplice hijacked a helicopter is a mystery. There may have been an insider. The Greek Secret Service are very concerned, because an eyewitness described the man holding a gun to the pilot's head as 'Greek-looking.' How did you get on with their agent, by the way?"

At first Bond didn't know who M was talking about. "Ma'am?"

"Mirakos. That was her name, wasn't it?"

"Oh, right. She seemed very . . . capable, ma'am."

"Hmpf." M could see right through him.

"Other than the possibility of the hijacker being Greek, why are the Greeks so concerned? These were our people."

"Cyprus is a very touchy issue with them. You're aware of all the trouble that island has gone through. When we allowed the Cypriots to form their own country in 1960, it opened up a can of worms. There aren't many races who hate each other more than the Greeks and Turks. It's gone on forever, and it's one of those things that *will* go on forever, I'm afraid. It's as bad as Northern Ireland, or Israel and the Arab states."

"Do you think the attacks on our troops have something to do with the Cyprus problem?" Bond asked.

"Yes, I do," she said. "The Cypriots look at our presence there with disdain. In my opinion, the Greek Cypriots would like to see us out of there, although if it came down to a matter of life or death—such as a further Turkish invasion—then I'm sure they would reverse their stance and be grateful we were there to help. On the other hand, I have a feeling that Turkey doesn't mind our being there. They want to propagate the notion to the world that they are peace-loving and cooperative."

"So you think that Greek Cypriots are behind this?"

"If the terrorists aren't Cypriots or Greek nationalists, then their sympathies lie with that side. I think the attacks on our bases were meant to be warnings of some kind."

"The numbers would indicate that there will be more attacks," Bond said.

"It will be interesting to see what the next target or targets are."

"What would you like me to do, ma'am?"

"Nothing at the moment except study everything you can get your hands on about terrorist factions in Europe and the Middle East. Brush up on the history of Greece, Turkey, and Cyprus. I'm afraid we haven't much to go on until they strike again. Just be where I can find you should I need you in a hurry. Don't go running off."

"Of course not."

"Good. That's all, 007."

He stood up to leave and she asked, "Will I see you tonight at Sir Miles's dinner party?"

"I thought I might make an appearance," he said.

"There's someone I'll want you to meet," she said. "Until tonight then."

Did he detect a hint of excitement in her clear blue eyes? If he wasn't mistaken, M had just betrayed the fact that she would be accompanied by a man. Interesting . . .

Bond stepped out of the office and caught the ever faithful Miss Moneypenny at the filing cabinet.

"Penny?"

"Yes, James?"

"M's divorced, isn't she?"

"Yes. Why do you ask?"

"Just wondering."

"James, really. Now I *know* she's not your type."

Bond leaned in to kiss Moneypenny's cheek. "Of course not. You know the truth, as always." He opened the door and turned back to her. She was looking at him expectantly. "I don't have a type," he said as he closed the door.

Major Boothroyd lit the cigarette, puffed once or twice, then threw it as far as he could across the room. The cigarette landed in a pile of hay in the middle of a fireproof container. The hay burst into flames. Technicians immediately rushed in with fire extinguishers to put it out. Boothroyd coughed and gasped for air.

"I don't know how you can smoke those things, 007," he said, wheezing. "Didn't you cough the first time you inhaled tobacco smoke?"

"I'm sure I did. I really don't remember," Bond said.

"Well, it's the body's natural way of warning you to stay away! I need a glass of water . . . "

The major had been with SIS longer than Bond could remember.

Boothroyd had run Q Branch with a keen eye for detail and the imagination of a science fiction author. His knowledge of weaponry and technical devices was unmatched. Bond enjoyed teasing him, but the truth was that Boothroyd would always have Bond's respect.

"How are you getting on with the P99?" Boothroyd asked.

"It's quite an improvement, I must admit," Bond said. "I like the way I can operate the magazine release, the decocker, or the trigger without changing the position of the gun in my hand."

"Yes, Walther has certainly stepped up the technology," Boothroyd added. "I like the way the magazine release is ambidextrous and can be operated with the thumb or index finger."

The Walther P99 9mm Parabellum was a new gun, advertised by Carl Walther GMBH as the gun "designed for the next century." It was a hammerless pistol with single and double action, developed in strict conformity with the technical list of requirements of the German police. With a high-quality polymer used for the frame and other parts, the weight of the gun with an empty magazine was only 700g. The steel-sheet magazine had a capacity of sixteen rounds, with an additional round in the chamber. A very special advantage of the P99 was the ability to fire more rapidly than most other semiautomatic pistols. Due to the missing hammer, the barrel was positioned low over the hand, which reduced recoil. Bond loved the new gun, but he still preferred to carry the thinner PPK in his shoulder holster. He used the P99 when he didn't need to conceal the weapon under clothing.

"How's the new car coming along?" Bond asked.

"It's nearly finished. Come and have a look." Boothroyd led Bond into another area of the laboratory. The Jaguar XK8 coupe sat on a platform as technicians made last-minute modifications to it. It had a solid blue base paint with a zinc coating, giving it a sheen that was undeniably glamorous. Bond had been wary of the car's future when Ford took Jaguar under its wing, but the move proved to be a wise one. While it remained a British-made and -designed car, Jaguar adapted Ford's maintenance program. This improved its service reliability immensely in other countries, particularly the U.S.

Bond had given the XK8 a test drive when they first hit the market in 1996 and he fell in love with it, but the price tag had prevented him from purchasing one himself. When he learned that Q Branch had bought a coupe for company use, 007 took an active interest in it. For once, he made the time to collaborate with Major Boothroyd on the features it would have, something that was unprecedented.

The vital thing was the engine, a completely new four-liter V-8 of advanced specification that set it apart from Ford and maintained Jaguar's individuality. The AJ V-8 four-valve-per-cylinder engine normally had a maximum output of 290 horsepower at 6,100 rpm and 284 foot pounds of torque at 4,200 rpm. It was the first V-8 engine designed by Jaguar. Major Boothroyd, however, commissioned Jaguar's Special Vehicle Operations unit to improve the car's power to do 400 bhp. The rev limiter, which would otherwise limit top speed to a paltry 155 miles per hour, was removed. The car was equipped with a Z 5HP24 automatic transmission, which offered five forward gear ratios to optimize performance. First through fourth gears were selected for sharp response and effortless acceleration, while fifth was an overdrive ratio for fuel economy. The transmission's versatility began with two driver-selectable gear modes, Sport and Normal. Switching into Sport mode timed the gear changes for peak response. Bond had never cared for automatic transmissions, but the XK8 offered something different.

"I'm sorry to say that M has decided that you are to be the lucky man to test-drive it in the field," Boothroyd said. "It was nice knowing this car. I'm sure I'll never see it again."

"Bollocks, Major," Bond said. "I'm in love with this car. I promise I'll take good care of it. When can I have it?"

"It'll be ready in a day or two. I don't know where you'll be, but I'll have it shipped to you. We want to find out how the car handles in extreme conditions."

"So you're giving it to me."

"Right."

"I'm glad to hear that everyone thinks so highly of me."

"Now pay attention, 007," Boothroyd said, stepping up to the car and tapping the hood. "We've coated the car with chobam armor, which is impenetrable. We use it with reactive skins that explode when they're hit. This deflects the bullets. It's a case of an equal and opposite force negating the energy of the bullet."

"Naturally," Bond said.

"Not only that," Boothroyd said, very proud of himself, "the metal is self-healing. On being pierced, the skin can heal itself by virtue of viscous fluid."

"Remarkable."

"We've also used certain paints that have electrically sensitive pigments which will change color. Used in conjunction with the electronically controlled standard interchangeable license plate, the car can change identity a number of times.

"Now, as you know, the Jaguar is fitted with an intelligent automatic gearbox, and gears are changed by means of a combined manual and automatic five-speed adaptive system through a 'J' gate mechanism. When you want to use the manual system, you merely select the left-hand side of the J gate mechanism and change gear in the normal way, except that there is no clutch pedal. On the right side of the J gate is the switchable adaptive system, which electronically changes to suit individual styles of driving. If you want to wind the engine up and drive aggressively, electronic software will recognize that you're in a hurry and will allow the engine to reach higher revs before changing to the next gear—thus giving you better performance. Alternatively, if you choose to drive the car more gently, which is highly unlikely in your case, the adaptive system will switch and change up earlier. The gear patterns are computer-controlled, yet driver-dependent."

"I knew that," Bond said smugly.

"Well, did you know that there are sensors which recognize wheel slip? If that happens, the power will be cut until traction is established again. Sensors on the rack tell the gearbox not to change gear when cutting a corner. You can behave like a complete lunatic and floor the throttle midway through a bend—but you'll find that the electronics will take over and never permit the car to go out of control. Clearly, the combined gearbox system has advantages over manual only. Specifically, in your case, in conjunction with GPS navigation, it's a matter of hands off the driving and hands on your female passenger!"

"I resent that remark," Bond said. "What about offensive features? Did you get what I asked for?"

"If you're referring to satellite navigation . . . yes. The car will drive to a set of coordinates and can actually drive itself with you in place or not. I daresay that it runs less of a risk on the road without you."

"Thanks."

"Now, look here"—Boothroyd got into the car and pointed to various devices—"the heat-seeking rockets and cruise missiles are used in conjunction with the satellite navigation. They're deployed to a set of coordinates, or they can follow a moving target selected by the screen and joystick on the dash.

"Inside the car you have a deployable air bag on the passenger side—guaranteed to smother someone with safety. Notice the windscreen. Optical systems magnify available light or heat at night to produce an image on this screen." Boothroyd pulled down a sun visor. "You can drive in the dark without headlamps, through smoke, fog, whatever—and because of the satellite navigation and intelligent cruise control, the vehicle will drive, steer, and avoid obstacles electronically. By the way, the car's microprocessors are stored in a box in the boot."

The major released the latch of the center-console armrest storage compartment. "Under the storage tray you'll find a holster for your P99."

"Very handy," Bond said.

Boothroyd got out of the car and pointed at the headlamps. "Holograms can be projected from both the front and rear headlamps. Additional holograms can be projected inside the car to give the appearance of a driver when there's no one there. We have a wide range of holograms that we can project outside the car. You'll want to go through our library and select a few to store into the computer."

"I'll bet you're saving the best for last," Bond said.

"You're absolutely right, 007," Boothroyd said with a wide grin. He walked over to a table. On top of it was a device that looked like the wings of a small model airplane, the size of a boomerang.

"This is our flying scout," he said. "It stores underneath the chassis until you activate it from inside the car. It will fly out from under the car and reach an altitude of your choosing. You can manually steer it by a joystick, or it can follow a predetermined flight route using the satellite navigation. The scout can send back pictures and coordinates of targets to you. It can tell you what's around the bend ahead. It can tell you if you're about to get caught speeding."

"That's quite handy, Major."

"As an afterthought, I equipped the scout with the ability to drop mines. Just be sure you're not underneath it if you happen to use them."

"Is that all?"

"*Is that all?* What do you want, 007, a tank?"

Bond shrugged. "I am quite good in tanks."

"Hmmm . . . Well, we can always add accessories as we think of them. That's the beauty of the XK8—it's so adaptable."

"Well, thank you, Major, I look forward to giving her a spin around the world."

"Oh, I almost forgot." Boothroyd opened up a steel cabinet and removed a remote control device and some goggles. "These are now standard issue. This control box will fit in the heel of your standard field-issue shoe. It's an alarm-sensor nullifier. It's guaranteed to deactivate any alarms within a twenty-five-yard radius. Just push that button there and aim it at the walls, the furniture, the doors—whatever you want. And these are our latest improvement in an old reliable—the night-vision goggles. If you find yourself outside of the car at night, you can always use these."

Bond tried them on. "I can't see a thing," he said.

"Oh—you've got them on sleep mode. I installed an extra feature. You can completely black out all vision so that the goggles perform like night shades. They're perfect for taking naps on aeroplanes."

Bond was mortified but did his best not to show it.

▶3.
AN EVENING IN THE COUNTRY

After a thirty-minute drive out of London and into Berkshire, James Bond reached what once was one of the more beautiful areas of England. The old farmlands on his left and the forest on his right had unfortunately been overtaken by urban development in the last twenty years; yet the amount of rural scenery still provided him with the feeling that he was in the country. The Bentley sailed across the Windsor-Bagshot road, and thankfully the familiar landmarks were still there—the Squirrel public house on the left and the modest stone gateway of Quarterdeck on the right.

The former M, Sir Miles Messervy, had lived in the rectangular Regency manor house made of Bath stone as long as Bond had known him. The property was remarkably well kept. The dense growth of pine, beech, silver birch, and young oak that grew on three sides of the house had been recently trimmed. There were already a number of elegant motorcars parked in the short gravel drive, and Bond was forced to park the Bentley near the end behind a Mercedes. He would be arriving at a fashionably reasonable hour—precisely half an hour before the scheduled eight-thirty dinner and just in time for a couple of stiff drinks.

The brass bell from a long-forgotten ship still hung on the front door. Bond fondly remembered the Hammonds, who had looked after Sir Miles for many years. They had met their untimely deaths during the Colonel Sun affair and were afterwards replaced by the Davisons. Like Hammond before him, Davison was a former chief petty officer.

The door opened and Davison stood there smiling broadly. "Good evening, Commander," he said. "Sir Miles was just asking about you."

"Good evening, Davison," Bond said. "I hope I'm not too late?"

"Not at all, sir. We're still expecting some of our guests."

Bond stepped into the hall. The smell of polish from the pine paneling was as strong as ever. The meticulously detailed 1/144 scale model of the battle cruiser *Repulse* was still the focal point on the table in the hallway. A dull roar of conversation and the soft strains of Mozart came from the main room. The smell of roast beef filled the air, and Bond suddenly felt very hungry. Davison took his overcoat, and he made his way through the open Spanish mahogany door.

The entire roomful of people couldn't help but notice James Bond, a splendid figure of a man dressed in a black three-piece single-breasted Brioni dinner suit with peaked lapels and no vents. He wore a deep bow tie, and the tucked-in white silk pocket handkerchief made the picture complete.

Bond walked inside and went straight to one of the servants and asked for a vodka martini. He then surveyed the guests. There were about twenty people in all, mostly faces he recognized. There was an MP and his wife in the corner speaking to a retired admiral and his spouse. Three women of various ages were eyeing him from the bay window. Sir James Molony and Major Boothroyd were locked in conversation near the fireplace. Miss Moneypenny waved to him and began to edge her way toward him. Some stray wives were huddled around a table covered with hors d'oeuvres. More voices came from the library through the double doors. He could see Sir Miles standing by a leather armchair, smoking a pipe. Two other retired Royal Navy officers sat across from him, speaking animatedly. Sir Miles nodded every ten seconds or so in response to whatever the men were saying.

As Bond's martini arrived, Moneypenny joined him. "You always cut a dashing figure, James," Moneypenny said. She was dressed in a gray satin gown which revealed a little more cleavage than usual.

"Moneypenny, you look marvelous. Have I missed much?"

"Not really. Only some delicious nibbles."

Bond lit one of his Simmons cigarettes and offered one to Moneypenny.

"No, thank you," she said. "I gave them up long ago. Have you forgotten?"

Bond shrugged. "I must have. Forgive me."

"You become distant when you have nothing to do, did you know that?"

Bond shrugged. "It's just the soft life slowly eating away at me. I hate being on call."

"I know. But I do like you better when you're all chirpy."

Bill Tanner, M's chief of staff and Bond's longtime friend in the Service, walked over to them. "Go easy on the vodka, James—there're at least twenty other people here tonight who'll want some."

"Hello, Bill." Bond put down his glass. "Guard this for me, will you? I'm going in to say hello to the Old Man. I'll be right back."

The smell of his old chief's distinctive blend of Turkish and Balkan tobacco filled the library. Sir Miles's damnably clear blue eyes looked up from his weather-beaten face and actually twinkled when he saw Bond. "Hello, James," he said. "Glad you could make it." Since his retirement, Sir Miles had dispensed with calling Bond 007. While Sir Miles was M, he never called Bond "James" unless something out of the ordinary was up for discussion. Now it was always "James," spoken as if Bond were the long-lost son whom he'd never had.

On the other hand, it was difficult for Bond to call Sir Miles anything but sir. "Good evening, sir. How are you feeling?"

"I'm fine, I'm fine. James, you know Admiral Hargreaves and Admiral Grey?"

"Yes, good evening," Bond said, nodding to the other men. They mumbled hello in return.

"Well, enjoy yourself. Dinner won't be for a few minutes. We'll have a chance to talk later, all right?" Sir Miles said.

"Fine. It's good to see you, sir." Bond walked back into the other room.

A mousy but not unattractive woman in her thirties nursing a gin and tonic intercepted him as he came through the double doors. "Hello, James," she said.

Bond thought she looked familiar but couldn't place her. "Hello," he said hesitantly.

"I'm Haley McElwain. My maiden name was Messervy."

"Oh, of course!" Bond said, slightly embarrassed. "I must admit I didn't recognize you at first." He hadn't seen Sir Miles's eldest daughter in years. The old man had been a widower for as long as Bond could remember, and had two grown daughters from the marriage that few people knew anything about. "How are you? You're looking well."

"Thank you," she said, gushing. "You look splendid yourself."

"Are you still living in America?" Bond asked.

"I was," Haley said with a hint of disgust. "My husband was an American. We're *divorced* now." Bond thought she accentuated the word a bit too pointedly.

"So you're back in England?"

"That's right. I'm living with Daddy for the moment. With Charles and Lynne, of course." She meant her two children.

"Oh, yes, they must be quite grown up now . . ." Bond's eyes wandered around the room looking for an escape route.

"Charles is nine and Lynne is six. I'm sure they'll find an excuse to come downstairs and join the party at some point during the evening. Daddy will have a heart attack." She giggled too much for Bond's taste. Haley McElwain was not holding her drink too well.

"Well, it's good to see you," Bond said, starting to walk away.

"It's good to see *you* too!" she said, unwittingly licking her lips. "I hope you'll come by Quarterdeck more often. I'll fix us a lunch sometime."

"That would be lovely," Bond muttered softly. He forced a smile and moved toward Bill Tanner, who was watching the entire scene with amusement.

"You know, James," he said, "it's quite all right to flirt with the boss's daughter now. He's not the boss anymore."

"Go to hell, Bill," Bond said, taking a large sip from the martini which he had left with Tanner.

"She's really quite lovely," Tanner said.

"Then *you* go and have lunch with her," Bond said. "She's a divorcée with two children, and that's enough to keep me away."

"James, you're becoming more and more misanthropic every day. Keep it up and you'll be living in a cave somewhere in the highlands of Scotland before long."

"That's not a bad idea, Bill. Someplace where M would never find me . . ."

Right on cue, the grand lady of SIS walked into the room. M

was escorted by a tall, distinguished-looking gentleman in a dinner jacket. He had snow-white hair, a mustache, and dark brown eyes. He appeared to be in his sixties, but he looked fit, tanned, and he was very handsome. M was dressed in a formal black evening gown that was low-cut in a V, revealing more of their boss than anyone at the office had ever seen. Accentuating the overall effect was a spectacular diamond necklace that gracefully caught the light. She looked dazzling. Together, the couple made a striking pair, and all heads in the room turned toward them. Nearly everyone was surprised to see who the man was.

"Hello, Chief of Staff, er, Bill. Hello, James," M said, smiling broadly at the two men. She was glowing with happiness. Bond immediately confirmed his earlier suspicion. M was in love.

"Good evening, ma'am," he said.

"Oh, please, we're not at the office. Call me Barbara," M said. Unlike the way the Service operated in the old days, everyone knew what M's real name was. "How are you, James?"

"I'm fine, ma'am. You're looking great this evening."

"So are you, James. Do you know Alfred Hutchinson?" She indicated the man who was escorting her. She held on to his arm and looked at him with pride.

"We've never met." Bond held out his hand. "Bond. James Bond."

Alfred Hutchinson shook his hand. It was a firm, dry handclasp. "How do you do?"

"And this is my chief of staff, Bill Tanner," she continued.

Tanner and Hutchinson shook hands and greeted each other; then Hutchinson turned toward the hallway. "What happened to Manville? Did he have to park the car on the other side of Windsor?"

"Well, we did come a bit late," M said. "Oh, here they are."

Another couple came into the room, slipping off their overcoats and handing them to Davison. They were younger, a man and woman in their thirties.

"I had to park at the Squirrel," the man said. "You'd think there was a party or something going on here!"

"James, Bill, I'd like you to meet Manville Duncan. He's Alfred's lawyer. And this is his wife, Cynthia. These are James Bond and Bill Tanner—they work for me."

Manville Duncan and his wife shook their hands. Bond noticed that Duncan's handshake was cold and soft, like a woman's. He was probably the type of man who had spent his life in an office pushing pens and using computers. He was of medium height, with dark, curly hair and deep brown eyes. Bond thought he had Mediterranean blood in him. Cynthia Duncan was plain, pale-skinned, thin, and seemed intimidated by her surroundings.

"I'm going to see if I can get us some drinks straightaway," Hutchinson said.

"I'll come with you," M said. She nodded and smiled at Bond and Tanner. "I'm sure we'll run into each other later on."

She followed Hutchinson. Manville Duncan and his wife smiled sheepishly at Bond and Tanner, then moved past them into the room.

"Well, I'll be damned," Tanner said quietly.

"Did you know she was seeing Alfred Hutchinson?" Bond asked.

"No. It's unbelievable. She actually looks human."

"Bill, if I'm not mistaken, that's a woman in love. She's radiant."

"But . . . Alfred Hutchinson?" Tanner shook his head. "This could bring SIS some publicity that we don't really need."

Alfred Hutchinson wasn't just a dapper, distinguished English gentleman. He was already world-famous. He was Great Britain's "Goodwill Ambassador to the World." Two years ago, the British government had created the position for him in an attempt to improve worldwide public relations. Prior to that time, Hutchinson was a respected university professor, author, and historian. He had spent several years as a foreign relations adviser, although he had no real experience in politics. Hutchinson was a man who was very outspoken, and his frequent appearances on BBC news programs brought him national fame. Two of his books about the history of English politics and foreign relations were best-sellers. Hutchinson now traveled all over the globe, speaking on behalf of Britain and spreading "goodwill." Among his accomplishments, at the very least, was simply making news—"Hutchinson visits Beijing," "Britain's Ambassador to the World in Tokyo" . . . Although he had no political power whatsoever as a real ambassador, Hutchinson managed to re-create a British presence in the world where many felt that it had drastically waned.

The fact that Barbara Mawdsley, otherwise known as M, was romantically involved with him astonished everyone at the party that night. It was obvious the two had planned to make their relationship public on this very occasion. Bond quickly got over the shock of realizing M had a sex life, and found that he was amused by the situation. He wondered what the press would have to say about the Goodwill Ambassador to the World dating the head of SIS. On the other hand, why should it matter? They were human, like anyone else. They were both divorced. Bond wasn't sure, but he thought that Hutchinson had been married twice before.

Bond didn't know Manville Duncan. His first impression of the man was that he smoothly fitted the role of a sycophant to someone with a far greater intellect. Bond could imagine Duncan leaping to fill Hutchinson's coffee cup if his boss wished him to do so.

The main course at dinner was roast beef, new potatoes, fresh peas, and what Bond thought was a rather disappointing Saint-Emilion. He watched M and Hutchinson throughout the meal. They were obviously fond of one another, for Hutchinson would whisper something into her ear every now and then and she would smile broadly. At one point, Bond could have sworn that she must have squeezed the man's inner thigh, for he suddenly registered a look of surprise and then they both laughed. Bond glanced over at Sir Miles, who was also watching the couple. He had a frown on his face that could have been chiseled in stone.

After coffee, several of the men retired to the library. Sir Miles passed out A. Fuente Gran Reserva cigars, one of the few brands that Bond would put in his mouth. After a few minutes of chitchat, he was motioned into a corner by Sir Miles.

"How are you, James? Enjoy the meal?" he asked.

"Yes sir, it was splendid. I must give my compliments to Mrs. Davison."

"Oh for God's sake, stop calling me sir. I've told you a hundred times."

"Old habits die hard, Sir Miles."

"You didn't answer my first question. How are you?"

"I'm fine, I suppose. We have a curious case at the moment. We're not sure what to make of it."

"Yes, I've heard. Serial terrorists. Sounds messy. No leads at all?"

"Not yet. The Greek Secret Service is doing most of the investigation at the moment. We have some military investigators looking into matters in Cyprus. I may have to go out there again. We have to wait and see."

"How are you getting on with M?"

Bond hesitated, then smiled. "She's not you, sir."

"That doesn't answer my question."

"We get on fine, Miles. She's on top of it. We may not see eye to eye on everything, but I respect her."

"Well, if you ask me, she's making a bloody mistake in her choice of men."

This surprised Bond. "Oh?"

Sir Miles shook his head and made a face as if he'd just bitten into something bitter. "Despicable man."

"Really! I thought Alfred Hutchinson was one of the most revered men in Britain these days. He's quite popular in Parliament and with the PM." Sir Miles didn't reply. "Isn't he?"

"The man cheated on his ex-wife, he's a liar, and he has the manners of a pit bull."

"I guess that just shows you how much I know about politics. Actually, he seemed very charming to me. It's fairly obvious that M is attracted to him."

"It's just my personal opinion, of course. This is between you and me," Sir Miles said gruffly. "Goodwill Ambassador to the World, indeed. What a bloody joke."

"Why is that?"

"Let's just say I know a few things about his family. I shouldn't have said anything—forget about it."

"Do you know him well?"

"Not really. We've played bridge at Blades a few times. He gets into a terrible temper when he loses. He reminds me of that man we played against a while back . . . you know, the German with the disfigured face and the rocket."

"Drax?"

"That's right. Oh, never mind. There's just something about Hutchinson that I don't like. That's all. Forget I said anything about it."

For a moment Bond caught a hint of jealousy in Sir Miles's voice.

Could it be that he was attracted to the new M himself and was merely sounding off against her choice of suitors? Bond quickly dismissed the absurdity of that idea.

They were interrupted by M herself. She stuck her head in the door and spotted Bond and Sir Miles. "Oh, there you are, James. Might I have a word with you? Excuse me, Sir Miles."

"Quite all right, my dear," Sir Miles said with charm.

Bond followed her out and over to where Hutchinson was standing, admiring a new watercolor print that Sir Miles had recently completed.

"The old man has an extraordinary gift for capturing light and shadow, doesn't he?" Hutchinson said, peering closely at the painting.

"James," M began, "Alfred has some information about the Cyprus case which might be useful."

"Is that so?"

"Be at my office at ten o'clock tomorrow morning, please? Is that good for you, Alfred?" she asked.

"Yes, my dear," he said conspiratorially. "That will be fine."

"Why not just tell us now?" Bond asked.

"My dear man," Hutchinson said, "we're here to enjoy ourselves, aren't we? Let's not discuss business now, for heaven's sake. I'm going to have another drink. Can I get you something?"

"Thank you, no," Bond said. Sir Miles was right. There was something inherently sleazy about the man. "Ten o'clock, then," he said. He nodded at M and walked away.

Bond went into the hallway to find Davison. He had had enough socializing for one night. He was surprised to find none other than Helena Marksbury sitting alone. She was just putting out a cigarette in a glass ashtray. Bond had seen her earlier conversing with other SIS personnel, and he didn't want to join them. Now that she was alone . . .

"What's the matter, Helena? The bus doesn't stop here."

She smiled. "Hello, James. I was wondering if you were ever going to talk to me this evening."

"I've been trying to, but you were always engaged. Care to take a walk outside?"

"It's a bit cold and damp, isn't it?"

"We'll put on our coats. Come on, let's find them."

A few minutes later, they had their overcoats on and they quietly stepped out of the house. The air was chilly and the night was full of dark clouds. Bond lit two cigarettes and passed one to Helena. They walked around the side of the house to a sunken patio. A large fountain with a statue of Cupid in its center stood in the middle of the patio, but the water had been turned off.

"I felt a bit lost in there," she said. "They're really not my crowd."

"Would you believe me if I told you they're not my crowd either?"

"Yes, I would," she said. "You're not like the others at the office, James." She laughed to herself. "Not at all."

"I suppose that's a compliment," he said.

She smiled but didn't elaborate.

A bit of light from windows at the back of the house shone across the patio. He gazed at her oval face, the short brown hair and big green eyes. She was very beautiful. She returned his stare and finally said, "What would you like to do now?"

"I want to kiss you," he said.

She blinked. "You're very direct," she said.

"Always," he said; then he leaned forward and kissed her. She welcomed the embrace and opened her mouth to make the kiss more intimate. After a few seconds, they separated, but Bond kept his face close to hers. He felt a raindrop on his forehead.

"It's starting to rain," she whispered.

He moved in and kissed her again, and this time she responded even more passionately. The raindrops began to increase in tempo.

Eventually, she pulled away gently. Breathlessly, she said, "I know this isn't sexual harassment, but I'd better point out that you're my boss, James."

He kept his hands on her shoulders. He nodded. "I know. We . . . I shouldn't do this."

"We'd best go back inside. We're getting wet."

A thunderclap roared and the rain started to come down in earnest. Bond held her as they ran around the house to the front door. By the time they got there, she was laughing. They stood beneath the awning for a moment. Now there was an awkward silence between them.

"I was about to leave when I saw you," he said finally.

"It's pouring now, you'll have to wait. You couldn't possibly drive home in this."

"No. I'm going now. I'll see you tomorrow."

He gave her shoulders a squeeze and said, "Forgive me." Then he walked out into the rain and onto the gravel drive. Helena Marksbury watched him go and muttered under her breath, "You're forgiven."

Bond let the rain soak him as he walked to the end of the drive where he had left the Bentley. He cursed himself for what had just happened. He knew better than to get involved with women at the office. If only she wasn't so bloody attractive! What was it in him that made him want to seduce every woman he found desirable? Temporary recreational love was satisfying and always had been, but it certainly didn't fill a greater need Bond had. Was it possible that what he craved was a woman to love—*really* love—in order to fill that hole? The bitter answer to that was that he got burned every time he allowed himself to truly love someone. The scars on his heart were many and deep.

He got into his car and set off through the torrent toward London. Bond's darker side took hold of him once again as he pondered his lonely, wretched life. He would have liked the rain to wash away the familiar melancholy, but he ultimately accepted and embraced it as an old friend.

▶4.
TOO CLOSE TO HOME

The phone woke Bond abruptly out of a deep sleep. The illuminated digital clock read 2:37. He switched on the light and went for the white phone, but the ring continued. Bond felt a sudden rush of adrenaline when he realized that it was the red phone that was ringing. The red phone rang only in an emergency situation.

"Bond," he said into the receiver.

"James, code sixty." It was Bill Tanner.

"I'm listening."

"M's orders." Tanner gave an address and flat number. "You know where it is? Just off of Holland Park Road. It's the block of flats called Park Mansions."

Tanner rang off and Bond jumped out of bed. "Code sixty" meant that the matter had a special security classification. In other words, Bond must use utmost discretion.

It took him ten minutes to get to Holland Park, an area of affluence on the western edge of Kensington. The district grew as a result of the reputation of Holland House, a mansion built four hundred years ago primarily for the purpose of entertaining king and court. Town houses sprang up in the early to mid-nineteenth century on various streets and squares west of the park. Many MPs and governmental elite lived in the area.

Park Mansions was a long block of brown and red brick buildings three stories high. A security gate provided protection from traffic, but at the moment there seemed to be a lot of activity in front of one of the buildings. An ambulance was parked there, its lights flashing. A police car and two unmarked MI5 cars were double-parked in front as well. Bond left the Bentley outside the gate and walked through. He showed a constable his credentials and was shown through the front door of the building.

Bill Tanner met him at the open front door of the flat. Police tape had been stretched several feet away from the door, preventing any curious neighbors from peering inside.

"James, come inside," Tanner said. "M's in here."

"What's going on, Bill?"

"It's Hutchinson. He's dead."

"What?"

Tanner leaned in closer and kept his voice down. "This is his flat. M was here spending the night with him. She's quite distraught."

"Do we know what happened?"

"You'd better have a look. I phoned Manville Duncan after I called you. He's on his way."

Tanner led Bond inside the flat. MI5 Forensics were taking photographs and examining the scene. M was in the sitting room, dressed in a white and pink silk housecoat. She looked pale and frightened. She was holding a cup of coffee in her lap. When she looked up, Bond could see that she was extremely upset, not only because her lover was dead, but because she was embarrassed to be seen by her staff in this condition.

Bond knelt beside her and took her hand. "Are you all right, ma'am?" he asked gently.

M nodded and swallowed. "Thank you for coming, James. Poor Alfred. I feel so . . . exposed."

"Don't worry about that, ma'am. What happened?"

She shook her head and trembled. "I don't even know. One minute he was fine, and the next . . ." She closed her eyes, attempting to get hold of herself.

Bond stood up and said, "I'm going to have a look at him, ma'am. We'll talk in a moment."

He followed Tanner into the bedroom.

Bond had seen many cadavers and crime scenes, and this one was no different. Death brought an unnatural chill to an otherwise warm-hued room with oak wall paneling, a king-sized bed and ornate headboard, and distinctly masculine furnishings. Alfred Hutchinson lay naked on his back on the bed. He might have been asleep but for the fact that his eyes were wide open, frozen in fear. There were no marks on the body. There were no signs that there had been any violence. He looked as if he might have been a victim of cardiac arrest. In this state, Alfred Hutchinson was no longer the distinguished Goodwill Ambassador to the World Bond had met a few hours earlier. Now he was simply a chalk-skinned common corpse.

"Heart attack?" Bond asked the MI5 medical examiner, who was sitting by the bed, writing in a notebook. A member of the MI5 forensic team was taking photographs of the body with a multi/fixed-focal length Polaroid Macro 5 SLR instant camera, one of several special-purpose cameras that the team was using at the crime scene.

"That's what it looks like," the doctor said. "We'll have to conduct a postmortem examination, of course, but I don't think that's the whole story."

"What do you mean?"

"Hutchinson died of cardiac and respiratory failure, but he was in perfect health. After hearing Ms. Mawdsley's statement and examining the body, it's my preliminary opinion that he was murdered."

"How?"

"Some kind of poison. A neurotoxin, most likely, a substance that stops your heart and the automatic function of breathing. It's something that is irreversible once it's been introduced into the bloodstream. It acts fast, but not fast enough, I'm afraid. The man suffered terribly for several minutes."

"Any marks on the body?"

"One suspicious contusion on the anterior of his right thigh. See the little red mark?" The doctor pointed to a small, swollen puncture wound on Hutchinson's upper leg. "At first I thought it was just a pimple, but further examination revealed that he had been jabbed with a needle."

Bond looked at the body again. The man in charge walked into the bedroom.

"Commander Bond?"

"Yes."

"I'm Detective Inspector Howard. We're ready to take the body away if you are."

"Have you had a good look at all his personal effects?" Bond asked.

"We're just getting around to that now. Might I ask you to have a talk with Ms. Mawdsley? I wasn't able to get much out of her earlier."

Bond nodded and left the bedroom. He found that M had not moved, nor had she drunk her coffee. He sat down next to her in an armchair.

"Ma'am, we need to know exactly what happened tonight," he said softly.

M sighed heavily and shut her eyes.

"I'm still trying to piece it together," she said. "We left Sir Miles's house around eleven. Maybe eleven-fifteen. We were all together—the Duncans, Alfred, and me. We decided to stop at the Ritz for a nightcap."

She paused and took a sip of the coffee. She turned to Tanner. "Mr. Tanner, this is cold. Could you please get me a fresh cup?"

Tanner nodded and took the cup from her.

"What time did you get to the Ritz?" Bond asked.

"I think it was around midnight. We were there three quarters of an hour, I suppose."

"What did Mr. Hutchinson have to drink?"

"He had a brandy, as did I. We all did."

"Then what?"

"It was raining heavily. Alfred offered to drive the Duncans home, but they insisted on calling a taxi. They live out of the way, in Islington."

"So you and Alfred drove here together?"

She nodded. "He had parked near the hotel. We both had umbrellas, so I didn't mind walking in the rain. We got to the flat twenty minutes later. He seemed fine. We . . . got undressed . . ."

Bond knew this was extremely difficult for M. She was exposing a personal, intimate side of herself that no one else ever saw.

"It's all right, ma'am," Bond said. "Go on."

"We made love," she said. "Afterwards, he—"

"Excuse me, ma'am, but did he show any signs of fatigue or illness during your lovemaking?"

"No," M said. "He seemed completely normal. Alfred is . . . was . . . very energetic."

"I see. Go on."

"I got up to go to the loo. While I was in there, I heard him gasping for breath. I ran out to him and he was struggling for air, clutching at his throat. Oh, James, it was horrible. I reached for the phone to call an ambulance, but he grabbed my arm. All he could say was, 'Your hand . . . your hand . . .' So I let him hold my hand. He went into a terrible convulsion, and then he died. I called the ambulance and Mr. Tanner immediately afterwards. I thought about dressing him, but I knew that wasn't the thing to do. I . . . left him . . . like that . . ." She started to sob.

Bond put his arm around his chief and let her cry on his shoulder for a full sixty seconds until she finally pulled herself together.

Tanner brought another cup of coffee. "Manville Duncan just arrived. Here you go, ma'am."

Duncan's face was white when he hurried into the room. "What happened?"

Tanner gave him a quick rundown of what they knew so far.

"Christ, was it a heart attack?" Duncan asked.

"That's what it looks like," Bond said, "but I'm afraid that's not the case. Alfred Hutchinson was murdered."

M's eyes grew wide. "How do you know?"

"It's the medical examiner's suspicion. Mine as well. You see, ma'am, what you described is not consistent with a heart attack. Mr. Hutchinson was alive for several minutes, apparently choking, correct?"

"Yes."

"Then he went into convulsions?"

"That's right."

"Ma'am, can you come look at the body again? I'd like to show you something."

A complete change came over M. When she heard the word "murder," she summoned all of her professional integrity. Even though she was dressed in only a housecoat, she became the head of SIS once again. She stood up and gestured toward the bedroom for Bond to lead the way.

Bond took her in and showed her the tiny wound on Hutchinson's leg. "The medical examiner believes that's where the poison entered the bloodstream."

"Oh my God," M said. "I know how it happened. I remember now."

"What?"

"It was outside the hotel. We had just said goodbye to the Duncans.

We were walking toward his car. There was someone with a broken umbrella on the pavement. He was struggling with it, trying to open it."

"What did he look like?"

"I don't know," she said, angrily. "I don't even know if it was a man or a woman. They were dressed in a hooded yellow raincoat—completely covered."

"And?"

"As we walked by, the person accidentally poked Alfred with the end of the umbrella, I think. I know it struck him somehow, and he said, 'Ouch.' "

"What did the person with the umbrella do?"

"Nothing! They didn't even realize what had happened, for they moved on without apologizing or saying a word. Alfred shrugged it off and we kept walking toward the car, although now that I think about it, he seemed a little shaken up by the incident. He did act a little strange until we started driving. While we were walking, he kept looking behind us. And he insisted on holding my handbag until we got into the car, for fear that it might get snatched. In two minutes we got to the car. It all happened so fast that frankly I had forgotten all about it."

"You know what this reminds me of?" Tanner asked.

"Yes," Bond said. "Markov."

"By God, you're right," M said.

"What?" Duncan asked. "Who's Markov?"

"Georgi Markov," Bond said. "He was a Bulgarian defector. He was assassinated on Waterloo Bridge in . . . 1978, I believe, in this same fashion. Someone poked him with an umbrella. The tip of the umbrella injected a tiny capsule of ricin into his bloodstream."

"Ricin?"

"It's a toxic protein-based poison derived from castor beans. Depending on the dosage, it can be effective in fifteen minutes to an hour. It's lethal, and it leaves no trace in the bloodstream. To all intents and purposes, the victim dies of respiratory and cardiac failure. It attacks the nervous system and shuts off those basic motor functions."

"But . . . who would want to kill Alfred?" Duncan asked.

"That's the big question," Bond said. "Who would?"

M sat down. "He never mentioned anything to me. It's not as

if anyone were after his job. Manville, was there anything going on diplomatically that we should know about?"

"I can't think of a thing!" Duncan said. "He was . . . well, he was loved by everyone who met him!"

"You ever play bridge with him?" Bond asked Duncan.

"No. Why?"

"Never mind."

There was silence in the room and everyone pondered the situation. Detective Inspector Howard came into the room with an overcoat.

"Is this the overcoat Mr. Hutchinson was wearing tonight?" he asked M.

"Yes."

"There's something you should see. This was in the pocket."

He had a small white alabaster statuette in his gloved hand. It was the Greek god Ares.

"That's just like the statues found in Cyprus," Bond said. "Anything else in the pockets?"

"Just a coat check receipt," Howard said. He held it out. It had been carefully placed in a clear evidence bag to protect it from contamination. Bond took it and saw that the receipt was from the Ritz Hotel, and the number "173" was printed on its face. He almost dismissed it, but as he handed the receipt back he turned it over. Scrawled in a red marker was the number "4."

"It's the Number Killer," Bond said. "Alfred Hutchinson was victim number four."

"The bastards have brought this a little too close to home," Tanner said.

"Would you please explain what's going on?" Manville Duncan asked.

Bond looked at M for approval.

She nodded and said, "As his lawyer, Manville will be taking over for Alfred. I suppose it's information he should be aware of. Manville, please understand this is all strictly confidential."

"Of course," he said.

"Mr. Duncan," Bond said. "I have just returned from Cyprus. Over the past week, three separate incidents killed some British citizens. The first was one of our SIS people, in Athens. A fellow named Whitten. Did you know him?"

"No."

"His body was found in the Ancient Agora with the number '1' painted in red on a rock nearby. The second incident was on our Sovereign Base at Dhekelia in Cyprus. Several soldiers were killed—by poison. The number '2' was painted nearby, and one of these Greek god statues was left at the site. Just the other day, another group of soldiers at Episkopi were killed by another chemical weapon. The number '3' and another statue were left at the scene. This makes number '4.' "

"You're sure it's the same killers?"

"It seems obvious," Bond said. "I wonder if he was silenced to keep him from telling us what he knew about the case? Ma'am, does Mr. Hutchinson have any family? Where are his former wives?"

"His first wife is in Australia, I think," she said. "The second one lives here in London."

"Any children?"

"He has a son by his first wife. His name is Charles. He lives in America somewhere. In Texas, I think."

"That's it?"

"Charles is all I know about," M said.

"Then we'll have to get in touch with him."

"I'll do it," Tanner said.

"Oh hell," Duncan said.

"What?"

"Alfred was due to fly to the Middle East tomorrow. He had an appointment in Syria!"

"You're his lawyer, Manville," M said.

Duncan nodded, realizing the implication of that remark. "I'll have to go in his place."

"You'll have to fill his shoes until the powers that be decide what to do about his position," she said. "Are you up to it?"

"I'll have to be," Duncan said. He looked at his watch. "I'd better go home and get some rest, if I can, then get up early and go to the office and get ready. He had—"

"A five o'clock flight," M said. "I know."

"Look, uhm, Mr. Bond," Duncan said. "Please, I want to help all I can. If you have any more questions for me or simply want to pick my brains, call me at the office. They can get a message to me and I'll call you back."

"When will you be back in England?"

"In two days, I think. I'll have to check his schedule."

"Fine. Go on. Have a good trip. Don't mention to anyone what really happened to Mr. Hutchinson. We'll make sure that the public and the rest of the world believe that he died of a heart attack. Naturally."

"We'll have to keep me out of it," M said.

"That goes without saying," Bond said. "Let's get you out of here. You had better get dressed before any reporters get wind of this."

M nodded, turning to accept Manville Duncan's condolences before he left the flat.

Just before fetching her clothes, M said to Bond, Tanner, and Inspector Howard, "MI5 will handle this investigation here in Great Britain. But as it is linked to the events in Greece and Cyprus, 007, you're going to have to handle that end. This is obviously an international incident, and that gives MI6 full authority to act. Let's meet at ten A.M. in my office and discuss strategy, shall we?" Without waiting for an answer, Barbara Mawdsley turned and went into the bedroom where her lover lay cold and stiff.

Bond was relieved that she was beginning to sound like her old self again.

▶5.
RENDEZVOUS ON CHIOS

Approximately two days later, a meeting was called to order in a remote and secret fortress hidden away on the Greek island of Chios.

The island is only eight kilometers from the Turkish peninsula of Karaburun, one of the closest of all Greek territories to the country with which Greece has had such a precarious relationship for centuries. Not one of the major tourist islands, Chios has several Greek Army bases and camouflaged enclaves of weaponry.

Crescent-shaped, Chios is hilly and cultivated with olives, fruit, vines, and most important, gum trees. The capital, locally known as Chios Town, sits on the edge of a plain facing the Turkish coast on the site of its ancient ruins. Approximately twenty-six kilometers west of the capital, at the end of a winding, mountainous road that leads to nowhere, is a quiet, forsaken ancient village called Anavatos. It is built on a precipitous cliff, with narrow stepped pathways twisting between the houses to the summit—an empty, dilapidated medieval castle. Virtually a ghost town, Anavatos's abandoned gray stone buildings stand as memorials to one of the island's great tragedies. Nearly all of the inhabitants were killed in the atrocities committed by the Ottoman Empire in 1822, and today the village is inhabited only by a few elderly people at the base of the cliff. The villagers chose to throw themselves off the cliff rather than submit to capture and torture.

At noon on this early-November weekday, there wasn't a single tourist in sight. Anavatos never lured many sightseers, and those who did venture there to make the climb to the top never stayed long. Once visitors have seen the deserted ruins, there is nothing else to do. There are no shops, tavernas, or hotels. One restaurant at the base of the cliff serves its small population, every now and then enjoying the business of a tourist or two. Neither sightseers nor the current residents of Anavatos could ever have guessed that within the bowels of the decrepit medieval castle at the top of the lonely village were the sophisticated, modern headquarters of a peculiar group of people.

Since many notable legendary figures such as Jason and Homer reportedly visited the island, it was entirely conceivable that the noted sixth-century B.C. mathematician Pythagoras set foot on Chios. He came from neighboring Samos, where he founded a brotherhood called the Order of the Pythagoreans, or the Pythagorean Society. Pythagoras was a respected scholar of mathematics and philosophy, and his lecture rooms were often packed. Even women broke the law that prohibited them from attending public meetings, just to hear him speak. It wasn't long before the Pythagoreans began to revere their leader as a demigod. They believed in, among other things, transmigration of souls, and followed moral and dietary practices in order to purify the soul for its next embodiment. According to the Pythagoreans, all relationships—even abstract concepts like justice—could be expressed numerically.

Deep within the silent and desolate medieval castle at the top of Anavatos, Pythagoras was about to address his followers once again.

The man who professed to be him was dressed in a white robe. He had dark, curly hair with traces of gray, cut short and neat. His large, round, dark brown eyes were set deeply into a handsome, chiseled face, with dark eyebrows and a hawk nose. He had a tanned Mediterranean complexion and ruddy lips that seemed to be permanently formed into a frown. The fifty-five-year-old man was clean-shaven, tall and broad-shouldered. He could have been a film star, a priest, or a politician. The man had an indefinable charisma that captivated those who knew him. When he spoke, everyone listened. When he explained, they all understood. When he commanded, no one dared to ignore his instructions.

After the several minutes of silence that traditionally began their meetings, he would begin. During this time, the man who believed that he was Pythagoras reincarnated gazed at the nine people reclining on cushions on the floor in front of him. They were also wearing robes. Nine men and women looked at their leader with anticipation. There were an American and an Englishman. Three of them were Greek, two Greek Cypriots. One was Italian and one was Russian. Number Ten was a brilliant physician and chemist; Number Nine was an expert in transportation—he could fly anything anywhere. There was Number Eight, the prestigious president of a Greek pharmaceutical company and a distinguished biologist and chemist; Number Seven, a man extremely close to the leader in that they were related by blood; and Number Six, a banker, someone who knew the ins and outs of stock markets, investments, and foreign exchange. Number Five was a loyal friend who normally wore a Greek officer's military uniform; Number Four was a woman in charge of buying and selling on the black market. Number Three had been in charge of the first four strikes and normally handled overseas business, and the lovely Number Two was one of the most highly skilled assassins and terrorist soldiers on earth. The leader fondly gazed upon Number Two, whose work clothes included a gas mask and a protective suit.

They were in a room designed to replicate an ancient Greek interior. The large square area was made entirely of stone. Benches lined the perimeters, but the middle of the floor was devoid of furniture. An archway with curtains the colors of the blue-and-white Greek flag led to a completely different room. It contained modern office equipment—workstations, computers, monitors, and machinery. Beyond that again were living quarters as elegant as those of a luxury hotel. Here group members slept if they needed to stay overnight in Anavatos. At a lower level lived the various personnel employed by the ten people in the Greek meeting room. These included personal bodyguards and trained, armed "soldiers" who were so well paid that their loyalty was without question.

A cache of military weapons was stored in an armory. This consisted mainly of guns and ammunition stolen from Greek military bases. Some of the more sophisticated equipment had been stolen from NATO, or purchased from underground organizations operating in the Middle East and southern Europe. The most impressive device in the complex was an empty missile silo and launching pad. Its cover, which could be opened at the touch of a button, was cleverly disguised as a flat, dirt roof of the medieval castle that housed these unusual secret headquarters. The roof could easily be used as a helicopter pad. It had all been built under the noses of the villagers. They had been paid to turn their backs.

The period of silence was over. The leader picked up a lyre and strummed a perfect fifth. The Pythagoreans knew that vibrating strings produced harmonious tones when the ratios of the lengths of the strings were whole numbers, and that these ratios could be extended to other instruments if desired.

The meeting had begun. Pythagoras set down the lyre and smiled wryly at the nine people before him. They were ready. They leaned forward slightly, waiting for the soothing voice of reason. They were impatient to hear him speak, for he was the Monad, the One. And they were called the Decada.

"Welcome," he said. "I am happy to report that Mission Number Four was successful in preventing sensitive information concerning the Decada from reaching British intelligence. Unfortunately, the information the targeted man possessed is missing. Retrieval of it is essential. We cannot complete the *Tetraktys* without it. I have given Number Ten full responsibility for recovering it."

Number Ten nodded in acknowledgment.

"In the meantime, the Decada will continue its goal of achieving worldwide recognition. The first four strikes were simply samples of what the Decada can do. We were testing the waters, getting our feet wet, so to speak. And thus we have successfully warned the British not to interfere in our future plans."

The Monad turned and moved toward the stone wall behind him. He slipped his index and middle fingers in between the edges of some stones and released a catch. The panel of fake stones slid across, revealing a metal square embedded with red light bulbs. The bulbs were positioned to form points in an equilateral triangle:

The bottom four bulbs were lit.

"The foundation of the holy *Tetraktys* is complete. Four base digits have been completed. Note the perfection of the triangle—how it can be rotated and it will remain the same. A base of four always leads to a line of three, then to a line of two, and finally to a single point.

Ten points in all. Ten—the holy *Tetraktys*. The basis of the Decada. The creative connection between the Divine Mind and the manifest universe."

The Monad indicated the line with three unlit bulbs.

"Our next three strikes will build upon the first four. Two will follow these, and they will be the pivotal actions that will set up the Decada for its ultimate assault. After that, we will simply start again with a new *Tetraktys* of ten points. I can assure you that the world will be paying attention to us after the first *Tetraktys* is complete."

He turned to one of the followers sitting before him. "What is the Principle of Oneness, Number Four?" he asked.

Number Four, a woman, replied by rote, "The Principle of Oneness is Unity, and that is represented by the Monad. Completeness, perfection, eternity, the unchanging and the permanent are all qualities of the Monad, the number One."

"And how can One become the Many?"

"One can become the Many only through the manifestation of the *Tetraktys*, the Ten."

"And when One becomes the Many, what happens?" the Monad asked the entire group.

As if in a trance, they all replied together, "The Limited will become Unlimited. Limit is a definite boundary. The Unlimited is indefinite and is therefore in need of Limit. We will meld with the Monad. We will all have the power."

The Monad nodded with pleasure. "Let us recite the Decada of Contraries. I'll begin with Number One: Limited and Unlimited."

Number Two said, "Odd and Even."

Number Three said, "One and Many."

The remaining members of the Decada spoke in turn, repeating what they had learned from the Monad.

The Monad continued, "The Ten points of the *Tetraktys*. They are the perfection of Number and the elements which comprise it. In one sense, we could say that the *Tetraktys* symbolizes, like a musical scale, an image of Unity starting at One, proceeding through four levels of manifestation, and returning to Unity. Ten. Everything comes to Ten. And who are the Ten?"

"The Decada!" the group shouted.

The Monad was pleased. His followers were totally under his control. He paused and looked at each of the other nine members. He stared into their eyes for a full minute, person by person. They could feel the man's strength and power filling them as he looked into their souls. They felt invigorated and whole.

"The gods are pleased," he said. "Our first tribute was to the ancient Greeks, who built the Agora in Athens at the base of the holy Acropolis. We owe our allegiance to these ancestors of all mankind. It was in Greece where true Western thought materialized. They built the Temple of Hephaisteion, where Zeus and the other gods of Mount Olympus were worshipped, and it was there that we left our little . . . sacrifice. Our second tribute was to Hera, queen of the gods. The third was to Poseidon, god of the sea and brother of Zeus. Our fourth was to Ares, the god of war."

The Monad smiled. "How fitting that Ares be associated with the final point of the first four strikes, for he was a bloodthirsty god. Yes, with Ares we have declared war on our enemies. The British have been marked. It is a pity that our attempt to eliminate the Greek Secret Service investigator in her shower failed. But now we turn our attention to the Turks and the Turkish Cypriots. Once we have completed our first set of goals, the ones that will make us a force to be reckoned with, the Turks will be run out of northern Cyprus forever. My friends, we will move through the holy *Tetraktys* like lightning! I am happy to report that Number Eight is progressing with her work in the laboratory and we are now ready to break all ties with our American soon-to-be-former partners. It will not be long before we strike with our own swords, and the world will remember us forever!"

After the meeting, Number Two, Number Eight, and Number Ten huddled together in a private room in the complex. The three women spoke quietly.

"Deaths have already been reported in Los Angeles," Number Ten said.

"How quickly does the virus gestate?" Number Two asked.

"The quickest way is direct injection into the bloodstream," Number Eight explained. "A person will get sick in about eight hours. It's during these hours that the virus is most contagious. Otherwise, it takes ten to twenty-four hours for an onset of symptoms after exposure to someone who is already infected."

"Then it's working," Number Two said.

"More or less."

Number Ten replied, "By the time we've completed the tenth mission of the *Tetraktys,* all the deliveries will have been made. It will be too late to stop the process."

"Good," said Number Two. "Number Eight, keep perfecting the virus and the vaccine. Number Ten, you have your assignment. I have my own work for the Monad ahead of me. Ladies, by the time we're through with this, we shall be wealthy beyond our wildest dreams."

They hugged each other. Number Eight left the room. Number Two gazed into Number Ten's eyes.

"I must leave," Number Ten said. "There's a plane waiting for me."

"I know. Take care. I'll see you soon," Number Two said. They kissed each other intimately, on the mouth, then parted.

Number Two watched her lover leave, then made her way to her room. As she expected, the Monad was there, waiting in her bed.

▶6.
TEQUILA AND LIMES

London's cold, rainy weather continued, giving way to a bitter high wind that chilled one to the bone. It was unseasonably cold for the first week of November. Walking outside for more than a few minutes was an ordeal, and people had to make sure every inch of skin was covered to avoid being miserable.

James Bond looked out the window of M's office on the eighth floor of SIS headquarters and yearned for Jamaica. The weather wouldn't be perfect there either; it would most likely be raining too, but at least the temperature would be tolerable. He imagined hearing the warm laugh of Ramsey, the young Jamaican he had hired to look after Shamelady during his absence. Ramsey would have cheered him up with his broad smile, white teeth, and good humor.

Bond breathed deeply, attempting to motivate himself to go over the paperwork on his desk once again. The lack of progress on the case was certainly part of the problem, but he knew that the only way he would feel like he was accomplishing something was to get out of London. He was restless and irritable. The previous evening he had put away half a bottle of The Macallan and had woken up in the middle of the night in the armchair of his sitting room. He had crawled into bed, and didn't wake up until Helena Marksbury phoned him to inquire if he was coming to the office. Now he not only had a pounding headache, but he felt he was coming down with a cold.

"You look terrible, 007," M said behind him. "What the devil is the matter with you?"

"Nothing, ma'am," Bond said, turning away from the window. "This weather is dreadful."

"You're not catching flu, are you? It's going around."

"I never catch the flu," Bond said, sniffing.

"Nevertheless, I want you to see the doctor. I need you in top form if we get a break in the case," she said.

Bond sat down in the black leather chair across from her desk. M didn't look so great either. The stress and heartache she felt at the loss of her lover were all too apparent. To her credit, she had shown up for work every day since Hutchinson's murder.

"Have you located Charles Hutchinson yet?" she asked.

"No, ma'am, he's nowhere to be found," Bond said, suppressing a cough. "I'm thinking it might be a good idea if I took a trip to Texas. There may be some clues at Mr. Hutchinson's house there."

Bill Tanner had quickly gathered some useful information on Alfred Hutchinson. He owned a house in Austin, Texas, where he had spent time as a guest professor at the University of Texas. His twenty-three-year-old son, Charles, lived and worked there and Hutchinson had continued to make frequent trips there. Hutchinson's ex-wife was insisting that funeral arrangements be postponed until Charles Hutchinson could be reached. All attempts to contact the young man had failed. Either he was out of the country or something had happened to him.

"I suppose it couldn't hurt," M said. "Yes, I think that's a good idea. Should I get in touch with the CIA and let them know you're coming?"

"That won't be necessary, ma'am," Bond said. "I know someone in Austin who will be much more helpful than they would be."

Bond flew to Dallas on American Airlines and changed planes for the short hop down to Austin. It was late afternoon when he arrived, and the weather was better there than in London. The sky was overcast but it was pleasantly warm.

Bond hadn't spent much time in Texas. He had been to the area known as the Panhandle during the case a few years back that involved the last heir of Ernst Stavro Blofeld, but he had never been to Austin or any of the other more scenic areas in central Texas. He was surprised by the lush greenery, the hills, and the stretches of water that could be seen from the air. He had no idea that any part of Texas could be so beautiful. It was no wonder that his friend and longtime associate

Felix Leiter, who actually hailed from Texas, had gone back to settle in Austin.

At the airport, an exotic Hispanic woman dressed in tight-fitting blue jeans and a western shirt with the bottom ends tied together above her bare midriff approached Bond as he came out into the terminal. She appeared to be in her early thirties, had long black hair and small brown eyes that sparkled.

"Mr. Bond?" she asked with a Spanish accent.

"Yes?"

"I'm Manuela Montemayor. I've come to pick you up." The way she said "peek you up" was tantalizing. "Felix is waiting at the house. He's very excited to see you again."

"Lovely. I'm all yours," Bond said with a smile.

Bond collected his luggage and followed Manuela outside into the fresh warm air. She led him to a 1997 red Mitsubishi Diamante LS in the parking lot.

"Felix said you would hate the car, but I like it," she said.

"Looks fine to me." It felt good to get into the passenger seat after the long flight from England.

Manuela drove out of the parking lot to Interstate 35, then headed south. Bond looked to his right and saw the expanse of the University of Texas at Austin, an enormous campus well known for its American football team, fine arts department, and beautiful girls. The main building, or UT Tower, stood twenty-seven stories tall, overlooking the campus and city with the grandeur of an all-seeing sentinel.

"You been to Austin before?" she asked.

"Never. I've always wanted to come, especially since Felix moved here."

"We love it. The people are friendly, the music is great, and the climate is perfect."

"How's Felix doing?"

"He's fine. You know he's not so good on his legs anymore. The one leg with the prosthesis has deteriorated, so he stays in his wheelchair most of the time."

Christ, Bond thought. He hadn't known that Felix was in a wheelchair. He wondered how he would feel when he saw his friend in that condition. Bond never forgot that fateful day in Florida when Leiter lost the leg and an arm to a shark owned by Mr. Big and company. At the time, Leiter worked for the CIA. After the mishap, the Texan had been with Pinkerton's Detective Agency for a number of years. He had then spent a few years with the DEA, before going into private practice as a freelance consultant on intelligence and law enforcement matters.

Eventually, the car crossed the Colorado River, locally known as Town Lake. Manuela turned off of the interstate and headed west, entering the section of Barton Springs Road populated by trendy restaurants and nightspots, and on through Zilker Metropolitan Park.

"Now we are in West Lake Hills," Manuela said. "It's where we live."

This suburb of Austin seemed more fashionable than what Bond had seen along the way. The area was very hilly, and the houses were elegant and impressive. The car turned into a long, narrow drive surrounded by large oak trees that disclosed a wood-and-stone ranch house at the end.

"Here we are," she said.

As they walked toward the house, the cicadas were making a tremendous racket in the trees. Bond felt he was really out in the wilderness.

"You should hear them in the summer," Manuela said. "They're actually pretty quiet now. We have a lot of critters here in Texas."

A wheelchair ramp had been set up on the steps leading to the front porch. Manuela unlocked the door and held it open for Bond. "Hello!" she called. "Where are you, sweetheart?"

"In here!" It was a familiar voice, and Bond smiled.

"Put your luggage down," she said. "Felix is in the den."

A full-grown dalmatian jumped out from around the corner of the hallway. She immediately growled and barked at Bond.

"Esmerelda!" Manuela commanded. "Stop that. This is our friend, James."

Bond held out his hand, palm upward, then stooped down to the dog's level. The dalmatian sniffed his hand, then gave it a solid lick.

"Oh, she likes you already," Manuela said.

Bond scratched the animal's head and behind her ears. The tail started wagging; he had made a friend.

Bond and the dog followed Manuela through the long hallway, past a dining room and kitchen area, and into a large wood-paneled room full of furniture and high-tech equipment. There were large windows on two sides of the room, facing out into the woods behind the house. They were open, but the mesh screens kept the bugs out. It was an extremely pleasant atmosphere.

Felix Leiter turned away from the computer terminals and faced Bond with a big grin. He was sitting in an Action Arrow power chair, which silently turned on its wheels, steered by hand controls. Felix was still thin, and the way his knees stuck out from the chair reminded Bond how tall the man was. His straw-colored hair had gone a little gray, and his chin and cheekbones seemed sharper. What hadn't changed at all were the gray eyes, which had a feline slant that increased when he smiled broadly. The right hook had been replaced by a prosthesis that looked more like a hand, and it seemed to operate quite well. He held out his left hand.

"James Bond, you old horse thief!" he said. The slow drawl was warm and friendly. "Welcome to Texas, you goddamned limey!"

Bond clasped the hand. It was a firm, dry handshake. "Isn't the word 'limey' a bit old-fashioned, Felix?"

"What the hell, *we're* old-fashioned," Leiter said. "You can call me a bloody Yank for old times' sake, if you want."

"It's good to see you, Felix."

"Likewise, my friend. Sit, sit! Manuela will rustle us up some drinks. You met my lovely Manuela?"

"I did indeed."

"Hands off, James. She's mine, and she's loyal as hell."

"That's what *he* thinks!" Manuela called from the other room.

Bond laughed. "Don't worry, she couldn't do better than you. How long have you been together?"

"Two years. She's great, I tell you. Smarter than me too. She's a hell of an investigator. She's a field agent for the FBI. We hooked up when I did some freelance work on one of her cases. We've been on it ever since. We make a good team. She does all the dirty work while I stay at home and play with all these toys you see around the room."

"Glad to hear it. I take it you got my faxes?"

"Yes indeed, and I've already got some information for you. But drinks first!"

Bond smiled. It seemed that the most enduring element of their friendship throughout the years was their rather adolescent penchant to try to outdrink each other. He would never forget the barhopping they used to do in New York City, or Las Vegas, or in the Bahamas. Despite the fact that they came from two countries separated by a common language, Bond and Leiter understood each other. They were made of the same material. Both were men who had lived on the edge and survived to tell the tale. Leiter was also a man who, despite his handicap, could never be satisfied with retirement or inactivity.

Esmerelda settled down at Bond's feet, claiming him as her territory. Manuela brought in a tray with three shot glasses, a bottle of José Cuervo Gold tequila, some sliced limes, and a saltshaker. She set the tray on the small coffee table.

"What the hell?" Bond asked.

"You're in Texas now, James," Leiter said. "You're gonna do shots like the Texans do!"

"Oh for God's sake," Bond muttered, shaking his head.

"You know how, don't you?" Leiter asked, laughing. "Manuela, show him how we do it." Leiter poured tequila into one of the little glasses.

Manuela held her left hand to her face and licked the back of her hand just below where the thumb and index finger meet. She then took the saltshaker and sprinkled a little on the wet spot, so that the salt stuck to her skin. With a sly grin and her eyes glued to Bond's, she sensuously licked her hand again, this time lapping up the salt. Quickly, she took the shot glass and swallowed the entire measure of tequila in one gulp. She then grabbed a slice of lime and bit hard into it, sucking the juice and savoring it. She closed her eyes and her body shivered for a second.

"Now you try it," she said, holding out the saltshaker and pouring tequila into a glass.

"Are you serious?" Bond asked.

"You bet we are," Leiter said. "And later we'll go out for some real Tex-Mex cooking and have frozen margaritas!"

"Margaritas! You must be joking!"

Leiter laughed. "Come on, James, you'll love 'em. You know me. I was a hard liquor man like yourself . . . wouldn't touch anything but bourbon, whiskey, or vodka . . . but my Texas blood just took over once I moved back here. We all drink margaritas in Texas."

"And frozen ones are the best," Manuela added.

"Fine," Bond said with sarcasm. He went through the ritual of putting the salt on his hand, drinking the tequila, and biting the lime. It certainly wasn't the first time he had done it, but he felt a little silly. He had to admit that the tequila was good and strong, and the shock of lime added a burst of flavor which he had forgotten.

"Hell, you did that like an old pro," Leiter said, taking the bottle and pouring one for himself.

"I wasn't born yesterday," Bond said.

"Neither was I, my friend, neither was I," he said, licking the salt and going through the ritual himself.

The threesome polished off a couple more shots as they continued to talk. Bond and Leiter reminisced about past adventures together, and eventually the conversation got around to the Texan's condition.

"I got the chair a year ago, James," Leiter said. "It's been a big help. Not as much as Manuela, though."

Manuela blushed and looked down. She was feeling the effects of the alcohol and her face was glowing.

"Invacare is the company that distributes it—and this Arrow model is the top of the line in power chairs," Leiter said. "The sensitivity of the controls is amazing. Watch this."

Leiter's chair suddenly bolted forward and smashed into the coffee table, knocking over the tequila and glasses. Esmerelda yelped and jumped out of the way.

"Felix!" Manuela shouted. Luckily, she caught the bottle of tequila in midair.

Leiter, laughing hysterically, maneuvered the chair to the center of the room and spun it around three times very fast, then stopped on a dime. He popped a wheelie and landed hard, showing off the durability of the shocks, then backed up, spun around three times again, and started chasing the dog around the room. By then, everyone in the room was laughing.

Leiter stopped the chair and drove back to its earlier position. "I can go seven and a quarter miles an hour. That's fast, man. And I've also installed a few features of my own."

He popped open the right arm to reveal a cellular phone. Then he opened the left arm and had an ASP 9mm handgun in his left hand before Bond could blink.

"Very nice, Felix," Bond said. "That's the weapon I was using for a while."

"It's a great piece. You're not using it anymore?"

"No, I went back to the Walther."

"That old thing? Not much stopping power compared to some of today's stuff," Leiter said, replacing the pistol.

"I also use the new P99. It's a fine weapon."

"Yeah, I've seen that, it's a beauty. I've also got a baton under the seat." Leiter reached under the chair quickly and produced an ASP expandable police-style baton. "They get too close, I'll just whack 'em on the head."

Bond chuckled. "As long as you're happy, Felix," he said. "That's all that matters."

"What about you? How many women in your life these days?"

"None," Bond said, lighting a cigarette. He offered one to Leiter, who took it. Manuela refused.

"You're still smoking this shit?" Leiter asked. "You always liked them gourmet cigarettes. Give me a pack of Chesterfields or Marlboros any day. I want to *feel* that tar and nicotine poisoning my body!"

"Felix, you haven't changed a bit," Bond said. "I can't tell you how happy I am to see you."

"The pleasure's all mine, James. Oh . . . while I'm thinking about it . . ." He wheeled over to a desk and grabbed a cell phone.

"Take this," he said, handing it to Bond. It was an Ericsson, light and compact. "You might need it while you're here. My number is programmed into the speed dial. Just punch it and I'll come running . . . well, rolling, I suppose. Now . . . how can we help you?"

"Have you found out anything about Charles Hutchinson?"

"Yeah. Manuela did some digging after we got your fax. Seems like the boy's gone missing for a few days. He might be on a business trip. He works for a big-deal infertility clinic in Austin, one of those sperm bank things, and we've gathered that he travels around the world on their behalf. They're called ReproCare, and apparently they do business all over Europe and the Far East. It's owned by a European pharmaceutical company called BioLinks Limited."

"What a coincidence. One of our people was killed in Athens. He had confiscated a cache of chemical weapons smuggled into the country in frozen sperm."

Leiter and Manuela looked at each other. "We didn't know that," Leiter said. "That just confirms what we've been thinking all along. There's something between that infertility clinic and an underground militant outfit that operates around here called the Suppliers. This is the case we've been working on for two years."

"The Suppliers?" Bond asked. The name rang a bell. Of course! They were one of the terrorist organizations he had spent some time reading about recently.

"They've been under investigation by the FBI for some time now," Manuela said. "They reportedly deal in arms and military weapons. Lately they've been pushing chemical weapons and maybe even biological stuff. We do know that they're not picky about who they sell to. They've been known to supply some Middle Eastern terrorist factions with stuff. They've sold to the IRA. I've come to the conclusion that their main headquarters is right here in Austin or in a neighboring town."

"Where do they get their goods?"

"This is America, my friend," Leiter said with a sigh, as if that explained everything.

"Where did Alfred Hutchinson live?" Bond asked.

"It's actually not far from here. It's in West Lake Hills too. We've taken a look at it a couple of times, and it seems deserted. Charles has an apartment in the city, over in the Hyde Park area. It's an older section of town, but a lot of college students live there. The young man apparently has a thing for the young coeds. Can't say I blame him."

Manuela slapped Leiter on the shoulder. "Just kidding, dear," he said.

"We need to locate Charles," Bond said. "We're not sure if he knows his father is dead."

"We haven't made contact with ReproCare yet. We've been observing them, but I think it's about time we did make contact. How would you like to handle that, James? The doctor in charge is a woman who frequents the restaurant where we're going later. You've always been good at bringing out the best in women. Charles Hutchinson hangs out there too, because it's one of those college nightspots that are so popular."

Manuela spoke up. "He is some kind of playboy, this Charles. He drives a fancy sports car and always has a lot of girlfriends. He came to Austin a few years ago to attend the university, but he dropped out when he discovered he could get by on his good looks, English accent, and his father's notoriety."

"What's interesting is that once his father became a roving ambassador in England, Charles would accompany him on trips around the world. He's a real jet-setter. I imagine he's got a lot of money too. A spoiled rich kid," Leiter said.

"But that's not all," Manuela added, with an inflection that hinted that the best was yet to come.

"We suspect Charles Hutchinson may be involved with the Suppliers," Leiter said as he poured another shot of tequila.

"How do you know?"

"We have a list of people who we think are members of the Suppliers. We haven't got any hard evidence yet. We're on a wait-and-observe status, but we certainly have our suspects. Charles has been seen in their company . . . at the restaurant and in other public places. And these people aren't normally who you would expect an ambassador's rich kid to associate with. They're the type of people who still flaunt Confederate flags and look like Marine recruits."

"What evidence do you have that links this sperm bank with the Suppliers?"

Leiter shook his head. "None. We haven't found it yet. We're working on hunches. The connection just might be our little friend Charles. You coming here looking for him just might be the break we've been waiting for."

"Then we've got to find him."

"Agreed. Are you hungry?"

"Starving."

"Good. Prepare to feast at one of Austin's most popular and best restaurants. It's nothing fancy, but you can't get better Mexican food."

"It's Tex-Mex, not Mexican," Manuela said huffily.

"Manuela's a purist when it comes to Mexican food," Leiter explained. "Let's go."

With that, Leiter stood up and got out of the wheelchair. Bond was surprised at the ease with which the lanky Texan did so.

"What are you staring at, limey?" Leiter asked. "I can still walk!" He limped over to a corner of the room and grabbed a mahogany walking stick. "I just use the chair around the house 'cause I'm lazy and enjoy the ride. And it's got a great built-in vibrating lower lumbar massager in it. That's the best part! Let's hit the road, Jack."

▶7.
THE SUPPLIERS

Manuela drove Bond and Leiter back to the area of Barton Springs Road just east of Zilker Park. The sun had set and the college kids were out in force. "Restaurant Row" was lined with several establishments specializing in trendy Texas-style foods and other cuisines, plus a sports shop featuring Rollerblade and surfboard products. She pulled into the crowded parking lot of Chuy's Restaurant, a gaudy establishment that resembled the drive-ins of the late fifties and early sixties.

Bond had changed into casual wear—navy trousers, a light blue Sea Island cotton shirt, and a light navy jacket. He wore his Walther PPK in a shoulder holster underneath the jacket. Manuela had assured him that he was "casual" enough.

When they walked in the door, they were assaulted by loud pop music and the cacophony of a large crowd. Bond felt like a fish out of water, for many of the patrons around him were twenty years younger or more. Here was the youth of America in all their glory, and in all shapes, sizes, and colors. There were clean-cut yuppies dressed in designer clothes, and shabby pseudohippies with long hair and tie-dyed T-shirts. Some of the men were dressed like cowboys; others wore jackets and ties. The women wore anything from business suits to T-shirts and cutoffs.

This onslaught on Bond's senses was nothing compared to the shock he got when he focused on the interior design. "Overly festive" and "much too colorful" were the descriptions that came to mind. In the front entryway was an Elvis Presley shrine behind glass. It was decorated with a bust of "the King," a toy guitar, colored wooden fish, and other odd items. The *mil pescado* bar was decorated with a thousand colored fishes hanging from the ceiling. It was all designed to evoke a hip, pop-art style with a slightly off-center sensibility. Bond realized that some people would find it amusing, but he was put off by the atmosphere. It wasn't his kind of place.

"So you really recommend this spot?" he asked.

"You'll love it," Leiter said.

"I'm not loving it so far."

"I know, it's crowded and noisy, and it looks like your worst nightmare, but the food is incredible. Look at those women. Christ. You know, Texas girls are the most beautiful in America."

"I thought that's what they said about California girls."

"No way, José. Just look around."

"He's right, James, the women are beautiful in Texas," said Manuela. "Too bad the men are all jerks."

Leiter had some pull with the manager, so they didn't have to wait the usual forty-five minutes before being shown to a table at a booth. A waiter placed a basket of hand-fried tortilla chips with fresh homemade salsa in front of them. The utensils were inside a wax-paper packet which read, "This silverware has been SANITIZED for your protection!" Leiter ordered two rounds of frozen margaritas, much to Bond's dismay. Made from silver tequila, squeezed lime juice, and triple sec, margaritas were a staple in Texas, and the frozen variety made a slushy beverage that Bond liked to call "a musical comedy drink." It was served in a salted wineglass with a lime wedge. When he tasted it, however, he was surprised by its satisfying flavor. It certainly went well with the hot salsa. Leiter and Bond were soon laughing and reminiscing about old times.

The menu featured a variety of Tex-Mex specialties. Leiter and Manuela ordered fajitas for two. They recommended that Bond try either the fajitas or the enchiladas. He chose the latter. As an appetizer, they shared a bowl of chile con queso—a hot cheese dip made from cheddar and American cheeses, red peppers, and roasted tomatoes. When the food arrived, Bond could hardly believe his eyes. It is said that everything is big in Texas, and that certainly applied to the food portions. The enormous enchiladas were hand-rolled corn tortillas stuffed with ground sirloin and topped with the restaurant's special Tex-Mex sauce—a red chile sauce with chili meat—and then with melted cheese. On the side were refried pinto beans cooked with garlic and onions. The Mexican rice was mildly flavored with onions and tomatoes.

"All right, Felix, you win," Bond said after tasting the food. "This is good."

"What'd I tell you?" Leiter said, his mouth full of chicken. He and Manuela were sharing chicken fajitas which were marinated in beer, oil, and spices, then grilled with onions, cilantro, and bell peppers.

"Do you see any of our targets?" Bond asked, once he had finished with the rich food.

"As a matter of fact, Dr. Ashley Anderson just sat down at the table over by the aquarium," Leiter said.

"She's the boss at ReproCare," explained Manuela. "She was brought into the company when it was sold to BioLinks. ReproCare was about to go bankrupt when BioLinks stepped in and took it over."

Bond glanced across the room. A tall blonde woman who looked like a model a bit past her prime was just sitting down opposite a large cowboy. She was still quite striking, probably in her late thirties, and was dressed conservatively in a business suit. The skirt was short, revealing long shapely legs in high heels. Dr. Anderson exhibited an aura of self-confidence and authority. Bond might not have guessed that she was a physician, but he certainly would have placed her at the top of a large corporation.

The cowboy, on the other hand, was in his forties and looked like redneck white trash. He was bulky and overweight, but most of the mass was muscle. He was dressed in a sleeveless blue shirt, revealing large biceps. Tattoos were prominent on both arms. Sewn across the back of the shirt was a Confederate flag. He wore a large Stetson, blue jeans, and brown cowboy boots. His round baby face was distinctively marked by a scar that ran down the length of his left cheek. He was the complete antithesis of Dr. Ashley Anderson.

"Well, well," Leiter said. "This could be our first big break."

"How is that?"

"The fellow she's with is Jack Herman. He's a lowlife who's been on our list for a long time. If he's not a member of the Suppliers, then they're missing out on an excellent employment opportunity."

"What do you know about him?"

"He's been convicted of a couple of crimes, served some time, got out. He's probably on parole as we speak, but ten to one says he's breaking it. He was busted for selling drugs about fifteen years ago and spent three years in the penitentiary. His next biggie was armed robbery. He got ten years for that but only served six. I can guarantee you that he's not sitting with Dr. Anderson discussing how he can become a donor to the sperm bank."

"You thought that the clinic might have connections to the Suppliers . . ."

"I never would have thought Dr. Anderson would be involved," Manuela said. "She always seemed so respectable. But then again, she tends to enjoy the nightlife quite a bit. She's been seen with all kinds of men — and women — when you think about it, Felix. I actually wouldn't be surprised if she swings both ways."

"Yeah, and don't forget our friend Charles Hutchinson. They were an item for a little while."

"I don't know if it was sexual," Manuela said. "But yes, they were often seen in public together for a couple of months."

"If they were an item, it was sexual. She is, after all, a woman who collects sperm," Bond said in mock seriousness. Leiter burst out laughing. Manuela rolled her eyes.

"How can they sell sperm outside the U.S.? I find that very odd. Can they do that legally?" Bond asked.

"Apparently so," Leiter said. "You're right, it *is* unusual. Other sperm banks just deal their stuff domestically. ReproCare, however, is touted as having 'the finest sperm' in America. They sell it to other infertility clinics all over the world. I guess people think they're getting a good deal if it came from America."

"Tell me more about the Suppliers," Bond continued.

"They've been around about six years," Manuela said. "The FBI caught one of their leaders three years ago, before I was on the case. Fellow by the name of Bob Gibson. He was suspected of organized crime, selling illegal weapons and smuggling arms overseas, but the only thing we could convict him on was possession of illegal arms. He's still in prison. We're not sure who's in charge now, but as we told you, they operate out of Austin or somewhere nearby. They have tentacles that reach all over the country, though. There was a fellow who was driving a truck from Alaska to Canada, en route to Arkansas, who was implicated in carrying a deadly material called ricin."

"I know about ricin," Bond said.

Leiter continued the story. "When the Canadian customs agents searched the truck, they found four guns, twenty thousand rounds of ammunition, thirteen pounds of black powder, neo-Nazi literature, and three books that you can't buy at most bookstores, but that can be purchased by mail order or over the Internet. They were all about subversive warfare. A couple of the books detailed how to extract ricin from castor beans. Also in the truck was a plastic bag filled with white powder, and about eighty thousand in cash."

"What happened?"

"The man actually warned the inspectors not to open the bag of white powder. He told them it was deadly. The computer check on the guy was clear, so they let him go—without the powder. It turns out that it was enough ricin to wipe out a large suburb—it's one of the deadliest nerve poisons, and there's no antidote."

"I'm familiar with it," Bond said.

"Well, what was he doing with it? Even though it's not against the law to possess the stuff, the FBI became interested in him and he was arrested later in Arkansas on a minor traffic charge. He hung himself in his cell before any answers could be found. It turned out he lived in Austin."

Manuela picked up the story from there. "We searched his house and found a tin can filled with a pound and a half of castor beans and more recipe books for making ricin. His lawyer said his client had planned to use the ricin for peaceful purposes, such as killing coyotes that threatened his chickens or something like that. He claimed people had the right to have rat poison or coyote poison, just like they had the right to carry a handgun. The federal prosecutor in Arkansas replied to that one by saying it was tantamount to insisting you could use an atomic bomb to protect your property from a burglar. The most important thing we found in the house was literature about the Suppliers. That's what really clued everyone in on the organization. He was one of their couriers."

"It's believed that he was supplying ricin to the Minnesota Patriots, another nasty group of right-wing freaks," Leiter said.

The cowboy, Jack Herman, stood up and shook Dr. Anderson's hand. He left the restaurant without looking back. Dr. Ashley Anderson sat at her table alone.

"Well, it's now or never," Bond said. He got up and strolled over to where she was sitting.

"Hello, Dr. Anderson?" he said. She looked up at him, prepared to brush him off. Before she could say, "Get lost," the words caught in her mouth. Who was this dark handsome stranger standing before her?

"The name is Bond. James Bond. I saw that you were sitting alone," he said. "I'm visiting Austin from England for the first time, and I'd like to talk to you. May I buy you a drink?"

"Well, I don't normally accept drinks from strangers," she said in a broad Texas accent, "but since you're here all the way from England you can't be all bad. Have a seat. How did you know my name?"

Bond extended his hand. She shook it briefly; then he sat down.

Before answering her question, Bond caught the waiter and ordered two frozen margaritas.

"I'm a friend of Alfred Hutchinson. I'm looking for his son, Charles. I understand you know him."

Ashley Anderson blinked. Bond was sure that he had caught her completely off guard, but she rebounded quickly and said, "Yes, he works at my clinic."

"Do you have any idea where he is? It's imperative that I find him."

"Why?"

"Well, his father died three days ago."

The woman blinked again. Bond searched her face for signs that she might be surprised at hearing this news, but his instincts told him that she already knew.

"Oh dear," she said. "I'm sorry to hear that."

"I've been dispatched over here to find Charles, as Mr. Hutchinson's lawyers have been unable to contact him. He's wanted for funeral arrangements and other matters."

"I see," she said. "I haven't seen him in over a week. I've been in Europe for several days. In fact, I just got back today. Charles is one of our couriers. He carries sperm for our clinic—I run an infertility clinic—"

"I know," Bond said.

"Unfortunately, I really don't deal with our couriers' schedules. I think he left for Europe while I was gone. I'm not exactly certain when he's due to be back, but he's never gone more than a few days."

"Where did he go?"

"France? Or Italy. I'm not sure. I could check tomorrow at the clinic. I can find out when he'll be back too. Maybe we can get hold of him. Why don't you give us a call tomorrow? I'll give you my card."

"Could I come by the clinic instead of phoning? Maybe we can have lunch and you can tell me what all I'd have to do if I wanted to become a donor."

Ashley Anderson smiled. The English stranger worked fast.

"If you'd like to do that, come on by. I can't do lunch, though." She handed him her card. "I'm tied up until the afternoon. Can you come about two o'clock?"

"Fine, I'll be there." The drinks arrived and there was a short silence. Bond studied Ashley Anderson's face now that he was close to her. She had a wide mouth and large blue eyes. Her blond hair was shoulder-length, thin and straight. She was looking at him as if she were evaluating prize livestock. He finally broke the silence by saying, "Tell me a little about the clinic. I've always been curious about how those things work."

"Sperm banks? Well, we basically serve two functions. The first is we supply sperm to patients with infertility problems. The second is we provide the means for cancer patients to freeze and store their sperm before undergoing radiation therapy."

"So how *does* one become a donor?"

"There is a rigorous screening process," Dr. Anderson said. "We only take the best." She said that with a seductive smile. "You look like you have good genes. Are you serious about applying?"

Bond laughed. "Oh, I don't think so. I doubt that I'd meet your requirements."

After a moment's pause, she said, "I don't know if you'd meet the clinic's requirements, but you definitely meet mine."

Bond had hoped that she might be attracted to him. Throughout his long career as a secret agent, he had often gained the most ground with the enemy by sleeping with them. Seduction was a method used by spies dating all the way back to the time of Cleopatra. James Bond happened to be very good at it.

"Two o'clock, then."

The waiter brought Dr. Anderson her meal, breaking a moment of sexual tension that seemed to have generated from nowhere. She had ordered cheese enchiladas, refried beans, and guacamole.

"That looks good," Bond said.

"I love Tex-Mex," she said. "As long as there isn't any meat. I'm strictly a vegetarian."

"I'm not sure I could live that way," Bond said. "I do eat animals."

"I'm sure you do," she said suggestively.

"Well, look, I think I'll let you enjoy your meal. I'm going to rejoin my friends over there. I'll see you tomorrow afternoon, all right?"

"I look forward to it, Mr. Bond, but don't rush off on my account," she said.

"Believe me, I'd stay if I could, but I must get back. Have a lovely evening." He got up and went back to Leiter and Manuela.

"She swallowed it, hook, line, and sinker," Bond said. "Charles is in Europe on a business trip for the clinic. So she claims. We'll find out tomorrow where he is."

"Great," Leiter said. "I thought we'd go take a look at Hutchinson's house on the way back home. Or are you too tired?"

"No, no," Bond said. "I'm getting my second wind. Let's do it."

Alfred Hutchinson's American home was in a secluded wooded area off the beaten track on the western outskirts of West Lake Hills. The house wasn't visible from the road, so Manuela had to park out by the mailbox at the entrance to the drive. Bond got out of the car.

"Give me an hour," he said.

"We'll pick you up back at the top of the road," Leiter said. "Use the mobile phone if you need us before then." The car quietly sped away and left Bond standing in the dark. There were no streetlights, and the dense woods blocked all available moonlight. The cicadas were out in force, so he doubted that anyone could hear his footsteps on the dead leaves.

He slipped on the Q Branch night-vision goggles, which brought the surroundings to life. He could now make out everything clearly.

Bond crept down the path about a hundred meters and came to the broad ranch house that had a rustic, log cabin feel to it. It was dark and quiet. He paused long enough to open the heel of his right shoe and extract the alarm-sensor nullifier which Major Boothroyd had given him. He turned it on and pointed it at the house. A red light indicated that alarms were indeed set to go off if someone tried to break in. Bond pushed the green button and the red light stopped blinking.

He moved around to the side of the house, looking for a window that he might open without having to cause any damage. He found a back door. It had a standard lock—no dead bolt—so he thought he could pick it easily. He deactivated the alarms at the back of the house, then removed a wire lockpick from his belt buckle. He worked for two minutes on the lock, and the door swung open.

The house smelled damp and felt cold, as if it hadn't been occupied for a while. Bond moved through what was apparently a laundry and utility room into a kitchen. Beyond the kitchen was a dining room and a hallway to the rest of the house. He made a quick survey of the living room, then moved down the hall, past two bedrooms, and finally found what he was looking for. He took a deep breath when he saw what had happened.

Hutchinson's office had been ransacked. The room was covered in papers and opened manila filing folders. The filing cabinet drawers were left open. A large rolltop desk dominated the room, and it had been broken into as well. Its drawers were out and on the floor, the contents scattered over the gray carpet. A Gateway 2000 IBM-compatible computer sat on the desk.

Bond carefully stepped through the rubbish, looking for anything of interest. Most of the papers were teaching materials or nonsensitive diplomatic information. Nothing was left in the filing cabinets. Whether or not whoever did this had found what they were looking for was unclear. What could Alfred Hutchinson have been hiding? Was he involved with the Suppliers? Could they be behind the attacks in Greece and Cyprus? Did they kill Alfred Hutchinson?

Bond went to the computer and booted it up. After a minute, the familiar Windows 95 desktop glowed on the monitor. Bond clicked on the "My Computer" icon and perused the names of file folders on the hard drive. A personal folder called "My Data" was the only thing that wasn't a part of any normal system. Inside that folder were a couple of internal folders, one labeled "Teaching," and one labeled "Ambassador." Bond clicked on the "Ambassador" folder and found about four dozen files of various subjects. They all seemed innocuous and useless. The "Teaching" folder also contained nothing of interest.

Bond was about to perform a search for the word "Suppliers" on all the files when he heard a car door slam outside. He froze. Another door slammed. Someone was out in front.

He quickly shut down the computer. The front door of the house opened and he heard a man's voice say, "Hey, the alarm's turned off."

A woman said, "That's weird. I could have sworn I turned it back on when I left."

"You've left it off before."

"I know. Come on, let's hurry. It's in the office."

Whoever it was, they were walking down the hallway straight for Bond!

►8.
MANSION ON THE HILL

There was no time to leave the room. Bond leaped across the floor to the empty filing cabinets. He gently pushed one away from the wall and squeezed in behind it. From here, he had a narrow view of the desk and the computer terminal. He held his breath and waited.

The man and woman entered the office and flicked on the lights. The shock of illumination nearly blinded Bond. He switched off the night-vision goggles but kept them on.

"Place is still a mess," the man said.

"What did you expect? The maid to clean up after us?" the woman said sarcastically. Bond thought he knew the voice. He noted that the couple knew about the condition of the room before entering.

She stepped over the debris and went to the computer on the desk. Bond could see her back now, and he wasn't surprised to see the business suit and long blond hair. Dr. Ashley Anderson booted up the computer and then sat down in the office chair on wheels. The man came into view and stood at her side, looking at the monitor. It was the cowboy, Jack Herman.

"How do you know how to find it on that thing?" Herman asked.

"Haven't you ever used a computer, Jack?" she asked. "You can ask it to find any file that's on the hard drive."

"Is it there?"

"Hold your horses. I'm looking."

The cowboy shrugged and moved away from the desk. He started kicking some of the debris. Bond was afraid he might wander over to his side of the room. If he looked too closely, he would see Bond hiding behind the filing cabinet. Bond leaned back against the wall, now unable to see anything in the office. He listened and waited. The cowboy's boots were shuffling the papers on the floor. The sound was coming closer. He was just feet away from Bond.

"Would you stop that noise?" Dr. Anderson commanded. "It's annoying."

"Sorry," the cowboy said, and sauntered back to the desk. "I just don't understand why we're doing this. Who is this guy, anyway? What does he have to do with the Suppliers?"

"Don't worry about it and just do what you're told, Jack."

The cowboy grunted. "Found it yet?"

"Hell, no," she said. "It's not here. The file must have been deleted. Listen, I've got to get to the clinic. Remember the man I introduced you to the other day?"

"You mean that guy from Greece?"

"Yes. He's out at the mansion. I need you to go there and let him know we couldn't find the file. Would you do that?"

"I was going over there anyway. Shut that thing down and let's go," Herman said.

She turned off the computer; then they switched off the lights and left the room.

"Reactivate that alarm, would you?" Dr. Anderson said.

Bond waited a moment, until he heard their footsteps at the front door. He slipped out from behind the cabinet and reactivated his goggles. He quickly moved to the back of the house, used the sensor nullifier on the alarm once again, and went out of the door he had come in by. As quietly as possible, he moved over the crackling dead leaves to the front of the house.

Dr. Ashley Anderson was getting into a pink Porsche. The cowboy was inside a beat-up Ford F-150 pickup truck. Tied down in the back of the truck was a Kawasaki Enduro motorcycle. Dr. Anderson drove off down the path out of the property. The cowboy started the pickup.

It was now or never. Keeping low, Bond ran and climbed onto the back of the pickup truck just as it was leaving. He slipped over the tailgate and flattened himself on the bed of the truck. The cowboy drove out onto the street and followed the Porsche. Bond was unable to watch where the truck was going because he had to stay down. He removed the goggles and tightened the strap so that they clung to his neck. Luckily the cowboy was alone in the cab. Bond could see a shotgun propped up on a rack behind him.

The two vehicles separated when they reached Bee Caves Road. The Porsche turned left and headed toward Austin. The pickup turned right and went west out toward the hills. It eventually reached Loop 360, also known as the Capital of Texas Highway, and turned right.

While officially still in Travis County, this was the country. A half-moon shone through a dark cloudy sky, casting a soft glow on the rolling hills. Most of the autumn leaves had fallen, giving the trees a skeletal, ghostly appearance. The wide road curved up and around the cliffs, every now and then passing side roads leading into the darkness. After nearly twelve minutes, the truck turned off the highway and headed west again on Farm Road 2222, a somewhat treacherous highway that led to Lake Travis. The cowboy drove recklessly, taking the curves too sharply. All Bond could see, though, was the sheer cliff towering above him on one side of the truck, and the night sky on the other.

Soon the truck turned left onto City Park Road, an uphill winding two-lane road. Raising himself slightly, he could see the vast city lights spread out to the east of the truck. He would have liked to be able to remember the route they had taken, but he was a stranger and totally lost.

The truck finally stopped on a gravel road that sliced through some dense trees. Bond pressed himself against the side of the truck bed, hoping that the cowboy wouldn't look in the back when he got out of the vehicle. The door opened and Bond heard the boots stomp down onto the gravel. The door slammed shut, and the footsteps moved away from the truck.

Bond peered over the edge of the truck bed and saw a mansion designed to look like an ancient Greek temple. The cowboy was walking toward an archway at the front of the house. Old-fashioned gas pole lamps were positioned around the mansion, and there were even caryatids sculpted along the perimeter of the roof, matching those that still remained on the Erechtheion of the Acropolis in Athens. Full-size statues of Greek gods and heroes were scattered around the front lawn. The place was decidedly sinister, and it was obvious that this was its owner's intention.

As soon as Jack Herman was out of sight, Bond leaped over the tailgate and hugged the back end of the truck. After making sure no one was outside the house, he ran to the side of the building. The front of the house was well lit, but luckily the sides were not. He crept up to a large window and looked inside.

The cowboy was greeting a large, swarthy man dressed in a black turtleneck cotton shirt and black trousers. He had black curly hair, a black beard and mustache, and black eyebrows. The size of the man was extraordinary. Jack Herman was a big guy with plenty of muscle, but the swarthy man was even larger—obviously a bodybuilder with the biceps to prove it. He probably weighed 250 pounds or more, but there wasn't an ounce of fat on his body. He had no neck, just a large block of a head sitting on a wall of shoulders.

Another man dressed as a cowboy appeared next to the bodybuilder and shook hands with Jack Herman. He was tall and blond, another roughneck type who seemed to be part of the same team as Herman. The bodybuilder, in contrast, looked out of place with his swarthy Mediterranean features. Bond recalled Jack Herman saying that the man was Greek.

The three figures moved from the entry hall into a living room which matched the ancient Greek design theme of the house. The floor was made of marble. The furniture was a chic wooden fake antique, and a collection of swords, shields, and maces adorned the stone walls. Bond moved along the side of the house to the next window and looked in. The three men joined another man sitting in an armchair. He was much younger, probably in his twenties. He was a good-looking fellow with brown hair and blue eyes, dressed sharply in a tweed jacket and dark trousers. Bond recognized him from the file photos. He was Charles Hutchinson.

Bond couldn't hear what the men were saying, but inside the room Jack Herman was shaking his head at the European. Bond figured that the cowboy was breaking the bad news that they didn't find whatever it was Ashley Anderson was looking for on Alfred Hutchinson's computer. Charles Hutchinson stood up, an expression of uncertainty and fear on his face. The swarthy bodybuilder turned and gave Charles a glare that Greeks would have called "the evil eye." Charles was distressed, and he attempted to say something. The Greek backhanded Charles, who fell to the floor. The two cowboys just stood there and grinned. The bodybuilder dismissed them and they left the room.

After a moment, Charles pulled himself up off the floor and rubbed his chin in humiliation. He sat on the wooden armchair he had been in before and stared straight ahead. The bodybuilder said something to him, then walked out of the room.

Bond could hear the two cowboys leave by the front door. He crouched down into the shadows and watched as the two men proceeded to open the tailgate and remove the Kawasaki from its cradle. After five agonizing minutes, the men got the cycle out of the truck and wheeled it onto the gravel driveway in front of the house, out of Bond's line of sight. He stood up again and looked in the window. Charles was still sitting there, looking glum.

Bond moved down to the next window in line. The bodybuilder was sitting at a desk, typing on a computer terminal with one finger. His hands were so large that his fingers were easily the size of cigars.

The room was a small office with some modern furnishings. Bond was particularly struck by the strange flag on the wall above the desk. It was roughly four feet square and it pictured an equilateral triangle made of ten red dots on a black background. There were four dots along the bottom, then three, with two on top of those, then one—much like the setup of bowling pins seen from above. A large mirror was on the opposite wall, and Bond was fortunately at just the right angle so that he could see the bodybuilder's back and the computer monitor in the mirror. It was too far away to read what was on the screen, but Bond could glean that the man was on-line, talking "live" with someone over the Internet. He knew this because lines of text appeared at the bottom of the screen, and then the bodybuilder would type with one finger and hit the return key. New lines of text would appear, followed by another set of lines.

The sound of one of the cowboys kick-starting the motorcycle came from the front of the house. One of them yelled, "Yee-ha!" The machine sat there idling, and every now and then the engine would rev up. It was quite loud.

It wasn't half as loud as the sudden dog bark that Bond heard a few yards away from him. The noise had attracted the attention of a Doberman that had been at the back of the house. She was full-grown, black as coal, and had fierce eyes that practically glowed in the dark. She growled and barked again at Bond, ready to pounce if he so much as twitched.

He knew he couldn't wait for her barking to bring out the men, so he braced himself for the attack and faced the dog. She leaped at him, teeth bared. Bond deftly rolled onto his back as the dog made contact and at the same time he grabbed her neck. In a maneuver that could only be equaled by circus acrobats and other Double-O agents, Bond used the dog's forward momentum to pull her over his body and into the glass window. The Doberman shattered the pane, howling. That set off the alarms.

Without hesitation, Bond got to his feet and ran to the front of the house. The dog would certainly jump back through the window in pursuit. The two cowboys were frozen in stunned amazement at the sudden flurry of activity. Jack Herman was standing by the motorcycle, and the blond fellow was sitting on it. Bond made a running jump and kicked Jack Herman in the face, knocking him to the ground. He then swung his leg around and caught the other man on the chest, knocking him off the Kawasaki. Bond caught the cycle before it fell on its side, and jumped on. He revved it up and took off down the gravel path.

"Hey!" he heard one of the cowboys shout, followed by the barking of the Doberman, hot in pursuit.

The Kawasaki KDX200 is a bike specifically made for heavy-duty off-road riding. Its single-cylinder two-stroke motor is fast and tractable. Ideal for heading into rough country, its dogleg control levers are covered with plastic handguards. Bond was extremely lucky that it had been made "available" to him!

He sped out of the gravel drive and onto City Park Road. In no time he was doing seventy miles per hour, which was particularly precarious on the winding, two-lane road. He had left the dog in the dust, but the Ford pickup was not far behind. With one hand, Bond slipped on the night-vision goggles again and cut off the lights on the bike. He then increased his speed to eighty and leaned into the motorcycle. Becoming one with the machine, he cut through the air and concentrated on curves in the road. There were very few oncoming vehicles.

The truck was gaining. A shotgun blast rang out behind him, but from too far back for the shot to be effective.

Bond felt his heart stop as he rounded a blind curve to see two on-coming cars—one in his lane! Its driver had been foolishly attempting to pass the other car and was two seconds away from colliding with the motorcycle!

Bond swerved to the right and the Kawasaki shot off the road into the woods. The terrain went into a dangerous incline, and 007 held on for dear life as the cycle plummeted down—remarkably, staying upright on its wheels. He dodged trees the best he could, but a branch hit him in the face and shoulder, nearly knocking him off the vehicle. The incline got worse and Bond realized that at any moment the cycle would lose its traction and they would begin to fall down what was to become a sheer cliff. He attempted to brake, but that only caused the Kawasaki to skid. Gravity took over, and the motorcycle fell sideways down the side of the mountain. Bond jumped and tried to grab hold of a tree, but he missed. He started rolling down the side of the cliff behind the cycle, unable to stop. He fell hard against a large rock, getting the breath knocked out of him, but he continued to plummet downward.

The incline ended abruptly at a sharp cliff edge. The Kawasaki sailed over the cliff into the air. Bond rolled and exerted a superhuman effort to grasp a tree branch that extended out over the cliff. He hung there, gasping for air.

Twenty-five feet below him was Farm Road 2222. He was hanging over the highway. The cycle had crashed onto the road and lay there beneath him. He could probably drop down and roll without injuring himself any more than he already had. For the moment, he held on to the tree branch and caught his breath. His face and shoulder were in great pain, and his right side was injured. He was afraid he might have broken a rib.

Then the pickup truck came barreling down the road below him. The driver didn't see the wreckage of the Kawasaki in time. He plowed into it, causing the pickup to swerve into the lane directly beneath Bond; 007 let go of the branch and dropped into the bed of the truck. The Ford kept going and got back into its lane. The passenger, the blond cowboy, had a pistol of some kind. He leaned out of the window and shot back at Bond, but he was in an awkward position and couldn't hold the gun steady. Bond removed his Walther PPK from its holster and blasted a hole in the back windshield of the truck. The blond cowboy caught the slug in the face.

Bond moved up to the driver's side of the truck, stuck his arm through the broken windshield, and put the Walther to Jack Herman's head.

"Stop the bloody truck," he commanded.

Herman nodded, but kept driving.

"I said stop it, or I'll make you stop it," Bond said.

There was traffic behind the truck, and more was beginning to appear in the oncoming lane.

"I can't stop it here! Let me pull over up ahead where there's an extra lane," the cowboy pleaded.

"Just make sure you do."

Instead of slowing down, though, Jack Herman floored the pedal and swerved the truck into the slow-traffic lane. To the right of the truck was a serious cliff—it made the one Bond tumbled down seem like a sand dune. Christ! Bond thought. The bastard intended to kill them both rather than be arrested!

Bond pulled his arm out of the broken windshield and jumped over the side of the truck just as the Ford careened over the guardrail. He hit the pavement hard and rolled with the impact. The pickup seemed to sail through the air in slow motion. He heard Jack Herman scream, and then the truck disappeared from view. Bond heard the impact a second later as the truck smashed into the side of the cliff and exploded.

He pulled himself off the road and limped to the side. The truck was aflame and was continuing to roll down the cliff into the darkness below.

Bond examined his body. His forehead and the left side of his face were scraped badly and bleeding. His shoulder hurt like hell, but nothing seemed out of joint. His right side was the worst. He had experienced broken ribs before, and this sensation was aggravatingly similar. It was a miracle he could walk away from what had just happened.

Bond found his Walther lying nearby and holstered it. He reached into his pocket and found that Leiter's cell phone was smashed. Cars were zooming past him, unaware of the fireball at the base of the cliff to their right. Bond limped along the road, heading east back toward town. No one stopped to see if he needed help, and he wasn't about to hitchhike.

Two hours later, Bond saw a small bar called the Watering Hole off the road to the right. A sign on the door warned, "Don't Mess with

Texas." He stumbled inside and surveyed the place. A saloon would have been a more appropriate description, as it was full of an odd mixture of cowboys and long-haired biker types. The jukebox was blaring one of George Jones's more famous beer-drinking songs at an extraordinary volume. Everyone stopped what they were doing and looked at Bond. A pool player in the middle of a shot scratched the table as he looked up and saw the battered figure in the doorway.

Bond ignored them all and went straight to the bar.

"Whiskey," he ordered. "A double."

The bartender didn't say a word and poured him two glasses of Johnny Walker. "Have a double double, mister. What the hell happened to you?"

"Nothing much," he replied. "Just fell off a cliff."

Bond drank one glass quickly and felt the warmth invigorate him. He closed his eyes tightly, then coughed. Considering that he was still suffering from jet lag and fighting a cold, it was a wonder that the ordeal he had just been through didn't kill him. He was exhausted.

He drank the other glass of whiskey, then asked to use a phone. The bartender pointed him to the pay phone, then said, "Nah, forget it. Here, use mine." He placed a phone on the bar and let Bond call Felix Leiter for free.

The old adage that Texans were genuinely friendy people was apparently true. Most of them, anyway.

▶ 9.
THE SPERM BANK

The mysterious malady that struck Los Angeles had attracted the attention of the Centers for Disease Control in Atlanta. A special investigative team arrived to find that fifty-two people had died from what was being called "Williams's disease," named after the man who had the first known case. Health officials in the city were opposed to making a public announcement for fear of creating a panic. The team from Atlanta began the tedious task of locating anyone who may have been in contact with the victims in the last twenty-four hours of their lives. At this point, no one could discern where the disease came from or how it worked. Preliminary tests revealed that the virus died shortly after its host did, leaving biochemists without a sample to study.

In Tokyo, things were worse. The death toll had risen to seventy. In twenty-four hours, the disease would surface in New York City and London, leaving in its wake a total of twelve people dead in one day.

Bond slept late to allow his body to recover from the previous evening's exertions. Manuela had examined him thoroughly—she turned out to be a qualified registered nurse as well as a damned good investigator—and had determined there were no broken ribs. Bond had one hell of a bruise, though, and his side was quite tender. His forehead and cheek had been scraped, but that would heal quickly. The left shoulder had been knocked out of joint, but wasn't completely dislocated. Manuela performed a bit of chiropractic therapy and got it back in place.

Since he was unable to say exactly where he had been the night before, after lunch Manuela and Leiter took Bond back over Farm Road 2222, past the bar where they had picked him up. He recognized the City Park Road turnoff, so it was only a small matter of time before they found the mansion in the hills. Leiter said he'd work on finding out who lived there, while 007 kept his two o'clock appointment at ReproCare. Bond's revelation of seeing Charles Hutchinson in the house was most interesting. Manuela had gone to Hutchinson's apartment in the Hyde Park area and learned from the manager that the young man had vacated it. The manager was very angry, because Hutchinson had broken a lease and taken off without a month's notice. Movers had taken away his things yesterday. The manager had not seen Charles Hutchinson personally, but received word of his departure from a lawyer. Manuela impressed the manager with her FBI credentials and gained access to the empty apartment, and also saw the letter from the lawyer. An hour later, she had confirmed that the lawyer didn't exist.

Either Charles Hutchinson was in with the bad guys or he was a prisoner being held at the mansion against his will.

Before they took Bond into town, Leiter gave him another cell phone. "Let's not break this one, it's the last spare I've got," he said.

"You're beginning to sound like an armorer I know in London," Bond replied.

ReproCare was located on Thirty-eighth Street in an office park near the large medical center that serviced much of north central Austin. A glass door carried the inscription "ReproCare— Infertility Therapy, CryoCenter."

Manuela and Leiter dropped Bond off and he went inside. The waiting room was small but typical of a doctor's office. An attractive young nurse with a Dictaphone headset in her ears was typing inside the reception office. She looked up at Bond and smiled broadly.

"May I help you?" she asked in a thick Texas accent.

"Uhm, yes, I have a two o'clock appointment with Dr. Anderson? The name is Bond. James Bond."

The nurse consulted her book. "Oh yeah, I have a note here. She's been detained for a while. But she wanted you to fill out all these forms, and when you're done someone'll take you back to a room for your first specimen."

"My first specimen?"

"You're here as a donor applicant, aren't you?" She smiled knowingly, quite used to having to deal with men who were embarrassed by what they had come to do.

It wasn't exactly what Bond had in mind, but he went along with it. "Right."

"Read the instructions on the forms and that'll explain what'll happen today. The doctor will talk to you beforehand, so don't worry."

Bond took the clipboard from the nurse and sat down in the waiting room. The forms numbered about ten pages, front and back. The cover sheet explained that donors needed to be over the age of eighteen and must go through an intensive screening procedure that included completion of a medical and genetic history questionnaire, a personal interview by the laboratory supervisor and complete semen analysis, a physical examination by a physician and testing for major infectious diseases. The first step to being accepted as a donor was to complete the questionnaire. If the applicant met the requirement of sexual abstinence for at least forty-eight hours prior to visiting the clinic, a first semen specimen would be taken after a brief interview. All information about the donors was kept completely confidential.

The questionnaire was very thorough. It asked about the applicant's medical and ethnic history. There were questions about personal interests and hobbies. Lifestyle and behavioral questions took up a large portion of the document. There were queries on nearly every disease known to man, sexual preferences, current and past medications and surgeries. Bond figured that the clinic had extremely high standards and that nearly everything in the questionnaire must be answered satisfactorily. He chuckled as he pondered that it was probably more difficult to be accepted as a semen donor than it was to become an agent with SIS.

It took him nearly an hour to fill out the forms. He falsified much of the information, but for his own amusement he attempted to remember all of the various injuries and hospitalizations he had sustained during his illustrious career. He handed the forms back to the nurse, who told him to have a seat and that someone would be with him in a moment. Ten minutes later, a man wearing a white lab coat opened the door to the back and said, "Mr. Bond?"

Bond stood up. The man held out his hand. "Hi, I'm Dr. Tom Zielinski." They shook hands. "Come on back," he said.

They went into a small office. "Have a seat," Dr. Zielinski said.

"Where's Dr. Anderson?" Bond asked. "I think I was supposed to see her."

"She had an emergency or something, I'm not quite sure. Don't worry, we'll take good care of you." Dr. Zielinski was of medium build and looked to be in his late thirties.

Bond really didn't want to go through with this. He wanted to talk to Ashley Anderson and see what he could get out of her, but perhaps if he played along with these people he could find a way to have a look around.

"I've gone over your questionnaire briefly, Mr. Bond," the doctor said. "We'll have to look at it more thoroughly, of course, but on first glance it looks very good. It says here your father was Scottish and your mother was Swiss?"

"That's right."

"You wrote that their deaths were accidental. Can you be more specific?"

"It was a mountain-climbing accident. They died together."

"I see. I'm sorry," the doctor said with no emotion. He scribbled on the form. "How old were you at the time?"

"Eleven. I went to live with an aunt. She was very doting."

"I see. I'm sorry." He turned the pages and landed on the hospitalizations section. His eyes grew wide. "Well, you've sure been hospitalized a lot! This is pretty remarkable. What kind of work did you say you were in?" He looked back on the front page. "Oh, here it is. Civil servant?"

"That's right."

"What's a civil servant?"

"I worked for the British government."

"I see." He added, "I'm sorry," out of habit, then cleared his throat, embarrassed. "And you'll be in this country for a while?"

"I'm now a permanent resident," Bond lied.

Zielinski nodded, still staring at the form. "This *is* quite a medical history. Broken finger . . . second-degree burns . . . barracuda bite? . . . hospitalization for nerve poisoning . . . bullet wounds . . . you have a pin in your ankle . . . and severe depression?"

"That was due to my wife dying."

"I see. I'm sorry." He continued scanning the document. "Knife wounds . . . concussion . . . electric burns . . . What's this here about trauma to your testicles?"

"That happened a long time ago."

"What was it?"

Bond shifted uncomfortably. "I was kicked in a fight," he lied again. The memory of Le Chiffre's carpet beater was all too vivid.

"I see. I'm sorry," the doctor said. "But you've never had any problems with ejaculation since then?"

Bond smiled wryly. "None."

The doctor scribbled something on the form and then explained that the specimen taken today would be analyzed for the number and motility of sperm cells and other qualities. If Bond passed the first test he would come in for a complete physical, blood work, and another specimen. He then asked Bond why he wanted to become a semen donor. Bond sincerely told the doctor that he would gain satisfaction if he could provide help to a couple who couldn't have a child on their own.

Satisfied with his patient, Dr. Zielinski led Bond down a hall and through a door to another section of the building. There were four closed doors in the hallway, each with a sliding sign that could be set to "Occupied" or "Vacant." Dr. Zielinski opened one and led Bond into a small room that looked more like a bedroom than an examination room. There was a vinyl couch, a table, a sink, a television, and a VCR. On top of the table were empty specimen containers, a box of tissues, and a towel. There were some X-rated videotapes on the VCR and a few men's magazines in a rack by the table. There were no windows, and the door locked from the inside. A phone was attached to the wall.

The doctor said, "You'll need to wash your hands with soap and water before beginning. Please collect a specimen without using lubricants or condoms. They're toxic to sperm. Label the specimen with your name, the time, and hours of abstinence since your last ejaculation. Take your time. You can lock the door for privacy. When you're done, just put the specimen in this incubator." He pointed to a small white machine on the table. "It'll keep the temperature of the sperm stable until it's ready to process. If you need anything, just dial 'O' on the phone. Okay?"

"Fine," Bond said.

The doctor shook his hand and said, "I probably won't see you again today. I have to go freeze some sperm."

"I see," said Bond. As soon as the doctor shut the door and left him alone, Bond added, "I'm sorry."

He waited five minutes, then opened the door. There was no one in the hall. Bond slipped out of the room and went farther down the hallway to a door marked "Personnel Only." He opened it quietly and glanced inside. It was another hallway with offices, and it was empty. He carefully closed the door behind him and walked purposefully down the hall. Some of the office doors were open. Unnoticed, he saw doctors and technicians busy with paperwork or microscopes. At the end of the hall was a large metal door. A keycard was needed to gain access. Bond presumed it was where they kept the tanks that stored the frozen sperm. He wanted to know if ReproCare kept anything else in there as well.

The outer door opened and he heard voices. Bond ducked into the nearest office and flattened himself against the wall. He closed the door slowly but kept it ajar. As the voices approached his end of the hall, he recognized Ashley Anderson's Texas accent.

"Your plane gets into Heathrow at eight forty-five tomorrow morning," she was saying. "Your connection leaves at noon, so you've got a bit of time."

Dr. Anderson and her male companion stopped just outside the office. Through the crack of the open door, Bond could see her use a keycard to open the unmarked metal door. She replaced the keycard in her lab coat pocket, and then held the door open for her companion, Charles Hutchinson. She followed him inside the inner sanctum and closed the door.

Bond emerged from the office and listened at the metal door. It was too thick for him to hear anything. He had to find a keycard and break into the clinic later after hours.

He made his way out of the "Personnel Only" area and back to the examination room where Dr. Zielinski had left him. Ashley Anderson and Charles Hutchinson would have to come back this way, unless there was another exit from the lab. He kept the door slightly ajar and waited.

Sure enough, in ten minutes Dr. Anderson and Hutchinson came down the hall. Through the ajar door, Bond saw that Hutchinson was carrying a metal briefcase.

Dr. Anderson was saying, ". . . and under no circumstances should you open the vials. I'll see you later. Have a good flight."

Bond heard Hutchinson go out into the waiting room; then he made his move. He quickly removed his jacket, shoulder holster, and gun, and hid them in a drawer. Next he grabbed an empty specimen container and held the door to his room wide open. He stood in the doorway and waited for Ashley Anderson to come back down the hall.

When she saw him, she smiled and said, "Well, hello there. How are you? Jesus, what happened to your face?"

Bond said, "I had an accident last night. It's nothing, really."

"I hope so. Sorry I wasn't available earlier—I had to tend to something. Did you fill out all your forms?"

"Yes, and now I'm ready to deliver a specimen." Bond held up the empty container.

"I see that. Well, don't let me stop you," she said with a grin.

Ashley Anderson was one of those women James Bond was very familiar with. He instinctively knew that certain members of the opposite sex immediately found him desirable. Bond was quite aware of the sexual impact he had on them, and he had always been able to use that gift to his advantage.

"As a matter of fact, I was, uhm, having a little difficulty getting in the mood. I mean, it's all so . . . clinical here, isn't it?" he said, flirting with her.

Her eyebrow went up.

"I thought perhaps you could join me and tell me a little more about your company . . . or something." He gestured with his hand for her to enter.

Ashley Anderson was certainly tempted. She looked up and down the hall, then came into the room with Bond. She closed the door and locked it.

"All right, Mr. Bond, what is it you need help with?"

Bond moved closer to her, backing the woman up against the door.

"I lied to you and to that doctor who interviewed me," he said softly, looking into her blue eyes and examining her mouth. He gently ran his fingers through her blond hair.

"Oh yeah?" she whispered.

"Yeah," Bond said, mimicking her accent. "I'm not interested in being a semen donor. At least not this way." He held up the empty container and smoothly tossed it across the room into the sink.

"I could get into a lot of trouble doing this. What's your game, Mr. Bond?" she asked, breathlessly.

"You're my game," he said as he moved in for the kiss. Their mouths met, and she wrapped her arms around his neck. They kissed passionately, and he felt her tongue explore the inside of his mouth. She started breathing very heavily and running her hands over his strong shoulders and back.

"Well, I'm sorry," she said in between kisses, "you committed yourself . . . to the program . . . I'm obligated to make sure that you're a . . . desirable donor."

Bond removed her lab coat and slowly unzipped her dress at the back. Underneath she wore a black lace bra and panties, and a black garter belt. He picked her up and carried her to the couch as she wrapped her legs around his waist. Ashley became enthusiastic very quickly, even breaking off one of the buttons on his shirt in her attempt to remove it. Her feline qualities extended to the lovemaking, for she spent most of the time clawing Bond's back with her fingernails and moaning with delight.

Afterwards, as they lay naked on the vinyl couch, their clothes scattered around the room, Dr. Ashley Anderson was satisfied that James Bond was indeed a desirable donor.

"How did you get into this business?" he asked her.

"I was always interested in reproductive issues. I thought I would be a gynecologist, but then I became more interested in infertility. That led to a job with a European pharmaceutical company called BioLinks Limited. When they bought out ReproCare a year ago, BioLinks put me in charge. So it's all mine now."

"Where is BioLinks based?"

"Athens. The president is a brilliant physicist by the name of Melina Papas."

"And you sell the sperm all over the country?"

"All over the world, actually," she said, sitting up. "We're one of the leading distributors, especially in Europe and the Middle East."

"How do you keep it alive?"

"In liquid nitrogen. We have some freezing machines in our lab.

They're computerized, and they use liquid nitrogen vapor to do the work. It takes about two hours to freeze the sperm. We lower its temperature to minus eighty degrees centigrade, then store it in tanks at minus a hundred and ninety-six degrees centigrade. The samples are stored in vials in separate boxes, and then kept in our special fifty-five-gallon drum tanks. When we transport them, we have special metal briefcases that keep them frozen for several days."

"Fascinating."

"Sure," she said, laughing. "I find you fascinating too, Mr. Bond. How did you get that horrible bruise on your side? What happened to you last night?"

"I fell off one of those spectacular hills you've got here in central Texas," he said.

"I'll bet you did," she said, standing up. Bond admired her long legs and muscular physique. For a doctor who spent her time indoors, she was remarkably well built. She had firm, tight buttocks and a thin waist. "I've got to get back to work."

Bond stood up and helped her gather her things. He picked up her white lab coat and discreetly reached into the pocket and palmed the keycard. When her back was to him, he dropped the card on his own pile of clothes and used his foot to move his shirt over it. He then helped the doctor get dressed. He was still naked when she turned and kissed him again.

"I hope that you'll consider making some more specimen donations," she said.

"I might," he said. "How about dinner tonight first?"

"All right."

"Want to meet at that restaurant?"

"Chuy's? Sure, why not. I can eat Tex-Mex twice in a row. What time?"

"When do you leave here?"

"I think I can get out at five today. The clinic normally closes at five-thirty. I could meet you there at six."

"Six o'clock then. Oh, one other thing. The primary reason I came here today was for Charles Hutchinson. Did you manage to find out where he was and when he'll return?"

Ashley Anderson nonchalantly said, "Yeah, he's been in Italy. He's not scheduled to be back until next week, but we got a message to him. He's going to London today, I believe. I hope that doesn't mean you'll be leaving Austin?"

"We'll have that date first," Bond said.

She kissed him again and left the room. Now the only trick was to find a way to get back in the building after everyone left at five-thirty.

He got dressed quickly, retrieved his gun, and stuck the keycard in his pocket. He left the room and went out into the reception area. The nurse there smiled at him knowingly, quietly acknowledging the little secret she shared with all the men who visited the clinic.

Bond went outside. It was nearly four-thirty. He walked a block to get out of sight of the clinic, then called Leiter on the mobile.

"Felix, you need to get on to Charles Hutchinson right away. He's probably at the airport as we speak. He's headed for Heathrow with a metal briefcase. Probably somewhere in Europe after a layover. I have reason to believe there's something quite deadly in the briefcase, and it's not just someone's sperm."

"I'll get right on it. So I take it your visit to the clinic was profitable?"

"It was one of the more pleasant doctor's appointments I've ever had. I'm going to try and sneak back in when they close. There are some things I think I need to see. I need you to do one more thing. Can you or Manuela phone ReproCare at exactly five twenty-five? Here's what I want you to do." Bond took a minute explaining his scheme.

"Okay," Leiter said. "You have my number. We'll alert the authorities at the airport now."

After they hung up, Bond went into a small coffee shop to wait.

▶10.
OFFENSIVE ACTION

Five o'clock came, and Ashley Anderson left ReproCare, crossed Thirty-eighth Street to a parking lot, got into her pink Porsche, and drove away. Bond waited awhile longer, until 5:25. He had watched many of the employees already leave the building.

He sprinted across the street to the clinic and went inside. The nurse behind the partition was packing her purse and putting on a light jacket.

"Hello," he said. "I think I left something in the room I was in earlier today. May I look?"

The phone rang and the nurse answered it. She listened to Leiter's voice and frowned. Bond mimed his question once again and the nurse nodded and waved him through. He went inside and quietly made his way to the examination rooms. Instead of going into the room he had been in earlier, he stepped into a different one, left the door open, and stood behind it.

Leiter's distraction had provided the right amount of confusion to the end of a busy day. The Texan had asked about a nonexistent account and the nurse had to look it up on the computer. By the time she had confirmed to the caller that no such account existed, it was 5:31. She hung up the phone, gathered her things, and looked in the hallway. She wandered down to the examination rooms and saw that they were all open and empty. The nurse shrugged, assuming that Bond had got what he had left behind and slipped out the front door while she was looking in the files. She turned and left the building, locking the front door behind her.

Bond waited a couple more minutes before emerging from his hiding place. The building was completely quiet. He was fairly sure that no one was around. He stuck his head through the "Personnel Only" door to verify he was alone, then went into the hallway and down to the unmarked metal door. He slipped Ashley Anderson's keycard in the slot and heard a click. He opened the door and went inside.

It was a large laboratory with several workstations. Sixteen Taylor-Wharton 17K-Series Cryostorage tanks sat along two walls. They resembled top-loading washing machines. Complete with solid-state automatic controls, each refrigerator was equipped with an adjustable low-level alarm with visual and audible signals, as well as a delayed remote alarm signal. If Bond tried to open any of the tanks, someone's pager would go off.

What was most curious were the shielded workstations. Two glass-enclosed booths contained mechanical arms and hands which a technician would normally operate to handle volatile or dangerous chemicals. Why would there be a need for such protection in a sperm bank?

To Bond's amazement, another door led into a small greenhouse. The ceiling allowed the sun to shine directly into the place. Several plants were growing in trays on two tables. He took a close look at the plants and he was sure that they had nothing to do with infertility or the storage of sperm. The three plants he recognized were the castor bean plant, a jequirity bean vine, and hemlock. All three of them could produce toxic substances.

Bond went back into the lab and found a PC displaying a colorful screen saver. He moved the mouse, and the desktop appeared on the monitor. It was an in-house system, but the menu was quite clear. Bond selected a folder marked "Shipping" and opened it. There were hundreds of files; Bond opened the most recent one. A list appeared that detailed sperm shipments since the beginning of the month.

DATE	CLIENT	QUANTITY	COURIER
11/2	Family Planning Inc. New York, NY	1 s/1 b	C.H.
11/4	Reproductive Systems Los Angeles, CA	1 s/1 b	C.H.
11/6	The Family Group London, UK	1 s/1 b	C.H.
11/7	Rt. 3, Box 2 Bastrop, TX	1 b	C.H.
11/8	BioLinks Ltd. Athens, Greece	1 case	C.H.

Bond scanned the log for other shipments with those initials. Other couriers' initials had made deliveries in other parts of the world. The Bastrop, Texas, address was odd. It didn't sound like a medical clinic. Bond memorized the Bastrop address and shut down the program.

He restored the computer to the way he found it, then studied the controls on one of the refrigerated storage tanks. He wondered if the handy alarm-nullifier that Major Boothroyd gave him would be effective on the tanks. It was worth a try. He opened the heel of his right shoe and extracted the device. He aimed it at one of the tanks, and the red indicator light switched from "Alarm Set" to "Alarm Off." Bond made a mental note to offer to take Major Boothroyd to lunch when he was back in London.

He opened the tank and was hit by a blast of cold air. Bond looked around the lab quickly and found some heavy insulated gloves. After his hands were protected, he took a look at the racks inside the tanks. There were several boxes filled with vials on the racks. Bond made a rough guess that there were anywhere from five to seven thousand vials of substance in one tank. He picked up a couple of vials and examined them. They were labeled with the donor number, date of specimen, and other pertinent information. It looked like sperm.

Bond tried three more tanks before he found one that didn't contain sperm. He knew he had hit the jackpot when he opened the tank and saw that the boxes on the racks were labeled "Danger! Use caution when handling!"

He took out one box and examined the vials inside. Some were marked "cyanogen chloride" and others were labeled "hydrocyanic acid." Powerful stuff. Another box contained vials marked as "soman" and "abrin," both deadly materials. A third box contained "ricin," "rabun," and "sarin." Finally, a fourth box was filled with vials of "botulin." Not only were they dealing with toxic chemicals, but the bastards were playing with biological warfare materials.

"Don't drop that," an all too familiar voice behind him said.

"Dr. Anderson," Bond said without turning to her. "Since when do couples experiencing infertility need botulin to have a baby?"

"Put the box down very carefully and turn around. Slowly."

He did. Ashley Anderson was holding a briefcase in one hand and a Colt .38, pointed at Bond, in the other. "I'll use this. Don't think I won't," she said. Her flirtatious, snappy personality was gone. She stared at him with cold eyes and a sneer. "Take those gloves off and drop them."

"My dear Ashley," Bond said as he removed the gloves. "If you shoot me at this range, the bullet will go right through me and into this tank. I'd hate to think what would happen to you if the materials in those vials were exposed to the air. I might be dead, but you'd never make it out of here without being contaminated."

She knew he was right. "Lie down on the floor. Do it!"

"What, you want another semen specimen so soon?" he quipped.

"Shut up and get down. I mean it!"

"It's a stalemate, Ashley. You won't shoot me."

She fired a round at the floor near his feet. The gunshot was deafening inside the laboratory.

"The next one will be your foot," she said. "Get on the goddamned floor!"

Bond complied. He did his best to conceal the fact that he had managed to grasp her stolen keycard in his right hand.

"So, am I correct in assuming that ReproCare is the front for the Suppliers?" he asked.

Ashley Anderson set the briefcase on a worktable and opened it with one hand, the gun in the other still trained at Bond. "Since you're going to die in a few minutes, I suppose it won't hurt to tell you. Yes, this is the laboratory for the Suppliers. It has been for a year, when I made a very lucrative deal with them."

She removed from the briefcase four cylindrical objects the size of coffee mugs, which appeared to be blocks of plastic explosive. She began to distribute them slowly on tables around the room, keeping the gun aimed at Bond. "But now my job with the Suppliers is finished. My orders come from a higher authority. Your people—I assume you're a cop of some kind—your people won't have to worry about the Suppliers anymore."

"Where's Charles Hutchinson going? What's he got with him?" Bond asked.

"You ask a lot of questions for a dead man, Mr. Bond, if that's your real name. Hutchinson's a little worm. He's the courier for the Suppliers. He delivers chemical and biological weapons that the Suppliers create to the various clients around the world. They're hidden inside vials of sperm. It's the perfect method for smuggling. There are not a lot of customs officers who want to start digging around in frozen sperm."

"Ingenious," Bond said. "Who's the higher authority you're working for?"

"That's knowledge you won't even take to your grave," she said. She punched some buttons on a device inside the briefcase. All four explosives beeped. "There. This building will be on another plane of existence in five minutes." She stood about six feet away from where he was lying. "So, this is goodbye, Mr. Bond. Too bad. You really were an excellent donor candidate."

"Aren't you worried that the explosion will release the deadly toxins?"

"The fire will consume them. They won't be dangerous. Not the ones we keep *here*, anyway." She grinned. "You know, the last few shipments Charles made had something totally original in them. I don't mind telling you that it was state-of-the-art shit. But it's all gone. Now shut up."

She assumed a firing stance and pointed the gun with both hands at Bond's head.

Using the skills he had trained for and practiced all of his professional life, Bond rolled to his left and onto his back. Dr. Anderson fired a shot and barely missed him. Bond threw the keycard at her with a jerk of the wrist. It was a technique he had developed and taught in his own class at SIS, "How to Turn Everyday Items into Deadly Weapons."

The corner of the card struck Ashley Anderson hard in the face, piercing the skin about three centimeters. The pain and surprise threw her backward. The card was stuck directly into the bridge of her nose, between the eyes. Bond leaped to his feet, ran to her, knocked the revolver out of her hand, and slugged her on the chin. She fell to the floor, unconscious. Bond pulled the card out of her forehead. She would live, but she might have a nice little scar to remember him by.

He picked her up and carried her out of the laboratory. He didn't have the time or the inclination to attempt to disarm the explosives. If the Suppliers' headquarters and laboratory were destroyed, it would be fine with him.

He carried her body out of an emergency exit and onto Thirty-eighth Street, and ran across the road. Cars screeched to a stop when the drivers saw a man rushing across the street carrying a woman with blood on her face. They assumed he was rushing her to the hospital just down the block.

ReproCare exploded with a boom that could be heard for a mile around. The blast had a direct effect on the electric and utility lines underneath the building, immediately cutting off power and water to the surrounding streets. Two cars collided in the road, and pedestrians screamed. The entire block turned into chaos.

Bond laid Ashley Anderson down on the pavement and grabbed his mobile phone. The first call he made was to the local fire department and police. The second call was to Felix Leiter.

Bastrop, Texas, is a quiet farming and ranching community about thirty miles southeast of Austin. It is known for its lush greenery and fields of cattle and is on a well-traveled route between Austin and Houston.

At sunrise on the morning after the ReproCare clinic was destroyed, an FBI SWAT team assembled on the perimeter of a ranch property that was a mile away from Highway 71. Manuela Montemayor had requested a raid after James Bond supplied the address he had found in the computer at the clinic. Bond and Leiter went along as "observers" and were told to stay back and let the FBI do their job.

"That's easier said than done," Felix told Manuela. "If we start shooting, James here is going to go absolutely nuts. He'll want a piece of the action, and so will I! Isn't that right, James?" He looked at his old friend for approval.

Bond shook his head. "Don't look at me, Felix. I'm just an observer."

"Quiet," Manuela said.

They were crouched in the trees just beyond a barbed-wire fence surrounding the property, which consisted of a ranch house, a barn, a silo, and thirty acres of grazing land. About thirty cows were lazily chewing their cud on the field. Leiter was in his Action Arrow power chair, but Bond could tell he was itching to jump out and join in the fun. They were both dressed in borrowed FBI team jackets and bulletproof vests, just in case.

Manuela introduced Bond to the man in charge of the raid, Agent James Goodner. He was a tall man with a cruel jowl but sparkling, pleasant eyes.

"Any friend of Felix Leiter's a friend of mine," Goodner said, shaking Bond's hand. "Just keep yourselves back and out of trouble. Hopefully this will be over quickly."

"What do you know about this place?" Bond asked.

"The property is owned by a rancher named Bill Johnson. He legitimately raises cattle and wasn't on any of our lists. If he works for the Suppliers, then he's done a good job hiding it. We're going to send some men to the front door of the ranch house there and present him with a warrant. If a team is allowed in to search the place peacefully, we may not be needed. Somehow, though, I don't think that's going to happen."

"We don't want to end up with another Waco," Leiter said. Bond remembered the disastrous raid the FBI made on a militant cult group in that Texas town a few years ago.

Manuela approached Goodner and said, "Your men are ready. I'm going to the door with them."

"What for?" Leiter asked.

"Sweetheart, it's my case. This is my territory. It's my job!"

"Well then, be careful, honey," Leiter said. She leaned over and kissed him on the cheek.

"Don't worry. Just think about what tonight will be like," she said. She winked at Bond, then left with two other agents.

"Tonight?" Bond asked.

Leiter shrugged and had a mischievous grin on his face. "There's something about gunfights that really turns her on. Must be that spicy Hispanic blood in her, I don't know. She turns into a hot tamale. One night—"

"Quiet," Goodner whispered. They could see Manuela and two agents approaching the front of the house, fifty yards away. From their vantage point, they could see the house, the barn, and part of the silo. Another group of men had assembled on the opposite side of the property. The place was surrounded.

Goodner was watching through binoculars. "They just knocked on the door. They're waiting. . . . All right, the door's opening. Manuela's presenting her credentials and warrant. A woman answered the door. Must be Mrs. Johnson. She's letting them inside."

He spoke into his wireless headset. "All right, keep cool, everyone. They're inside the house. Hopefully this will all end peacefully."

Three minutes went by, and the house was still quiet. Suddenly, the back door flung open and a large man dressed as a cowboy ran outside. He was headed for the barn and was carrying a shotgun.

Goodner held up a loudspeaker and said, "Stop where you are! This is the FBI! Halt or we'll shoot!"

Bill Johnson swung the gun up and fired in the direction of the voice. At the same time, three other men emerged from the house with what looked like AK-47s. They began to sweep the trees with bullets.

"Go! Go! Go!" shouted Goodner into the headset.

The FBI team shot a tear gas shell at the cowboys, then fired their own guns.

The barn door opened and more men with automatic weapons poured out. There were at least ten of them. They ran to various objects in the yard for cover.

"Where's Manuela?" Leiter shouted. "Is she okay?"

"Quiet, Felix," Bond said, watching intently. He felt like joining the action too. "I'm sure she's fine."

The volley of bullets continued for several minutes. Two FBI agents were hit, but their bulletproof vests saved their lives. Three of the Suppliers went down.

Bill Johnson made a run back to the house while his men covered him with a barrage of gunfire. He got inside, then returned holding Manuela in front of him. He had a pistol to her head.

"Put down your guns, or the bitch gets it!" he yelled. Manuela was struggling against him, but he was just too big.

"He's got Manuela!" Felix cried.

"Easy, Felix," Bond said. "Let the FBI handle it."

Goodner said into the headset, "Hold your fire, men."

After the tremendous cacophony, the abrupt silence was unnerving.

"All right, we're gonna get in a truck and leave," Johnson yelled. "You're gonna let us out of here or the bitch gets a hole in her head!"

Goodner held up the loudspeaker. "You'll never get away with this, Johnson. The place is surrounded. Let her go and tell your men to put down their weapons. None of you will leave here alive if you don't!"

"Bullshit!" Johnson yelled back. He moved, clutching Manuela, toward the barn.

Bond glanced at the supply of weapons the FBI had at their disposal. There was an American M21, a modified version of the old M14. It was a perfect sniper rifle. He picked it up and whispered to Goodner, "I'm pretty good with this. Let me move over there and see if I can get a bead on him."

"This is highly irregular, Mr. Bond," Goodner said. "We have our own sharpshooters."

"But we're in the perfect spot. If he moves into the barn with her, our chances will be slimmer."

"All right, but I know nothing about it."

"Keep him talking," Bond said, then moved a few yards away, next to a large oak tree. He quietly climbed up to a large branch. From there he could see the entire area.

Goodner said into the speaker, "Johnson, just what is it you want? Talk to me!"

"Fuck you!" Johnson yelled.

"Let me at that bastard," Leiter said. He opened the secret compartment in the wheelchair and pulled out the ASP.

Johnson moved Manuela closer to the barn. There were several of his men around him, crouched behind food troughs and barrels.

"We need to distract the asshole so James can get a better aim," Leiter said.

"Don't do anything stupid," Goodner said.

Johnson got to a large door on the barn and gestured for one of the men to open it. Inside was a Ford pickup truck. The man got in and started it.

"Damn it, they're going to get away!" Leiter mumbled. He looked up at Bond and said, "Can you get that son of a bitch, James?"

Bond aimed the rifle. Johnson was not in a good position: Manuela's face was in the way. "Not yet," he whispered.

"Fuck it," Leiter said. He suddenly burst out of the cover of the trees and drove the wheelchair at full speed onto the field toward the house.

"Leiter! What the hell . . . !" Goodner shouted.

"Yeeeee-haaaaa!" Leiter hollered.

It was such an incongruous sight that both sides stared in disbelief. There, in the middle of a gunfight standoff, a man in an electric wheelchair was barreling out into the wide open and yelling like a madman.

"Felix!" Manuela shouted.

The surprise proved to be enough for Johnson to involuntarily loosen his grip on her. She felt the release, then elbowed the man hard in the stomach.

At that moment, James Bond got a clear aim at Johnson's forehead. He squeezed the trigger. Bill Johnson's face burst into a red mess, and his body flew back against the barn door. Manuela ran away from him and toward Leiter.

The other Suppliers started firing into the trees again. The FBI resumed shooting as well. James Bond watched in horror as Leiter and Manuela met each other in the middle of the field, yet somehow the flying bullets avoided them. Manuela jumped into Leiter's lap, and together they sped in the chair back toward the trees.

Before they were safely out of there, Leiter let out another "Yeeee-haaaa," popped a wheelie with the chair, turned, and soared over the field into the midst of the cattle. The cows, totally unnerved by the gunfire and the sight of the strange wheeled vehicle, began to panic. Backed up against the barbed wire, they had no choice but to run forward, toward the barn. Rushing past the wheelchair, the cattle began to stampede, driving the Suppliers out from behind their cover. The cattle also supplied adequate cover for Leiter and Manuela, who rolled back into the trees and safety.

Bond couldn't help but shake his head and laugh.

In five minutes, it was all over. Once the Suppliers were running in the open, they were easy targets. Two more of them were killed, and the rest surrendered. The cattle were rounded up and penned with the help of one of the arrested men, who gladly cooperated with the FBI.

The barn was full of containers of chemical weapons and crates of illegal arms. Goodner said there was enough material there to start a small war. Bond was especially interested in the chemical and biological weapons.

"We have a special team for that stuff," Goodner said. "We ain't touching it."

Bond found Leiter and Manuela at the side of the barn. She was still in his lap.

"James! Great shot!" Leiter said.

"Thank you," Manuela said. "You saved my life. Well, you both did."

"Felix, you damned fool, you could have been killed!" Bond said.

"Hey, the risk was worth it," Leiter said, nuzzling Manuela's neck. "We've been in worse situations than that, my friend." He held up his prosthetic hand. "I've got nine lives, remember? I've only used up a couple of 'em."

Bond glanced over at the team and noticed that one man was carrying a metal briefcase similar to the one Charles Hutchinson had been carrying.

"Wait!" he called. The man stopped. Bond took a look at the case. He called Goodner over to see it.

"Your chemical and biological weapons team should open this one. I have a feeling there's something nasty inside."

"Will do," Goodner said. "After hearing about what's going on in L.A., you couldn't pay me a million bucks to handle that thing."

"Oh? What's going on in L.A.?"

"Haven't you heard? There's some kind of weird epidemic. One of those Legionnaires' disease things. Only in L.A.—wouldn't you know it? Well, thanks for all your help, Mr. Bond."

"Don't mention it."

Bond paid little attention to the irrelevant news about Los Angeles and forgot about it completely when he turned back to his friends and saw that they were fixed in a passionate embrace. He quietly withdrew, allowing them a little more breathing room. He walked round the barn, lit a cigarette, and thanked his lucky stars that they were alive.

▶11.
THE NEXT THREE STRIKES

Nicosia, the capital of Cyprus, is a fortified, tight-walled city with a circumference of just three miles. The Turks and Turkish Cypriots call their side of the city Lefkosia, Nicosia's official name prior to the twelfth century, when the country was under Byzantine rule. The Turks reverted the city's name to its former one after the invasion of 1974. They refer to the occupied northern area of Cyprus as the Turkish Republic of Northern Cyprus, founded in 1983 by Rauf Denktash, once a friend and colleague of Archbishop Makarios, the first president of the Republic of Cyprus.

Largely supported by the West, the Greek Cypriot side of the city and country has managed to become a tourist attraction and formidable political voice in the Mediterranean during the last several years. In contrast, the Turkish Republic of Northern Cyprus must work at getting tourists to visit. Travelers wishing to travel from Greece or southern Cyprus into the north can only do so for a day trip, and only if they are not Greek Cypriots or Greeks. Travelers who enter the TRNC from Turkey or other countries cannot enter the southern side. As a result, the prosperity of the TRNC has not been equal to that of its southern neighbors. Where the Republic of Cyprus expanded its half of the city to include modern shopping malls and business centers, the TRNC's side remains underdeveloped, underpopulated, and in a state of poverty.

The Greek and Turkish Cypriots have always been passionate in backing their respective sides of their history. The two viewpoints conflict in their interpretations of the facts, and there is often outright denial of them. Objective parties such as Britain or the United States have been working with the Cypriots in an effort to help settle their problems, but both sides seem to have dug in their heels. A stalemate has been in existence for years. When incidents of violence erupt sporadically in what is now called "the last divided city," as they often do, further escalation of the tensions between the two factions is an unavoidable outcome.

A so-called buffer zone along the Green Line ranges from one hundred meters in one spot to up to five hundred in another. It is an eerie no-man's-land in which time has stopped since the Turkish "intervention" of 1974. Patrolled by the United Nations, the strip cutting through Nicosia and the rest of the country is lined with barbed wire, high fences, and signs forbidding photography. The buildings that remain in the buffer zone are abandoned, bombed out, and achingly quiet. Propaganda of both sides is displayed on the respective borders so that any visitors who choose to cross the line will get both points of view. A banner hangs over the northern gate so that people traveling to the south can read it. "The Clock Cannot Be Turned Back" is what it proclaims in English.

The buffer zone gateway between southern and northern Nicosia is known as the Ledra Palace Checkpoint. The Ledra Palace was once the most luxurious hotel in Nicosia. Now it is the headquarters for the UN and lies in the middle of the buffer zone between two military gates. Visitors are allowed to walk across the no-man's-land during the day, but at night access is denied. During the five-minute walk between gates, visitors will see numerous soldiers. On the southern side are the dark brown camouflage uniforms of the Greek Cypriots and Greek Army. On the northern side are the Turks' green camouflage outfits, and in the middle are the light brown uniforms of the United Nations.

At five o'clock on the day after the Suppliers' headquarters was blown to bits in Austin, Texas, things were relatively peaceful along the Green Line in Nicosia. The four Turkish soldiers who manned the gate on the northern side officially closed down for the day, and if there were any tourists still in the TRNC then, they would be forced to spend the night at one of northern Lefkosia's run-down hotels. A small parking lot behind the two-story white guard post was just emptying itself of taxicabs and vehicles belonging to the administrative staff that worked in the building.

Not far from the guardhouse, a dark green 1987 Plymouth moved slowly along Kemal Zeytinoglu Street. The word "Taksi" was printed in English on the bubble on top of the car, as on all cabs in Lefkosia. The driver waited a minute, watching the empty street leading south. At precisely 5:10, the car tore into the silence of the dusk with squealing tires, bursting out onto the street and speeding down to the avenue. It cut the curve to the right without stopping and was now headed south, straight for the checkpoint gate.

The Turkish soldiers saw the car coming and thought at first that a taxi driver had had too much to drink. As it approached, however, it increased its speed so that it would smash through the gate and enter the buffer zone illegally. The four men simultaneously jumped up and ran out to the street, ready to draw their weapons. The driver of the Plymouth slammed on the brakes and spun the wheel so that the car made a screeching 180-degree turn in front of the checkpoint building. A figure dressed in a gas mask, hood, and camouflage protective gear jumped out of the back seat of the taxi. The soldiers, who were spread out in a semicircle facing the cab, shouted at the figure and prepared to open fire. Before they could, the figure tossed a grenade onto the ground in front of the men. It took them completely by surprise, and they had no time to react before it exploded in their faces.

The chemical grenade produced an immense white cloud. The four soldiers were not hurt by the blast, but they were blinded by the smoke. There was something in it that irritated their eyes and made breathing extremely difficult. They fell to the ground and groped their way toward what they believed would be safety. One man heard the taxi's engine roar into life as it sped away a half-minute after the explosion. When the smoke finally cleared three minutes after that, the men were still coughing and gasping for air. They didn't notice that the number "5" had been spray-painted on the wall of the checkpoint building. Sitting on the ground below the number was a small alabaster statue of Athena, the Greek goddess of wisdom.

The soldiers made it to their feet, and one crawled into the guard post to call the authorities. He was able to dial the number and tell his superior officer what had just happened. He then became violently sick and was stricken with cramps.

When the police and more soldiers arrived at the checkpoint, two of the soldiers were dead and the other two were nearly so. In the half hour since the grenade exploded in front of them, the men experienced a number of symptoms that came on suddenly and escalated

from one to the other without warning. The difficulty in breathing
led to excessive nausea and vomiting, cramps, involuntary defecation,
spasms, and finally reduction of the heart rate. They had been killed by
the nerve agent sarin, a particularly nasty chemical that acted quickly
and aggressively.

As for the Plymouth and the mysterious masked figure that made
the attack, the car had been abandoned three blocks north of the checkpoint. The assassin had jumped into a 1988 Volkswagen and was now
heading innocently toward the port city of Famagusta.

The Turkish Republic of Northern Cyprus uses two major ports on the
northeastern part of the island. Kyrenia, directly north of Lefkosia, is
mostly a passenger harbor, the point of entry for mainly Turkish tourists
or immigrants. Famagusta, on the east coast of Cyprus, is the harbor for
shipping and trade. Like Nicosia/Lefkosia, it is a walled city, and it has
certainly seen better days. Probably the city with the longest and most
colorful history on Cyprus, Famagusta has changed hands a number
of times. Now the TRNC's flag, which is similar to the Turkish red and
white flag except that the colors are reversed, blew in the wind at the
dock along Shakespeare Street.

Dominating the northeast shoreline are the docks themselves, an
entrance into the city called the Sea Gate, and an impressive ancient
citadel known as Othello's Castle. Shakespeare supposedly based his
famous play on the citadel and a legendary dark-complexioned Italian
mercenary who fought for the Venetians and was called *il Moro,* "the
Moor."

The lone man standing in the dark on the roof of the castle could
just see the long boardwalk projecting southeast. He could also see
the small white Turkish guard post, the one crane in operation, and
two ships that were docked at the port. One of the ships was loaded
with food and supplies from Turkey. Looking through binoculars, he
panned the edge of the dock and finally saw the camouflaged figure
emerge from the shadows. Right on time.

The figure turned toward the castle and flashed a penlight three
times. It was the signal for the man to get the escape route ready. He
made an acknowledgment of one flash with his own penlight, then

made his way down the dark stone steps to the first floor of the castle. He had paid admission to get inside the citadel during business hours and had found a place to hide until dark. Now all he had to do was use the long wooden ladder he knew would be in the maintenance shed, and climb over the wall of the castle to the street.

Meanwhile, on the dock, the figure in camouflage protective gear, gas mask, and hood slithered up to the lonely white guard post. Only two Turkish soldiers manned the booth at this time of night. The unloading of the supply ship would take place in the morning. Security was normally reliable and there wouldn't have been a need to post extra guards around the ship. The soldiers had no reason to believe that the Famagusta dock was about to become the latest target of the most skillful trained assassin in the Mediterranean. The Number Killer was probably right to think there was no one in the world better at this job.

The murderer boldly walked up to the guard post and stood in the doorway. The two Turkish guards looked up in surprise at the frightening shape before them. For the brief moment the men were able to gaze upon their killer, all they could see was the gas mask and its likeness to an insect's head.

The Number Killer shot both men with a Daewoo DH380, a double-action semiautomatic pistol made in South Korea. The silencer muffled the sound of the .380 caliber bullets that slammed into the soldiers and knocked them back against the wall. They slumped into a heap on the floor, bleeding profusely.

The camouflaged figure moved quickly to the ship docked a few meters away. One lone sailor was on deck, smoking a cigarette. The assassin calmly walked to the end of the ramp and proceeded to climb aboard the ship. The Turkish sailor saw the bizarre creature appear in front of him and was too frightened to scream. The Daewoo let off another round, kicking the sailor over the rail and into the water.

Another sailor called from below in Turkish. "What's going on?" he yelled. The Number Killer confidently opened the hatch and descended the steps into the bowels of the ship. It took two more bullets to make sure that no one was alive to witness the assassin's next act.

He opened the cargo hold and stepped inside. The ship was full of much-needed food from the mainland. There were crates of vegetables, cartons of eggs, bags of potatoes and other types of produce. There was enough food to stock all the grocery markets in northern Cyprus for at least three days. If all went as planned, when the goods were unloaded and shipped to diverse parts of the TRNC they would be covered with an invisible and deadly germ.

The figure in the protective suit removed a backpack and set it on the floor. He opened it up quickly and removed a metal canister. He unscrewed the top to reveal four glass vials full of liquid attached to the inside of the canister. The Number Killer then removed a spray gun from the backpack. It was a type of everyday garden tool used for pesticides. The canister with the vials fitted perfectly onto the back of the spray gun.

The assassin stood up and began to spray the crates of vegetables. The heads of lettuce and potatoes were covered with the fine mist. The breads and eggs were blanketed by the tasteless, odorless chemical. After ten minutes, the Number Killer had efficiently emptied the spray gun, and the entire cargo room was covered with the already drying liquid. There was still one more task left to do. Reaching into the bag of tricks, the assassin pulled out the spray paint can and drew the number "6" on the wall of the cargo hold. He then carefully set a small alabaster statue of Hermes, the ancient Greek god of trade, commerce, and wealth, on the floor. He quickly packed up his equipment and left the ship the same way he had come in.

There was still no activity on the dock. No one had discovered the bodies of the two guards yet. The Number Killer walked calmly across the boardwalk to the Sea Gate. The rope he had left earlier was still there. He climbed up the wall and over the barbed wire. This time he pulled up the rope as he perched on top of the wall, straddling the barbed wire. Down below, on the other side of the wall, was a public utility truck. It was the kind used for highway building and maintenance, and the back was full of sand. The killer calmly jumped into it.

The man who had been on top of Othello's castle was sitting in the driver's seat of the truck. He heard the thump of the assassin landing in the sand. That was his cue, and he started the truck and headed northwest out of Famagusta on the main road, Cengiz Topel.

If it hadn't been for the anonymous phone call to the Famagusta police one hour later, the food aboard the ship would have been sent out to feed over eighty thousand Turkish Cypriots. The voice on the other end of the line spoke English and sounded neither Greek nor Turkish. The message was that the food in the cargo ship at the dock must be burned. Under no circumstances should the hold be entered without protective clothing and gas masks, for a deadly biological agent had been distributed inside. The call was dismissed at first as a hoax, but one Turkish Cypriot policeman decided it wouldn't hurt to go take a look. When he found the dead soldiers in the guard post, he sounded the alarm.

By noon the next day, the authorities had determined that if the food had been shipped to its final destinations, within a week northern Cyprus would have been hit by a devastating anthrax plague.

The sun shone on Anavatos and produced an unseasonably warm day for November on Chios. There had been a couple of tourists from Italy early in the day, but they were gone by midafternoon. The Italians had no idea that the medieval fortress at the top of the cliff masked the modern headquarters complex of the Decada. They walked right over a trapdoor made of stone, completely unaware of the meeting going on below in the square meeting room.

The Monad was not pleased. Eight members of his elite group were present. The cushion usually occupied by Number Ten was vacant. The Monad had dispensed with many of the formalities of the meetings, and began after only five minutes of silence. He strummed the lyre and spoke.

"Welcome," he said in the quiet voice that mesmerized his followers. "I am happy to report that Mission Number Five was entirely success-ful. Four Turkish soldiers in illegally occupied northern Cyprus were eliminated. Mission Number Six was also implemented quite success-fully, and I must commend Number Two, the Duad, for bravery and two jobs well done. However, I am distressed to inform you all that Mission Number Six was not a total success. While Number Two com-pleted the mission, it was not carried through to our ultimate goal of spreading anthrax over northern Cyprus. The deed was discovered by the authorities before the cargo ship was unloaded."

The other members of the Decada looked concerned. Number Two was especially angry.

The Monad raised his hands to reassure them. "Do not trouble yourselves, my friends. I have the answer. I know what happened. The gods have been good to me and have revealed to me the source of betrayal in our organization. But before I have the traitor brought in for trial, I have other grave news. Number Ten will no longer be joining us. Dr. Anderson was arrested in the United States two days ago. I have not received official confirmation yet, but I believe that she is probably dead by now. I am sure that she would have followed our strictest policy and taken her own life rather than subject herself to interrogation. It is a shame."

Number Two did her best to control her emotions. She looked over at Number Eight, who acknowledged her pain.

The Monad continued, "The Decada has cut its business ties with the militants in Texas. We don't need them anymore. The One will become the Many through the actions of our own efforts from now on. Unfortunately, we have to revise our plans somewhat. Mission Number Seven must now be used to deal with a traitor to the organization."

The Monad clapped his hands twice. A soldier in a dark green camouflage uniform entered, dragging a young man by the arm. The rest of the Decada didn't know him by sight, but they knew who he was.

"Loyal members," the Monad said, "I present to you Charles Hutchinson, an Englishman. He is, as his father was, an enemy of the Decada. He alerted the Cypriot authorities that the cargo ship at Famagusta had been infected. Do you deny this charge, Mr. Hutchinson?"

"You killed my father, you bastard," Hutchinson spat out.

"Your father failed to provide us with some valuable information that we needed. Instead of supplying it to us, he attempted to go to British authorities and expose us before we had accomplished our first set of goals. He had to die."

Charles Hutchinson suddenly realized what his fate was. He began to tremble with fear.

"Look," he stammered, "I'm sorry . . . I was just upset about my father . . ."

"Spare us your pleading," the Monad commanded. "Are you aware of what has happened to the Suppliers in Texas? And to our loyal Number Ten, Dr. Ashley Anderson?"

Hutchinson, now speechless with fear, shook his head quickly.

"They are no more. The laboratory was destroyed by Number Ten, as instructed. The names of the major personnel in the Suppliers' organization were supplied to the FBI in America, along with incriminating evidence. They are being rounded up as we speak. The headquarters was discovered and raided. We will have to find a replacement for Number Ten. I will recruit one of our more loyal employees."

The Monad stood and stepped over to Charles Hutchinson. He placed his hand at the base of the young man's head and gripped him tightly.

"Decada!" the Monad said with force. "I present to you Charles Hutchinson, traitor and enemy to our principles. What say you, guilty or not guilty?"

"Guilty!" the eight followers cried.

The Monad turned to Hutchinson and said, "I do so love a brief trial. It is decided. You have become Limited. Now you must join the One. Perhaps when the One becomes the Many, you will be forgiven."

The Monad nodded slightly to the guard, who pulled Hutchinson out of the room.

The medieval castle at the top of Anavatos was at the edge of a cliff wall that dropped virtually straight down a quarter-mile to a wooded, hilly landscape. It was a breathtaking sight when one stood at the small stone wall which served as some protection to visitors to the ruins.

The stone trapdoor opened and three guards forced Charles Hutchinson out. He was screaming and crying, but there was no one around to hear him. Even the elderly residents who lived at the base of the ruined city wouldn't hear him. Only the few birds circling the foreboding precipice in front of him could hear his cries.

The guards led him to the edge of the cliff and offered him a blindfold. He was too shaken to realize what they were asking. The guards shrugged and put the blindfold away. Hutchinson knew he was going to die, but he didn't know how. He figured they were about to take him off Anavatos and drive him somewhere remote.

When the push came, he was surprised.

Watching on a video monitor from inside the complex, the Monad nodded his head and said a prayer to the gods. He was pleased. They told him that he had been adequately avenged.

Number Two stood behind him, struggling to keep her feelings to herself. At least Number Ten had set their plan in motion before she died. It was now up to her and Number Eight to see it through to the end.

▶ 12.
HIDDEN AGENDA?

Bond spent another two and a half days in Texas, then returned to London in time to receive the news of the Number Killer attacks in Cyprus. He stopped by the flat and quickly examined the neatly stacked pile of post and newspapers from the past several days. Bond took a couple of hours to freshen up, then drove the Bentley to the office in time for a debriefing. It was still rainy and cold.

The green light flickered above the door just as Bond walked into Moneypenny's outer office.

"Looks like there's no time for chitchat, James," she said. The green light was a signal for Bond to come inside. He raised his eyebrows at Moneypenny and went on through.

M stood with her back to Bond, gazing out the large picture window that overlooked the Thames. He waited a moment before saying, "Good afternoon, ma'am."

She turned around and gestured to the black chair in front of her desk. "Sit down, 007," she said, then moved back to her desk and sat across from him. The lines on her face seemed to be more prominent. Bond thought she looked tired and pale.

"Are you all right, ma'am?" he asked.

"Yes, yes," she sighed. "It's been a difficult few days."

"I can imagine."

"I was called on to help Alfred's solicitors with his estate. His former wives wanted nothing to do with him, although I daresay he's probably left something tidy to them in his will. Now I know how celebrities feel when their personal lives are displayed in public. It hasn't reached tabloid stage, but my name was mentioned in the *Times* obituary. I would like to go away to the country for a month or so."

"Perhaps you should," Bond said.

"That would be cowardly. Forget it. I was just speaking with Manville Duncan. He returned from the Middle East quite distraught. Manville is almost as upset about Alfred's death as I am. He's not cut out for Alfred's job, but he'll do fine as a temporary replacement, I suppose. You've heard about what happened in Cyprus?"

"Yes, I've read the briefing."

"Two more attacks. One in Nicosia and one in Famagusta. Both directed against the Turkish side. More numbers. More Greek god statuettes. It was a blessing that someone called the Turkish Cypriot authorities and warned them of the poisoned food. Someone is on our side, at least."

"It makes no sense," Bond said. "Why attack our British bases, then go and strike against the Turks? It's not as if we're on Cyprus to protect the Turkish presence. If anything, we disapprove of their occupation as much as the rest of the Western world."

"Quite so," M said. "Turkey is the only country to sanction their government in northern Cyprus. We do not recognize the TRNC as a true republic, it's just easier to say than 'illegally occupied northern Cyprus.' I'm afraid the world has tolerated the occupation far too long, mainly because, in many ways, the Turks were right to intervene. According to them, the Greek Cypriots did unspeakable things to the Turkish Cypriots in the 1960s before the Greek military coup. Turkey was supposedly protecting her people. Mind you, I'm not defending the Turks. They've committed horrible atrocities on Cyprus. But never mind that. Tell me about the Suppliers."

"We won't have to worry about the Suppliers anymore," he said. "Their organization has been completely dismantled. I stayed around for two days assisting with the investigation. They raided the homes of all suspected Suppliers members and made a number of arrests. The main headquarters and storehouse for weapons was a barn in Bastrop, a small town near Austin. The amount of chemical weaponry they found was simply staggering. It is now believed that the Suppliers were one of the largest and most powerful distribution organizations in the world. The FBI found evidence that sales were made to over fifty clients worldwide."

"Who was the mastermind behind it all?"

"They're still trying to find out. That's the only glitch. The original boss is in prison. We don't know who the interim chief was, but apparently he got away. None of the arrested members will talk. There was nothing more I could do for the FBI, so I came back. It's their show now."

"What happened with the woman from the clinic?"

Bond frowned. "She died."

"Suicide?"

He nodded. "She didn't give them a chance to interrogate her. Swallowed a tablet of concentrated potassium cyanide."

M tapped the desk with her fingers. "Why would she do that? What did she know?"

"She was working for someone other than the Suppliers. She mentioned that her orders came from a 'higher authority.' I definitely got the impression that she had no loyalty to the Suppliers."

"Was she connected to our Number Killer?"

"I believe so, yes. The Number Killer's arsenal came from the Suppliers. I don't have proof, but I'm sure of it."

"And what about Alfred's son?"

Bond shook his head. "The FBI tracked him after he left Austin. He took a flight to London and apparently spent a day here taking care of the arrangements for his father. Did you speak to him?"

"No. I tried to reach him but he was tied up with solicitors all day. The next thing I knew, he was out of the country."

"That's right. He flew to Athens. He had already arrived by the time we all learned where he was. It was too late for customs to stop him."

"So he's somewhere in Greece?"

"That's what we presume. ReproCare was owned by BioLinks Limited, a large pharmaceutical firm in Athens. We'll have to look into that."

M got up and poured two glasses of bourbon. She handed one to Bond without asking if he wanted it.

"Now that he's delivered his package of chemicals to whomever the Suppliers sold them to, don't you think he'd come home?" she asked. "Surely he knows that the Suppliers are no more."

"He's either on the run, or he's hiding somewhere."

"Or he's dead."

"There is that possibility too." Bond took a sip of the bourbon. "The men in that house in Austin did not treat him as an equal. My first thought was that he was being held captive. The Suppliers were after a file on Mr. Hutchinson's computer. They didn't find it. If we knew what the file contained, it would be a big help."

"Do you remember that Alfred was going to show us something concerning the Cyprus case?"

"Yes. What was it?"

"I don't know. He didn't tell me. We've had a good look through his flat too. I wonder if Charles was connected to this information?"

"The FBI raided that mansion on the hill in Austin and it was completely empty. The occupants had made a hasty departure. Even the furniture was gone. Leiter found out who owns the house, though: a Greek fellow by the name of Konstantine Romanos."

"I've heard of him," M said. "He's some kind of teacher/tycoon?" She began to punch up his name on her computer.

"That's right," Bond said. "Independently wealthy, he's a respected mathematician at Athens University. He's also a writer and a philosopher. I don't know a lot about him yet, I just looked him up on the computer myself."

He tapped a file folder in his lap and opened it. "The man in this photo, though, is not the man I saw in the house." Bond took out a black-and-white publicity shot of Konstantine Romanos. The man he had seen in the house was a bodybuilder with huge hands, dark hair, and a thick mustache. The man in the photo was in his fifties and was tall and thin. His curly hair was dark, but it had hints of gray. Strikingly handsome, he had the looks of a screen idol now in the autumn years of his career.

"There's not a lot here. I've already put in a request to Station G and to the Greek Secret Service for more information on him. According to Records, Romanos is clean, but I found something interesting. He has one living family member, a second cousin, Vassilis, who was a champion bodybuilder in his hometown in Greece. There's no photo of him, but the man in charge of the Romanos mansion the night I was there looked a bit like Romanos. It could have been his cousin."

"Why would Romanos have a house in Texas?"

"One of Konstantine Romanos's several accomplishments was serving as a guest professor for five years in the University of Texas philosophy department. This was around the same time that Alfred Hutchinson was also a guest professor at the college."

It was a frightening coincidence. M said nothing, so Bond continued, "We know that Charles Hutchinson carried a supply of chemical weapons to Athens for the Suppliers. Where he's gone from there is a mystery. We need to find him."

She nodded. "I agree. You're to go on to Athens. Find out what happened to Charles Hutchinson and see if you can meet this Romanos fellow. Observe him. I'll make sure you get complete cooperation from the Greeks, and we'll try to get more information on that pharmaceutical company."

M stood up and slowly walked toward the window. It was raining again. "You know, Alfred might have been killed because he found out what his son was up to. He never spoke of Charles. The only time he did was to say that his son had been an 'embarrassment' to him."

Bond didn't want to say that he suspected Alfred Hutchinson of much more than simply not nurturing a positive father-son relationship. The coincidence of Hutchinson and Romanos being in the same Texas city for five years was too compelling. They had to have known each other. What if Hutchinson himself was involved with the Suppliers? He could have used the diplomatic bag as a means to deliver weapons to other countries.

"I'm concerned about the pattern in the attacks," M said. "Our people are trying to determine what the significance of the Greek god statuettes might be. The numbers, I'm afraid, are just there to add up. There will be more, but when and where? You have to find out. The severity of the attacks is also escalating. That anthrax could have caused a terrible epidemic. Many people would have died. My own personal stake in this matter aside, this could turn into a predicament that might threaten national security."

Bond waited for her to go on.

"The Cyprus situation is a tinderbox waiting to explode. Greece and Turkey are both members of NATO. If they were to go to war against each other, all of Europe would suffer. The government of Turkey has been unstable for some time now. The fundamentalist Muslims would welcome an opportunity to take control away from the seculars. If they did, it wouldn't be long before they formed dangerous alliances with countries like Iran or Iraq. A war with Greece would put quite a strain on a country that already has twenty percent unemployed. The fundamentalists could take advantage of the situation."

. M handed the file folder back to Bond. "I'll have Chief of Staff contact the Greek Secret Service and let them know you're coming in the morning. One of their people will meet you at the airport. I want to know what happened to Charles Hutchinson. Follow his trail. If it happens to cross one made by Konstantine Romanos, you'll know what to do."

"Yes, ma'am."

"You've always had a knack for uncovering the mountain after first finding the molehill. I'm counting on you to do it again. That's all, 007."

Bond stood up to leave, then hesitated.

"What is it?" she asked.

He shook his head. "Nothing."

"No, I know." She paused a moment, then said, "You want to say that you suspect Alfred had something to do with all of this. The thought has crossed my mind as well. I'm trying not to let my personal feelings cloud my reasoning, but I refuse to believe it until I see some strong evidence."

"Of course," Bond said.

She looked at him intensely. After a moment, her eyes dropped. "I'm sorry about the other night, James. People that work for you should never have to see you in such an exposed condition. I feel so . . . humiliated."

"Don't give it another thought, ma'am," Bond said. "We all go through traumas in our lives. Just take comfort in knowing you were among friends."

She raised her eyes and said, "Thank you. I also want to thank you for how you're handling all of this. Tanner almost called 004 that night, but I asked him to call you. I knew that you would . . . understand."

Bond didn't know what to say, so he nodded reassuringly and left the room.

He would always remember that moment in the months to come.

From then on, the level of mutual respect they had for each other was significantly strengthened.

Bond looked into his office and found a message to call Felix Leiter. When he got through to him, Leiter said, "James! Glad you reached me!"

"What is it, Felix?"

"Listen, you know that metal briefcase you spotted in Bastrop?"

"Yes?"

"It had some kind of weird shit in it, my friend. It was opened in quarantined conditions, but everyone who was exposed to it is *dead*. I'm telling you this bug is unlike anything we've ever seen. It produces symptoms similar to ricin poisoning, but it's a germ—it's contagious! The stuff has been sealed off and sent to the Centers for Disease Control in Atlanta."

"Christ. What exactly was inside the case?"

"Sperm samples. There were tiny vials of liquid hidden in the sperm. One of them was broken. We think the bug was in the vial. And that's not all."

"What?"

"Apparently there's a strange epidemic happening in L.A. and over in Tokyo too. Mysterious diseases, killing off people right and left."

"I remember your FBI man mentioning it."

"I'm just now learning what details there are, but this has been going on for days. Anyway, they're in a panic there. They've sealed off buildings to keep the sick people in, and health officials are working like mad to figure out what's going on. We're just now hearing about it because the authorities in the respective cities wanted to keep it quiet at first. I'm wondering if the germ you found is identical to the bugs in L.A. and Japan."

"My God, Felix, I think Charles Hutchinson may have delivered a lot of those cases recently. Not just Los Angeles or Tokyo!"

"That's what I'm thinking too, James. And all of ReproCare's records are destroyed. The FBI is suddenly very worried. We need to track down those cases and quarantine them. They've already begun to check every medical clinic in the cities you saw on the computer at ReproCare.

Damn, New York and London. Do you realize how long that's going to take?"

"I understand. I'll alert M immediately and we can help out over here."

"That's my man. Thanks. Don't panic yet. There's no proof that the bug you found is the same one as in L.A. and Tokyo."

"Fax me any other information as you get it, all right?"

They wished each other luck and said goodbye.

Bond hung up the phone and went back up to see M.

Little did he know that a sixty-two-year-old woman had already contracted the first London case of Williams's disease after receiving a blood transfusion at a hospital in Twickenham.

Alfred Hutchinson had kept an office near Buckingham Palace in Castle Lane. James Bond got out of the taxi, stepped over a large puddle of dirty rainwater to the pavement, and entered the building. He gave his name to the security man and was told to come on up.

Manville Duncan was holding the door open and waiting for Bond when he stepped off the elevator.

"Mr. Bond, this is a surprise," he said. "I just got back from the Middle East. I'm off to France tomorrow."

"I'll just take a minute of your time," Bond said. They shook hands and Bond noted once again that Duncan's handshake was clammy.

"Come in, come in."

The office was elegantly decorated in a grand Edwardian style. Bond felt he had entered the library of a stately mansion.

"This is where Alfred worked," Duncan said. "I've barely had time to move things in from my old office. I find that it's easier just to stay where I was!" He led Bond to an outer office where Bond spotted a portrait of Manville Duncan's wife on a desk. Papers and file folders were scattered about, indicating that the temporary ambassador was a bit disorganized.

"Sit down, please—oh, just move those books out of the way. Now, what can I do for you?" Duncan sat behind the desk and faced Bond.

"On the night of Sir Miles's party, Mr. Hutchinson told us that he had some information about the Cyprus case. He was planning to turn it over to M and me the next day. Do you have any idea what that was?"

"M mentioned that to me. I'm afraid I haven't a clue."

"There was a file on his computer in Austin. Something important. He might have had a copy here. Any thoughts as to what it might have contained?"

Duncan thought a minute and shook his head. "No, and MI5 went though his hard drive here. I can't imagine what it was."

"What do you know about Charles Hutchinson?"

"I know he's a bad lot. He's done a few things which were never made public, thank God."

"Oh?"

"Shortly after his father became Ambassador to the World, Charles was arrested in Germany for being drunk and disorderly. A few months later, he was almost brought up on rape charges in the Philippines. His father got the charges dismissed. I don't know if it was true or not, but Charles got away with it."

"How often did they see each other?"

"More frequently than Alfred let on. He took frequent trips to Texas, because he loved it there. I'm sure he saw his son when he was in Austin."

"M says that Hutchinson was disappointed with Charles."

"You wouldn't know it. The boy often accompanied Alfred on diplomatic trips. Charles went along for free under a diplomatic umbrella. He got to see the world. He got to perpetuate his playboy image and get himself into trouble without really getting into trouble. Diplomatic immunity has its advantages."

"Do you know anything about the clinic in Austin where Charles worked?"

"No. Alfred rarely spoke about what Charles was doing in Austin. I do know that he wasn't happy that Charles had dropped out of university. He thought the boy wasn't measuring up to his potential. But as far as his occupation or activities, I don't think Alfred really cared. If you ask me, I think Alfred *knew* that Charles was up to something illegal."

"How do you know?"

"I can't really put my finger on it. It was the way he often spoke about his son. It was as if he were protecting him from something. That reminds me—I just remembered that he had an argument on the phone with Charles about a week before he died. I couldn't make it out, but I did hear Alfred tell Charles that something was 'too dangerous.' When I walked into the office, he was just ringing off. His last words to his son were, 'I have no other choice.' "

"What do you think that meant?"

"I'm afraid to speculate, but do you really want to know what I think?"

"Yes."

"I think Alfred himself was up to something," Duncan said gravely. "I think his fingers were in places they shouldn't have been. He was using his position to achieve something. He had some kind of ambition, a goal. I can't explain it, because I don't know what it was. It's just that I always got the impression that Alfred had a hidden agenda. While he was working for England, he was also working for himself. He had some kind of grand scheme."

"Something criminal?"

Duncan shrugged. "It's just speculation. The fact that his son has a dark cloud over him makes me more suspicious."

"Did Hutchinson ever talk about Cyprus?"

"Only within the context of work. He was very concerned about the situation there. He felt that Cyprus was one of his priorities."

"Do you think he favored any particular side?"

"If he did, he didn't mention it. I think he was fairly neutral on the subject. He always said that both sides were wrong and that they knew it. Neither side wants to admit they're wrong, so it's a contest of stubbornness. Alfred hoped to be a part of the peace process there. Maybe he wanted a Nobel Prize."

"Ever hear of a man named Konstantine Romanos?"

Duncan frowned, then shook his head. "Who's that?"

"A philosopher and mathematician. He's a teacher in Athens who once had a guest stint in Texas at the same time as Hutchinson. You don't recall our late ambassador mentioning him?"

"No."

Bond was grasping at straws. It looked as if Manville Duncan didn't know anything. Even his speculations were dubious. Still, Bond's instincts told him that Duncan was right about one thing: Alfred

Hutchinson *did* have a hidden agenda. He was up to something that didn't fall under his duties as an ambassador. Bond didn't know what it was either, but he was determined to find out.

"Thank you, Mr. Duncan," Bond said, standing. "That's all I need for now. Have a good trip tomorrow. When will you be back?"

Duncan sorted through some papers and found his diary. "I'm in France for two days."

"If you think of anything, please get in touch with us. A message can be sent to me."

"Where are you going?"

"I'm trying to find Charles Hutchinson."

"I see. Any clue to where he might be?"

Bond didn't want to say. "He's in Europe somewhere. Probably hiding."

Duncan nodded. "Probably. Well, good luck."

As Bond left the office and walked out into the rain, he couldn't help feeling that the ghost of Alfred Hutchinson was laughing.

▶13.
THE GREEK AGENT

Sergeant Major Panos Sambrakos of the Greek Military Police was usually up at the crack of dawn, ready for his routine monthly inspection of the camouflaged military storehouses on the island of Chios. This time, though, the sun was setting over the horizon, casting a hazy orange glow over the Aegean. He looked over at the coast of Turkey, plainly visible to the east, and still found it amazing that they could be so close to their enemies and shots were never fired.

Sambrakos, a tall young man of twenty-five, enjoyed his role as an MP. It gave him an elite status that allowed him and his fellow policemen access to any area on the island. The opportunity for meeting women was also a perk that he didn't ignore. Most of the time, though, he used his position to exert authority over common soldiers. It gave him a feeling of power to put on the uniform and assume a different, authoritative persona. He enjoyed strutting down the streets and writing citations as the servicemen cowered in front of him. He had originally dreaded his compulsory military service, but after landing a position with the Military Police, Sambrakos had come to the conclusion that he was having the time of his life.

He also felt important because he was working on top-secret projects for one of the commanding officers on Chios, Brigadier General Dimitris Georgiou.

The general had approached him two months ago, requesting someone to replace a recently deceased officer, a man who had been the general's personal assistant for twelve years. The officer had died tragically in an automobile accident. The general asked Sambrakos if he would like to be considered for the job. The duties would involve highly classified material, and everything they discussed would be privileged information. Sambrakos was surprised, flattered, and intrigued by what

General Georgiou had said. He readily agreed to perform clandestine duties for the general as some kind of test.

One of these duties turned out to be a simple, mundane chore. Sambrakos had to inspect the several weapons bunkers scattered over the island which the general had personally shown to him. Large caches of weapons and equipment were hidden in these bunkers, all camouflaged so that they couldn't be seen from above. The areas were blocked from the public by barbed-wire fences and intimidating signs forbidding the use of cameras. Sergeant Major Sambrakos's job was merely to drive a jeep alone to each storehouse and make sure everything was safe and secure. The monthly inspection took him an entire morning, since he had to travel all over the island.

Tonight was different. The general had asked him to perform an inspection beginning at sundown. This was Sambrakos's third inspection and he was eager to do well. Unfortunately, he also had a terrible headache. On the previous day, he had drunk a little too much ouzo in the afternoon, then attended a dinner party that lasted until three o'clock in the morning. With no sleep, the sergeant major had reported for regular M.P. duty at four o'clock in the morning.

Sambrakos climbed into the 240GD Mercedes military jeep, still half asleep, and drove away from his encampment. He would begin with a base located at the northern end of the island and work his way down. The storehouse there, near the small village of Viki, was different from the others for two reasons. For one thing, it was not marked like the other supply posts. From the outside it appeared to be an abandoned barn. Secondly, it contained an old Pershing 1a missile that was missing a warhead. General Georgiou had told Sambrakos personally that the Greek military had acquired the missile from NATO in the early eighties. It was delivered with the understanding that if there was ever a need to arm it, NATO would supply the warhead. General Georgiou convinced Sambrakos that because of Greece's vulnerable geographic position with enemies on three fronts, he had managed to get the missile "on loan" from NATO. The Pershing even came with its own Ford M656 transport truck, from which it could be launched. One day Sambrakos had to familiarize himself with the truck so that he could drive it if necessary. Georgiou told Sambrakos that he was one of the handful of men who knew of its existence. Sambrakos was sworn to secrecy, for it was essential that Turkey never learn that Greece had a Pershing on an island so close to its shores.

That was the story the general told Sambrakos, and the sergeant major naively believed him.

The jeep moved over the rolling hills of the island toward the north shore. At one point, he drove along the coast. He admired the silhouettes of the hollow stones that had been placed at intervals along the shore by the ancient Greeks. They looked like rooks on a chessboard and had been used to warn villagers of approaching pirate ships. Firewood was permanently kept inside the stones so that a blaze could be lit when an enemy ship was sighted. The smoke signal could be seen by others along the line, and the people were thus ready to repel the pirates.

The sky was black when Sambrakos eventually stopped the jeep on the road a hundred meters from the dilapidated old barn. He jumped out and unlocked the two padlocks that secured the gate.

Sambrakos approached the barn and noted that the padlocks on the double doors were unlocked. Feeling a rush of adrenaline, the sergeant major swung the doors open.

When he stepped inside, his heart nearly stopped.

General Georgiou was standing there, waiting for him. He held a flashlight and a briefcase.

The missile and its truck sat in the barn behind the general, gleaming in the work lights. The American-made Pershing 1a, or MGM-31A, is nearly thirty-five feet long with a three-and-a-half-foot diameter. It has a range of 100 to 460 miles, and is one of the most successful mobile nuclear missiles ever created. Its support equipment includes an automatic azimuth reference system which allows the Pershing to be launched from unsurveyed locations, and a sequential launch adapter which reduces the response time in a quick-reaction role.

"Ah, you're here," the general said. "Get in the truck. We're taking the missile somewhere. We're on a classified mission."

Sambrakos was surprised. "Sir?"

"You heard me, let's go," Georgiou said, pulling the sergeant major inside.

Sambrakos didn't feel right about it. There was something about the general's behavior that bothered him.

Two other men dressed in Greek MP uniforms stepped out from behind the truck. Sambrakos didn't recognize them, and he thought he knew all of the other MPs on the island.

"Oh, this is Sergeant Kandarakis and Sergeant Grammos. They'll be coming along," the general said, turning to walk toward the truck.

Sambrakos stood his ground. It wasn't right, whatever was happening. He didn't know exactly why he felt that way, but he instinctively rebelled against the order.

"Sir, I need to have a little more information about this," Sambrakos said. "Who are these men? I've never seen them before."

The general turned to his aide and said, "I gave you an order, Sergeant Major. Do not question it. Let's go."

Now Sambrakos knew something was terribly wrong. The general sounded scared himself. It was obvious that *he* was doing something wrong and he didn't want to be challenged.

The general turned back to him again and said, "Sambrakos? Are you coming?"

"No, sir," Sambrakos said.

The general narrowed his eyes at the young man. He shook his head and said, "I knew I shouldn't have brought you in on such short notice. I had no time to see if you would really work out. Well, it looks like this *isn't* going to work out."

The general turned and walked away, nodding to the two other men.

Sambrakos was too stunned to react when one of them raised a handgun and shot him in the chest. The MP crashed backward to the floor as blackness overtook him.

The assassin looked outside to make sure no one had heard the shot; then he pulled the body over to the side.

"You'll have to drive instead," the general told the other man. "I hope you can do it. Let's go."

The three of them boarded the M656 and drove out of the barn. Brigadier General Dimitris Georgiou, Number Five of the Decada, was angry about his choice for a new recruit. The sergeant major had been useful for a while as a buffer between him and the rest of the Chios military administration, but the test of loyalty came too soon. At least the boy wouldn't talk. Now the general was the only one in the Greek military left alive who knew about the Pershing missile he had stolen from a NATO base in France twelve years ago.

James Bond arrived in Athens midmorning. There was a time when Ellinikon International Airport's security record was considered poor. Its reputation had improved after the terrorist-plagued eighties, but Bond never felt completely comfortable there. It was a place where he felt compelled to keep looking over his shoulder.

He entered the country under the name "John Bryce," an alias he had not used for many years. He carried the two Walthers—the PPK and the P99—in a specially lined security briefcase that prevented X-ray penetration. The gruff customs agent sent him through quickly, and Bond stepped into the arrivals terminal. His eyes scanned the faces for the agent from the Greek National Intelligence Service who was supposedly meeting him. Even though he didn't know who it would be, Bond was trained to recognize fellow agents simply by their posture, clothing, or accessories. There was no one who caught his eye.

He was walking through the crowd toward the exit when Niki Mirakos stepped up to him from nowhere and said, "The guided tour of Greece begins in five minutes. Do you have your ticket?"

Bond smiled broadly and responded, "Yes, and it's been punched twice."

"Then hold on to it and follow me," she said with a smile.

"How are you, Niki?" he asked.

Her brown eyes sparkled. "I'm fine. It's good to see you, James . . . er, John."

"I must say this is a surprise and a pleasure."

She led him outside to the parking lot. "They came to me and said that you would be in Athens. Since we had worked together briefly in Cyprus, I got the job."

"Lucky you."

Niki looked at him warmly. "You're the lucky one—you just don't know it yet."

They eventually found a white 1995 Toyota Camry. Niki opened the passenger door for Bond, then went around and sat behind the wheel. As they drove away, she said, "Sorry I have to use this old thing. You're probably used to something better."

"You're the second person in a week that has apologized to me about their car," Bond said. "If it gets you where you need to go on time, then it will do."

"I just wondered, because your company car arrived late last night from London. It's parked in your hotel lot."

So the XK8 had arrived ahead of him. That was something.

"Yes, well, the Service was a bit extravagant with the Jaguar, mostly due to my insistence."

The sun was shining brightly. Compared to London's dreadful weather, Bond thought, Athens was a tropical paradise.

"It's still very pretty," Niki said, reading his thoughts. "You know, Hellas has the best three hundred and sixty-five days a year of any country on the face of the earth. I think the climate had a lot to do with the evolution of society. People migrated to ancient Athens because the sun was always shining." She had used *Hellas,* the Greek word for "Greece." Bond was not fluent in Greek. He could read it, but he couldn't speak it, except for a few common words and expressions.

Bond had been to Greece on a number of occasions. He always found it to be a warm, friendly country. The people are hard workers, but they play even harder. The afternoon ritual of drinking ouzo, eating *mezedes,* and discussing the meaning of life is standard procedure in Greece. He particularly liked the fact that nearly everyone smoked and he had no problem lighting a cigarette in a public place. Greece has the dubious distinction of having the highest number of smokers per capita in Europe.

"I'm glad you flew to Greece on Thursday, and not Tuesday," she said.

"Oh, why?"

"Don't you know Tuesdays are bad luck in Greece?"

"How come?"

"It was a Tuesday when the Byzantine Empire fell to the Ottomans. Many Greeks won't do anything important on a Tuesday, like have a wedding, or start a journey, or sign a contract."

"I'm afraid I'm not very superstitious."

"That's all right. We Greeks tend to be overly so." She fondled the chain around her neck. It contained a blue glass stone resembling an eye. Bond knew that it was a charm to ward off the evil eye.

Niki drove Bond to the Plateia Syntagmatos, the heart of the modern city of Athens. A large, paved square is at its center, just across from the old royal palace. It was from the palace balcony that the *syntagma,* or constitution, was declared in 1843. The building now houses the Greek parliament. Bond's hotel was directly across from the palace, to the northwest. The Hotel Grande Bretagne at Constitution Square is arguably Athens's grandest hotel, built in 1862 as a mansion to accommodate visiting dignitaries. It was converted into a hotel in 1872 and became the preferred destination for royalty. The Nazis occupied it as their headquarters during World War II, and it was the scene of an attempted assassination of Winston Churchill on Christmas Eve in 1944. The hotel is still aptly referred to as "the Royal Box of Athens."

"Are you hungry?" Niki asked.

"Famished," Bond said. It was time for lunch.

"Why don't you check in and I'll meet you at the hotel restaurant in half an hour? I'll go park the car."

"Fine."

Bond hadn't stayed at the Grande Bretagne since the Colonel Sun affair, many years ago. Memories of the hotel came back to him as he walked into the lobby. It has a large and lofty foyer with stained glass, green marble pillars, and a good copy of a Gobelin tapestry featuring Alexander the Great entering Babylon. Bond was given a corner suite on the eighth floor. It had a sitting room with a window overlooking the parliament building. The bedroom contained a king-sized bed and a terrace with a magnificent view of the Acropolis.

He dressed quickly in a sharp Nassau Silk Noile outfit of tan trousers, a white mesh crew knit shirt, and a tan waistcoat. The Walther PPK fitted snugly in the chamois shoulder holster underneath a white, fully lined silk jacket. Normally the Walther wouldn't have fitted into the Berns-Martin holster, but Q Branch had commissioned the company to make one specially for Bond.

The two-story GB Corner Restaurant was decorated just as elegantly as the hotel it served. The booths, benches, and chairs were covered in maroon leather, and frosted glass lamps at each table cast cool light around the room.

Niki was waiting for him in a booth. She had already ordered a bottle of Chatzimichali red wine.

"Welcome to Athens, Mr. Bryce," she said conspiratorially. "Everything on the menu is quite good."

"I was here several years ago. I remember the food. I take it you live in Athens?"

"Yes, I live west of the tourist areas. I've been here most of my life. I spent some time in the country when I was a girl."

"How long have you been with the service?"

"Would you believe ten years?"

"You've kept your youth remarkably well," Bond said. He guessed that she was in her mid-thirties. Her tan skin glowed in the soft light. Bond found Mediterranean women exotic. She was a delight to look at and talk to. Besides being extremely attractive, Niki was also very professional. He normally preferred working alone or with other men, but this time he looked upon the prospect with a positive attitude. He had a sudden recall of how soft the inside of her thighs had been, and forced the memory out of his head for the moment.

"Thank you. As I said before, it's probably the climate here. Let's order, then we'll talk."

They both started with traditional dishes of moussaka, which was similar to lasagne but made with ground beef, fried eggplant, onions, and béchamel cream and baked. For a main course, they each had souvlaki with rice. Bond knew he was really in Greece when he tasted the succulent beef grilled on a skewer with peppers and onions.

They ordered coffee and she said, "Since we're officially working together, I can now share information with you. I can, how do you say in English, 'feel you in'?"

Bond smiled. "That expression, 'fill you in,' is more American than English, I believe. Yes, it's good to be working with your service. Station G, I'm afraid, was a casualty of one of SIS's administrative changes made during the last several years. Budget cuts eliminated the entire operation, save for a token agent. Old Stuart Thomas is still the head, but he only works twenty hours a week and uses a temporary secretary. Needless to say, the London office was disappointed with what little intelligence Station G had provided on the case. The late Christopher Whitten was a field agent working in Athens temporarily. But never mind that. Feel me in."

She laughed and lit a cigarette.

"As you know, the Greeks are very concerned about the Cyprus situation. The people do not tolerate the Turkish presence in the north. Many feel very passionate about it. Greece is in a constant state of readiness in case a war ever broke out with Turkey. Naturally, no one wants that to happen. Except for the joy of kicking some Turkish butts, a war would be very foolish."

"I understand."

"We believe the Number Killer is attempting to provoke a conflict between Greece and Turkey over Cyprus."

"How do you know?"

"Before it all started, the secret service received a letter from someone who called himself the Monad. It was untraceable. The letter said that a group called the Decada would commit ten acts of violence over the next two months. When the tenth act was completed, war would break out between Turkey and Greece. The southern Cypriots would be reunited with the north under a Greek flag. It was written in a flowery, poetic style, much like ancient Greek verse. It ended by saying that the gods would be watching and waiting, for this was their wish."

"That's it?"

"Yes. It went into the prank pile until the two incidents in Cyprus occurred. I mean, we get a lot of stuff like that. There are so many 'groups' out there and a lot of them claim to be militant ones with violent intentions but they turn out to be harmless. It's not the first time someone has threatened to start a conflict at the Green Line in Cyprus just to break the stalemate. There are a lot of people who might do something crazy. It isn't something to take lightly. Anyway, someone remembered the letter and pulled it out. We now believe the letter was not a hoax. The Decada, whatever it is, exists. We don't know a thing about them. We don't know who they are or where they're based."

"What can you tell me about Charles Hutchinson?"

"He's disappeared. We put a tail on him when he arrived in Athens two days ago. He rented a car and drove south to Cape Sounion. He successfully lost our man there. I suspect he got on a boat or aircraft and went to one of the islands. The rental car was found yesterday in a parking lot near the pier."

"What can you tell me about a man named Konstantine Romanos?"

She laughed. "Great minds think alike. We've had our eye on Mr. Romanos for a little while, actually. He has a very mysterious past."

Niki went through the details that Bond already knew—that Romanos was a lecturer at Athens University, was a noted author, and was considered one of the most brilliant mathematicians in the Western world.

"Where does he get his money?"

"He's extremely wealthy. That's one reason why he's been under suspicion for a few years. He spends a lot of time at the casino on Mount Parnitha. Wins big, loses big, wins it back. He's also the leader of a spiritual and philosophical organization called the New Pythagorean Society. They're a collection of mathematicians who follow the teachings of Pythagoras. It's all legitimate. There is one funny thing, though."

"What's that?"

"They're based in Cape Sounion. And Romanos lives there in a big house when he's not in Athens."

"Well well. Mr. Romanos has suddenly become more interesting to me. What do you know about his background?"

"We know he's a, how do you say, a 'self-made' man. He was a refugee from northern Cyprus in 1974, one of the many Greek Cypriots who fled the Turkish invasion. In Cyprus he had been a noted lecturer and mathematician as well. He had a good life in Nicosia. When he came to Athens he had very little money and was homeless. He had lost his wife and children in a fire caused by the Turks. He was given government housing and a job. Then there was a period of his life that is unaccounted for in our records. Between 1977 and 1982, no one knows where he went or what he did. In late 1982, he reappeared on the scene, with more money than a dozen people make in a lifetime. The tax boys investigated him and he claimed he got the money in the Middle East during those years by investing in and selling real estate. Since that time, he formed the New Pythagorean Society, secured his various teaching and lecturing affairs, bought and sold companies, and he now owns a big yacht called the *Persephone* that sails all over the Aegean."

"A real success story," Bond said.

"A year ago he acquired a pharmaceutical company in Athens called BioLinks Limited. The president is a fairly well-respected scientist named Melina Papas."

Bond smiled. "Great minds *do* think alike. BioLinks owned the clinic in the United States where Charles Hutchinson worked. It's also where he delivered some rather tainted sperm samples."

She nodded and said, "I just read the report. That is amazing. Our joint investigation is paying off, isn't it? We've already gone in with a court order to seize their entire sperm and blood supply until this is sorted out. No one's got sick yet, thank God. We can go over there whenever you'd like and take a look around. I can't imagine that our case is related to those epidemics in America and Japan, though. Do you think it is?"

"If the Americans match the bug I found in Texas with the one in L.A., then I would say it is. Unfortunately, that takes time. Why would Romanos want to own a pharmaceutical company?"

"Who knows. The company was in the red before he got hold of it. This year it looks as if it may turn a profit. They are in the research-and-development area of prescription drugs. We've looked into the company and it's all quite legitimate, but we have a good surveillance team watching them closely."

Bond shook his head, pondering the details. "What does maths have to do with pharmaceuticals?"

"If you ask me, the guy is nuts," she said. "I've seen him on television. I don't understand a thing he says. Then again, maths was my worst subject."

Bond laughed again. "Mine too. What do the New Pythagoreans do?"

"I'm not entirely sure. They pretend to hold philosophy symposiums. They offer courses, both in mathematics and philosophy. It's something of a religion with those people. They're also heavily into numbers . . . numerology, and that might mean something."

"I want to meet Mr. Romanos. What about this casino you mentioned?"

"It's pretty cool, you'll like it," she said, unconsciously dropping her businesslike persona. "It's up on a mountain, and you have to take a cable car to get to it. He usually plays on Friday nights."

"Sounds like my kind of place."

"So what would you like to do first? Where do you want to begin?"

"I believe we should pick up the Jaguar and take a drive down to Cape Sounion. I'd like to take a look at this New Pythagorean Society and see where Romanos lives. Tomorrow we'll go to BioLinks."

"Fine. Are you armed?"

"Certainly."

"Then let's get going."

The blue Jaguar XK8 sped smoothly into Attica, the tip of the Greek peninsula jutting out southeast from Athens. The coast road was perfect for Bond to try out the new car. It was a winding, twisting four-lane highway that eventually narrowed to two lanes with mountains on one side and the sea on the other. They passed resorts with deluxe beaches and hotels, such as Glyfada and Voula. Traffic wasn't very heavy, so Bond took the car at a safe but slightly accelerated speed all the way. He loved the grip of the wheel and felt the engine's power in his hands. He longed for a stretch of road where he could push the Jaguar to its limit.

Niki sat silently in the passenger seat, looking out at the sea. Her reverie was interrupted by the cellular phone in her handbag. She answered it, spoke in Greek, and hung up. "We need to go straight to the Temple of Poseidon when we reach Cape Sounion. Something's happened there. Do you know the story of Aegeas and the Temple of Poseidon?"

"Please enlighten me."

"There was an ancient king named Aegeas. His son went out on a long expedition. Aegeas told his son that when he returned, he should put white sails on his ship so that the king would know that the expedition was a success. However, even though the mission was a success, the son forgot to change the sails and approached the cape with black ones. The king thought his son was dead and threw himself into the sea. The sea was thereafter called the Aegean Sea, and the Temple of Poseidon was built there in his memory."

"I've seen it," said Bond. "It's a magnificent set of ruins."

The temple was built on a craggy spur that plunged sixty-five meters to the sea. It was erected in 444 B.C., around the same time as the Parthenon, and was constructed of Doric marble columns. Only sixteen of the columns remain.

"It is widely believed that the temple was built by Ictinus, the same architect who built the Temple of Hephaestus in the Ancient Agora," Niki said.

"That's where Whitten's body was dumped?"

"Right."

They reached Cape Sounion in just under two hours. They could see the monument from the road, gleaming white in the late-afternoon sun. As they approached the site, though, they were met by police vehicles and were prevented from going farther.

Niki spoke to the officer and then showed him some identification. Reluctantly, he let the car through and radioed his superiors at the ruins that Bond and Niki were on their way up the hill.

The popular tourist attraction was closed for the day, and several official vehicles were parked in the gravel lot. A group of people were up at the base of the temple, looking at something covered by a sheet. Bond parked the car and they walked up the hill to join the police. A sergeant spoke to Niki, then led them through the crowd to the white sheet.

The first thing they saw was the number "7" scrawled in red on a sign reading "Deposit Litter Here" in English and Greek. Under the sheet was a dead body. The policeman said something else in Greek, then pulled the sheet down so that they could see the victim.

Although the body was badly battered, Bond recognized him. It was Charles Hutchinson.

▶14.
THE NEW PYTHAGOREANS

Bond and Niki spent two hours at the crime scene speaking with Greek police inspectors and gathering what information they could. Before leaving the Temple of Poseidon, Bond stood at the edge of the cliff and looked out to sea. A wave of melancholy hit him inexplicably. He looked out at the horizon toward the west. The sun was on its way down, casting its orange glow over the water. Although the scenery was quite different, the view reminded him of Jamaica and his beloved Shamelady. He longed to be there. Niki came up behind him and watched with him for a moment before speaking.

"I feel a great sadness in you," she said finally. "What is it?"

Bond sighed. "Nothing. Come on, there's not much more daylight. We had better go and see Romanos's house."

Niki looked at him sideways, then let it go. "Look there, to the north."

She pointed toward the hills away from the temple.

"Do you see that building there? That's the Hotel Aegaeon. Now, just beyond that, do you see the mansion with red windows and beige walls?"

"Yes."

"That's where Romanos lives. Let's go. I'll tell you in the car what the inspector told me."

They got into the Jaguar and drove away from the site.

Niki said, "They have to perform a postmortem examination, but the medical examiner at the scene thought that Charles Hutchinson had been dead about three days. He obviously wasn't killed here, but his body was moved here overnight. It was discovered by tourists this morning."

Bond said, "The number 'seven'—if Charles was killed three days ago, that's around the same time as the two incidents in northern Cyprus. They were numbers 'five' and 'six.' "

"Yes, they were all done the same day."

"The first series of attacks didn't occur on the same day. And there were four of them."

"Yes, but they were committed very close together in time," she said. "I think the significance is in the numbers, not in the time frame."

"What else did you find out?"

"We'll get the full autopsy report, but from the looks of it, Charles Hutchinson was killed in a fall of some kind. His body was badly battered—not from a beating or torture, but from an impact. He also had an old Greek coin in his mouth."

"Just like Whitten. Payment for Charon the boatman to take him across the River Styx."

"I'm trying to figure out why the body was dumped at the Temple of Poseidon."

"Poseidon was one of the statuettes found at Episkopi."

They pondered the mystery in silence as the car pulled up to the gate of the large mansion they had seen from the temple. A stone fence surrounded the property, and an intercom screened visitors before the automatic gate would open. The two-story house was built in the 1920s. Some lights were on in a few of the windows, but the only other sign of activity was that a man dressed in black was washing a black Ferrari F355 GTS on the drive. He looked up and saw them peering through the gate, but kept on washing the car.

"We've just been spotted. Where is the headquarters for the New Pythagoreans?" Bond asked.

"Just down the road. Let's see if the office is still open."

They drove away from the mansion and got on the main road. She directed him to a large white building of stone and plaster. It was a modest structure that might have been a restaurant or a shop. A sign outside the building read in both Greek and English, "The New Pythagorean Society." There were three cars parked in front, and the front door was propped open.

They got out of the Jaguar and went inside. The entryway was lit by candles. Literature was piled on a table by the door. Bond examined the pamphlets which outlined the organization's tenets and provided membership applications.

"May I help you?" came a voice, speaking Greek.

They turned to see a man of about forty wearing a white robe. He had come in through an archway that led to the rest of the building. He had dark hair and bright blue eyes.

Niki answered him in Greek, and then he spoke English. "You are welcome. If you have any questions, feel free to ask."

"I'm very interested in your organization," Bond said. "I'm from England and am writing a book about the ties between philosophy and religions. I'd be grateful if you could tell us a little about the New Pythagoreans. If I end up using the material in the book, you'll get some publicity out of it."

The man smiled broadly. "I'd be delighted to help you. I am Miltiades. I run the facility here at Cape Sounion. And you are . . . ?"

"I'm John Bryce, and this is . . ."

"Cassandra Talon," Niki said. "I'm serving as Mr. Bryce's guide in Greece."

"I see. Well, do you know much about Pythagoras?"

"Just a little," Bond said.

"He was a great mathematician who founded his own group of philosophers. It was called the Pythagorean Society, and they based everything in life on numbers. They believed that everything in the universe could be explained or defined with numerology. It's not something I can make you understand in ten minutes, mind you."

"That's all right. What does your group do?"

"We follow the teachings of Pythagoras, which often went beyond mathematics. He was one of the first philosophers to link spirituality with the challenges of everyday life. For example, he believed that one's diet was important in achieving a soul that was at peace with the body. We believe that animals and man are on the same journey, and that man is a little farther along than his animal brethren. Knowing this, we are expected to refrain from the eating of flesh. Our members are noted mathematicians and philosophers, mostly Greek, but we have members all over the world. We publish a quarterly magazine that is read in universities. Some of the greater minds in the Western world write for us. We donate a sizable amount of our income to various charities. We also provide a scholarship in mathematics at Athens University for qualified students."

"I've heard of your leader, Mr. Romanos. Is he here?"

"No, I'm afraid Mr. Romanos is away. He rarely shows his face here these days, he's such a busy man. He leaves me in charge, which was quite a leap of faith on his part, I must say!" He chuckled to himself.

"He lives nearby, doesn't he?"

"Yes, he does. You may have seen the mansion with the red roof on the way here. That's where he lives. Mr. Romanos is a man who enjoys his privacy. He has become very famous over the last few years."

"Can we see the rest of the building?"

"Certainly. Follow me."

Miltiades led them through the archway and into a large room that resembled a sanctuary. Pews covered the floor, facing a podium at the front of the room. Bond's heart skipped a beat when he saw what was printed on a tapestry hanging on the wall behind the podium.

It was an equilateral triangle of ten points, just like the one that he saw at Romanos's house in Austin, Texas.

"What is the significance of the triangle?" Bond asked.

"Ah, that is the symbol of the New Pythagorean Society. It is our logo, I suppose you can say. You see, Pythagoras and his followers believed that the number ten was sacred. This triangle consists of ten points. Notice that if you turn the triangle, it will always rest on a base of four points. The next level has three points, then two, and the tenth point is at the top of the triangle. It represents perfection."

Miltiades then led the couple out of the sanctuary and into a sitting room and library. The place was lined with full bookshelves. There were tables and chairs for studying, some occupied by young men and women.

"This is our library, where we keep over five thousand works on mathematics and philosophy. Students are allowed to use the library for a small fee. They come from all over Europe to use our resources." Miltiades had a kind of patronizing attitude that rubbed Bond the wrong way.

Niki and Bond stepped over to a wall to study some framed photographs. There was one of the board of directors, all dressed in white robes. Several photos featured Konstantine Romanos at various public functions. In one he was accepting an award from the prime minister of Greece. In another he was shaking hands with Melina Mercouri.

Still another photo featured Romanos sitting at a dinner table with several other men dressed in tuxedos. Next to Romanos was none other than Alfred Hutchinson. The photo was dated "1983."

"Do you know where this photo was taken?" Bond asked Miltiades.

Miltiades peered at it and shook his head. "Alas, no, I'm not sure. I think it might have been some kind of banquet for the university."

Bond and Niki exchanged glances. Here was proof that Alfred Hutchinson knew Konstantine Romanos. Bond feared what the news might mean to M. Had she been "sleeping with the enemy"?

The rest of the tour was unremarkable. Bond politely asked for some of the organization's literature and took Miltiades's card. They thanked him and left the building.

Back in the Jaguar, he said, "That triangle was the same as the one I saw in Texas. I think I'm beginning to understand the pattern of numbers. They're following that triangle. The first four attacks occurred around the same time: Whitten's murder, the two attacks on the Cyprus bases, and Alfred Hutchinson's assassination. There were only three in the next group—the next line up in the triangle: the two attacks in northern Cyprus and Charles Hutchinson's murder. I would wager that the next group of attacks will consist of only two, and they will be big ones. They're leading up to the coup de grâce, the tenth and biggest one yet."

"I think you're right," Niki said. "So do you think the New Pythagoreans might be a front for the Decada?"

"That's what I want to find out. I think the sooner I meet Konstantine Romanos, the better."

The sun had set and they were hungry. Niki suggested that they eat dinner at a taverna she knew before setting off back to Athens. They stopped at a quaint little place called Akroyali, which means "the edge of the beach." It was a white wooden building with blue trim and blue tables. Blue-and-white-checked tablecloths covered the tables both indoors and on a patio outside.

At first the taverna didn't appear to be open for business, until the proprietor, a woman named Maria, recognized Niki and hurtled out of the kitchen with an enthusiastic greeting. They chose an indoor table because the wind had come up outside, but they had a full view of the beach and sea.

Maria went on and on in Greek about that evening's "special," which apparently was the only dish they happened to be serving on a November weekday. Niki whispered to Bond that the taverna was normally closed for the winter season during the week, but because Maria was her friend, she would make something for them. It was another example of Greek hospitality.

Maria brought out a bottle of Villitsa, a local white wine, some water, and two small bottles of ouzo. For the ouzo, she provided two glasses with ice.

Bond poured the ouzo. The clear liquid turned milky when it touched the ice in the glass. The licorice taste was refreshing, and it reminded Bond of drinking sake.

"May the poisons go down with the ouzo," Niki said as she took a sip.

Someone in the kitchen turned on the radio. A Greek folk song was playing, and Bond and Niki listened to the energetic but plaintive music until the tune was over.

"Did you feel the pain in that song?" Niki asked. "All Greek music has pain in it. In a way, we enjoy the pain. The songs are really about sad things, but they *sound* happy."

Bond poured the wine. They raised their glasses and clinked them together.

"Do you know why we clink glasses when we drink wine?" Bond asked her.

"No, why?"

"Drinking wine satisfies all but one of the senses. We can see the wine, touch it, taste it, smell it . . . but we can't hear it. So we—" He tapped her glass again to make the clink sound. "To hear the wine."

Niki smiled. "It's good to see you chirpy again. I really saw a dark cloud come over you earlier."

"I'll always be chirpy if you're going to ply me with ouzo."

Niki laughed and Maria brought out an overflowing bowl of Greek salad and two forks. It was a true Greek salad, consisting of tomatoes, cucumbers, onions, olives, feta cheese, and olive oil, and there were also plates of fried octopus and bread. Niki showed Bond the Greek way of eating bread and salad—she took a piece of bread and dabbed up some of the olive oil on the bottom of the salad bowl, then fed it to Bond.

The main course was sargi, a saltwater fish about a foot long. Maria's husband caught the fish just outside the taverna, where they congregated around the rocks in the sea. It was grilled with a mixture of eggs and lemon shaken over the fish. It went well with the wine.

Maria beamed as she spoke at a furious pace over their table as they ate. She used her hands expressively as she talked.

Niki translated. "She says it's wonderful to see two romantic people again for a change. Usually all she gets are people doing business on cellular phones. 'How is one supposed to enjoy a meal if one is doing business at the same time?' she asks."

"Are we romantic?"

"We were once. Maybe it shows."

When they had finished, Bond paid for the meal and left a large tip. Maria happily fussed over them as they got up to leave.

The coast highway was very dark by the time they left Cape Sounion in the Jaguar. They didn't notice that a black Ferrari F355 GTS had pulled out onto the road behind them.

Bond drove at seventy-five miles per hour, feeling the car grip the two-lane road as it twisted and turned along the mountains. The darkness of the sea was on the left side of the car. The only thing preventing a vehicle from shooting off the road and down the cliff was a useless short metal rail. Traffic was light, but every now and then an oncoming car would pull around a curve and pass by the Jaguar.

He noticed the headlights after ten minutes had passed. The car behind him was keeping a good pace with the Jaguar.

"Tell me, Niki, do Greek drivers always drive as fast as I do?" Bond asked.

"No one drives in Greece like you do, James. I love your car too, but you could slow down."

Bond decreased the speed to see what the car behind him would do. Once he had slowed to nearly fifty-five, the Ferrari crossed the yellow line and illegally passed him. Bond caught sight of a dark, hulking shape looking over at him as the car went by.

"That was the black Ferrari we saw in front of Romanos's mansion," Bond said.

He immediately activated the GPS navigation controls. A screen popped up inside the windshield. An aerial view of the coast road rendered in real-time Silicon Graphics appeared on the screen. A flashing yellow blip indicated the Jaguar. The Ferrari was speeding ahead, a flashing red blip. In a moment, Bond felt the wheel turn independently, following the route transmitted by satellite navigation. If he had wanted to, he could have let go completely and used his hands for other tasks, but he preferred to control the car manually. He continued to slow down, putting some distance between the Ferrari and the Jaguar.

"He must not have been very interested in you," Niki said. "He's gone pretty far ahead." The red blip soon disappeared off the screen. It was more than three miles ahead of the Jaguar.

"You spoke too soon," Bond said as two more red blips appeared behind the Jaguar on the screen. They were traveling at a tremendous speed toward Bond.

He responded by increasing his own speed back to seventy-five. Bond flipped another switch and the outline of the flying scout appeared on the screen. The graphics revealed that it was stored neatly beneath the Jaguar. He pushed a button and the readout proclaimed: "Readying Scout." A small joystick popped out of a compartment on the dashboard. In three seconds, the display changed to read: "Scout Ready." Bond pushed a red launch button and they felt the car lunge. At the same time they heard a sudden whoosh behind the Jaguar as the scout ejected from its bay. The batlike vehicle soared out and up into the air, then turned so that it was traveling thirty feet above and parallel with the Jaguar.

Keeping one hand on the wheel, Bond used his left hand to manipulate the joystick. He guided the scout so that it changed course and flew back toward his pursuers. Once it was above the two cars, Bond pushed another button. The viewscreen on the dash displayed the makes and models—they were both black Ferraris and they were gaining fast.

Bond sped up to a hundred. He heard Niki gasp slightly as she clutched the armrest on her door. The tires screeched when he pulled around a curve, but the Jaguar's control was outstanding. Then they heard gunfire.

Three bullets hit the back of the Jaguar in rapid succession. One of the Ferraris was about thirty yards behind Bond. He could see in the rearview mirror that someone was leaning out the passenger window and was firing at the car.

More bullets hit, but the chobam armor deflected them. Major Boothroyd's reactive skins exploded as they were hit. Viscous fluid spread around the bullet holes in the metal, and within seconds a new patch of coating had covered the penetrations.

He shut off the headlights in order to take advantage of the night-vision capabilities. The optical systems intensified the available light and projected a view of the road on the secondary screen inside the windshield. The gunfire continued, but the shooter's aim was hampered now. The bullets whizzed past the Jaguar without hitting it.

An oncoming car shot around a curve, nearly hitting Bond. The horn blared. Bond punched another button so that the scout would transmit the aerial view of the road again. Now he could "see" around the curves ahead and determine if there were any oncoming cars in the opposite lane. Bond drove around slower-moving vehicles in his path, speeding past them in the dark. The Ferraris, however, kept up with him.

Bond slowed a little to let one of the pursuers catch up.

"What are you doing?" Niki asked.

"Let's see how badly these fellows want us."

The Jaguar's speed went down to seventy-five, and the Ferrari was on its tail. Confused as to why his bullets weren't piercing the car's body, the shooter let loose a volley of gunfire from the Uzi he was carrying. The driver pulled into the opposite lane, taking a chance that there were no oncoming cars.

Bond let the Ferrari pull up alongside him. The two men inside glared at Bond, attempting to peer in the dark window to see his face. Bond punched a button. Suddenly, the lights from an oncoming car zoomed around a bend in front of the Ferrari. Niki screamed. Bond could see the surprised looks on the pursuers' faces as the driver swerved to the left to avoid the car. Unfortunately, he swerved off the road, through the metal rail, and out into space. The Ferrari crashed on the cliffside below two seconds later and burst into flames.

Bond punched another button and the hologram of the oncoming car disappeared.

"What happened to the other car?" Niki asked, her eyes wide.

"It was a projection of your imagination," Bond said.

The other Ferrari sped forward, attempting to shorten the distance between the two cars. Another man leaned out of the window and fired. This time the bullets sprayed across the back of the Jaguar. Bond pushed down the accelerator and increased his speed to 120. The GPS navigation showed that the original Ferrari, the one that went ahead of Bond earlier, had turned around and was now coming back.

"Do you think they recognized you from Texas?" Niki asked.

"Unless there were hidden cameras at the infertility clinic, they couldn't have. No one saw me at Romanos's house except men who are dead now. I suppose the clinic is a possibility. Hang on, this fellow behind me is asking for it, and our old friend in the first Ferrari is coming back."

Bond used the joystick to maneuver the flying scout directly over the Ferrari behind them. There was about twenty feet between them now. At one point, the Ferrari inched up close enough to ram the Jaguar's rear bumper. The scout's targeting mechanism locked onto the Ferrari and maintained its speed. Now, there was nowhere the Ferrari could go without the scout flying directly over it.

The headlights of the first Ferrari appeared around a curve ahead. It was coming toward him at a high speed. The lights were on bright, but luckily the night-vision optics prevented the beams from blinding him. The Ferrari pulled into his lane, ready to meet the Jaguar head-on.

Bond was about to swerve into the westbound lane, but the GPS navigation screen indicated that another car was there, slightly behind the Ferrari. It was probably a civilian. The Ferrari behind him was gaining and the man was shooting again. In a few seconds the Jaguar would collide with the oncoming Ferrari. If he swerved to the right, he would crash into the mountain. If he pulled into the other lane, he would hit the civilian car or go sailing off the cliff.

Bond flipped two switches, one right after the other, and felt the car lurch as a cruise missile shot out from beneath the chassis. The Ferrari in front of him exploded into a huge ball of flame and went careening into the mountainside. The civilian car went on past. The driver's eyes were wide with terror as he passed the Jaguar.

The Ferrari in back was very close now. Bond manipulated the joystick so that the flying scout inched ahead of his own car. He pressed a couple of buttons and the computer made instant calculations comparing height, speed, and distance. He moved the flying scout into position and once again locked onto the target behind him. Bond pushed a button and looked in the rearview mirror.

The flying scout released a swarm of mines on tiny parachutes. The computer had carefully calculated the time it would take for the mines to reach the ground. Then it had positioned the scout far enough ahead so that the Ferrari would be in the right spot on the road when the mines hit. When they did, the Ferrari was blown out of the lane and off the cliff.

Now that the threat had been eliminated, Bond turned on the car's headlights and proceeded toward Athens at a safe speed. He slowed down long enough for the flying scout to dock underneath the car. Once it was in its bay, Bond locked it down.

"Well, I'm impressed," Niki said. "I'm going to have to speak to our armorer. We never get any toys like these."

"Do girls use toys like these?"

"This girl does."

Bond opened a small compartment in his armrest. He pulled out a set of keys and handed them to her.

"These are spares, in the event that you might need them."

She took them, wide eyed. *"Efharisto!"*

"And just in case we meet any more Ferraris, I'm going to give the Jaguar a little face-lift. It won't change the car, but it will confuse the enemy for a few minutes." He flipped a switch, and the electrically sensitive pigments in the car's paint changed. The Jaguar went from blue to red. Another switch turned the license plate from an English registration to an Italian one. Bond then reached out to turn off the GPS satellite navigation device, but decided not to. He set the cruise control to maintain the car's speed and punched in the commands for the car to guide them along the coast road straight into Athens. With his hands free now, he turned in his seat and put his arms around Niki.

"Oh my God," she said. "The last time I ever did anything like this in a car, I was a teenager."

Bond kissed her and slowly put his hand on her breast. He could feel the nipple harden beneath her cotton shirt. She let out a tiny gasp and arched her back so that he had easier access to her erogenous zones.

"We probably have another hour and a half before we reach Athens," he said. "The back seat can barely hold one person, much less two. Unfortunately, bucket seats are not my idea of comfort for this sort of thing either."

She said, "Who says we have to be comfortable? I think we'll manage just fine—at least until we reach a little viewpoint I know up ahead where we can stop for a while."

Then she pulled off her shirt.

▶15.
BIOLINKS

Inexplicably, Bond awoke with a start. He looked over and saw the curves of Niki's body beneath the sheet next to him. She was sleeping soundly.

He looked at the clock and saw that it was late morning. It had been an extremely pleasant night. They had made love on the terrace of his Grande Bretagne suite with all of Athens before them. There was something appropriate about the act of copulation in full view of the Acropolis. They had continued the lovemaking on the large bed inside. Niki's cries of passion were loud and were probably heard in other parts of the hotel, but Bond didn't care. He enjoyed lively women, and this girl was definitely a fiery Mediterranean. She seemed to be insatiable. They had finally fallen asleep in the early hours before sunrise.

As he watched her breathe quietly, Bond wallowed in the melancholy he now felt. The night had been an assault on the senses: a terrific meal, a brush with death, then hours of sex. Bond had felt completely alive when Niki's legs wrapped around his waist and she looked into his eyes with her own deep brown ones. Now that it was morning and a new day, all that had vanished. The previous night was just a shadow of a memory and now he felt empty.

Niki must have sensed him watching her, for she stirred and stretched. She turned to him and reached out, saying, *"Kalimera,"* in a sleepy voice. He took her in his arms and kissed her. "Good morning," he replied.

"What time is it?" she asked with a yawn.

"Nearly eleven o'clock. I never sleep this late."

"You needed your rest after last night."

He ran his hand along the contour of her side, following the curve across her ribs to her waist, then up and over the hip.

"I'm going to make a phone call," he said. He kissed her again, stood and slipped on one of the hotel's terry cloth robes, and walked into the sitting room. He used a small standard-issue Q Branch device to check the phone for any bugs, then picked up the receiver.

There was a two-hour time difference between Greece and England. Sir Miles Messervy was probably up by now, pottering around his garden at Quarterdeck or sitting drinking coffee and reading *The Times*.

A gruff voice answered, but it lightened considerably when Bond said who it was.

"Hello, James, where are you?"

"I'm abroad, sir. I wanted to ask you something. I hope it's not too early."

"Not at all. I was just sitting here drinking coffee and reading *The Times*. I take it you're on the Hutchinson case?"

"Right. Do you remember the night of your party, you said that you knew something about his family. What was it?"

Bond heard the former M sigh. He said, "I think I was reacting to my own prejudices against the man. We just didn't like each other much, I suppose."

"You can tell me, Sir Miles."

"I don't know if you remember any of the brouhaha that occurred when Hutchinson was first given the post of Ambassador to the World?"

"I only remember it was greeted with an enthusiastic response."

"There was one article, buried somewhere, I don't know, in the *Daily Express* or some such paper, about his father's court-martial during the war. It raised a few eyebrows but it disappeared quickly."

"I didn't see that. What was it about?"

"Hutchinson's father, Richard Hutchinson, was an officer stationed in Greece. He was court-martialed for 'mislaying' a horde of Nazi gold. That sort of thing was happening all over the place in Europe. The Swiss didn't get it all. It was a similar situation as that other officer you investigated in Jamaica, I don't recall his name. The one who died on his beach."

"Smythe."

"That's right. Anyway, Richard Hutchinson was accused of stealing a large amount of the Nazis' gold supply from a cache in Athens. He was eventually acquitted for lack of evidence and he got an honorable discharge. That's why nothing more was ever made of it. Hutchinson went on into civilian life. Needless to say, the gold was never found."

"Interesting. Do you believe the old man was guilty?"

"If he had been *Alfred* Hutchinson, I'd say yes, because I know . . . er, knew the man. I didn't know his father. But the army doesn't usually go court-martialing officers unless they have a damned good reason."

"Why did Alfred Hutchinson rub you up the wrong way, Sir Miles?"

"He had an air of superiority that was obnoxious. He thought he was a cut above everyone else. I wouldn't have bought a secondhand motorcar from him. I never trusted him. That's all. Only gut feelings, I'm afraid."

"No, that's fine, Sir Miles. You've been enormously helpful."

"Goodbye, James," the old man said. "Be careful."

They had an appointment with Melina Papas, the president of BioLinks Limited, after lunch. It would not be a pleasant meeting. The Greek police force had already confiscated the building's entire sperm and blood supply and had put a serious deadlock on the facility's business operations, but it couldn't be helped. Bond and Niki expected to get an earful from Ms. Papas about that.

Niki drove the Toyota while Bond studied a file marked "BioLinks Limited." Inside was a black-and-white photo of a woman in her forties with dark hair, a hawk nose, and a puckered mouth. The caption read, "Melina Papas, President." Her résumé was impressive, as she had worked in research and development for three major international drug companies before founding BioLinks six years ago.

BioLinks Limited was located near Athens University in a large, three-story modern complex. The lower floor held medical offices that served patients with infertility problems and acted as a family-planning unit. The upper floors contained offices, laboratories, and drug manufacturing equipment.

They were taken to the elevator by a plump woman with a mustache and eventually brought into the executive office of the president. It was a large, well-lit, and comfortable room with a conference table at one end and an elegant desk at the other. Medical and biochemistry books lined the walls.

After a moment, a frumpy woman with a hawk nose walked into the office. She was short, roughly five feet tall.

"I'm Melina Papas," she said. She didn't look happy.

Niki introduced them in Greek, but before she could finish, the woman said in English, "When can we have back our sperm and blood supplies? Do you realize what this has done to our business? Our research and development has completely halted!"

"We want to make sure that there isn't anything wrong with your bodily fluids, Ms. Papas, or rather, the company's bodily fluids," Niki said. "You wouldn't want to give someone anything that might hurt them, would you?"

"It's been twenty-four hours. How long will this take?"

"Ms. Papas, I think you can count on not getting any of it back. It will probably be destroyed."

"This is outrageous! You will hear from our lawyers." Melina Papas clenched her puckered mouth even more tightly.

"That's fine," Niki said, "but we have the law on our side. Now, we'd like to ask you some questions if you don't mind."

"I do mind, but go ahead and let's get it over with."

"Do you know Charles Hutchinson?" Bond asked.

"No."

"He delivered a case of sperm from your clinic, ReproCare, in Austin, Texas."

Ms. Papas shook her head. "We haven't had any deliveries from them in weeks. I told your other inspectors that."

"Ms. Papas, we know that Charles Hutchinson delivered a case here, and we'd like to know what was in it," Niki said.

"Why do you have samples shipped here from the United States?" Bond asked. "Can't you get your own sperm here in Greece?"

"Yes, of course we can. It's just that our clients tend to think they get better quality if it comes from America."

"Being Greek, I consider that an insult," Niki said.

"Surprisingly, it's true, to an extent," the woman said. "The sperm tends to be healthier and have better motility. I'm not saying that really makes it better, but it sounds better to our clients. It's marketing, that's all. You understand that many races are represented by the sperm we market. We get people who want an Asian father, or a Caucasian, or a Hispanic . . . We have to get what sperm we can."

"What kind of research and development are you doing here?"

"We make drugs, Mr. Bryce. That is our primary business. We also have a small team working on fertility issues. There is a team working on vaccinations for various diseases. We have an AIDS researcher. We have a cancer researcher. Our facility is one of the most highly respected medical research laboratories in Greece."

"How well did you know Dr. Ashley Anderson?" Bond asked.

"I met her three times, I think. She came here on business a few times. I was certainly unaware that she was involved in criminal activity."

"ReproCare *was* owned by BioLinks, wasn't it?" Niki asked.

"Yes, but it was an independent clinic. They operated on their own."

"Then why were you getting sperm samples from them?" Bond asked.

"It was just part of our business! Really, I was terribly distraught when I learned what happened in America. I couldn't believe that she was using our laboratory and clinic there to distribute chemical weapons. She was a talented and intelligent biochemist. I think the Americans must have got the wrong person or something. It just can't be true."

"I'm afraid it is true," Niki said.

"Luckily our insurance will cover the loss of the clinic. I still don't understand how she died, though."

"She took her own life, Ms. Papas," Niki said.

"I see."

"Do you know a man named Konstantine Romanos?" Bond asked. He noticed that the woman flinched a little.

"Of course I do—he owns the company," she said. "He doesn't have anything to do with the day-to-day operation of it. That's my job. I think he's been in the building only a couple of times."

"He's put a lot of money into BioLinks, has he?"

"Well, yes. We would have gone bankrupt two years ago if he hadn't purchased us. Now we're worth millions."

It was difficult to pin anything on her or the company. The Greek police and secret service had absolutely nothing out of the ordinary on BioLinks. Melina Papas had a clean record. Bond thought it was possible that whoever was behind all of this was just using BioLinks as a tool of convenience, but his intuition told him otherwise.

"Did you know a man named Christopher Whitten?"

"No, I don't think so. Is he English?"

"Yes."

"I don't know him."

"Does the name Alfred Hutchinson mean anything to you?"

Again, Bond detected an involuntary blink. "No," she said.

Bond looked at Niki. They silently acknowledged that they weren't getting anywhere.

"Thank you, Ms. Papas," Niki said. "We're sorry to have troubled you. I'm sure arrangements will be made to reimburse you for the loss of the, uhm, bodily fluids."

"Can I have your guarantee?"

"I'm not authorized to do that, but I'll see what I can do."

They were shown out of the office and led to the elevator by one of Ms. Papas's aides. Once they were alone, Niki whispered, "So how good a liar was she, James?"

"A good one," he said. "But not good enough."

Back in her office, Melina Papas poured a glass of scotch and sat at her desk, trembling. She picked up the phone and dialed her secretary.

"Christina," she said, "I have to go away for a few days. I'm leaving now. Please handle all my correspondence and phone calls. . . . No, I can't tell you where I'm going. If you need to get hold of me, leave a message on my voice mail. I'll call you. . . . Right."

She hung up, then opened a cupboard behind the desk. She removed a travel bag and stuffed it with some of her more treasured office possessions. Melina Papas fought back tears, for she knew she would never be returning to work in this capacity again.

After she was finished, she picked up the phone again and placed a call to the island of Chios.

By the end of that day, fifteen people in London had died of Williams's disease. One of them had brought it across the English Channel to Paris. New York's casualties numbered in the thirties. In Japan, the death toll had climbed to well over a hundred. In Los Angeles, ninety-eight people had met their end from the mysterious affliction.

Inevitably, the news agencies realized what was going on. That night, it was reported on CNN that a deadly epidemic was threatening to spread worldwide.

▶16.
ROMANOS

The Au Mont Parnes Casino sits atop Mount Parnitha, one of the three hills surrounding Athens. It is in the Thrakomakedones area, a suburb at the outer limits of the city. While it is possible to drive up the mountain to the casino and park a car right outside, almost everyone who visits the establishment chooses to park down below and ride the cable car. It is a pleasant five-minute ride, and at night the view of Athens is spectacular. The city lights fan away from the mountain and spread across the dark vista as far as the eye can see.

At ten P.M., James Bond parked the Jaguar in the cable-car parking lot and joined a group of twelve people in the waiting room. He was a bit overdressed in a gray Brioni tailored three-piece suit, but he wanted to make an impression on Romanos when he met him.

After their visit to BioLinks, Niki had gone back to her headquarters in Katechaki Street. Bond told her that he would call her in the morning after his night at the casino. He had wanted to do this alone. Partners were fine in most situations, but Bond didn't like distractions when he gambled, and he thought a partner like Niki would be distracting for what he had to do tonight. Besides, Niki needed to follow up on the police investigation of Charles Hutchinson's death. Frankly, he wanted a little distance. It was a familiar malaise, and unfortunately, it was a vicious circle. She had called him twice during the evening, probably in an attempt to get him to change his mind and allow her to accompany him. As usual, it seemed that women always became more interested in him when he tried to avoid them. As Felix Leiter once said to him, "Women are like stamps—the more you spit on them, the more they get attached to you."

The casino itself was a bit of a letdown after the spectacular cable car ride. Bond had to walk through nondescript hallways to the main room. Not nearly as opulent as Bond had expected, the Au Mont Parnes was small. It consisted solely of one room containing all of the various gaming tables. Although there were no slot machines and the red carpet was ornate, little else in the casino was striking. Off to the side of the room near the bar was a section for sitting and drinking that contained several tables covered in white tablecloths.

Despite its overall shabbiness, the casino attracted a crowd. The place was already full, and smoke filled the room. Several blackjack tables were in operation, the roulette table was packed with players and spectators, and the poker tables were unreachable.

Bond went over to the only baccarat table in the casino. It too was crowded, with no vacant seats. He lit one of his cigarettes from H. Simmons of Burlington Arcade and ordered a vodka martini from a waitress. When his drink came, he stood casually to one side and observed the people around the table.

Konstantine Romanos had the "shoe." There was a singular aura around the man, as if he exuded an invisible, yet tangible, charisma. He was very handsome, sat very tall in his seat, and had a dark complexion. His eyes were cold as steel. He incongruously smoked a thin cigar in a cigarette holder, the smoke circling his head in halos. Romanos was apparently doing very well. He had a large stack of chips in front of him.

Bond recognized the cousin, Vassilis, standing behind Romanos. He was the bodybuilding, swarthy man he had seen in Texas. Vassilis wasn't fooling anyone—he was there as a bodyguard for his boss. The man was simply a mountain.

Baccarat is closely related to chemin de fer and its rules vary from casino to casino. Bond observed that the game in the Au Mont Parnes was closer to chemin de fer in that the bank was held by a single player until he lost. The bank, and shoe, then rotated around the table to the players willing to put up an amount of cash. The object of the game was to obtain cards totalling as close to 9 as possible. Court cards and 10s were worthless.

A woman sitting at the table said, "Banco," and placed a large bet in the Players' field on the table. Calling "Banco" was a bet against the entire bank's worth, which in this case was around a million drachmas. No one else at the table was betting, except a Middle Eastern man wearing a fez. Bond studied the woman, who looked to be in her late twenties or early thirties. She had fiery red hair and was extremely attractive, with pale white skin and blue eyes, and a hint of freckles on her face and bare shoulders.

Romanos dealt the cards. He had a natural 8 and turned his cards over.

"Eight," he said. The redhead lost her money.

A man shook his head and stood up from the table, leaving a seat open for Bond. He casually took the chair and said, "Banco." He matched the bank's bet of two million drachmas. At the exchange rate of roughly 365 drachmas to the pound, this amounted to almost 5,500 pounds. Earlier Bond had drawn out the cash from an SIS fund specifically for "nonreimbursable" business expenses.

Konstantine Romanos looked up at Bond and nodded his head slightly in a greeting. He dealt the cards from the shoe. Bond had a 1 and a 3. Romanos examined his cards and left them facedown. Bond asked for a third card. It was dealt face up—a 4. Romanos was forced to stand, then turned his cards over. Bond's 8 beat Romanos's 7.

"Lady Luck is on your side, Mr . . . ?" Romanos said in English.

"Bryce. John Bryce," Bond said. "It's not luck. I say a little prayer to the gods before playing. Don't you?"

Romanos blinked slightly and smiled. Bond wasn't sure if the man knew who he was. Vassilis, the cousin, was staring hard at him. Up close, Bond thought Vassilis looked like a circus freak of old. Once again he was amazed that the man had practically no neck—just a large football-shaped head on top of a wall of shoulders. His biceps were so large that Bond doubted he could get both hands around one.

Romanos forfeited the shoe. It was offered around the table, but no one wanted it. It finally came to Bond, who set the bank at half a million drachmas.

Romanos called, "Banco." Bond deftly slipped the cards out of the shoe and slid them across the table. Bond had a total of 7. He had to stand. Romanos asked for a third card, which was revealed to be a 5. The two men revealed their cards.

"Eight," Romanos said. "Seems as if the gods forgot about you that time."

Bond offered the bank and shoe to the next person, but it eventually found its way back to Romanos. He set it for one million drachmas.

"Banco," Bond said. Another two cards came across the table. This time Bond had a natural 9, but so did Romanos.

"Push," said the croupier.

The cards were dealt again. Bond had a total of 7 again and had to stand. Romanos drew a 3, then revealed a court card and a 2. The spectators gasped as Bond raked in the chips.

"It's too bad that nine is the best possible number in baccarat," said Bond. "It really should be ten, don't you think?"

Romanos flinched and the thin smile disappeared. "What do you mean?"

"You *are* Konstantine Romanos, aren't you? Head of the New Pythagorean Society?"

Romanos smiled and nodded. "You know something of our little group?"

"Just a little, but I'd love to learn more."

"Perhaps that can be arranged," Romanos said. Everyone at the table felt a sudden tension between the two men. Play continued in a back-and-forth fashion until Romanos ended up with the shoe once again. Bond glanced at the other people. The attractive redhead was watching him intently. She placed a large bet against the bank.

Romanos dealt Bond two totally useless court cards. Luckily, Bond's third card was a 7. Romanos had a total of 6, barely losing. Bond glanced at the redhead, who was smiling knowingly at him.

"Mr. Bryce, you're going to clean me out before I've had time to finish my drink," Romanos said. "Might I buy you one, and we can adjourn to the bar?" The man's English was very good.

"One more," said Bond. He declined to take the bank. Romanos held on to it, and it was worth nearly four million drachmas.

Romanos nodded his head as if to say, "Very well." He dealt the cards. Bond had a total of 5, the worst possible number to get in baccarat. He had to draw a third card, which could very well push him past 9. The third card came across the table and was revealed to be a 4. Romanos drew a card, then turned the hand over. He had a total of 7. Bond won again with his 9.

"My compliments," Romanos said, passing the shoe. "I shall quit while I still can." Although the man was polite, Bond could tell he was perturbed at losing so much. He had forfeited nearly five million drachmas to Bond. As Vassilis pulled back his chair, Romanos stood up. He was well over six feet tall, statuesque and authoritative. It was no wonder he had followers who would do his bidding. Did that bidding extend to murder and terrorism?

Bond politely passed the shoe, tipped the croupier, then joined Romanos at one of the tables near the bar. He asked for another vodka martini. Romanos ordered a gin and tonic.

"Tell me, Mr. Bryce," he said, "why do you want to learn more about the New Pythagoreans? Are you a mathematician?"

"Lord, no," Bond said. "I'm a writer. I'm preparing a book about philosophy and religion. I thought your group was interesting. I know that you base much of your teachings on Pythagoras."

"That's correct. Pythagoras was much more than a mathematician. Socrates and Plato owed a great deal to Pythagoras. You should come to one of our gatherings down in Cape Sounion sometime. It is a wise man who looks and listens. Pythagoras argued that there are three kinds of men, just as there were three classes of strangers who went to the Olympic Games. The lowest were those who went to buy and sell, and next above them were those who came to compete. The best of all were those who simply came to observe. We are all lovers of either gain, honor, or wisdom. Which do you love, Mr. Bryce?"

"I love a little of all three, I think," Bond said.

"The Master—that is, Pythagoras—demanded that those desiring instruction should first study mathematics. The Pythagoreans reduced everything in life to numbers because you can't argue with numbers. We usually don't get upset about mutiplying two and getting four. If emotions were involved, one might try to make it five and quarrel with another who might try and make it three, all for personal reasons. In maths, truth is clearly apparent and emotions are eliminated. A mind capable of understanding mathematics is above the average, and is capable of rising to the higher realms of the world of abstract thought. There, the pupil is functioning closest to God."

"I should have studied harder in school," Bond said.

"The Master said that we are all part of the world in an unlimited boundary. When, however, we come to the process by which things are developed out of the Unlimited, we observe a great change. The

Unlimited becomes the Limited. That is the great contribution of Pythagoras to philosophy, and we must try to understand it. Life is made
up of many contraries, Mr. Bryce. Hot and cold, wet and dry, one and
many. The most consistent principle underlying Pythagorean philosophy and mathematics is a dialectic procedure involving the relationship, and usually the reconciliation, of polar opposites. We believe that
when the One becomes the Many, a new order will take its place on
earth."

"And who is the One? You?"

Romanos shook his head. "That is not for me to say. The One is
perfection. I'm certainly not perfect. You saw me lose at baccarat a few
minutes ago."

"No, you're not perfect, Mr. Romanos. Not yet. Only when you
reach the number ten will you be perfect, am I right?"

Romanos looked hard at Bond. "What do you mean?"

Bond tried to make light of what he had said. "The ten points of
the equilateral triangle. Your logo. I've seen it. You haven't reached the
number ten yet, have you?"

"No. It is difficult to do in a lifetime."

"Is it something like nirvana? Getting closer to God?"

"You might say that."

"Well, seeing that you've completed number seven, you don't have
too far to go."

Bond could see Romanos stiffen at that. In those few minutes,
Bond perceived that Romanos might be a genius, but he was also a
madman. He had taken basic and inherently positive principles of Pythagorean philosophy and twisted them into something bizarre. If he
were truly the leader of the Decada, then it wasn't difficult to believe
that weak-minded fools would follow him.

Sensing something was wrong, Vassilis stepped up to Romanos and
whispered in his ear. Romanos never took his eyes off Bond. Romanos
nodded slightly and said something to his cousin in Greek that Bond
didn't understand.

"I must step out for a minute. Please enjoy yourself, Mr. Bryce. In
parting, let me tell you something that was attributed to Pythagoras. In
mathematics, the logical process is to first lay down postulates—that
is, statements that are accepted without proof—and then go through

deductive reasoning. I apply that logic to everyday life, Mr. Bryce. Proof must proceed from assumptions. Without proof, an assumption is meaningless. Remember that the next time you start making assumptions. I'll be back at the baccarat table in a little while if you'd care to try your luck again."

"Thank you. It was nice meeting you, Mr. Romanos," Bond said. Romanos got up and followed Vassilis out of the room.

Bond finished his martini and had started to get up when he noticed the redheaded woman eyeing him from an adjacent table. She was sitting alone, sipping a glass of wine.

"Whatever did you say to Mr. Romanos to upset him so?" she asked in a thick Greek accent.

"Did I upset him?" Bond asked.

"He looked upset to me," she said. "I don't think it was because you beat him at baccarat."

"Do you know Mr. Romanos?"

"I know who he is. He is something of a personality in Greece."

"And you are . . . ?"

She held out her hand. "I'm Hera Volopoulos. Please sit down . . . Mr. Bryce, was it?"

"John Bryce." Bond took a seat beside her and admired her even more than before. She was absolutely stunning. The blue eyes stood out like jewels against her white face and red hair. He removed his gunmetal cigarette case and offered her one. She took it; then he lit hers and his own with the Ronson lighter he always carried in his pocket.

"What brings you to Greece, Mr. Bryce?"

"I'm a writer," he said.

"Have I read anything you've written?"

"I doubt it. Mostly articles in obscure English journals. They're not widely distributed."

"I see."

"And what brings you here on a fine Friday night?"

"I come here because I enjoy gambling. My late husband used to come here often, and I suppose I got into the habit. I have friends whom I see here every now and then. Sometimes it's a pleasant way to meet men."

She exhaled audibly, accentuating the last thing she said with a billow of smoke. Bond interpreted that as an invitation. He briefly thought of Niki and wondered if she might turn up at the hotel unexpectedly. The possibility was remote.

"What do you know about Mr. Romanos?" Bond asked.

"Only that he's very rich, and he's supposed to have a better than average brain. I think he's very handsome."

As she said that, Bond noticed Romanos and his cousin reentering the casino. They went straight for the baccarat table without looking in their direction.

"I can see that he has a certain charm," Bond said.

"How long will you be in Greece, Mr. Bryce?" she asked.

Bond made a whimsical gesture and said, "As long as the gods will have me."

Hera smiled. "I was named after one of the gods," she said.

"The queen of the gods, if I remember correctly."

"Yes, but she wasn't a very nice queen. Very jealous. She made poor Hercules go mad and kill his wife and children. She came between Jason and Medea. She was always doing something nasty. However, she did possess the ability to renew her virginity every year by bathing in a magical pool."

"Is that really an advantage?"

"I suppose to Zeus it was. He was a lecherous old fool, chasing after virgins all the time. It was the only way she could keep him interested."

"And what do *you* do to keep someone like Zeus interested? Do you have a magic pool?"

Hera smiled seductively. "I like you, Mr. Bryce. Why don't we have dinner? I can show you around Athens."

Bond was tempted. He thought briefly of Niki again, then discarded any feelings of loyalty to her. He was on an assignment. It was his way, he couldn't help it.

"It's awfully late for dinner, isn't it?"

"In Greece we eat very late and stay up until the early hours. Come on, you can follow me to my home in Filothei. It's pretty there. I'll fix us a light snack. We can sit on my balcony and enjoy the night air."

He had to admit that she was irresistible. "All right," he said. "Are you parked down below?"

"Yes, we'll ride the cable car together."

He got up and took her hand to help her up. As he looked into her eyes, her pupils dilated slightly.

As they walked out of the casino, he looked over at the baccarat table. Romanos was glaring at the cards. His luck hadn't improved. He had relit his thin cigar and was puffing on it furiously. Vassilis, the big man, was staring in Bond's direction. Bond nodded slightly to him, but the bodyguard only scowled at him.

They walked out through the plain corridors to the cable car entrance. There were two men waiting for the car, which was on its way up. When it arrived, one of the two men gestured graciously for Bond and Hera to step inside first. They got in and settled themselves at the back of the car so they could look at the view of the city. The two men got in, the door closed, and the car began its five-minute journey back down to the base of Mount Parnitha.

As soon as the cable car left the platform and was in the air, Bond glanced back at the two men. Each held a semiautomatic handgun, cocked and ready to fire.

▶17.
QUEEN OF THE GODS

One of the men barked something in Greek and gestured with the gun for Bond and Hera to get down on the cable car floor. Bond figured that these goons worked for Vassilis Romanos. Perhaps they knew his identity after all. He had been so distracted by the woman that he had carelessly let down his guard.

Hera asked the man something in Greek.

"Markos says lie down on the floor," the other man said in English. "This will only take a second."

Hera looked at Bond with fear in her eyes. He whispered to her, "Don't worry, just do what they say."

The cable car was approaching the first support tower. There were three such towers between the casino and the ground terminal. Bond remembered from the earlier trip that when the car passed one of the support towers, it lurched slightly as the wheels moved over the metal housing the cable. If he timed it just right . . .

Bond held up his hands. "What is this? A robbery? I really didn't win that much, fellows."

"Move!" the second man commanded.

"Look, I'll give you my wallet." Bond slowly reached for the inside of his jacket.

"Keep your hands up," the English-speaking thug said. The one called Markos asked the second man something in Greek. Bond caught the words "Ari," "money," and "wallet." This aroused the curiosity of the second man, who Bond presumed was called Ari. He hadn't planned on robbing his victim. Perhaps the Englishman did have a bit of cash on him. Markos spat out an order in Greek.

"All right, give us your wallet first. Slowly. No tricks," Ari said. "And we'll take the lady's handbag too."

The cable car was two seconds away from the support tower. Bond reached inside his jacket and grasped the Walther PPK. The car moved over the cable housing in the tower and the entire cabin lurched. Bond jumped up and landed on the floor hard, causing the cable car to tilt. The two men lost their balance. Bond drew the gun and fired at Markos, hitting him in the shoulder. He dropped his gun. Ari began firing his pistol wildly. Hera screamed and cowered in a corner of the cable car. Three bullets smashed windows behind Bond. Shards of broken glass scattered all over the floor of the car. Bond leaped to the floor, slid forward, and tackled the thug. Both Bond and Ari dropped their weapons.

The cable car was rocking now, still descending to the ground. The guns slid to the opposite end of the car and lay out of reach. Bond rolled on top of Ari and punched him hard in the face. Markos, bleeding profusely from his bullet wound, climbed on top of Bond and attempted to pull him off. Bond brought his left elbow back hard into the man's nose. He cried out in pain.

By now, the element of surprise had worn off. Ari raised his knee into Bond's stomach. He then landed a blow on Bond's chin, knocking him over and onto the floor. Both men jumped on top of Bond and began to pummel him with their fists. Trying desperately to protect himself, Bond brought his arms up in front of his face. The two men were strong and tough. Their ugly faces were right above him, snarling.

Out of the corner of his eye, Bond saw Hera huddled on the floor at the other end. One of the guns was inches from her, but she was frozen with fear. Bond realized that he couldn't rely on her to help.

Bond reached out quickly and grabbed the men's heads in his hands. He slammed them together hard, then thrust his fists into their noses. They fell back, giving Bond time to get to his feet. Ari leaped for his gun but Bond grabbed his legs. He couldn't reach it. This gave Markos time to make a move for his weapon. Bond stuck out his leg and tripped him, and Markos slammed into the side of the car, breaking more glass. Ari grabbed a large shard of glass and swung it at Bond. The edge cut through Bond's jacket and sliced the front of his shoulder along the collarbone. Bond released the man's legs and jumped to his feet. He immediately attacked Markos with a *Ushiro-geri* back kick, causing the thug to bend forward, out of breath. Bond took hold of his shoulders and pulled him up and over. Markos crashed through the opposite window and out of the cable car. He screamed loudly as he fell to his death.

Ari got to his feet and lunged at Bond with the glass shard. Bond grabbed his arm and struggled with him. They fell to the floor. The glass was inches away from Bond's face. The thug held it so tightly that it was cutting his own hand; blood was seeping out through his fist. Bond summoned all of his strength to twist the man's arm back toward him. They were evenly matched and it was now simply a matter of who would give out first.

The cable car went over the second support tower. In another minute or so they would be on the ground. Bond knew he had to avoid any police action or his cover would be blown and the assignment would be compromised.

The two men's arms trembled. Bond took a deep breath and strained harder to push Ari's arms backward. They slowly moved so that the shard was now pointing at the man's throat. His eyes widened as he realized he was losing the struggle. Bond kept pushing. The point of the shard was now touching the assailant's Adam's apple.

"Who are you working for?" Bond asked through clenched teeth.

Ari spat in Bond's face.

Suddenly, Hera came to life and got up from her position on the floor. She knelt behind Ari, reached for his hair, and pulled it. Ari yelled but kept his attention on Bond and the glass shard. Enraged, Bond used his last remaining ounce of strength to shove the man's arms. The glass shard pierced the man's throat, cutting through his windpipe and severing his spinal cord. His eyes glazed and his head rolled over in a final, ghastly exhalation of bad breath and bloody spittle.

Bond stood up and retrieved his gun. Hera collapsed back against the wall of the car, breathing heavily.

"Are you all right?" he asked.

She nodded. "You're hurt."

He examined the wound on his shoulder. It was minor, but he had to get it treated. He looked out the front window of the cable car and saw the ground terminal approaching. He didn't want to be in the car when it stopped.

"It's not so bad. Look, you don't have to come with me, but I'm going to jump out of the window. I can't let the authorities question me about this."

"Of course," she said. She reached into her handbag and pulled out a card. "This is my address. Go there. I'll handle the authorities. I have some influence at the casino. They all know me. I'll be home shortly and tend to that wound. Don't worry, I'll be fine."

Bond climbed through one of the broken windows and prepared to leap out to the ground before the car entered the terminal. He counted to three as the cable car brushed the tops of the trees on the ground, then jumped, landed hard on the ground, rolled, and got to his feet. The cable car entered the terminal. Bond ran to the parking lot and got into the Jaguar before any of the authorities knew what had happened.

Hera lived in a luxurious suburb of Athens called Filothei. It was full of green parks, quiet wide roads, and many large houses and villas with big gardens. Using the Jaguar's satellite navigation and road map features, he drove onto Kiffisias Avenue, a large three-lane street with trees in the middle. Eventually he found L. Akrita Street, and the three-story building of flats where she lived. Bond parked the Jaguar and waited. Nearly an hour later, he saw her pull up in a Mercedes-Benz, get out, and walk toward the front. He got out of his car and called to her.

"Oh, there you are, Mr. Bryce," she said. "Come on up, I live upstairs. How do you feel?"

"All right. Call me John. How did it go?"

"Not a problem, John," she said. "I just flashed a smile at the manager and said that we were almost robbed and that you jumped out the window and ran. It was the truth! The only thing I didn't tell them was your name."

They got to the third floor and entered a tastefully furnished flat that was filled with artwork and statuettes. She threw her handbag on a chair and went straight into the bedroom.

"Get yourself comfortable and come on in. We'll take a look at that shoulder of yours," she called from behind the door.

Bond took off his jacket. His shirt was very bloody. He went into the bedroom, where she was standing next to the bathroom. He removed his shirt and looked at the wound. The gash wasn't too bad—just messy. He had managed to sop up most of the blood in the car on the way to the flat.

"You poor thing," she said, leading him into the bathroom. She wet a cloth, then took her time cleaning the three-inch wound. Afterward, she led him back into the bedroom.

"Press that cloth against it," she said. "Just hold it there awhile."

He sat on the edge of the bed and watched her undress. She did it slowly, sensuously, like a professional striptease artist. When she was naked, she pulled down the sheets and slipped under them. Her long red hair spread out over the pillow.

"I was afraid you'd cancel our date," she said. "I'm glad you didn't. I wanted to see what was under that hood of yours," she said.

"I don't want to bleed on you," he said. "It's closed a bit. If you're not too rough with me, I don't think it'll open up."

She raised up, letting the sheet drop to her waist. Her naked breasts were firm and full. She had large, red nipples that complimented her hair. There was a concentration of freckles on her chest, a physical trait that Bond always found tantalizing.

"Oh, I'll be gentle," she said, reaching out to him and sliding her hands around his shoulders. She started kissing the back of his neck and nibbling on his ear. Her right hand moved across his hairy chest and down to his abdomen. He was immediately aroused. "As gentle as a little tiger," she whispered.

He turned to her and pressed his mouth on hers. She pulled him back onto the bed and then climbed on top of him, straddling his torso.

"You just lie back and let me do all the work," she whispered.

Hera leaned over him, giving him access to her breasts. She moved down a little, guiding him into her, then kissed him on the mouth.

Konstantine Romanos sat in a stretch limo, traveling from Mount Parnitha to his Athens residence. Vassilis sat across from him, his eyes closed. All in all, the evening wasn't a total loss. He had made back most of his money that was taken by the Englishman.

He opened up a laptop computer and logged on to the Internet. An E-mail with an attached JPG file was waiting for him.

"Ah, here's the information I wanted," Romanos said, but Vassilis was asleep. Romanos downloaded the JPG file and in a moment, a grainy black-and-white photo that was obviously a still frame from a roll of videotape appeared on his screen. It showed James Bond in the hallway of the ReproCare clinic in Texas, most likely shot from a hidden security camera. Typed underneath the photo were the words "Man Responsible for Suppliers Shutdown."

Well! Romanos thought.

He kicked Vassilis awake. The big man snorted and shook his head.

"Take a look at this," Romanos said, showing him the screen. Vassilis stared at it.

"The guy at the casino," the brute said. "He killed Markos and Ari."

"Right. Now, are you sure you didn't see him in Austin?"

"I don't know who it was. I didn't see the guy. The two cowboys chased him and they both died. It could have been him, who knows? After what he did to Markos and Ari, I'd believe it was him. It took someone with balls to mess up the clinic in Austin. It took someone with balls to do what he did to Markos and Ari. If this is the same guy, then we'll just have to make sure he has his balls for dinner."

Vassilis grunted and rubbed his hands eagerly.

"Vassilis, please," Romanos said. "I have a difficult decision to make. Our plans may have to be altered. I haven't spoken to Number Two yet. This man may be the same one who was in Cyprus."

Romanos took back the computer and studied the photo. He then created an E-mail and attached the JPG file to it, and addressed the correspondence to someone named "Three."

Romanos typed: "Am sending you copy of JPG file. Find out who this man is. Currently using alias John Bryce. Was responsible for incidents in Texas. Was seen snooping around Cape Sounion HQ. Believed to be man responsible for destroying three of our security vehicles and the murder of six security men near Cape Sounion. He killed two of our security men tonight in Athens. He may have been in Cyprus when Number Two implemented Strikes Two and Three. My guess is that he's a British Secret Service agent."

He signed the E-mail "Monad" and sent it.

The limo drove into the heart of the city and ended up near Athens

University. Romanos had a flat that overlooked the campus. The driver let him and Vassilis out inside a garage. They went into an elevator and made their way to Romanos's flat.

"Vassilis, I have an assignment for you," Romanos said, walking to the bar and taking a bottle of brandy. He poured two glasses and gave one to his cousin. Vassilis would do anything for Konstantine.

He continued. "This man Bryce, or whoever he is—I'm afraid he may have to replace our current target for Strike Eight in the *Tetraktys*. This will alter our plans significantly, but it must be done. The man is a menace to us. The gods have spoken to me. He must not be a menace any longer."

"Number Two made a backup plan in case Ari and Markos failed, my cousin," Vassilis said.

"Really! She has more initiative than any of us. She is a true warrior, Number Two. She will not fail."

The men finished their brandy, then Vassilis hugged his cousin and left the flat. Konstantine Romanos sat at the desk and booted his own computer. Within moments he was back on the Internet, setting up an IRC channel with which he could talk live with someone. In a moment, three users popped into the virtual room.

It only took a few minutes. Romanos typed out his instructions. The three users acknowledged and signed off. He then shut down the computer and stood up.

Looking out of his window at the university from the sixth floor, Romanos reflected on what the gods had told him. The destiny he was to fulfill was near at hand. There were just a few little obstacles in the way, and he would have to make sure they disappeared. Soon, very soon, the Decada would strike again.

The Monad began to plan his next move.

An hour had passed. Bond and Hera sat up in bed smoking cigarettes.

"Why is it such a cliché to smoke a cigarette after lovemaking?" Hera asked.

"I suppose for those of us who enjoy smoking, it adds punctuation to the statement," Bond said.

"Make it an exclamation mark, then," she said.

Hera snuggled against him and ran her fingers through the hair on his chest. After a moment, she got up and threw on a terry cloth robe.

"I'm going to get some snacks and something for us to drink," she said. "Stay there, handsome. I'll be right back."

Bond heard her clanging around in the kitchen for a few minutes. She came back carrying a bottle of Taittinger, two glasses, and two covered dishes.

"You open the champagne, and I'll fix our plates," she said.

He rolled out of bed and took the bottle. He expertly opened it, popping the cork out at the ceiling. He poured the champagne while Hera uncovered the plates of Greek salads, bread, and cheese.

She removed her robe, and they sat on the bed naked, eating and drinking. The champagne was cold and tasted wonderful.

"So what do you do with your life besides visit casinos and take strange men home with you?" he asked.

"I don't make a habit of the latter!" she said, laughing. "I'm in real estate. I manage some properties in north Athens and have an interest in a hotel or two."

"Must be lucrative."

"It's not bad. One of these days, though, I will be a very rich woman."

"Oh?"

She smiled. "It's in the cards. So, what are you writing about in Greece?"

"Philosophy and religion."

"Rather broad topics, aren't they?"

Bond smiled. "I don't like to talk about my work. I let it speak for itself."

"You don't strike me as the shy type, Mr. Bryce. From what I saw in that cable car tonight, it didn't look like you spend all of your time writing."

"John, please."

"Well, John, where did you learn to fight like that? That was quite impressive."

"I learned it in the army," he lied. "Luckily I rarely have to use it. I was just glad you weren't hurt."

"So you're really a writer, huh? You'll have to send me some of your work so I can read it."

"Your English is very good."

"I'm fluent in Greek, English, and French," she said. "I did have an education."

"I can see that."

"You must try to hear Konstantine Romanos speak somewhere. Just sitting in on his lectures at the university can be interesting."

"I thought you said you didn't know him?"

She blinked and said, "I don't. But I have heard him speak. At the university. So am I going to show you Athens when the sun comes up?"

"I'm afraid I have some business to attend to," he said. "Perhaps we could get together tomorrow night . . ."

"Of course. I'll take you to one of my favorite restaurants. You'll love it."

A sudden wave of nausea came over Bond. He wasn't sure what hit him, but it was like a ton of bricks. Then there was a ringing in his ears.

He barely heard her continuing to talk. "It's all healthy food, no meat at all, a lot of vegetables and fruits . . ."

Bond struggled to speak, but his speech sounded slurred. "Are you on some kind of diet . . ."

"I don't eat meat," she said. "Strict vegetarian."

The warning bells went off in Bond's head, but it was too late. The drug in the food was acting too quickly.

How could he have been so stupid? he thought. He had waltzed right into their trap. A vegetarian! Ashley Anderson had been a vegetarian. The man at the New Pythagorean Society at Cape Sounion said that the members don't eat meat. Was Hera a member of . . .

The wall of confusion rapidly enveloped Bond's mind. He looked at Hera, who was watching him intently. She didn't ask him if anything was wrong.

Then she said, "Sorry, John . . . or whoever you are. You're going to wish that Ari and Markos had got you in the cable car. The fools didn't know who I was, or they wouldn't have tried to rob us. I could have intervened and finished the job, but you impressed me. I wanted your body, and now that I've had it and have no more use for it, we have to say goodbye."

"You . . ." he began. He tried to stand up, but the room spun wildly. He fell to the floor with a thud. He opened his eyes and saw Hera standing above him.

". . . bitch," he managed to say. Then the darkness spread over him like a blanket, and he was dead to the world.

▶18.
A MURDERER'S TOMB

Darkness and vibration. A low rumbling noise. Movement. Cramped muscles.

These were the sensations Bond felt as he slowly inched back into consciousness. He was curled up in a small, dark space. Some kind of box? No, there was movement and vibration. He was in the boot of a car.

Sore and stiff, Bond attempted to flex his muscles as best he could and shake away the drug's cobwebs. He was dressed in a shirt and trousers, but was barefoot.

So Hera Volopoulos was on the side of the enemy. Bond cursed himself for being such a fool. Once again his libido had got him in trouble.

Bond could hear two men speaking Greek inside the car. The voices were faint and he couldn't understand them. Where were they taking him?

He couldn't see a thing. He felt along the interior of the boot, looking for anything that might be of use to him. There was a box of some kind—a compact disc changer? Eventually he found a couple of buttons. Bond pushed them and the interior boot light switched on.

He immediately recognized where he was. He was inside his own Jaguar XK8. Apparently whoever it was that was driving was planning to destroy all traces of him. They were probably taking him to some remote place where they would kill him and bury him, then get rid of the car.

Bond examined the latch and determined that he couldn't open it from the inside. If he had some tools, perhaps . . . What should he do? Wait until they stopped the car, then make his move? They would most likely be ready for him. Was there anything that Major Boothroyd told him about the car that he could deploy?

Inside the car, Vassilis Romanos was driving. Next to him in the passenger seat was another brute, named Nikos. Vassilis had never had the pleasure of driving a Jaguar and he was enjoying it immensely. Too bad they had to get rid of the vehicle after they killed the Englishman. He would have liked to keep it.

"What time is it?" Vassilis asked Nikos in Greek.

"Four-thirty." The sun would come up in a little less than two hours. "How much farther?"

"About another hour."

"Is he still out back there?" Nikos asked.

"I haven't heard anything, have you?"

The car sped west on the highway. They were already an hour out of Athens and were approaching the Peloponnese, the southernmost section of the Balkan Peninsula, which contains some of the more beautiful parts of Greece, but the two men didn't care about the area's natural beauty. They had no appreciation for such trivialities.

Bond tried his best to relax and regain his strength. It was terribly uncomfortable in his cramped position, but he practiced a technique of flexing and stretching one limb at a time. He also took the time to examine every inch of the boot. Besides the CD changer, the microprocessor box was fastened to the back. Perhaps he could hot-wire some of the internal defense systems . . .

He opened the box, revealing a mass of circuits and wires. Luckily, a wiring diagram was printed on the inside of the lid. The light wasn't adequate—he had to strain his eyes to read it—but he was able to trace an auxiliary power feed which he could maybe connect to one of the terminals. He studied the various options. The passenger or driver air bags were possibilities. If he got rid of one of the men, his job would be that much easier when the time came to open the boot.

After another half hour, the car approached the barren foothills of Mount Agios Ilias and Mount Zara, where the ruins of ancient Mycenae lie. They were the remnants of a kingdom occupied mostly by Agamemnon, who had been murdered by his wife, Clytaemnestra, and her lover after he returned home from the Trojan War. Both Agamemnon's and Clytaemnestra's tombs are located in the ruins of Mycenae.

Bond felt the change as the car went from a paved highway to a gravel road. Perhaps they were approaching their destination.

The car had in fact turned onto the path leading to the ancient ruins. It came to the wire gate and stopped. Nikos got out of the car and used a key to unlock it. The car's headlamps provided the only illumination. The sky was pitch-black and the ruins were dark silhouettes of slabs, arches, and columns.

Bond felt the car stop and one of the doors open and close. He had managed to pull the auxiliary feed and was ready to connect it to a terminal. He figured that thirteen amps for thirteen microseconds would be enough to do the trick.

Nikos got back into the car, and Vassilis drove through the open gate and up the hill past the closed concession-and-souvenir stand.

When he was sure that the man was back in the passenger seat, Bond brushed the auxiliary feed across the "Air Bag—Passenger" terminal.

The dashboard in front of Nikos exploded in his face, releasing an oversized air bag that totally enveloped him. It surprised Vassilis too, for the car swung out of control and came to a sudden stop against an embankment. Vassilis struggled with his door and got out. He could barely hear Nikos's muffled screams. He turned, stooped to the ground, and pulled a commando knife from a sheath attached to his shin under the trouser leg. Vassilis then climbed back into the car, attempting to cut away the air bag. The material was too thick. This was no ordinary air bag, Vassilis realized. Before he could think of anything else to do, the struggling beneath the air bag ceased.

Vassilis replaced the knife, drew a Sig-Sauer P226, walked around to the boot and unlocked it. He raised the lid and stepped back, pointing the gun at the back of the car.

"Get out," he ordered. "Keep your hands up."

Bond was finally able to straighten his body and climb out of the boot. He kept his hands behind his head, but he took the opportunity to stretch his back.

"I can't tell you how good this feels, thank you," Bond said. "Oh my, did something happen to your friend? Personally, I think the automobile manufacturers are going a little overboard with all these new safety features, don't you?"

"Start walking!" Vassilis said. He gestured to a path leading up the hill to the ruins.

Bond had no choice but to do as he was told and stall for time. He turned, and Vassilis followed him away from the light of the Jaguar's headlights. The path grew very dark, and it didn't help that he was barefoot. The stones were hard and sharp. At one point, Bond tripped over a rise in elevation that he couldn't see.

"Get up!" barked Vassilis. "Keep those hands up."

Bond managed to palm a stone, then stood up and replaced his hands on the back of his head. The stone felt rough against his scalp.

They walked past the ruins of a large stone pit called the Grave Circle. An even larger one, full of grave shafts, was farther up the path. They were very near the Lion Gate, the main entrance to the citadel, with its carved lintel showing two lionesses supporting a pillar.

"This way," commanded Vassilis. They turned right onto a smaller path moving away from the Lion Gate, then went around a bend to face a wide space carved out of the hill. The space was lined with stones, forming a passage leading to the tomb of Clytaemnestra. The open doorway was framed by carved stones and was supported by modern scaffolding. The lower portion of the door was a rectangle, but the upper portion was a triangle.

"Inside," Vasslis said, shoving the barrel into Bond's back. They went inside the dark tomb. After a few seconds, Vassilis turned on a flashlight and set it on the ground. They were inside a dome made of stones, about twenty meters high. One portion of the ceiling was held up by scaffolding. Apparently some restoration work was still in progress.

Vassilis aimed the gun at Bond.

Bond took just a second to memorize the room and get his bearings. "Wait," he said. His voice echoed loudly in the tomb. "Aren't you going to ask me anything first? Don't you want to know who I work for? What my real name is?"

Vassilis shook his head. "It won't make no difference." His accent was thick.

Without warning, Bond hurled the stone at Vassilis with all his might. It hit him dead on the forehead. The echo in the dome amplified his yell tenfold. Bond took the split second of opportunity to leap in the air and deliver a *Tobi-geri* jump kick to the man's sternum. Bond's bare foot slammed into one of Vassilis's vital points, causing him to drop the gun and fall back. But whereas the kick might have killed an ordinary man, Vassilis was only stunned. Before Bond could grab the gun, the

Greek rolled into him. Bond fell over Vassilis and landed hard on his wounded shoulder.

Vassilis got up and swung at Bond. The blow knocked him hard back to the ground. For a few seconds all he saw was a bright light, and the pain in his head was unbearable.

My God, Bond thought. This was possibly the strongest man he had ever encountered.

The big man was about to land another blow, but Bond responded quickly enough to roll to the side. Vassilis couldn't stop his fist, so he hit the ground hard. Instead of hurting his knuckles, he made an impressive indentation in the dirt.

Bond staggered to his feet and shook his head. He got his wits about him just as Vassilis got to his feet. Bond delivered a *Nidan-geri* double kick, in which he leaped into the air and slammed his left foot into Vassilis's stomach, and then kicked the right one, the jumping foot, into his face. It barely fazed the bodybuilder. With a deafening growl, Vassilis reached out, grabbed Bond by the shirt, and like a wrestler, swung him around and around. He let go after four rotations, sending Bond flying across the dome into the brick wall. The man had done it as if Bond were made of paper.

Before he could recover, Bond's opponent was on him again. He picked up Bond from the ground, raised him high over his head, and threw him once more across the room like a beanbag.

Bond landed hard on his back, sending painful sparks up his spinal cord and igniting every nerve in his body. In the dim light, he could see Vassilis searching for the gun. Bond could see it, three feet in front of him. He tried to roll toward it, but Vassilis jumped on his hand before he could grab it. Bond grunted in pain and pulled his hand away. Vassilis stooped down and snatched the gun.

"Okay, you had your fun for today," Vassilis said, grinning. "It is past your bedtime."

He aimed the pistol at Bond's head.

Bond kicked out with his foot and connected with the flashlight that Vassilis had left in the middle of the room. The light went out, plunging the dome into darkness. Bond rolled as the gun went off. The sound was amplified tremendously, the echo lingering for several seconds.

"You will not leave here alive," Vassilis said in the dark after the noise had died down.

The only light coming into the room was from the open entrance, but the door's silhouette was all that could be seen. It was all the way on the other side of the dome. Bond knew that Vassilis was somewhere between it and him. If he could lure the thug where he wanted him . . .

"Over here, you overgrown lump of lard," Bond said.

He ducked out of the way as he felt the big man lunge for him. He felt a brush of air as Vassilis barely missed him. The room was so dark it wouldn't have mattered if they had been wearing blindfolds.

"Nice try, you rotter," Bond said. "Now I'm over here."

He sidestepped Vassilis again, and they continued to play this bullfighting game in the dark for the next several seconds, until the big Greek became frustrated and angry. With every lunge he shouted something that sounded like an animal in pain.

Bond maneuvered to the side of the room where the scaffolding held up the ceiling. His lack of shoes gave him an advantage now—his feet moved quietly over the ground, whereas Vassilis's boots made loud crunching sounds. Bond reached out slowly and found one of the scaffolding supports. He carefully moved inside and under the scaffolding, keeping his hand on one beam.

"Hey, fathead. Here I am," Bond said.

Vassilis roared like a beast. Bond slipped out under the beam and ran for the entrance to the tomb. Vassilis crashed wildly into the scaffolding, knocking it to pieces. There was a loud rumble, and then a crash as the stones in the ceiling fell. Vassilis screamed. Bond waited until the noise settled and it was completely quiet in the tomb. Bond groped for the flashlight and shook it. It flickered on, illuminating the now dust-filled chamber. Coughing, Bond held it close to the pile of rubble. Vassilis was completely buried by the heavy stones, but he could see part of the henchman's arm sticking out from under a large rock. His head was somewhere farther beneath the rock, completely flattened. Bond tried to find the handgun, but it was buried along with its owner.

Bond left the tomb and made his way back down the path to the Jaguar. Thankfully, the strongman had left the keys. Bond found the hidden catch beneath the dash that released the inflated air bag. He pulled it out of the passenger side of the car, then tugged on Nikos's body and threw it to the ground. Bond found some loose change and a few drachmas in the corpse's pockets, all of which would come in handy. Then he went around to the driver's side and got in the car.

He backed up the Jaguar and sat there on the gravel road for a moment, catching his breath. The first thing he did was open the secret compartment where the Walther P99 was kept. He pulled it out and made sure the magazine was full of Teflon-coated, full-metal-jacket bullets. Underneath the storage compartment was a shoulder holster made especially for the P99 by Walther. He started to slip it on, wincing at the pain in his shoulder, and decided against it. He put the gun back into the compartment, then took a look around the car. Vassilis had left a black notebook on the floor by his feet. Bond picked it up and looked inside. It was a diary. The last entry was the new day's date and he could just make out the Greek words: "Number Two, Monemvasia, 11 A.M."

He took the cellular phone from its compartment and dialed Niki's number. A sleepy voice answered.

"Wake up, darling," Bond said. "I need your help."

"James! Where are you?" she said.

"I think I'm at the ruins in Mycenae. It's so dark I can't tell. The sun's just beginning to come up here."

"Are you all right?"

"I could use some shoes, but otherwise I'm fine."

"What happened?"

He gave her a brief rundown of the events. He left out what had happened with Hera.

"Wait, I didn't get one part," she said. "How did you get drugged, again? Where did you say you were?"

"I'll tell you later. Listen. I think there's something happening this morning in a place called Monemvasia."

"I know it. It's a medieval village on the east coast of the southern end of the Peloponnese."

"Can you meet me there today?"

"I'll leave right away. It will take me, uhm, four or five hours. Meet me at the entrance to the causeway between Gefyra and Monemvasia. Gefyra is the mainland village. They're connected by a bridge."

"Right. Before you leave, see what you can dig up on a redheaded woman using the name Hera Volopoulos."

"Will do. Take care, James."

Bond backed out of the ruins and drove to the main highway, leaving the two dead bodies for the site caretakers to deal with.

Before he got very far, Bond flipped a switch and changed the color of the car again. This time it went from red to a dark green. The license plate changed to a Greek registration.

He utilized the road map feature of the GPS navigation system and made his way to the E-65, the main highway that led to his destination. He passed through Tripoli and stopped at a roadside café to buy some coffee and a roll. The proprietor, who spoke no English, noticed that Bond wasn't wearing any shoes. He jabbered in Greek and gestured for Bond to wait a minute, then went into the back room and came out with three pairs of old shoes. Bond laughed and tried on the pair that looked closest to his size. Surprisingly, they fit snugly.

"How much?" Bond asked.

The proprietor shrugged and held up five fingers, meaning he wanted five thousand drachmas. Bond handed over a bill and thanked him. The proprietor saw the nice, shiny Jaguar that Bond got into, and kicked himself for not asking for more.

Three hours later, Bond drove into Gefyra and parked near the causeway leading to what was commonly referred to as "the Gibraltar of Greece." Monemvasia is a medieval town built on a rock which emerges dramatically from the sea off the east coast. It is topped by a fortress with a few scattered buildings at sea level.

Docked off of the edge of Gefyra and just visible from Bond's vantage point was Konstantine Romanos's yacht, the *Persephone*.

▶19.
THE NUMBER KILLER

Bond tucked the Walther P99 into the back of his trousers, left the Jaguar parked out of sight near the causeway, and walked along the narrow streets of Gefyra so that he could get a better view of the boat. He ducked behind a wall and peered around.

The *Persephone* was a new Hatteras Elite series 100 motor yacht, an impressive, hundred-foot-long white and black vessel with walk-around side decks. There were a few men dressed in black working with a hydraulic crane and loading material onto the boat. Bond saw Hera Volopoulos on the starboard deck, speaking with one of the men. She was dressed in a dark jacket and trousers.

After a moment, she was joined on deck by Konstantine Romanos. He was "dressed for sailing," in dark navy trousers, a white sports jacket, and a nautical cap. They spoke briefly. Hera nodded her head, then walked off the boat and down the plank to the shipside area of the dock. She spoke to a man at a forklift, then walked off the dock toward the causeway. The men continued loading crates onto the *Persephone,* and Romanos disappeared below.

Bond felt cold. It had become windy, and the temperature was much cooler here than in Athens. He was also tired and hungry, but he felt that he was onto a breakthrough in the case. Should he try to sneak onto the boat or follow the woman? There was a score to settle. He moved away from the safety of the wall and followed the woman.

Hera walked onto the causeway, crossed the strait, and headed toward the lower town of Monemvasia. Bond waited until she had passed the cemetery and gone through the main portal into the populated area. He sprinted across, and ran up the road to the town.

When he stepped through the opening, Bond thought he had entered some magical place in another time. It was as if the little village had been hidden for centuries from the entire world. Facing this quaint pocket of antiquity was the rich blue sea, which spread out to the southeast. The narrow streets were walkways between the many tourist-oriented souvenir shops, tavernas, and churches. There was even a former mosque from the time when the Turks occupied the town.

Bond started looking for Hera. The village was quiet except for the folk music playing on a radio in the distance. The streets were a complex maze of stairways and narrow passages, and as he moved along the stone path he spotted Hera's red hair disappearing around a corner ahead. He continued onward, moving like a prowling cat and staying close to the buildings in case he had to duck quickly into one of the shops. Along the way, small prune-faced old women sat in doorways and looked at him with curiosity.

Hera stopped at a shop and bought some bottled water. Bond waited behind a corner, then moved on when she did. She soon entered the central square of the town, where she stopped briefly to stand and drink some of her water.

What the hell was she doing? Bond wondered. Was she waiting for Vassilis to meet her here? Let's get on with it!

After finishing the bottle and tossing it into a rubbish bin, she turned and walked through a passage rising above the campanile of a large church in the square, then along the north side of another church. From there a path led uphill to the upper town. She started the climb up the zigzagging stone steps that took visitors to the upper town, which was virtually in ruins. All the way up to the summit of the rock, pieces of buildings still stood facing the sea—a wall or two here, a foundation and corner over there.

Bond waited a couple of minutes before starting up after her. He crouched down and moved from ruin to ruin, waiting until he saw her climbing higher and higher. It was not an easy ascent. Only the fittest of tourists ever made it all the way to the top.

Now that he was in the upper town, Bond felt totally alone. No one else seemed to be around except Hera. He saw her reach the top of the cliff and walk toward the twelfth-century Hagia Sophia, the church built on the ledge of the sheer cliff. It was the only building in the upper town that was complete and in use.

Bond watched her go in the front door. It must have been the designated meeting place with Vassilis. It was close to eleven o'clock. He waited several minutes, then stealthily moved to the front of the church. He drew his gun and carefully pushed the door open and stepped inside.

It was too quiet. He moved slowly around the perimeter of the nave and went into the diaconicon, the room behind the altar. Narrow, elaborately ornamented windows were set into the stone walls about six and a half feet up.

Bond heard a creaking sound in the prothesis, the area on the other side of the altar. As silently as possible, he stepped through a portal into the other room. The glass in one of the windows was broken and the frame was open. Bond waited and listened. There was no other movement around him. Was he being watched?

He tucked the gun back in his trousers, took hold of the window ledge, and pulled himself up to look out. A bit of ground was some twenty feet down below, but the church was extremely close to the edge of the cliff. He could just squeeze his shoulders out of the window to get a better view.

A muzzle of cold metal poked him in the back of the neck.

"I know you didn't come here to pray, Mr. Bryce, but you had better start," Hera said. The voice came from above his head. She was hanging upside down on a tension line above the window. The rope was attached to the roof of the church; she had simply climbed out of the window, pulled herself up, attached the rope to her belt, and waited for him to stick his head out the window. After spending a night with her, Bond knew that she was extremely agile.

"Hand me your gun, carefully," she ordered.

"We really must stop meeting like this," Bond said.

"Shut up. Do it."

He did as he was told. She took the P99 and stuck it into her utility belt.

"Now slowly move back inside the church. Keep your hands up."

Bond squeezed back through the window and jumped to the floor. Before he had time to run for it, Hera had lowered her body down on the line and was aiming her gun at him through the window. It was a Daewoo that looked vaguely familiar.

"Turn around and put your nose and palms against the wall behind you," she said. He did. In less than two seconds she performed a smooth maneuver of pocketing the gun, twisting her body upright on the rope, thrusting her legs through the window, and hopping to the floor. She retrieved the Daewoo and pointed it at Bond.

"I assume that since you're here and Vassilis isn't, Konstantine's cousin isn't with us anymore. Konstantine isn't going to like that. All right, start walking out. I'm right behind you. We're going down to the lower town. No stupid moves—I'm very good with this gun," she said.

He turned and looked at her. There was something very familiar now about her shape and her stance with the gun.

"The Number Killer . . . a woman," Bond said.

"Oh, you realize we've met before, Mr. Bryce? Or should I say Mr. Bond?" she said with a smirk. "It's too bad I didn't get you in Cyprus. Too bad for you. Now it will just make your ugly death that much more enjoyable. For me. But Konstantine would like to have a little talk with you first. You wouldn't want to miss a talk with Konstantine, would you? It's your chance to find out what all this is about, right? I know you'll cooperate. Now march."

They went back into the nave. Bond said, "So what was the other night about, Hera? Are you a praying mantis who eats the male after she mates?"

Hera found that image flattering. "I never thought about it that way," she said.

Bond turned around slowly and brought his face close to hers. "Or did you want to go to bed because you really are attracted to me."

She held the gun to his temple. "Back off and get those hands up," she said.

Bond leaned in and whispered, nuzzling her ear. "You don't mean it. You know we were good together. Now why don't you forget this nonsense and join me." He kissed her neck, but his hand was an inch from the Walther P99 in her belt.

"If you so much as touch your gun, I'll blow your brains out. I don't care if Konstantine does want to see you first." Bond froze. "Now put your hands up and step back."

Still not moving his arms from around her, Bond sighed audibly and said, "Very well. If that's the way you want it." He made an exaggerated shrug of the shoulders as he brought his arms up and away from her back. That shrug was enough to throw off Hera's concentration, for Bond snatched her wrist with a lightninglike strike with his left hand. The gun was knocked away from his head, but it discharged loudly into the ceiling. Bond grabbed her arm with his other hand and with both hands attempted to control the weapon. Hera coolly brought her knee up hard into his left kidney. Bond was momentarily frozen in pain. Hera took that second to strike him hard on the back of the head with the Daewoo. He bent over and fell to the floor.

Niki Mirakos drove her Camry at close to ninety miles per hour down the E-65 and twice had to radio policemen with her credentials. She got to Gefyra at just around eleven o'clock, and was going down a side street to find a place to park when she saw the green Jaguar. Could it be . . . She pulled over and parked near it. There couldn't be that many Jaguar XK8s in Gefyra—Bond must have changed the color again. She got out and walked toward the bridge. He was nowhere in sight, but the *Persephone* was docked in full view. Aside from two men walking on the decks, there seemed to be no one else about.

She had punched up the records on Hera Volopoulos before leaving Athens. According to the Greek Secret Service files, Volopoulos was suspected of being a trained soldier working eight years ago for the Greek Cypriot militant underground. She had been linked to an arms-smuggling racket in Cyprus before it was broken up by the Cypriot police. There was nothing else on file, except that she was last seen in Cyprus two years ago.

Niki knew that organized crime on Cyprus was big business. Because of its strategic location in the Mediterranean, the island was a convenient stopping place and temporary safe haven for smugglers, terrorists, arms dealers, thieves, prostitutes, pimps, and other forms of low life. Several factions of underground criminals developed on Cyprus during the last thirty years. Part of her training in the Greek Secret Service included extensive study of the Cyprus situation.

The file photo of Hera Volopoulos was not very good. It was a black-and-white picture of a woman wearing sunglasses, looking over her shoulder and running. The motion blur made it virtually impossible to identify her. Why did Bond want this information? Was she connected to the Decada? As a precaution, Niki put out an advisory to all law enforcement agencies to be on the lookout for the woman.

Niki supposed she should wait a bit to see if Bond showed up. If he weren't around in fifteen minutes, she would start snooping.

Sometimes she felt guilty working to protect the Turks and Turkish Cypriots. Here she was, a Greek, trying to make sure that Greek or Greek Cypriot terrorists didn't do something terrible to the Turks. She shook her head at the irony. She hated the Turks as much as she might hate a Greek Cypriot terrorist. She could remember her grandfather telling horror stories about Turks when she was a little girl. The Turks were always the bad guys, and she grew to fear them. It was how bigotry was always perpetuated, she realized—through the mouths of older generations. As legends, knowledge, religion, and art were all passed down from generation to generation, unfortunately so was hatred. It was one of the unpleasant side effects of history.

Niki was shaken from her musings when she saw James Bond emerge from the Monemvasia side of the portal and begin walking toward her across the causeway. Behind him was a redheaded woman wearing sunglasses. It was she. Hera Volopoulos. Niki knew it. Bond was walking slowly, looking a little dazed. He saw her but didn't register recognition. Niki knew something was wrong. The woman had a concealed gun on him. She was taking him to the *Persephone*.

Niki casually moved from her position and walked back toward the street where she had parked her car. She hid in the doorway of a taverna twenty feet away from the causeway entrance as Bond and Hera came across and started walking toward the dock. They would have to pass her on the way. She thought Bond glanced at her, but he kept on walking as if he had not seen her.

She could have stopped them. She could have pulled her gun and kept them from getting aboard, but something in Bond's face said not to do it. It was too dangerous. She needed backup. If they were taking him aboard the yacht, then it would be a far better plan to follow it and see where they went. Bond might be in danger, but he could handle himself.

It was gut instinct that told Niki to wait and see what happened. She would call for backup and arrange to follow the boat. They weren't going to kill Bond yet. They wanted him alive for a while.

She just hoped that she could find a way to get him off the yacht before they changed their minds.

Earlier, Hera had slapped Bond repeatedly until he regained consciousness. When his eyes fluttered open, she grabbed him by the chin. She dug her nails into his skin and said, "Don't ever try that again. I'm real good with a knife. It would be a great pleasure to remove the piece of equipment you seem to be so fond of using, James Bond. I'm sure thousands of rejected women all over the world would thank me. Now get up and walk."

His head throbbing, Bond got to his feet and staggered to the front of the church.

"Besides," she continued. "You're not supposed to fight in a house of God. This is a holy place."

"Since when do you care about what's holy?" Bond asked.

"Shut up and get going," she said.

Bond made up his mind to see it through. The woman had the upper hand now, and he should take no more unnecessary risks. Besides, she was right. He really wanted to hear what Romanos had to say to him. He had been in tight situations before. This one was no worse.

It took them twenty minutes to descend the steps to the lower town. Bond lost his balance once and fell. His head was throbbing and his vision was a bit blurred. She had struck him hard in the church.

They moved through the alleylike main path and out the portal. Bond saw Niki at the other end of the causeway, expertly playing it cool. She was as professional as they came. He hoped that she would remain so and not try to stop them; he wanted to get on the boat.

They walked past her and he looked at her briefly but intently. He thought she got the message. If she did her job right, she would get back to her people and have the yacht followed.

He stopped at the edge of the ramp leading onto the *Persephone*.

"Get aboard," she said.

Bond walked forward to the deck, wondering if he should have brought an ancient Greek coin to give to Charon the boatman.

▶ 20.
GODS NEVER DIE

The *Persephone* was a superb yacht. As Bond was led aboard and down below, he noticed that there were several rooms. A lavish galley and dinette were located on the main deck. There was a midlevel pilothouse with a complete control console, helm, and lounge seating, as well as steps to the flying bridge above.

What was extraordinary about the setup was that the interior didn't look like a modern boat. It was decorated in the style of an ancient Greek galley: The walls were covered in wood that looked hundreds of years old. The light fixtures were made to look like flaming torches. The pilothouse was indeed equipped with the latest technology, but it was all disguised by a bizarre facade of theatricality and make-believe. The entire ship was a stage setting for a Greek tragedy by Aeschylus or Euripedes.

Obviously Konstantine Romanos didn't mind flaunting his wealth. Bond thought he was two sandwiches short of a picnic.

Hera knocked on a wooden door that was the entrance to the master cabin. They heard a bolt draw back, then the door creaked open.

Konstantine Romanos stood in the doorway, still wearing the captain's uniform which was completely incongruous with the setting around him. His room was illuminated entirely by candles.

"Ah, Mr. Bond, come in," he said. He gestured to a chair at a table. Hera followed him in and shut the door behind her. From then on, she stood in silence like a sentry.

"Your costume and set designers need to communicate better," Bond said. "Are we in the twentieth century or in ancient Greece?"

Romanos ignored him. "Sit down. What would you like to drink? Wait . . . I know. You like martinis, don't you? Vodka martinis. I know that. It's in the information we dug up on you," he said. He was playing the gracious host, but his voice was laced with menace.

"Unfortunately, we don't have any martinis this morning, but we do have some nice red wine," he said, then walked over to a bar and poured two glasses from an unmarked wine bottle. "Would you like something to eat?"

Bond was actually starving, but he shook his head. "Let's just get on with it, Romanos."

"Tsk tsk," he said. "You look famished. I insist. Have some bread and cheese." He placed a wooden plate with a fresh loaf of bread and a chunk of goat cheese on the table. A large kitchen knife was stuck in the cheese.

"I trust I don't have to worry about you trying to take that knife," Romanos said. "Hera here will make sure that you remain sensible." He began to cut the bread and cheese and placed several pieces on a plate in front of Bond. Sitting down across from him, Romanos held up his glass and said, *"Yasou."*

Bond would have preferred not to eat and drink with the man, but he needed sustenance. He slowly began to eat, but he was eyeing the knife and trying to form a plan to grab it.

"Here you are again, Mr. Bond," Romanos said, as if Bond were a naughty child and had been sent to the school headmaster.

"The name is Bryce."

"Please, dispense with the spy stuff, we know who you are. You are a civil servant working for the British government. We got your picture from a closed-circuit television camera at ReproCare in the United States. That was quite a job you did on that place."

"I didn't set the explosives."

"No, of course you didn't. The late Dr. Ashley Anderson did. We shall miss her. That facility was due to be closed down anyway. What you did do, Mr. Bond, was hasten its demise. We wanted to rid ourselves of those awful Suppliers, and you helped us do that."

"So you *are* the leader of the Decada?"

"I am the Monad, the One," he said. He gazed intently at Bond. The man's eyes seemed to glow, and Bond couldn't look away. He found himself mesmerized by Romanos; there was something in his eyes that beckoned Bond to stare into them. It was several seconds before Bond's willpower alerted him to the fact that Romanos was attempting to hypnotize him. He managed to look away, but it was an effort to do so.

Bond realized that Konstantine Romanos was one of those rare men who possess a unique power of persuasion. If he could hypnotize weak-willed people, use his flowery talk and philosophical conundrums and eventually charm subjects into trusting and believing him, then he was the sort of man who might be looked on as a prophet (or a devil). Many men throughout history had had this kind of charisma, and they were always leaders.

Bond now understood why Romanos had a large following who believed his unique brand of mumbo jumbo.

"What are you after, Romanos? I know you're dying to tell me."

"Mr. Bond, it's quite simple. I'm on a mission from the gods. They do exist, you see. I know, because they speak to me. The soul of Pythagoras lives within me, and he was a very religious man."

"What is that mission?"

Romanos sipped his wine and glared at Bond with fire in his eyes.

"I suppose I can tell you, since you will be tortured to death very soon. You will be held accountable for the death of my cousin Vassilis. He was my Number Seven, you know. Very important to the organization. He was family. You will be made to suffer for what happened to him. But before that I will tell you the story of my life."

"If it's all the same to you, I think I'd rather just get on with the torture," Bond quipped.

"You won't have many witticisms left when we're through with you, Mr. Bond. I'm a Greek Cypriot, born and raised in the northern town of Kyrenia. In 1963, I was just out of university, having studied mathematics and philosophy. I had landed an important teaching job in northern Nicosia, was married and had two beautiful children. I was apolitical. It was a good life, but I was unenlightened at the time. The gods had not spoken to me yet. It took a crisis to open the communications between me and them. My life crashed around me that year, for violence broke out all over Cyprus. Our former president and spiritual leader, Makarios, was making too many concessions to the Turkish Cypriots. Your troops and the United Nations' so-called peacekeeping forces invaded the island and tried to keep the peace, and they succeeded, for a while."

"You forget that many Greeks and Greek Cypriots on Cyprus looted and destroyed many of the Turkish Cypriot settlements. The United

Nations and our troops came in to keep Greek Cypriots from killing Turkish Cypriots."

"That's what the Turkish propaganda wants you to believe."

"Romanos, these are facts. But go on, we can argue semantics later. We'll call an assembly, put on our sandals, and have a proper debate in the Parthenon."

Romanos smiled wryly at Bond's sarcasm, then went on. "Throughout the rest of the sixties, a very tentative peace existed, but there were always small outbreaks of violence. I moved my family to the outskirts of Nicosia, unfortunately to an area that became overpopulated with Turks and Turkish Cypriots. The worst was yet to come. As you know, a military coup d'etat occurred in Greece in 1967. Makarios retained control of the Republic of Cyprus, but he had many enemies in Greece. Seven years later, in 1974, the Greek National Guard ousted Makarios and set up a junta on the island. Makarios fled. It was . . . chaos. The Turks used the opportunity to invade the island. They began to systematically massacre Greeks and Greek Cypriots, working their way down from the north."

"Uhm, you forgot to mention that when Makarios was ousted and the junta was set up, the same thing was happening to the Turks and Turkish Cypriots. Turkey has always claimed that they were 'intervening,' not 'invading.' They were protecting their people."

"Again, that is the Turkish propaganda speaking. The Turks are animals. They are like jackals, waiting until their prey is in a weakened state. Then they strike and are merciless."

"I'm not defending the Turks, Romanos," Bond said. "They have done some unspeakable things on Cyprus. If you ask me, both sides are equally misguided and bigoted. It's simply another example of two races disagreeing with each other over centuries of misunderstandings."

"Do you expect us to get together, hold hands, and sing 'All You Need Is Love'? You're just like all the other British mediators who have tried to dictate policy on Cyprus. You know nothing about our people. If you think our problems can be solved by talking about them, then you're out of your mind."

"I'm not the one who talks to gods who don't exist."

Romanos looked at Hera and nodded sharply. She stepped over

and slapped Bond hard across the face. He jumped up and prepared to defend himself, but Romanos pulled a Walther PPK out of his jacket and pointed it at Bond.

"Sit down, Mr. Bond," he said. "Oh, is this yours? I believe we found this at Number Two's flat. Tie him to the chair, Number Two."

Hera laughed quietly and took some thick nylon cord from a cabinet. She wrapped it around Bond's chest and tied him tightly to the back of the chair.

"All right, you've got a captive audience, Romanos. You might as well continue your little story," Bond said.

"I will. There was a war. The northern third of Cyprus was occupied by the Turks, and they forced out or killed all of the Greeks and Greek Cypriots living there." Romanos paused a moment, as this part of his tale was obviously painful. "Our house was bombed. My wife and children died. I was wounded in the head and left for dead. All I remember was regaining consciousness in a hospital in southern Nicosia. My only memory is that shortly after the bombing I saw some British soldiers. I begged them to help me and they ignored me."

Bond figured that might explain the Decada's attacks on the British bases.

"I was in hospital for six months," Romanos continued. "I wasn't sure if I would lose my mind and the very faculties by which I made my living. I couldn't remember simple mathematical problems. I forgot my Latin. It was only after I was discharged and I fled to Greece that I regained what I had lost."

No wonder the man was mad, Bond thought. The serious head injury had left him unbalanced.

"I admit I was in a bad way when I got to Greece. I lived on the streets of Athens, homeless and poor. I drank. I was invisible to the people around me. Then, one day, I slept in the Ancient Agora in Athens. I had crept in and found a place among the ruins where I could sleep. It was there that the gods first spoke to me."

A change was coming over Romanos as he spoke. He seemed to be assuming the persona of an orator, preaching to a large crowd. His voice grew louder, and he stood up from the table. He walked around the room as he spoke, gesturing to the invisible masses around him.

"The Greek gods sent me messages which I, and I alone, was able to hear. One night, I experienced an epiphany of the highest order. Zeus himself spoke to me and entrusted me with the soul of Pythagoras. Konstantine Romanos died that night, and the Monad took his place. Divine assistance led me to an organization that helped homeless people get back on their feet. Once I could prove that I had teaching credentials before the war, I got a job in a university library. I read everything I could about Pythagoras and his philosophy.

"I went to lectures at the university and to student gatherings, for I met many young people through working in the library. I became involved with some students who were violently anti-Turk. They were Greek Cypriots who, like me, were forced out of their homes in northern Cyprus, and they wanted something done about it. It turned out that they were a little militia. They had smuggled guns and bombs into the country and were planning on instigating revenge against the Turks."

"Who were they?"

"It doesn't matter now," Romanos said. "They're all dead now. What's important was that I learned a great deal from them about guerrilla warfare and terrorist tactics. It was with this experience that I got my first job as a mercenary. I left Greece for Lebanon in, let's see, 1977, it was. While I was away, the group attempted an ill-conceived attack on a Turkish supply ship off the north coast of Cyprus. They were never heard from again. But the knowledge I took from them was invaluable. I applied Pythagorean philosophy to their lessons. They were seeking to make the One into the Many, which was what Pythagoras wanted to achieve."

Bond now understood that Romanos had combined the teachings of Pythagoras and the tenets of the militant group. The philosophies had blended together unnaturally and he believed them.

"But I digress," he said. "I spent the next few years working as a freelance mercenary in the Middle East. I performed jobs for various factions, for which I was paid handsomely."

"You mean acts of terrorism, don't you?" Bond interjected.

"I found that I had an extraordinary ability to organize men and lead them. The gods had given me a gift of persuasion. There was one particular excursion in 1981 in which I made a sizable amount of money. I decided to retire from the mercenary business and come back to Greece and do what I was ordained to do. I settled in Athens and made some wise real estate investments. I founded the New Pythagorean Society. Through connections I had made with the Greek government, I landed a teaching position at Athens University. I wrote and published a book. I suddenly found myself in demand, so to speak, and I became well known in Greece. People actually paid money to hear me speak. I received invitations from other countries to visit their universities and lecture. I spent five years in the United States, in Texas, in the late eighties, off and on, with frequent trips back to Greece. For the remainder of the decade, I expanded my power base and laid the groundwork for the future policymakers of Greece and Cyprus—the Decada."

Bond glanced at Hera to see what she made of all this. She was standing at attention, staring straight ahead, expressionless.

"I selected nine of my most trusted and faithful followers to occupy the other seats of leadership in the Decada. Each of them an expert in their own field, each with a sizable team of followers to perform the various tasks we needed done. Five men and five women, each representing the Pythagorean contraries of Odd and Even—odd being male, even being female. I, naturally, became the One, the Monad. I appointed Hera here to be the Duad, the Two. My late cousin Vassilis was the Seven. I regret that I must replace him. You are responsible for the deaths of two of my numbers, Mr. Bond. You will pay dearly for that."

"Why did you attack the British bases in Cyprus?" Bond asked.

"The gods commanded it. The British played no small part in what happened in Cyprus in 1974. They did nothing to stop the Turks from invading."

"And Alfred Hutchinson? Why did you kill him?" Bond turned to Hera. "It was you, wasn't it? You were the assassin with the spiked umbrella in London."

Romanos answered for her. "Yes, it was Hera. She is my sword. I met Hera in Cyprus in 1978. She was a mere youngster then, weren't you, Hera? She was the most vicious, hardened, and most dangerous twelve-year-old girl I had ever seen. We became very close, I'm not ashamed to say. She has been with me ever since."

"Lovely story," Bond said. "Sick, but lovely."

Hera reached over to slap him again, but, curiously, she hesitated. She resumed her silent stance as Romanos continued.

"But you asked about Hutchinson. As I mentioned before, I was in Texas for a while. Through my underground connections, I was put in touch with an American militant group there called the Suppliers. A go-between introduced me to Charles Hutchinson, a spoiled, rich playboy who was a courier for the Suppliers. He also happened to be the son of another distinguished guest lecturer at the University of Texas, where I was teaching. The boy and I—we did business together. The Suppliers began to transport biological and chemical weapons to the Decada via the Suppliers' front of selling frozen sperm to countries around the world. Eventually, I masterminded a plot to frame the Suppliers' leader, a redneck named Gibson. He was arrested and put in prison. From then on, I assumed leadership of the Suppliers from afar without the rest of their organization realizing it. I controlled all of their connections worldwide. It allowed the Decada to broaden its power base and make more money, but the militant group's usefulness soon wore out.

"The boy's father, your late Ambassador to the World—what a joke—obtained some vital information regarding the so-called Turkish Republic of Northern Cyprus. The Decada tried to obtain that information by employing Charles to get it. Charles made a complete mess of it, and his father got wind of what he was up to. Alfred Hutchinson threatened to go to your secret service with the information, so he had to be eliminated. His son betrayed us. Of course, once his father was killed, he foolishly tried to get even by alerting the Turkish Cypriot authorities in Famagusta of our little anthrax scheme. The Duad here kept close tabs on Charles when he got to Greece a few days ago. He was eliminated too. I can't abide traitors."

"Then you never got Hutchinson's information?" Bond asked.

"I didn't say that. Number Ten, Dr. Anderson, knew that Hutchinson had stored the information on his computer in his Austin home. She had infiltrated the ranks of the Suppliers on my orders, before Gibson was imprisoned. I felt it would be useful to have one of our own keeping an eye on those Texas rednecks. They had become a bit careless in the past few months—several of their couriers had been caught, and it was only a matter of time before Charles would have been arrested. Your agent in Athens, Whitten, he was onto them. Had he been alive when Charles made his next delivery, Whitten would have nabbed him. The link between the Suppliers and the Decada would have been discovered. Therefore, Whitten had to die. He was the target of the first strike."

"And you destroyed the Suppliers' laboratory because the authorities were onto you?"

"That's right. The FBI was too close to shutting them down. We didn't need them anymore. Our Number Eight is a brilliant biochemist. We're coming up with a little bug of our own. It is still in the experimental stage, but it will soon be ready to test. It will make the ebola virus seem like the common cold."

"I take it that Number Eight is Melina Papas, the president of BioLinks Limited?"

"You *are* clever, Mr. Bond!"

"Is this the same bug that is causing epidemics in Los Angeles and Tokyo?"

Romanos looked at him as if he were mad. "I don't have the slightest idea of what you're talking about."

Bond wasn't sure if he believed him. "Just what do you want, Romanos? What the hell are you after?"

"The gods have ordered the Decada to disgrace and humiliate Turkey for what they did to Cyprus, and to make a statement to the world about the power of the holy *Tetraktys,* the number ten."

"And how do you plan to do that? Are you attacking mainland Turkey or just northern Cyprus?"

"I've told you too much already, Mr. Bond. That part of our plan will remain a secret. Let's just say we have a little help from the Greek military. One of their senior officers, a brigadier general, is Number Five in the Decada."

Romanos finished his wine and set down the glass. "I must leave you now, Mr. Bond. I have business to attend to in Athens. You will be sailing on the *Persephone* for a short while. Hera will watch over you and see that you're made perfectly uncomfortable."

"Wait a minute, Romanos," Bond said, stalling for time. "You didn't tell me everything about Alfred Hutchinson. You knew him before you were in Texas. I saw your picture with him at the New Pythagorean headquarters in Cape Sounion."

Romanos shrugged. "I didn't say we weren't acquainted before then. As a matter of fact, we worked together. Remember that great deal of capital I told you I received in 1981 that allowed me to quit the mercenary business? I came into possession of a large cache of seized Nazi gold that was hidden in Athens since the war. It had been secreted away by Alfred Hutchinson's father, who was stationed in Greece. During my mercenary days, I became business partners with Alfred, and together we sold off the gold all over the world. It's how he financed his politcal career. Then, with Alfred's diplomatic connections, we were able to completely cover our tracks. We both became very wealthy."

Christ, Bond thought. Hutchinson *was* a crook. "And was he a member of your Decada?"

"I'm not going to answer that," Romanos said. "Oh, and by the way . . . we did eventually recover Hutchinson's information that he had on his computer. There was a copy of the disk that we got our hands on. We now know everything there is to know so that we can proceed with our next three *Tetraktys* attacks. It's a shame you won't be around to see them."

"You're a raving lunatic, Romanos!" Bond shouted. He turned to the girl. "Hera, you can't possibly believe this man! He's deranged, don't you see?"

"This is the Monad," Hera said. "His will is that of the gods."

Bond closed his eyes. She was as far gone as Romanos.

"Why the numbers, the statuettes of the Greek gods? Why were bodies dumped on sacred ruins?"

"It was how the gods ordered it. They wanted the world to know that we were working for them. The gods used to walk the earth, you know. All of those places were homes to them. If a location wasn't available, we were instructed to leave a small icon representing them at the site. The numbers were simply a count-off from the holy *Tetraktys*."

"You know your plan won't accomplish what you hope, Romanos," he said. "If you attack Turkey, they'll blame Greece."

"Bravo, you're not as stupid as I thought," Romanos said.

"But a war between Greece and Turkey? What good will that do? The entire Balkan area will be in ruins. NATO will find a way to stop it swiftly."

"If that is a side effect of our strikes, then I can't help that. The

Greek government is too cowardly and weak to initiate the war with Turkey. I have to lead them and show them the way. The Greeks will realize that I am the One and they will follow me to victory. We have the gods on our side, and the gods never die."

Romanos gave Bond a slight bow. "Goodbye, Mr. Bond. *Andio.* I hope you die a painful death so that my cousin's and poor Dr. Anderson's souls receive some satisfaction."

With that, he left the room. Bond had known some insane men in his time with equally mad schemes to bring destruction to the world. Romanos just moved to the top of the list. Only in a world full of fanaticism, bigotry, terrorism, and evil could such a scheme exist, much less be believed and implemented by a mass of people. What were the three remaining *Tetraktys* attacks? Could the virus that was found in the briefcase in Texas be the same homemade bug created by Melina Papas? If so, then it certainly was not still in the experimental stage—it was ready for mass murder. Could Romanos have something else up his sleeve that he wasn't revealing?

Bond was alone with Hera. She took the chair that Romanos had used and pulled it up in front of him. She sat on it with the back facing Bond, her arms draped around it. She reached over to the block of cheddar cheese and removed the kitchen knife.

"Now, let's see," she said. "What are we going to do to amuse ourselves while we're on our journey?"

Niki Mirakos waited on the causeway separating Gefyra and Monemvasia. It had been an hour since Bond was taken onto the yacht. What were they doing in there? Torturing him? Killing him? Three times during the hour, she was tempted to storm the boat alone, but she knew she was outnumbered. She had placed a call to headquarters in Athens as soon as Bond was on the boat. A team was on its way and would be there any minute by helicopter.

Suddenly there was movement on the boat and Konstantine Romanos walked down the ramp to the dock. He got into a black Mercedes and was whisked away. The men on the *Persephone* began to untie the yacht from the dock. The motors started. She was about to sail away.

Niki elected to stay with the boat rather than follow Romanos. She ran back to Bond's Jaguar and used her spare key to get inside. She then called her headquarters to see what was keeping the team.

The *Persephone* pulled away from Gefyra and out into the Mirtoön Sea.

▶ 21.
BY THE SKIN OF THE TEETH

Hera began by lightly sliding the sharp point of the knife over Bond's face. She took her time, slowly moving it along the skin. Any more pressure and the knife would penetrate the outer layer of tissue. Bond kept perfectly still.

She didn't say a word. She seemed fascinated by Bond's face, the way a young girl might gaze upon a new doll. She traced the nose and around the nostrils with the blade. She ran it along his lips and even placed it gently in his mouth and twisted it. She moved it around his eyes and eyebrows, and repeated these various patterns of sadistic massage for what seemed like an hour. In a way, it was a pleasurable sensation. If Hera had been a woman he trusted, it might have been an extremely sensual way of tormenting someone. Bond wondered, though, how long it would take before she got a little rougher.

She ran the knife along his right cheek and finally asked, "How did you get the scar, James? Shall I add a matching one on the other side? I do like things to be symmetrical. I've been studying your face. I think I know how I'm going to reshape it."

"It's only a matter of minutes before the Greek Secret Service stops this boat. My associates know I'm here," he said. "If I don't report in, they'll come for sure."

"And if you're nowhere to be found on the boat, they will have to admit their mistake and leave. We have nothing to hide here."

"What's in all those crates?"

"Food. Supplies. For our base."

"Oh? Where's your base?"

Hera placed the edge of the knife at Bond's throat. "You ask too many questions, James. Along with rearranging your face, I just might have to cut out your vocal cords. The Greek government knows

Konstantine Romanos. He's a respected citizen. His boat is known to the authorities. They wouldn't dare stop it."

"Can't you see he's mad, Hera?"

She slashed the knife lightly and swiftly across his neck. A thin stream of blood appeared.

"That was only a scratch. Next time I'll press harder."

Bond said nothing. He stared at her coldly, daring her to do her worst. The blood trickled down his chest onto his shirt.

"Did you see that film about those American bank robbers?" she asked. "You know, the one where a psycho bank robber tortures a cop? The cop is sitting there in the chair, tied up like you are. The bank robber cuts off the cop's ear. Did you see that movie?"

"No."

"It was bloody. Pretty violent. The cop gets beaten up pretty good. Then he gets his ear cut off. It was very realistic."

She circled his left ear with the knife.

"I saw another movie where a woman had an ice pick and she stabbed her lover to death in bed. She just stabbed him and stabbed him and stabbed him . . . It was very bloody. Did you see that one?"

"I don't go to the cinema much."

"There was another movie that had these two crazy killers—a man and a woman who were lovers—they went on a spree across America, killing people. They get caught and sent to prison. In the prison, they cause a riot and everybody gets cut up or shot. It was the bloodiest movie I ever saw. Did you see that one?"

"I'll bet you're loads of fun on a date, Hera," Bond said.

The nylon ropes were tied around Bond's upper arms and chest. His forearms were free and he could bend his arms at the elbows. She took his right hand and raised it from his lap.

"You have nice hands, James," she said, tracing the veins on top with the point of the knife. Bond had a sudden recall of a night many years ago, when a SMERSH assassin cut a Russian letter into the back of his right hand. The skin had been grafted, but a faint white patch remained. "Look at this," she said. "Looks like you burned yourself or something. That's not your original skin there, is it?"

Bond didn't answer her. She turned his hand over so that the palm was facing up. She peered closely at it.

"You have a very strong head line," she said. "The heart line is interesting. There are a few breaks in it. Your heart was broken . . . one, two . . . three . . . four times? You've been married once. Your life line . . . hmmm . . . it's very strong. Your head line is strange. You are not a happy man in your life, James. It seems that nothing completely satisfies you. Am I right? Why is that? I should think you would have everything your heart desires. Well, it's too late to do anything about it now. You know we can change the destiny that our palms foretell. We just have to redesign the lines . . ."

With that, she viciously and swiftly carved a triangle into the palm of his hand with three deliberate strokes of the knife. Bond almost cried out in pain, but he gritted his teeth and held it in. He clenched his fist tightly, pressing on the wound to stop the bleeding.

Hera stood up and kicked away her chair. "I think it's time we take that ear off. Which one shall it be? The right or the left? After we do the ears, we'll do the lower lip. Then I'll carve off the upper lip. You'll never kiss anyone again, lover boy. Doing the nose will be pretty messy, but I think it should be next. You'll still be alive by the time we get to your eyes. One at a time. Pluck. Pluck. We'll save the tongue for last. I'll split it in two, then I'll cut the entire thing out and feed it to the fish. I haven't decided if I want to examine other parts of your body after all that, but I probably will. It's going to be a slow, painful death, James. It's a pity, for you're very handsome. Well, you are now. You won't be too pretty in a little while."

She took hold of his right ear and placed the blade of the knife against his scalp. Bond closed his eyes, willing himself to fight the oncoming pain.

There was a buzz on the intercom. She picked it up and spoke impatiently. "What is it?" She listened a moment, looked at Bond, frowned, and said, "All right. We'll be right up."

She hung up and began to cut the nylon cords. "It seems we have some visitors. I'm going to take you out on deck so they can see you. You're not to try anything. Do not look at them. Do not give them any signals. Keep your hands to your sides. I'll give you something to wrap around that hand."

She found a handkerchief in Romanos's desk, used it to wipe the blood from around his neck and chest, then wrapped it around

Bond's right hand. She continued cutting the ropes until Bond was free.

"Let's go. Get up slowly and don't try anything foolish. Walk around like you're enjoying yourself. I'll have a gun on you the entire time."

She picked up Bond's Walther PPK that Romanos had left behind. He noted that she still had the P99 in her belt.

Bond stood up, clutching the handkerchief tightly around his hand. It was involuntarily shaking.

They went up the wooden steps to the deck above. Four men were there, dressed in wet suits, standing at attention with their arms folded.

A helicopter was hovering above the boat. It was an unmarked Gazelle, and Bond could see two people in it. He wondered if Niki might be the pilot, but it was too high to tell. He looked around the sea and saw other vessels on the water—a couple of sailing boats, a catamaran, and what looked like a cruise ship not too far away. There was an island about two miles off the bow of the ship.

"Where are we?" Bond asked.

"Near Santorini. Lie down on the deck chair," Hera said. "Act like you're enjoying the sun." Together they sat on two chairs side by side. Bond stretched out and did as he was told. Was there anything he could do to signal the helicopter? Surely they were Niki's people, keeping an eye on the boat.

Hera said something to one of the men in Greek. He acknowledged the order, then proceeded to put on a Dacor tank.

Hera turned to Bond and said, "We'll just make it look like we're having a nice time out here on the water, so relax."

Bond glanced around him. He didn't see any usable weapons. There were some doughnut-shaped life belts near the door, a coil of rope behind him. He had to get off the boat, regardless of whether or not Niki's people figured out that he needed help.

Inside the Gazelle, Niki and a National Intelligence Service agent studied the sea below them. Niki was piloting the craft, while the other agent peered through binoculars at the ship.

"Well?" she yelled over the noise of the helicopter.

"I see him. He's on the upper deck lying down. He's with the redheaded woman. He looks like he's not in any trouble to me."

"Are you sure?"

"There's three . . . four men standing on the deck, but they look like crewmen. Looks like one is serving drinks, another one is getting into diving gear."

"Then we'll wait," she said. "I'd hate to blow his cover. James is up to something, I know it. He's infiltrated them through that woman." A pang of jealousy streaked through her heart, as she suspected that James had slept with Hera Volopoulos. Niki clenched the controls of the helicopter and fought to contain her emotions.

He was doing a job, she told herself. Sometimes field agents had to do whatever was necessary to obtain information.

"We're going on to Santorini," she said. "We'll refuel and keep tabs on the boat."

"The records at Gefyra said they were headed for Cyprus."

"What a surprise."

Niki pushed away her feelings and concentrated on flying the helicopter. It hung in the air for another minute, then flew away toward the island.

Bond watched the helicopter move toward Santorini with disappointment, but he had put together a risky plan which he had to try.

"All right, get back up," Hera said. "We're going below."

"But it's such a nice day. Can't we get some sun while you torture me?" Bond asked, standing.

"Shut up." She stood and aimed the Walther at him. "This gun is puny. Why do you use it?"

"Why do you care?"

She marched him to the stairs leading back down. He eyed the life belts mounted on the wall by the door. Acting quickly, Bond grabbed one and, with all his might, flung it at Hera like a discus. It took her completely by surprise, temporarily knocking her gun hand away. The Walther went off, then flew out of her hand and sailed across the deck and off onto one of the lower decks. The stray bullet hit the man with the aqualung, and he plummeted over the side of the yacht into the water. Bond followed up the attack by ramming Hera in the chest with his head, which sent her tumbling to the deck.

"Bastard!" she cried. She was on her feet immediately. The three other guards made a move for Bond. He took a defensive stance, while desperately looking for an escape route. The men rushed him, but Bond easily warded off their attack and knocked them down. Hera pushed past the falling bodies and delivered a hard kick into Bond's stomach, but he managed to grab her leg and twist it. She fell to the deck again. Bond threw himself on top of her, grabbed the P99 from her belt, leaped over her body and ran.

"Get him!" Hera cried. The guards drew guns and fired at him, but the bullets missed as he jumped from the upper deck to one of the walk-around side decks on the port side. He landed on his feet and ran to the stern. As the bullets zipped past him, Bond stuck the P99 in his trouser pocket, took a breath, and dived neatly into the cold, blue water.

"We can't let him get away!" Hera cried. She ordered the three men to put on aqualungs and dive into the water.

Bond surfaced and gasped for air. He was about thirty meters from the boat. Getting his bearings, he saw that he was a good mile and a half from Santorini. Could he make it? The water was rougher than he had thought. It would be a challenging test of stamina.

Then he saw the cruise ship. It was approximately a hundred meters away. He began to swim toward it instead.

The three guards quickly equipped themselves with tanks, fins, masks, and harpoon guns. They jumped into the water and began swimming swiftly toward Bond.

Bond didn't look back, but he knew that the men were in pursuit. He was hoping they'd come after him. The water was indeed far too choppy, so he had to find a way to snatch one of their aqualungs. Then he remembered the man who was shot. Bond dived and swam deep, looking for the dead guard. A stream of bubbles marked the location, for he was caught on some rocks about thirty meters below the surface. Bond held his breath and fought the pressure, willing himself to swim down to the body. It took nearly two minutes to reach him. His lungs were about to burst and he felt the pain in his ears as he made the final approach—then grabbed the dead man's regulator and inserted it into his own mouth. He took a few gulps of air, then removed the aqualung and strapped it onto himself just as a harpoon shot past his head.

Diver number one caught up with Bond and attempted to stab him. Bond kicked him hard in the chest, then grabbed his arms. They struggled in the water, their bodies turning over and over like jellyfish. Bond, the far superior swimmer and fighter, easily chopped the knife out of the man's hand with a blow to the wrist. He caught the knife as it floated in front of him, then thrust it into the man's throat. Blood clouded the water as Bond struggled to get back to the dead man to remove his fins and mask. Bond had many years of experience compensating for the slow-motion delay that inevitably occurred while fighting underwater. He ripped off the dead man's face mask. Another harpoon shot toward him, but Bond swung the body into its path just in time. The spear plunged into the man's side but before Bond had time to think, divers two and three were on top of him. They were both armed with knives. Bond performed a somersault in the water, kicking the men as he turned. Still wearing the shoes he had bought in Monemvasia, Bond smashed the glass on diver two's mask with a heel. Blinded, the guard temporarily left the skirmish. That gave Bond enough time to pull the knife from diver one's throat and thrust it at diver three. His opponent was held at bay for the few seconds Bond needed to pull the fins off the first dead man's feet, kick off his shoes, and slip them on. Diver three swam toward Bond at full speed with his knife-wielding hand outstretched. Bond swung his own knife and caught the man's shoulder with it, but the attacker succeeded in nicking him in the side. Bond dodged another swing, only to discover that diver two had recovered his eyesight and was back, ready to tackle him from behind.

Bond broke away from the melee and swam to the cruise ship, which was almost on top of them. The two men chased him. He maneuvered dangerously close to the ship's rotor blades, hoping the men would follow. The force of the water was immense, and it took all of his strength to keep from being sucked into the propeller. He took hold of the metal casing around the blades, climbed up halfway out of the water and held on for dear life as the boat took him at top speed through the water.

Bond thought he had successfully escaped, when a hand grabbed his ankle. Diver three was hanging on to him as the ship pulled them along. Bond felt the man's knife slice into his calf. He kicked out and connected with something very hard, but the man refused to loosen his grip. Bond moved forward on the rotor housing by pulling himself along some metal rungs. His injured palm screamed in agony. He finally made it to a point in front of the rotors. His lower body and the diver attached to his ankle were being dragged into the current that flowed through the rotors and out the other side. The suction was extremely powerful.

The attacker attempted to pull himself up Bond's leg. Bond kicked him again and again until the man lost his grip. The force of the water immediately pulled him into the rotor blades, and the blue water turned to a dark red as bits of the body spread out into the sea.

Bond climbed back to his position above the rotors and held on to the housing again, allowing the cruise ship to take him toward Santorini. He had time to catch his breath and rest. Diver two, the one whose mask was broken, was nowhere in sight. Bond put the knife in his belt and examined his hand and calf. The wound that Hera had made in his palm was bleeding badly and hurt like hell. The cut in his leg was superficial and would not need stitches. He then checked the Walther P99 and found that the magazine was missing.

The area around Santorini is famous for its underwater volcanoes. The foam from the rotors prevented him from seeing them, but he remembered that the caldera was quite beautiful—white, black, and gray, with patches of multicolored, sparkling strata made of lava and pumice. The volcanoes were really just craggy rocks with large holes, dormant for centuries.

The ship began to slow down, signaling its approach to the island by blowing its siren. Bond rode the boat all the way in to the bay at Fira, Santorini's major port. Just as he was about to slip off the ship and swim to shore, a harpoon struck the hull by his head. He looked behind him and saw diver two swimming hard toward him. Bond let go of the rotor housing and swam down to the rocky volcanoes. Just as he had hoped, the diver followed him.

Bond swam into one of the dark holes and hid behind an outcrop of hardened lava. He watched and waited, ready to ambush the guard and slit his throat. Suddenly, two small bright lights appeared in front of him. Bond's heart skipped a beat when he realized that they weren't lights at all—they were eyes! He was face-to-face with a moray eel, what the Greek fishermen called a smerna. This one was snakelike, a meter and a half long, and it had shiny black skin which was speckled prominently with large golden-yellow spots. The eel had a huge mouth equipped with what looked like hundreds of sharp teeth. Bond knew that the bite could produce a toxicity and might take days to heal. Normally moray eels didn't bother divers unless they were disturbed, but they especially didn't like being threatened when they were sleeping on rocks or in caves.

Bond pushed back slowly from the lava as the eel watched him closely. At that point, the diver in pursuit appeared above him, knife in hand. Bond deflected a fatal blow just in time, but was nicked again in the shoulder. The two men struggled a moment until Bond managed to perform another somersault and sling the guard over him onto the rock where the moray eel was resting. The diver slammed into the eel, which reacted ferociously. The smerna swiftly clamped its huge jaws on the diver's neck and wouldn't let go. Bond watched in horror as the surprisingly powerful eel shook the man like a snake with a rat. The water turned dark red, clouding the gruesome sight. Bond turned away and shot out of the lava outcrop.

Back on the surface, Bond swam along the port side of the cruise ship to the dock. Exhausted, he climbed onto the rocks, removed his fins, and made his way onto the shore. A few tourists disembarking from the cruise ship saw him and pointed. A man wearing bloody street clothes and an aqualung had just climbed out of the water!

Bond dumped the diving gear and walked barefoot to the Fira Skala building, where he immediately contacted the local police.

▶22.
SECRETS OF THE DEAD

Hera Volopoulos ordered the men to open a hatch on the upper deck of the *Persephone,* disclosing a prototype of a new Groen Brothers Hawk H2X gyrocopter that sat inside. Only about twenty-two feet in length with a height of nine and a half feet, the Hawk was powered by an Allison 250 C20 turbine and had a range of 600 miles at its cruising speed of 140 miles per hour. It could also lift off without a runway, unlike most gyrocopters of the past.

Hera put on a helmet and got inside the little white vehicle that resembled the head of an ostrich. She gave the thumbs-up sign to the two men on the deck and started the motor. The Hawk rose gently into the sky and flew away toward Cyprus.

Exactly fifteen minutes later, the *Persephone* was met by two secret service helicopters and two coast guard ships. The remaining three men on board fought to the death rather than be arrested.

"I'm sorry, James, but it looked as if you were having a good time on that yacht," Niki said. "If I had known they had guns on you, we would have taken action."

Bond was sitting up in a village police station where the Greek National Intelligence Service had temporarily set up shop on Santorini. He was drinking hot coffee and eating a plate of scrambled eggs that Niki had prepared for him. A doctor had spent the last hour sewing up his palm. Bond would have to be left-handed for a while. The wounds on his neck and leg were superficial.

"Besides," she continued, "I was convinced you were screwing that woman and was a little pissed off at you. Well, I'm glad you're okay. You're like a tomcat—you have nine lives."

Bond grinned, but didn't address Niki's concerns.

The chief of police stepped in and said something in Greek to Niki.

"I have a fax coming in, I'll be right back," she told Bond as she left the room.

Bond sighed heavily, then took a sip of coffee. He was feeling better. The lack of food or sleep for so long, and his ordeals on the boat and in the sea, had taken their toll. Niki's comment about Hera had irritated him too. He hated being paired with a partner, especially a female one.

Niki returned and sat on the desk across from him.

"Romanos has disappeared," she said. "That is, he's nowhere to be found in Greece. They're on the lookout for him in Cyprus."

"Was he followed from Gefyra?" Bond asked.

"No, the team arrived too late, and I stuck with the *Persephone* because you were on it. We sent word all the way up the line to Athens to watch out for his car, but no one ever saw it. He must have gone somewhere else and hopped on a train, a boat . . . who knows?"

"And where's the *Persephone* now?"

"Within five hundred miles of Cyprus. We've sent a force out to intercept them. Your redheaded *friend* should be under arrest by now. Let me hear what Romanos told you."

"He's planning three big strikes, most likely against northern Cyprus or Turkey, and he said he had the help of the Greek military—some general or other is on his team. Melina Papas has been creating a new virus for him, and I suspect it's already made. It could be the one I found in Texas. If it is, then he's already attacked Los Angeles and Tokyo with it. He's going to want to hit a lot of people at once. Is there an event coming up that will bring a big crowd together in northern Cyprus or in Turkey?"

"Damn, there is. November fifteenth is the day the so-called TRNC declared its independence. There are parades and celebrations in Lefkosia."

"That's tomorrow."

"That's right."

"I had better get in touch with London. Can I use your mobile?"

Niki gave it to him and left the room so that Bond could call his office in privacy. After the series of code words and forwarded connections, Bill Tanner came on the line.

"James! Good to hear from you."

"I need to speak with M, Bill."

He put Bond through and soon he heard the weary voice of his chief.

"Double-O Seven?" she asked.

"Yes, ma'am. I have some news. I'm afraid you're not going to like it."

"Go ahead."

"Alfred Hutchinson's father was court-martialed during the war over some unrecovered Nazi gold."

"I knew that."

"Alfred and Konstantine Romanos were partners in selling it off all over Europe. It's how Alfred financed his political career. I fear that Ambassador Hutchinson was more involved in this affair than we realized. He may have been a member of the Decada."

"Are you sure, 007?" M sounded more angry than upset, as if she wanted Bond to prove it before she would believe it.

"That's what Romanos himself told me. They've known each other since the early eighties."

There was silence at the other end of the line.

"Ma'am, I understand how this news makes you feel, but I must ask you something. Romanos said that the information Hutchinson was going to give us the morning after his death was about the Decada's plans. It's imperative that we get hold of that material. I think they're going to strike very soon, possibly tomorrow. Please think very hard once again. Is there anything in your memory that might lead us to this information?"

M said, "His flat was searched thoroughly, but I'll have a team go over there again right now. Let me think about it."

Bond gave her the number of Niki's mobile.

"I'll ring you in three hours or less," she said.

It was now six o'clock and the sun would be going down soon.

"Right. Take care, ma'am."

"You too, 007." She hung up.

Bond went out of the room and found Niki talking on another

phone. She was agitated and speaking rapidly in Greek. She slammed down the phone and said, "She wasn't on the boat, James."

"What?"

"Hera Volopoulos. She wasn't on the *Persephone.* Only three men were found on the yacht and they were killed. She wasn't on board."

"The boat didn't make any stops after she left Monemvasia?"

"No."

"That's impossible. Unless she got away in another boat."

"That must be what happened. Now what?"

"M will call on your mobile in three hours."

Niki nodded. "We have a room where we can wait."

She made love to him as though the world would end that night. She was ravenous after having hungered for him for two days and she submitted enthusiastically to his caresses. Bond thought that Niki demonstrated a unique and earthy emotional response to sex. She made involuntary guttural sounds of pleasure that were somewhat primal, and which he found exciting.

They were at the Hotel Porto Fira, in a room made partly of volcanic rock. It was built on the caldera's edge and was one of the finer establishments in the port town. If he hadn't needed the release of tension that Niki had just provided, Bond would have been happy to light a cigarette, sit on the terrace, and gaze at the classic postcard views of colored balconies, blue-domed churches, and warm, sunny beaches that make Santorini one of Greece's most beautiful islands.

The lovemaking had eased the earlier tension that had risen between them. They each lit a cigarette, lay in bed and looked up at the white ceiling. They could hear the sound of the sea outside.

"James, you like me, don't you?" she asked.

"Of course I do. Why?"

"You seem distant, as if you were somewhere else."

"Am I?" he asked, but it was true. He was concerned about M and was thinking about the relationship she had with Alfred Hutchinson. Bond knew what it was like when a lover betrayed everything you stood for and believed in.

"James, listen. I ask nothing of you," Niki said. "You don't have to be afraid that I'm going to try and keep this relationship going after the assignment is over."

"I wasn't thinking that at all."

"I just—" Niki caught her breath, then continued. "I mean, I'm aware of your reputation, James. You have a girl in every port. It's all right. I don't mind being the girl in this one. I just thought you had only *one* girl in each port."

Bond looked at her and took hold of her chin. "Don't be a silly goose. You are the only girl in this port."

"I'm not sure I believe you, but anyway, we have an assignment to-gether and shouldn't be doing this in the first place. Why would we want to continue it?" She sounded hurt.

"Niki . . ."

"No, really, it's all right. Just promise me one thing."

"What?"

"Before the very last time we make love . . . that is, when you know it's the last time . . . before you leave Greece . . . tell me. Don't just leave without saying a word. All right?"

"All right."

Her lips were slightly open, an inch from his. She kissed him and explored his mouth with her tongue. Then she said, "The assignment isn't over yet. Put out that cigarette and let's do it again."

"M on hold for you, James," Bill Tanner said over the phone. The ring had awakened Bond and Niki in the hotel room. Bond looked at his watch. It was 8:10.

When she got on the line, M said, "We found it, 007, I think we've got it."

"Yes?"

"I've been going over and over the events of that night," she said. "Something compelled me to look inside the handbag I was carrying then. It's one I don't usually use. You see, when he was dying, he kept saying, 'Your hand . . . your hand . . .' He was gasping, he couldn't speak well. I thought he wanted me to hold his hand. What he was trying to say was, 'Your handbag . . . your handbag.' Well, I hadn't touched that handbag since the night of the murder. I got it out and looked inside, and found an envelope. Inside were instructions and a key to a safety deposit box at a branch of Barclay's. The instructions gave the address of the bank and authorization for me to open the box if anything happened to Alfred. He must have slipped the note inside when he insisted on holding it. He knew what had happened to him on the pavement. He knew that he was going to die."

"Go on."

"I just got back from the bank. Inside the box was a note he wrote to me, a piece of paper with a triangle drawn on it, a marked-up map of Cyprus, and a floppy disk. On the disk we found details of a meeting he had set up with the Rauf Denktash, the President of the Turkish Republic of Northern Cyprus. He was going to visit the President on their independence day."

"That's tomorrow."

"Yes, the fifteenth of November. There are some plans of the Presidential Palace on Tanzimat Street on the disk as well, an invitation to a breakfast celebration tomorrow morning, and something else far more disturbing."

"What's that?"

"Aerial maps of Istanbul. There is one large map of the Aegean, with the longitude and latitude of the city highlighted. There's a series of numbers on this map, and Bill Tanner confirmed that they were the target coordinates for a missile."

"And the note?"

"It's personal, but I want you to see it. It clears up the business with the Nazi gold. I'm going to fax all of this to you. Once you've had a look, call me back."

Niki opened her Compaq laptop and plugged it in. She set it up to receive faxes, and soon the data was being transmitted and downloaded onto her hard drive. Bond read Hutchinson's letter to M:

My Dear Barbara:

If you are reading this, then I am probably dead. I hope you will find all of this material useful in stopping the Decada. I believe they are planning to assassinate the President of the Turkish Republic of

Northern Cyprus on November 15. They have something else planned for Istanbul.

I took the precaution of placing a copy of this data in my safety deposit box because I recently discovered my computer had been tampered with. The files may have been copied. I have since deleted them.

You'll probably learn that I was involved with Konstantine Romanos in a scheme to sell off a large cache of Nazi gold that my father had secreted away after the war. I regret to tell you that this is true. Even though I became a wealthy man from the sale of the gold, Romanos cheated me out of 50% of my share, and I was unable to claim it. I couldn't go public, for it would have destroyed my political career. The suspicions about my father were damaging enough. The scandal would have been more than I could bear.

I attempted to extort the money from him, threatening to go to the authorities with the information that Romanos was a terrorist. When I learned that my son was involved with the Decada, I knew it was time to do something aggressive. Romanos used my son as a hold over me. He thought he could keep me from talking if Charles was under his wing. Instead, I resolved to give you all of this information.

The facts of life are such that we are all human and we all make mistakes. Alas, the facts of death do not allow us to properly correct those mistakes. By then it is too late to clear out the dark, dirty secrets from the closets of our souls.

I want you to know that I love you very much, and once this ghastly business is over, I hope you can forgive me and that your memories of our time together will be pleasant.

> *With all my love,*
> *Alfred*

So the man was somewhat honorable after all, Bond thought.

Bond studied the rest of the data and decided that the President of the TRNC was definitely one of the three *Tetraktys* targets. If Istanbul was another one, what was the third? There was no indication of what the Decada planned to do with Instanbul, except that there were cruise missile coordinates written on a map. Had they obtained a cruise missile? Was this the military connection? And what about that virus? Was there a connection to all this?

"Niki," Bond said. "Get on to your people and pull any reports from the last few months dealing with arms trading in the area. Look for missiles, anything relevant."

He phoned M back and told her that he had gone over the information.

"Romanos said he had recovered all of Hutchinson's information after all. I believe he has a missile that he's planning to use on Turkey. They're going to try and kill the President of Northern Cyprus in the morning. We have to put together a team and get there as soon as possible," Bond said.

"I agree," M said.

"We have to go into the north. That will be tricky with our Greek friends. They might refuse to cross the border."

"Damn it, convince them that their country will be blown to hell if they don't stop these fanatics. You're also going to need the assistance of the Turks. I'll call Station T in Istanbul and alert them that they are under attack, but *not* by Greeks or the Republic of Cyprus."

"Romanos admitted that his people were creating a virus. That may have been the bug we found in Texas. What's the status of the epidemics?"

"Just a minute, Chief of Staff is handing me something." She was silent as she read for a minute. "Christ."

"What?"

"The death tolls in Los Angeles and Tokyo are rising. There have been new cases reported in New York and London during the past forty-eight hours. Do you think this is his virus?"

"According to him, it wasn't yet ready for use!"

"Well, somebody's using it. All of the infected people have been quarantined, and the clinics where they got the blood have been sealed. Hospitals are on full alert to isolate anyone who comes in with similar symptoms."

"Then we need to find him fast. If there's really going to be an assassination attempt on the Turkish Cypriot president tomorrow, that may be our only chance of tracking him down. What I don't understand is how he is going to get to the President. It was Alfred that had the invitation to meet with him tomorrow, right?"

"Yes. He was supposed to be part of the President's entourage for the day's festivities. Of course, Manville Duncan had to step in. He's in Nicosia now at the British Embassy. I'll get hold of him and see if he can handle this situation with a diplomatic approach."

"That would help a great deal," Bond said. "How is he doing being Ambassador to the World?"

"Oh, he just complains that he's not very worldly about food. He's a picky eater, I suppose. He's especially at a disadvantage in a meat-eating country like Cyprus."

"Why is that?"

"You didn't know? Duncan is a strict vegetarian."

A cold chill ran down Bond's spine. "My God. Ma'am, it's Manville Duncan who is the member of the Decada. It was never Alfred Hutchinson. Hutchinson wasn't killed because of the secrets he knew. He was murdered so that Duncan would be free to replace him for this event tomorrow! He's a traitor, and *he's* the one who will try to assassinate the President!"

▶ 23.
INDEPENDENCE DAY

Manville Duncan nervously loaded the ricin pellet into the gold-plated ballpoint pen that would serve as the method of execution.

"Are you sure you can handle this?" Hera asked him impatiently.

"Don't worry," he said. "You just worry about *your* job."

The sun was rising in Lefkosia, and the two of them had met in Hera's room in the Saray Hotel on Girne Caddesi, probably the best hotel in Lefkosia.

"The parade begins at nine o'clock," she said. "You'll be meeting with the President at nine-thirty. He's supposed to address the people at ten. If you're on time, he'll collapse of a heart attack in the middle of his speech. Remember to place the number and the statue where they won't be found for a while. Then get the hell out."

Duncan felt his pocket to make sure that the piece of paper with the number "8" on it and the small statuette of Apollo were still there.

"What about your equipment?" he asked. "Was it here, as arranged?"

She nodded. "It's an old American M79 genade launcher, the kind used in Vietnam." She pulled it out from under the bed. It was a short, rifled, breech-loading weapon that fired a fixed cartridge. Its maximum range was about 350 yards.

"And four cartridges." They were in a metal briefcase, packed in Styrofoam, and looked like oversized short and fat bullets. "They're filled with sarin. I'm firing them at ten oh-five whether the President is dead or not. Make sure you don't follow him outside. If you breathe this stuff you'll die." The rest of her accoutrements—the gas mask, the protective suit and hood, the boots and gloves—already lay spread out on the bed. On the bedside table was a can of red spray paint and a small alabaster statuette of Hermes.

Duncan watched Hera prepare. He said finally, "I know what you're up to, Number Two."

"What do you mean?"

"I know what you and Number Ten and Number Eight were planning."

"And what is that, Mr. Duncan?"

"You're planning to split off from the Decada and form your own group. You're planning a mutiny."

"Why would we do that?"

"I don't know. I know that you and Number Ten were . . . well, that you were intimate with each other. Number Eight made it a ménage à trois. Am I right?"

"What if you are?"

"The Monad won't like it."

Hera suddenly seized Duncan by the throat and squeezed hard. His eyes bulged as he struggled for breath. After allowing him to feel the pain for thirty seconds, she said, "Listen, you worm. If you so much as breathe a word of that to the Monad, I'll cut out your liver and stuff it in your mouth, do you understand me? If you're smart, you'll keep quiet, and maybe we'll have a place for you when we form the *true* Decada. I've been with the Monad since I was twelve years old. I want to break free. It's my destiny. The gods have spoken to me too. Pythagoras himself experienced a mutiny among his own followers. This is meant to happen. Besides, the Monad is misguided. We all agree with his goal to teach the Turks a lesson, but after that, we have our own plans. Bigger ones. Once this *Tetraktys* is completed, we're moving on. I promise you that what we leave behind us won't be pretty, so you had better start choosing where your loyalties will lie."

She released him, then continued getting ready. Duncan gasped for breath and sat on the bed. He waited a few minutes to regain his composure. Then, as if nothing had happened, he stood up.

"I had better get going," Duncan said, clipping the gold pen in his jacket pocket. He straightened his tie and said, "Good luck, Number Two."

"You too, Number Three."

Manville Duncan left the room for his appointment with the gods.

———

It was nine o'clock in the morning. Hundreds of Turkish Cypriots had gathered in the streets of Lefkosia for the parades and celebration. The President of the Republic was due to speak from a stage set up near the Saray Hotel. A few blocks away, he was greeting visiting dignitaries at a special breakfast reception in the Presidential Palace. No one in the streets noticed the British helicopter that flew overhead. After all, British aircraft were seen in the sky all the time.

Niki Mirakos flew the Wessex helicopter from the RAF base in Akrotiri, carrying four Greek Secret Service commandos and James Bond. M had arranged the whole thing in secrecy with the Greeks. It was best that neither the Republic of Cyprus nor the TRNC knew what was happening for the moment. The government of Turkey, however, had been alerted to the situation.

They were all dressed in protective uniforms with gas masks hanging loosely around their necks. Armed with AK-47s, the commandos were a highly trained professional antiterrorism unit. Crossing the Green Line was something they had thought they would never have to do.

Down below, at the Presidential Palace, Manville Duncan was greeted by the President's aides and brought inside the splendid white building. He was led into a room full of diplomats and other important visitors from Turkey and abroad. Fruit juice, breads, and fruit were laid out on a table. Rauf Denktash, the President of the TRNC, was surrounded by friends and colleagues near a large bay window looking out over the street. The festive atmosphere of the place was infectious.

"Mr. President," the aide said, leading Duncan up to him, "this is the Goodwill Ambassador to the World from Great Britain."

"Mr. Hutchinson?" the President asked.

"No, Manville Duncan. I believe my office alerted yours—Mr. Hutchinson died suddenly over a week ago. I was Mr. Hutchinson's lawyer and have temporarily taken over his duties."

"I am sorry to hear about Mr. Hutchinson," the President said in English. "We had never met but had spoken on the phone. Nice man. But you are just as welcome here, Mr. Duncan."

"Thank you. I am here representing Her Majesty's Government in the interest of promoting peaceful relations between the TRNC and the Republic of Cyprus."

The President nodded his head in acknowledgment and said, "Ah, but Her Majesty's Government refuses to recognize the Turkish Republic of Northern Cyprus as a nation. What can we do about that, Mr. Duncan?"

Duncan displayed his most rehearsed, charming smile. "My dear President, now is not the time to get into *that* discussion, is it?"

They both laughed. "It is a pleasure to be here," Duncan continued. "Congratulations. Enjoy your day."

"Thank you," the President said, then rejoined his colleagues.

Manville Duncan stepped over to the table and picked up a glass of orange juice, then felt his inside jacket pocket to make sure the ballpoint pen was still there. As a precaution, he also wore a shoulder holster with a Smith & Wesson Bodyguard Airweight .38 Special.

The Wessex flew over the crowds toward the western side of the Venetian wall that surrounded Lefkosia. Looking down, Bond saw quite a different city than what was south of the Green Line. Lefkosia was not nearly as modernized as Nicosia was. The buildings below looked hundreds of years old. As a result, Lefkosia had distinctly more character than its southern counterpart. There were numerous historic monuments dating from the Middle Ages and subsequent eras, including many examples of Gothic and Ottoman architecture.

"Where do you want me to land this thing?" Niki shouted.

Bond pointed to a mosque. "There, that's it. Put it down in the courtyard."

He checked the AK-47 he was carrying, and then made sure the P99 was loaded. He had been lucky to obtain extra magazines and ammunition from the Akrotiri base.

The Wessex descended into the courtyard of the Kanli Mescit Mosque. The commandos jumped out and Bond followed them. He gave the thumbs-up sign to Niki, who then took the Wessex back up into the air.

For a few moments, nothing happened. Bond and the men waited and watched the walls surrounding the courtyard.

Suddenly the gates of the mosque opened, and twenty Turkish soldiers poured in, their rifles ready. They were wearing green camouflage uniforms. The men encircled the perimeter of the walls and within seconds had the entire courtyard covered. They knelt and aimed their rifles at the five men. A captain shouted in Turkish for the Greek commandos to lay down their weapons and surrender. For several tense moments, the Greeks and the Turks stared at each other without moving. Face-to-face with their ancient enemies, both sides were unsure how to proceed.

The four Greek commandos looked at Bond. "What happens now?" one of them asked. Bond scanned the faces of the Turkish soldiers, but he didn't see the man he was looking for.

"Steady, men," Bond said quietly. "This has to be a mistake..."

Then, two men in civilian clothes marched through the gate and spoke quietly to the sergeant in charge of the soldiers. The sergeant nodded and barked a command to his men. They immediately lowered their weapons and stood at ease. The two men in civilian clothes then walked toward Bond and the Greek commandos. One fellow, a large man with a thick mustache and big brown eyes, resembled someone from Bond's past.

"It's all right," Bond said to the men. "He's here."

Bond stepped forward and stood in front of the men, then held out his hand. The mustached man looked Bond up and down, then grinned broadly. He vigorously shook hands and said, "Mr. Bond, it is so good to see you again."

"You too, Tempo," Bond said. He had not seen Stefan Tempo, the son of Bond's Turkish friend Darko Kerim, in many years. Bond remembered well that fateful day aboard the Orient Express when he had found Kerim's body, murdered by the Russian assassin Red Grant. Later, Kerim's son Stefan had assisted Bond on that assignment, which seemed a lifetime ago. The mature Stefan Tempo was the spitting image of his father.

"How's Station T these days?" Bond asked.

"We do a lot of desk work now," Tempo said. "But when the British start requesting permission to perform commando raids in northern Cyprus with the help of the Greeks, we put down our pencils and take notice."

"Tempo, we don't have much time. We have to get to the Presidential Palace," Bond said.

"We'll lead the way," Tempo said. He barked an order in Turkish to the soldiers, then gestured for Bond to follow them out of the gates. The four Greek commandos looked at the Turks warily, but they went along with the group without complaint.

They all rushed through the gates and onto Tanzimat Street, which was packed with civilians. The men ran in formation, the crowd parting for them as they moved toward the elegant white building.

The TRNC guards in front of the palace were taken by surprise. Tempo and the Turkish sergeant approached the guardhouse and presented papers. They were to be allowed in quietly. Bond had planned it so that Duncan would not be forewarned of their arrival; hence, the TRNC knew nothing about it. At first the guards could not believe that they had a security breach on their hands. Tempo's credentials convinced them otherwise. Finally, the palace head of security nodded his head and let them through the gates.

The TRNC guards led the way into the building. Bond looked at his watch. It was precisely 9:30. They stepped quietly up the grand marble staircase to the second floor and were ushered to the President's greeting room, where the breakfast party was still in progress.

Manville Duncan had his gold ballpoint pen in hand. The President was standing at the food table, pouring a cup of Turkish coffee. All Duncan had to do was press the pen point into the President's arm or leg, and then push the button on the end to release the pellet. The President would feel only a slight pressure and maybe a pinprick.

"Mr. President," Duncan said, leveling the pen at his target's hip. "I am expected back at the British high commissioner's residence very shortly, and I wanted to thank—"

The door burst open. Three of the Turkish soldiers and a TRNC guard came into the room and pulled their guns. They shouted in Turkish for everyone to freeze. Bond pushed his way inside the door.

Duncan, panicking, lunged at the President and grabbed him around the chest. He held the pen at his neck and shouted, "Stay back!" He started to back up to the bay window with the frightened President in the crook of his arm, but the President tripped and fell backward. Duncan dropped the ballpoint pen and reached into his jacket for the .38 Special.

A shot rang out and caught him in the chest before the gun was out of its holster. He flew backward into the food table. Dishes crashed to the floor. Bond lowered the Walther P99 and replaced it in the holster he was wearing on his back. He approached Duncan and knelt beside him. The man was coughing up blood and clutching his chest.

Stefan Tempo rushed to the bewildered and frightened President and spoke rapidly in Turkish, taking him out of the room. Other TRNC officials began to reassure the rest of the guests that everything was under control.

"All right, Duncan," Bond said. "Now's your chance to tell me what you know. Where is Hera? What's Strike Number Nine?"

Duncan spat bloody phlegm from his mouth and gasped, "The One . . . will . . . become . . . the Many . . ."

He exhaled loudly and died. Bond searched his pockets and found a piece of paper with the number "8" scrawled in red and the alabaster statuette. In his other pocket was a map of Lefkosia and a piece of Saray Hotel stationery. A building on the map was marked in a yellow highlight. The notepaper had something scribbled in pencil—

#numbers, 17:00

Bond wasn't sure what that meant, but he put the paper in his pocket, then looked at the map again.

"Tempo, what's this building?" Bond asked, showing him the map.

"That's the Saray Hotel."

"Get your men and let's go. We're finished here."

The Saray Hotel was eight stories tall and provided a magnificent view of Lefkosia/Nicosia from the roof. Hera Volopoulos, dressed in her Number Killer uniform, had completed setting up the M79 grenade launcher and had armed it with one of the shells containing sarin nerve gas. The shells would explode in the air and distribute the chemical, and the breeze would do the rest. Hundreds of people would be affected. All Hera had to do was fire the four shells in different directions, take her previously prepared escape route down to the first floor, run to the rental car she had parked a block away, and drive to the area north of the city where she had hidden the gyrocopter. No one would notice her amidst all the celebration going on in the streets. The Turkish Cypriots were out in force, and nothing could distract them. Hera thought that it was devilishly appropriate that the strike was being made on their independence day.

At ten o'clock, she looked over at the temporary stage that was set up in the square across from the hotel. The President hadn't shown up. Had he died from Duncan's pellet too soon? Or had Duncan failed in his mission?

She wasn't about to wait until 10:05. She examined the grenade launcher one more time, checked her gas mask, and prepared to fire the first shell.

"Hold it, Hera!" Bond's voice rang out from the roof entrance to the lift. He stood thirty feet away, the P99 pointed at her, daring her to make another move. Behind him were several Turkish soldiers with their weapons trained on her. They were all dressed in gas masks and protective gear.

"Step away from the launcher." Bond's voice sounded metallic through the mask's filter.

Her finger was on the trigger. "Just one of these shells will be enough, James," she said through her mask. "It will only take a reflex to pull the trigger. If you shoot me, I can't guarantee that I won't fire the launcher involuntarily."

Bond knew that she would fire the launcher no matter what happened. If he had only been a little closer to her, a shot from the Walther might have knocked her away from the weapon. But at this range it wouldn't do the trick.

Before anyone could move, they all heard a low rumbling sound headed in their direction. Something they couldn't see was rising from the ground. It sounded like a lawn mower at first, but it grew louder. Bond recognized the noise and knew that the stalemate would be over in a moment. It was right on time.

The Wessex helicopter suddenly pulled up and over the Saray Hotel, skimming the edge of the roof where Hera was poised. Niki expertly brought the aircraft across the building, knocking her away from the launcher before the woman had time to react. Hera fell to the roof, rolled and jumped to her feet on the ledge of the building. She reached for a submachine gun strapped on her shoulder and swung it around at Bond.

"Fire," he said, and the men let loose a volley of ammunition. But before the bullets could slam into her, the woman had calmly stepped backward off the building.

Bond ran to the ledge and looked down. She was nowhere in sight! Then he saw the rope. It had been attached to a gutter on the side of the building, and ran down to an open window. Given the rope-climbing ability she had demonstrated in Monemvasia, Bond knew she had got away.

The commandos ran down the stairs and spent a half hour searching the hotel, but there was no trace of Hera Volopoulos except a protective suit and a gas mask which she had dropped in the hotel room. Giving up, Bond went back up to the roof.

The Wessex hovered over the hotel. Niki waved at Bond and he gave her the "okay" sign. He then carefully retrieved the four shells and put them back in the Styrofoam case.

Stefan Tempo stepped up to Bond and said, "We must go back to Turkey. This never happened. Our government has no record of these incidents today."

"Nor does mine."

"Thank you, Mr. Bond. You have done a great service for Turkey, Greece, and Cyprus. My father was a man of tolerance. He befriended everyone—the Gypsies, the Bulgars, the Russians, even Greeks. He was made of different substance than most of us."

"Your father was a great man, Tempo," Bond said. "I'm sure that had he lived, he would be working very hard to keep the peace between your people and the Greeks."

Tempo shook hands with the Greek commandos, then watched as

the Wessex came back around. A rope ladder was lowered to the roof of the hotel. Bond and the four men climbed up and into the aircraft. He looked down as the Wessex ascended, and waved to the son of his old friend. Bond then leaned over to the pilot's seat and kissed Niki on the cheek.

▶24.
GHOST TOWN

Even in mid-November the sun was shining brightly in Akrotiri, Cyprus. Bond and Niki sat in a hangar at a folding card table studying the material they had received by fax from the Greek National Intelligence Service, as well as the items found on Duncan.

"You think this might be related to the Decada?" Niki asked, reading him a translation of the report, as it was written in Greek.

TO: NIKI MIRAKOS

FROM: RECORDS

DATE: NOVEMBER 15, 1998

WITH REGARD TO YOUR QUERY ON ANY MILITARY INCIDENTS WITHIN PAST
    TWO MONTHS, WE HAVE FOUND THE FOLLOWING:

CASE 443383: Three privates charged with possession of marijuana.
    Athens.

CASE 250221: Stolen property (stereo, compact discs, computer, etc.)
    reported by colonel. Athens.

CASE 449932: Sergeant major found shot. Attempted murder under
    investigation. Chios.

CASE 957732: Four privates and two sergeants found guilty of disorderly
    conduct. Crete.

CASE 554212: Sergeant killed in traffic accident with civilian. Civilian
    arrested for driving while intoxicated. Crete.

"Where's Chios?" Bond asked.

"It's the Greek island closest to Turkey. It's not much of a tourist center."

"What is there?"

"Mostly military camps. Gum trees."

"Why would this sergeant major be murdered? Does that happen often in the Greek Army?"

"Not at all. You want more details?"

"Please."

As Niki sent a message via her laptop's E-mail system, Bond looked at the map with the coordinates of Istanbul that was on Hutchinson's computer file.

"They have a missile, that's got to be the answer," he said. "Have them search your records for anything unusual involving a missile."

"That's a rather broad search request, isn't it?"

"Just do it, please," Bond said. He was weary and hot. Someone brought them soft drinks, but he chose to drink bottled water.

Niki sent the request through and waited until a list appeared on the screen.

"There's . . . two hundred and thirty-three instances involving a missile," she said. "You want to take a look?" She saved the message and logged off the Internet.

Bond studied the monitor. Greece was a country that depended on NATO for any nuclear support. If the missile was something used to deploy nuclear weapons, NATO might be a link. He looked for any matches that involved NATO. There were twenty-three.

One entry struck him as curious. In 1986, a NATO Pershing 1a missile was reported missing in France. A thorough investigation indicated that the missile might have been lost in a transport accident that occurred outside of Paris. What was especially interesting was that a Greek officer, First Lieutenant Dimitris Georgiou, was in charge of the transport. There was some question as to whether there had been a Pershing in the shipment at all or whether it had been listed by mistake.

Niki was looking at the other materials on the table. She picked up the piece of paper that Bond had found in Duncan's pocket.

"What does this mean? 'Numbers seventeen hundred'?" she asked.

"I don't know. It's a code for something."

"Wait a minute," she said. "I know what it is. This is an IRC address."

"A what?"

"On the Internet, people can set up IRC addresses and 'chat' live in what they call a private room, or channel. If you know the location of the channel, or the name the creator or operator gave it, then you can join the chat."

"I knew that, I've just never used one. I know that the benefit of using an IRC channel is that it can't be traced."

"Right. Unless you know the name of the channel, it's totally secure."

Bond looked at his watch. It was 4:40 P.M. "It's almost seventeen hundred hours. Do you know how to find that channel?"

"Sure, it's easy. Let's go on-line again and I'll show you."

Niki took control of the laptop and logged on under her own screen name of "PilotGrl." Once she was connected, she started a program that handled IRC communications. She then scanned the active list of IRC channels. Sure enough, there was one in use called "#Numbers."

"Now we can see who is in that room." She used the mouse to click on the highlighted "#Numbers" designation, then a menu popped up that listed only one screen name, which meant that only one person was in the room. It was the name "monad." She used the mouse again to click on the "Who Is" icon. The information that appeared was "monad@ppp.chios.hol.gr."

"Monad," Bond said. "That's Romanos."

"And he's on an on-line service in Chios. See?"

"He's on Chios?"

"I would bet money on it."

"So Duncan and Hera were probably supposed to contact Romanos by this IRC channel at five today. Probably to make a report?"

"That's what it looks like."

"Say hello to Romanos."

"What?"

"Say hello to him. Shake him up."

"Since he's the operator of the channel, he'll have the ability to kick me out if he wants."

"Then say something immediately to him."

Niki entered the room with a couple of mouse clicks. Her screen name "PilotGrl@spidernet.com.cy" appeared on the list of room users. She began typing and downloaded the following transcript onto the hard drive as they "talked":

PilotGrl:	Hello. Number Two sent me. Is Number Three not here yet?
Monad:	Who are you?
PilotGrl:	No one you know.
Monad:	This is a private IRC channel. Please leave or I will kick you out.
PilotGrl:	You are expecting Manville Duncan, your Number Three? . . .
PilotGrl:	I don't think he's coming.

There was a long pause before Romanos responded.

Monad:	Who are you?
PilotGrl:	Just a friend. :) I don't think Duncan is going to show.
Monad:	Why not?
PilotGrl:	I'm afraid he got shot. Pity.
Monad:	You must be working for Bond.
PilotGrl:	Bond who? I don't know what you're talking about. Do you want to . . .
PilotGrl:	have cybersex?

At that point, the listing for "Monad@ppp.chios.hol.gr" disappeared from the list of users.

"He's gone," she said. "We scared him off."

"We have to get to Chios. Try your people again and see what they've found out."

She sent another E-mail and immediately received an Instant Message from her superior in Athens.

"They say that the sergeant major on Chios, a young man named Sambrakos, wasn't killed. He was shot and has been in a coma since the shooting. He's in a military hospital on the island."

"Ask them who the commanding officer is there."

Niki typed the question. After a moment, the answer came back.

"Brigadier General Dimitris Georgiou," she read.

"That confirms it," Bond said. "Let's go. Get them to alert the base that we're coming, but to keep the brigadier general in the dark."

She typed in the request, and in a moment got another reply. "They say that the brigadier general is currently on leave. They'll be expecting us at Giala—that's the military headquarters on Chios. Wait a second . . . there's a message for you. From F Leiter?"

"That's my friend Felix, in Texas. Let me see." Bond looked at the screen and read:

CENTERS FOR DISEASE CONTROL CONFIRMS YOUR BUG IS IDENTICAL TO BUGS IN L.A. AND TOKYO. THE CIA AND JAPANESE SECRET SERVICE ARE NOW AFTER YOUR GUY TOO. HOPE YOU GET HIM BEFORE THEY DO.
— FELIX

Bond jumped up to make yet another request of the British Forces Cyprus.

The RAF arranged for Bond, Niki, and the four Greek commandos to travel on an Olympic Airways flight that was leaving from Larnaca airport for Athens at six-thirty P.M. With the help of the Greek government, the flight was diverted to Chios, much to the chagrin of the thirty-six other passengers. They arrived there at approximately eight-thirty, after the sun had already set. A young Greek soldier met them at the gate and led them to a Mercedes jeep in the parking lot.

They drove to the military headquarters in Chios Town. It was a small but efficient base made up of several beige-and-white buildings of brick and plaster. Jeeps and trucks were kept under camouflaged nets. A large gate in front kept nonmilitary personnel out of the area.

The jeep was waved through and Bond and Niki were led to an office where a tall man awaited them.

He spoke English. "Hello, I'm Lieutenant Colonel Gavras. I'm in charge right now. Brigadier General Georgiou is on leave."

Niki showed the man her credentials and said, "This is James Bond of the British Secret Service. We have reason to believe that a terrorist is hiding somewhere on the island, and that General Georgiou is involved. It is imperative that we find the terrorist tonight."

"That's a tall order, Miss Mirakos, and quite an accusation."

"Where is the general?"

"He's supposed to be in Spain."

Bond interrupted. "Can we get a jeep and driver to take us around the island?"

"It's pitch-dark," Gavras said. "You'll probably want to wait until the morning."

"There isn't time," Bond said. "The man is probably planning something for tonight."

Gavras frowned and looked at Niki's papers again.

"My orders come from the head of the secret service, sir," she said.

"I see that. Well, I'll see what I can do."

"Another thing," Bond said. "This boy who was shot. Is he still in a coma?"

"Sergeant Major Sambrakos recovered consciousness yesterday, as a matter of fact."

"Can we see him?"

He frowned again. "Let me make a call."

Sergeant Major Panos Sambrakos lay with a dozen tubes connected to his body. He looked weak and disoriented.

"Panos?" the nurse said in Greek. "Panos, these people are from the Greek Secret Service. They'd like to ask you some questions."

Bond and Niki greeted him, and Sambrakos's eyes flickered.

"Ask him if he knows General Georgiou," Bond said.

Niki asked him and Sambrakos nodded.

"Who shot him and why?"

Again she asked the questions. Sambrakos replied and closed his eyes. Niki said, "He says it was General Georgiou who shot him and left him for dead. He doesn't know why."

"What about the missile? Ask him about the missile."

Niki spoke again, and the boy replied softly and slowly. "He says that there was a Pershing missile hidden in a barn up north. General Georgiou told him that it was a secret, and that if he wanted his military career to stay clean, he should keep it that way. On the night he was shot, the general and two strange men were planning to take it somewhere."

"Ask him if he knows if the missile was armed or not."

The boy looked at Bond and replied in English, "It wasn't armed."

Bond said, "Don't worry Panos, we'll get the bastard."

They thanked him and left the hospital room.

"My bet is that Romanos has fashioned his own warhead."

"How will we find him?"

"It's not *that* big an island, is it?"

They started by heading west toward Karyes.

"Where might a militant group set up camp?" Bond asked.

"There's nowhere they could do it without being noticed," Gavras said. He was driving the jeep himself.

"No abandoned villages, old buildings that are not in use anymore?"

He shook his head. "There are villages on the island that are small and practically invisible. But I doubt an operation like the one you're talking about could even exist on the island."

"Believe me, it does," Bond said.

Karyes wasn't promising, so the jeep moved on until it came to a crossroads. Avgonima was straight ahead, and Anavatos was to the right.

"Wait a minute," Gavras said. "There's Anavatos. No one lives there. Well, a few old people do down at the base of the cliff."

"What is it?"

"It's an ancient village built on a mountain. It's all in ruins now, but a few businessmen have bought some land and hope to turn it into a tourist attraction someday. They're slowly moving in and renovating the ruins."

"Let's see it."

"It's a long shot."

"Romanos would want to place his missile somewhere high up. I want to see this place."

The dark road snaked up into the hills until it stopped at the base of the village. The residents had all gone to bed, for there were no lights at all in any of the houses. The moonlight cast an eerie glow on the cliff. The whitish ruins stood out sharply in contrast to the blackness of the mountain. They looked like ghostly artifacts of another world and another time.

"How do you get up there?" Bond asked.

"On foot," Gavras said. "You just have to go up the path there, see? It winds all around the ruins and eventually gets to the top. Be careful, though. In the dark it can be quite dangerous. At the top is a sheer cliff drop on the other side. It's where the residents of the village jumped and committed suicide instead of being taken prisoner by the Turks a hundred years ago or so."

Bond thought briefly of Charles Hutchinson and wondered if he might have been thrown off that cliff.

"I'm going," he said. He reached into a backpack where Niki had placed his belongings that she had brought from his hotel in Athens. He pulled out Major Boothroyd's night-vision goggles, then checked his Walther P99 to make sure the magazine was completely full. He stuck two extra magazines in his pocket.

"I'm coming with you," Niki said.

"I think I had better go alone," Bond said. "I'm just going to do a quick reconnaissance. Give me a half hour."

Before Niki could protest, Bond walked away from the jeep toward the structures at the base of the cliff. Suddenly there was a flash of bright light. A tremendous explosion blew the jeep over on its side. Both Niki and Gavras were thrown several feet.

"Niki!" Bond shouted, and ran to her. She was dazed and confused, and there was a nasty cut on her forehead.

"What happened?" she mumbled.

"Someone fired a bazooka, I think," Bond said. "From up the cliff."

She tried to get up, but her leg was bent awkwardly behind her. "Oh God," she said, gasping. "My leg. I've twisted it. What about the colonel?"

Bond moved over to Gavras. His body was still and lifeless.

"We've lost him. I'm going to call for help if the radio is still working."

The smoking jeep had a large hole in the back end but was basically in one piece. Bond unclamped a fire extinguisher from the floorboard and put out the flames, then climbed inside to try the

Motorola radio. Surprisingly, he got a signal to the base and made a report.

He then ran back to Niki with a charred blanket he had found in the back of the vehicle, and wrapped it around her.

"Help is on the way," he said. "Stay here. I've got to go up and see what I can find."

She nodded. "Don't worry about me, I'll be okay. It only hurts if I think about making love to you."

He affectionately placed his left palm on her cheek. "I'll be back."

He left her there in the dark and went up past the closed taverna and onto the main stone path that ascended the cliff. She was a strong girl, she would be fine, he thought. He couldn't stop to help her—there was no telling when Romanos was planning to initiate his attack on Turkey. Now that Romanos knew they were there, he could set it off at any time.

At night, Anavatos was an eerie place. The ruins looked war-torn and skeletal in the moonlight. It was a black-and-white world of ghostly shapes and shadows. Bond kept thinking that specters were moving about, watching his every move. The spirits of the dead Greeks who threw themselves off the mountain were haunting him, taunting him, urging him forward so that he too could take the fatal plunge into blackness.

Bond put on the night-vision goggles and things improved immensely. The infrared filters turned the little moonlight into a warm green glow that enabled him to see the path clearly. The shapes and shadows were still all around him, and they weren't any less unnerving, but at least he could find his way up the cliff without groping.

The ascent reminded him of the ruins at Monemvasia, except that these were far more desolate and lonely. The narrow passages were claustrophobic, with broken buildings on all sides gaping at him like openmouthed tombs.

At one point, he was able to look down and note his progress. He could see the path he had traversed zigzagging down through the ruins to the base of the mountain below. He could barely discern the outline of the overturned jeep, and the two figures lying on the ground nearby.

Bond kept going up. At the halfway point, he stopped to get his bearings and take a look at what was above him. A large structure was at the summit of the cliff. There was no sign of any lights coming from it, of course, but Bond guessed that the Decada was hiding there. Turning a corner, he was met head- on by a man dressed entirely in black. A fist plunged into Bond's stomach, causing him to double over. A boot rammed into his face, and he fell to the hard ground. Another kick assaulted his ribs.

He had the wind knocked out of him and was struggling to catch his breath when he heard the unmistakable click of a semiautomatic handgun being cocked. Bond swung his right arm out and across the man's shin. His spear-hand chopped the bone with enough force to break a block of ice. The man yelped and fell down.

Bond jumped up and gave him a taste of his own medicine, kicking him twice in the ribs and once in the face. The man lay motionless.

Bond continued to climb, rubbing his side to make sure nothing was broken.

When he reached the top, Bond took a look at the ledge, below which was a seemingly bottomless canyon of trees and rocks. He then carefully moved around the large building, listening for the slightest sound.

He had completely circled the building before he saw the ventilation grille partially covered by a plant. It was built into the bottom of one of the walls, and smoke was trickling out of it. If Bond had not been wearing the goggles, he never would have seen it. The goggles had picked up the faint light coming from the vent, and the smoke was silhouetted neatly over the illumination.

Bond bent down and examined the vent. It would be easy to pry off but that might make too much noise. He tried to budge one side of the grille, but it squeaked from the rust. Bond used some natural lubrication to loosen the vent—he spat on his fingers and ran them across the edges. Once they were moist, he tried again. This time, the grille pulled out of the wall with only a slight scraping sound.

The opening was big enough to squeeze through. He looked inside and saw a floor of carved stone. It was dimly lit, probably by candlelight. He listened to see if anyone was in there, then he slowly put his feet through and wormed his way into the shaft. He turned over onto his stomach, held on to the edge of the vent opening, and hung over the floor of the room. He let go and dropped to the ground.

He was in some kind of temple, he thought. There was a stone altar at the front of the room, and there were benches around the perimeter. The middle of the floor was empty. There was only one way out of the room, so Bond stepped lightly to the hanging curtains and listened.

Hearing nothing, Bond parted the curtains and looked out. It was a hallway, lit by a single burning torch mounted on the wall. If the inside of the *Persephone* looked old, it was nothing compared to the interior design of this place. Bond felt as if he were really walking through a building in ancient Greece.

Bond removed his goggles and let them hang around his neck. He drew the Walther and held it in his left hand—his right palm still hurt too much to handle the weapon effectively. He took a step at a time, watching and listening.

He came to a closed wooden door and listened. Silence.

Bond tried the handle. It clicked softly and the door opened.

It was another dim, empty stone room, except that a large equilateral triangle made of ten points was on the wall directly ahead. The points were made of little red light bulbs, all of them lit except the last three on top.

When Bond walked into the room, lights flashed on around him.

Eight men held Uzis trained on him from all sides. Konstantine Romanos stood at the top of a stone staircase to the left.

"Welcome to Anavatos, Mr. Bond," Romanos said.

▶25.
THE FACE OF DEATH

Bond was disarmed and then led through a series of stone corridors to a large dark space. Romanos flicked a switch and electric lamps made to look like torches illuminated the room. It was a missile launch pad. The Pershing 1a was mounted on an M656 transport truck, aimed at the ceiling. The double hatch in the ceiling was closed.

Besides Romanos, Bond counted eight armed guards, a man in a military uniform whom he surmised to be General Georgiou, and four women dressed in civilian clothes. One of the women was Hera Volopoulos. He recognized another as Melina Papas, who had a metal briefcase handcuffed to her wrist. It was identical to the case that Charles Hutchinson had brought from America.

"You have done my organization a considerable amount of damage, Mr. Bond," Romanos said. "You don't deserve to die quickly. In ancient Greece, criminals were often tortured in public. They were kept alive as long as possible so that their suffering would be prolonged. Unfortunately, I do not have the time to indulge myself with the pleasure of watching your agony. I have my orders from the gods. We must abandon our headquarters here in Anavatos. I am sure that by now the Greek military and secret service are on their way."

Another guard entered and whispered something to General Georgiou. The general then said something to Romanos in Greek.

"Ah, our transport has just arrived," Romanos said. He turned to one of the women and issued an order. She nodded and left the room.

"Mr. Bond, this is not the end of the Decada. We will regroup at another location and continue our path. We will, however, complete the task we began here so many months ago."

He gestured to the missile. "As you see, a Pershing. It's been missing from NATO for a long time. We happened to find it and we fit it with a warhead we got through our Russian friend, Number Four. The

Russian mafia drove a hard bargain, but we eventually got a good deal. As you may have guessed, it will detonate over Istanbul. This is a small price for the Turks to pay for northern Cyprus."

"It's just going to cause chaos all over Europe, Asia, and the Middle East!" Bond said.

Romanos nodded to the guards. They grabbed Bond and pulled him down onto a table. The men held him in place as Romanos flipped a switch on a control panel. Metal cuffs shot out of the table and snapped over Bond's ankles and wrists. He was now horizontal, helpless and vulnerable.

"Do you like puzzles, Mr. Bond?" Romanos asked. "My maths students like puzzles. Well, some of them do. I give them fiendishly diabolical puzzles on their exams. I enjoy games of chance, crosswords, riddles . . . but I truly love mathematical puzzles. How were you as a student, Mr. Bond?"

Bond just stared at him incredulously.

"Don't tell me," Romanos said. "You were kicked out of Eton, after which you went to a military school. I would bet that mathematics was not one of your strong subjects. Am I right?"

Bond closed his eyes. The man was indeed correct. Although he was adept at many, many things, Bond was not a mathematician.

Romanos stepped over to the missile and pointed to a panel on the base of the launcher.

"I imagine you possess the capability of stopping the launch if you had access to the controls. A man of your expertise has probably disarmed hundreds of bombs, haven't you? Surely you can stop a Pershing missile from launching? Do you see this panel? Inside are the launching controls, covered by a thin glass cover that serves as a safeguard. You see, this entire complex is armed with explosives."

He pointed to four egg-shaped devices mounted in the ceiling.

"They will go off if that glass cover is broken without following a certain procedure. You must deactivate the alarm system to get to the controls."

He took a notepad from his pocket and scribbled on it for a few seconds. He tore off the piece of paper and opened the launching mechanism panel, then carefully placed the notepaper inside and closed the panel.

Romanos looked at his watch and twisted a timer knob on the control board. He then indicated a switch. "When I flip this switch, the timer will start. In four minutes from that instant, you will be released from the table. In four more minutes, the doors on the ceiling will open and the missile will launch automatically. *However,* I've written down a puzzle on the piece of paper that's now inside the panel. The answer to the puzzle will tell you how to disarm the alarm system. Once you've done that, you'll then have however many seconds left to stop the launch. If you can get to those controls, you have my permission and blessing to stop the launch. This was the gods' idea, not mine. They admire you for some strange reason. They have shown mercy on you and have ordered me to give you this one, slim chance, however hopeless. It also amuses the hell out of me. Think you're up to it? By the way, the puzzle I've given you has taken my students anywhere from fifteen minutes to an hour to solve. That's why I'm confident that when five minutes is up, you'll be scrambling around on the outside of this missile and scratching your head like a primate."

General Georgiou said something to Romanos.

Romanos nodded and said, "Number Nine has been good enough to fly a helicopter here to pick us up. We must go. One last thing. Alfred Hutchinson was never a member of the Decada. Manville Duncan obtained the copy of his disk and gave it to us, of course. Alfred was an old fool. He could have been my partner. We could have become rich together and perhaps ruled a country or two. Instead he chose to expose us and betray me. If he hadn't, you might have been spared all of this. Goodbye, Mr. Bond. May the gods . . . have mercy on your soul."

With that, he placed his hand on the timer switch.

"Wait!" It was Hera. She was pointing a handgun at Romanos. Bond recognized it as the Daewoo he had seen her use before. Five of the armed guards aimed their weapons at the other guards. Melina Papas stood away from General Georgiou and the others.

Romanos was confused. "Number Two?"

"The gods have given me orders too, Konstantine. The Decada has benefited greatly from your leadership. You supplied us with money, equipment, contacts, and a plan to make ourselves heard round the world. But as Pythagoras himself knew, it was possible that some followers might have other plans. Your leadership ends here, Konstantine.

You are no longer the Monad. The True Decada is born here and now."

"Hera, you fool, what are you talking about?"

The gun went off, wounding him in the shoulder. Romanos fell back onto the concrete floor, clutching his bloody arm.

General Georgiou lunged at Hera, but one of the guards turned to him and fired an AK-47. Bullets riddled the general's body, knocking him lifeless next to Romanos.

The other Decada members cowered against the wall. Hera turned to them. "You others can join me if you like. If not, you die here with him."

Eyes wide, they nodded their heads furiously.

"Then go and get into the helicopter." They complied, running outside, escorted by two guards. Melina Papas remained with Hera.

Hera walked over to Romanos and stood over him. She pointed the gun at his right leg and fired again. He yelled and bent over in agony.

Bond, helpless on the table, watched in fascination and horror.

Hera squatted beside Romanos and tenderly stroked his sweating head. "I once knew a little girl," she said. "She was only twelve years old. Her parents were killed by Turks in Cyprus when she was nine. For two years she lived on the streets and fended for herself in an extremely hostile world. Then, one day, she met a man. He was two decades older than she was, but he was very handsome. He had a magical way of speaking. He became a father to her. He promised to rescue her, to take her away to his land and teach her about life. And that he did . . . while he kept her a prisoner for ten years. It's true that he taught her many things and fed her and clothed her and took care of her. But it's also true that he systematically *raped her for ten . . . long . . . years!*" Hera said it with venom.

"Hera," Romanos gasped. "I never meant it that way . . ."

She stood up and kicked Romanos hard in the face. Then, tenderly again, she said, "I thought I loved you once. You were so many things to me at so many different times . . . You were my torturer, you were my father. You were my brother, my lover, my teacher. I worshipped you!"

She kicked him again.

"We share many ideals," she continued. "I promised myself that I'd help you see the Decada's first *Tetraktys* through to the end, because I hate the Turks as much as you do. But what I hate even more is how you corrupted me. Now I'm taking back the life you took from me so many years ago in Cyprus. Hera, the queen of the gods, was always a vengeful deity. I'm taking over the Decada, for it's my destiny to do so. I see our role in the world as being far bigger and more profitable than you ever did. You taught me well. You made me what I am today, Konstantine. Remember that!"

Her voice began to tremble with rage. She aimed the pistol at his chest.

"You always pushed me to be the best—the best climber, the best fighter, the best assassin, the best *killer*... the best... lover... Well, it's no wonder I was a good pupil. After capturing me and breaking me, it was easy to teach me to hate and murder. Now I know no other way."

She paused and took a breath as tears rolled down her cheeks. "You taught me more about life than I ever cared to know, Konstantine. Now I'm going to teach you about death."

With that, she pointed the gun at his head and fired. Romanos's skull blew apart, spraying blood and tissue several feet around them.

After a long, tense silence, Bond said, "My God, Hera, you're madder than he was."

She turned and looked at him curiously, as if she had completely forgotten that he was in the room. Then Hera stared past Bond blankly, traumatized by the act she had just committed. Melina reached out and touched her arm. Hera turned to Melina and the two women embraced. The metal briefcase dangled awkwardly.

"What's in the case, Hera? The BioLinks virus?" Bond asked.

After a pause, Hera moved away from Melina. She had regained her composure, but she was a time bomb of nerves just waiting to explode. She replied, "We call it the Decada Virus. It was a project that the Monad began, but that we're going to finish. Melina here extensively studied the effects that ricin has on the human body. There is no antidote for ricin poisoning. She successfully created a chemical compound from the castor bean which acts like a virus. In other words, she has made the symptoms that one experiences with ricin poisoning infectious. The germ lives and breathes like bacteria. Once a person is infected with it, everyone they come in contact with will also become infected. People will die, one after another, very quickly—unless they're given the vaccine. Yes, there *is* a cure, which Melina also created, and we have all been inoculated."

She pointed to Melina's briefcase. "In there are several samples of the Decada Virus in protective tubes, as well as all the information we need to create more. The only samples of the vaccine and its formula are in there as well. That's why we don't want that case to leave Melina's wrist, do we? Melina, why don't you go on out to the helicopter. I'll be there in a minute."

The hawk-nosed woman nodded and left the room. Hera was now alone with Bond and the dead bodies around them.

Bond looked at her and said, "You've sent that virus to medical clinics all over the world, haven't you? Hidden in sperm samples!"

"You never cease to amaze me, James. You are indeed a clever and resourceful man. Yes, the virus is out there waiting, swimming around and just waiting to be injected into someone. We have people on the payroll in clinics all around the world. Their instructions were simply to transfer the material from the sperm to an available blood supply. Cities like New York, London, Los Angeles, Tokyo—boom—they're hit with a deadly epidemic. It's not pretty."

"Why, Hera? Because you were abused as a child? Because Romanos twisted your mind and turned you into a killer? That's not a reason to set off a chain reaction that will destory all human life on the planet!"

"That's not going to happen, James," she said with confidence. "Once the virus starts spreading like wildfire, I will announce to the world that BioLinks have developed a cure. The price to receive it, though, will be . . . very high. The deaths of millions of people will simply be the example of what the virus can do. In order to sell a product, you have to prove to the world that there is a need for it!"

"Don't you think there are biochemists in the world who are smart enough to study your virus and come up with their own vaccine?" Bond asked.

"Of course, but by then it will be too late," Hera said. "As we implement new *Tetraktys* strikes in different parts of the world, there will be rapidly increasing outbreaks of the virus. The nations of the world will have no choice but to quickly buy the only available vaccine—ours."

Bond shook his head. "So you're just another cheap extortionist. You're only in it for the money. I might have known."

"Goodbye, James," she said. "I think I'll leave you with Konstantine's little maths problem. He always did have a perverse sense of humor. Maybe you can at least stop a war between Greece and Turkey. But that seems so *insignificant* now, don't you think?"

With that, she flipped the switch to set the timer in motion, then turned and left the room. The door slammed shut and Bond was left alone.

A Huey UH-1 Iroquois helicopter sat on a landing pad that had been built on the summit of the cliff outside. The pad was actually the launch doors for the missile, which would open in less than eight minutes. Hera emerged from the lair into the night air and joined Melina Papas, the loyal guards, and the remaining Decada members aboard the helicopter.

Back in the launch room, sweat was pouring off Bond's face. No matter how hard he tried, he couldn't free himself from the manacles. He would just have to wait until the three minutes was up.

Where was the bloody Greek Army? How long was it going to take them to get there?

Bond's heart was pounding. It felt as if it would push right through his sternum. What was happening to him? Was this the end? Was this what happened when you knew you were going to die? They said that your life passed in front of your eyes when the moment of truth finally came. Bond had been close to death before, but somehow he felt that this time it was real. Had he been placed in a hopeless situation? Was that it? Was he subconsciously accepting the fact that no matter what he did in the next few minutes, it would all be over soon?

No! he cried to himself. Not this way! He would not let it end like this. He was not about to give up. If he died, then so be it. He had seen plenty of death in his lifetime, but he had also seen an enormous amount of life. He had beaten the grim reaper so many times before . . . why would he think that it would all end now?

The manacles suddenly sprang open. He was free.

Bond leaped to the missile and pried the control panel off with such force that he cut the ends of his fingers. A wire-cutting tool and the piece of paper fell out. Underneath he saw a glass panel covering a control panel and a single toggle switch that was obviously the abort button. On top of the glass was the booby trap—three colored wires, one red, one blue, and one white. One or more of them had to be cut before he could get to the controls. Bond grabbed the paper and read it. In English, it said:

PYTHAGORAS WAS FAMOUS FOR HIS THEOREM WHICH STATES THAT IN A RIGHT TRIANGLE, THE SUM OF THE SQUARES OF THE LEGS IS EQUAL TO THE SQUARE OF THE HYPOTENUSE. THE CONVERSE IS ALSO TRUE. IF THE LENGTHS OF THE SIDES OF A TRIANGLE ARE "A," "B," AND "C," WHERE "C" IS THE HYPOTENUSE AND $A^2 + B^2 = C^2$, THEN THE TRIANGLE IS A RIGHT TRIANGLE. SO IF A TRIANGLE HAS SIDES 3, 4, AND 5, IT IS A RIGHT TRIANGLE, SINCE $3^2 + 4^2 = 5^2$ (9 + 16 = 25). FURTHERMORE, IF $A^2 + B^2$ DOES NOT EQUAL C^2, THEN THE TRIANGLE IS NOT A RIGHT TRIANGLE.

LET'S SAY YOU HAVE SIDES OF LENGTHS 17, 144, AND 163. DOES THIS FORM AN ACUTE, RIGHT, OR OBTUSE TRIANGLE?

CLIP THE RED WIRE IF YOUR ANSWER IS "ACUTE."

CLIP THE BLUE WIRE IF YOUR ANSWER IS "RIGHT."

CLIP THE WHITE WIRE IF YOUR ANSWER IS "OBTUSE."

YOU HAVE FOUR MINUTES. GOOD LUCK!

▶26.
THE WORLD IS NOT ENOUGH

The clock had ticked away forty-five seconds.

Bond stared at the puzzle in horror. It *was* impossible to solve in two minutes! He searched the depths of his brain to recall what he knew about the Pythagorean theorem. If it was a right angle triangle, the square of the sums of two sides must equal the square of the hypotenuse. Bond could mentally calculate that 17 squared was 289, but there was no way that he could calculate the squares of 144 and 163 in the time available.

There had to be a trick to this. Why would Romanos simply pose a routine problem made difficult because Bond had no calculator? It must be a logic puzzle, not a math problem. Did he have the time to think it through? Or should he gamble with life and death by selecting a wire and cutting it? How could he decide which wire to cut? Had his entire life come down to a flip of the coin?

Sixty seconds had elapsed. He had three more minutes to stop the missile.

Wait! What was it Romanos had said about "assumption"? It was at the casino in Athens. He had said that a mathematician begins with assumptions and must provide the proof from there. What was the puzzle's question again?

LET'S SAY YOU HAVE SIDES OF LENGTHS 17, 144, AND 163. DOES THIS FORM AN ACUTE, RIGHT, OR OBTUSE TRIANGLE?

The problem didn't actually say that the sides were part of a triangle. The question was what kind of triangle would be formed with the sides of 17, 144, and 163. Bond had been *assuming* that the lengths formed a triangle. The correct answer was that *it wouldn't be a triangle at all!* For a triangle to exist, the sum of the lengths of any two sides must exceed the length of the third side. In this case, $17 + 144 = 161$, which was not greater than 163.

Bond knew then that he should not cut any of the three wires. With one minute left to go, he made a fist and plunged it into the thin glass panel. The controls were at his fingertips.

Forty-five seconds . . .

He flipped the toggle switch and the timer stopped. All of the blinking lights around the control panel shut off. The missile was lifeless. A viewscreen indicated that the detonator was disengaged from the nuclear core. The conventional explosives in the warhead could still ignite, but critical mass could never be achieved.

Bond took a deep breath and slid down to the floor. Romanos had underestimated his ability to make a decision by making no decision. He thought wryly that it had been more of a Descartes-like action than a Pythagorean one, because it was Descartes who once said, "Not to decide is to decide."

He heard a loud boom on a floor below him. It sounded like an explosive demolishing a door. Bond got up and ran to the only exit from the room. Outside he could hear running footsteps and men speaking Greek. He pulled back the bolt and opened the door. Three Greek soldiers turned and pointed M16 rifles at him.

Bond held up his hands. "Don't shoot!"

"Mr. Bond?" one of them, a sergeant, asked.

"Yes."

"Let's go. We get you out."

Bond followed them out of the door in the nick of time, for the explosives inside the launch pad room went off full force. Bond and the three men were thrown several feet by the blast, and the stone walls around them began to crumble.

"Go! Go! Go!" the sergeant shouted.

The four men jumped up and kept on running. Another explosion went off near them, but by then they had made it into the Decada's conference room.

"What's the quickest way to the surface?" Bond asked. "The whole place is going to blow."

"This way," the sergeant said. He led them out of the conference room, through the control room, and up a flight of stairs, just ahead of more explosions below them. The steps fell apart as they climbed. They navigated around a ten-foot statue of the god Ares and entered a passageway that was shaking. Before they could get through it, a huge explosion rocked the entire structure. The walls, floor, and ceiling cracked open, leaving a gap of seven feet between them and the other side of the passageway.

"What now?" a soldier asked.

Bond looked back at the statue. "Help me with this thing!" He ran to it and started to push. The other men got the idea and helped tilt it over onto the ground. Together they shoved the statue across the gap, creating a bridge. One by one they crossed to the other side.

They reached the secret hatch to the outside world just as another explosion sent flames shooting up toward them from below. The men rolled out of the complex and could feel the heat as the entire mountain trembled.

More soldiers were outside. A lieutenant approached the sergeant and spoke rapidly in Greek. Bond caught the words "helicopter" and "Decada."

The sergeant turned to Bond and said, "We can still catch them if we hurry."

"What are we waiting for?" Bond asked.

They ran to the UH-60 Blackhawk helicopter that had landed on the same launch pad Hera had taken off from. They piled into the aircraft and it rose into the air.

The Blackhawk is one of many American-made machines that the Greek military have bought. It is equipped with an External Stores Support System, which includes the carriage and live firing of the Hellfire anti-armor missile. If they could catch up with Hera, the ensuing dogfight would be in their favor.

Once they were airborne, Bond asked the sergeant, "How is your agent, Niki Mirakos?"

"She will be fine," he said. "Her leg wasn't broken, but the knee was twisted badly. She will be on crutches for a while. She might need some surgery—it's too early to tell."

"What about the Decada? Where are they headed? They have a briefcase that must be retrieved."

"They took off toward the mainland ten minutes ago. We've alerted all bases between here and there to intercept them."

Bond took a moment to look around the cabin of the helicopter. There were three Stinger missiles with one-man portable launchers attached to the side of the craft. He immediately unfastened the harness on one and removed it. He realized that the sergeant was staring at him incredulously, so he asked, "May I?"

The sergeant shrugged and said, "Be our guest."

A radio communication came through, and the sergeant translated. "One of our Apaches has engaged the target three miles ahead."

They were there in a minute. In the dark, Bond could see only the streams of fire coming from the machine guns on the Huey and the AH-64 Apache. The Greeks' helicopter was at a slightly higher altitude, pursuing Hera's helicopter at top speed.

The Huey UH-1 was another American-made helicopter that was used extensively in the Vietnam War. Its 1,400-horsepower engine sat over the cabin instead of filling up the body, leaving plenty of room for troops or cargo. It was armed with machine guns, rockets, and grenades, and could cruise at 125 miles per hour.

Suddenly a bright streak shot from the Huey and hit the Apache, which exploded into a fireball. Hera apparently had missiles of her own.

"Now it's just us," the sergeant said. He gave an order over the radio for the backup units to hurry up.

Bond slung the Stinger launcher over his shoulder and got it ready to fire. "If you can get me in position, I'll hit them with this." He had to cripple the helicopter without completely destroying it. Hopefully, the metal briefcase would survive intact.

The Huey climbed, slowed down, and positioned itself above their Blackhawk.

"They're going to drop mines! Evasive action!" Bond shouted. The sergeant translated the order into Greek, and the pilot flung the aircraft into a dive as a volley of mines poured out of the Huey.

Then the Huey's turrets went into action, battering their vehicle with bullets. One man was hit in the face. Blood splattered in all directions as he was thrown back against the cabin wall.

The pilot managed to get the helicopter side by side with Hera. Bond thought he could see her next to the pilot, but it was too dark to tell. It looked like Melina Papas was behind her, issuing orders to men in the back.

One of the Greeks' other Apaches entered the arena from the other side, assaulting the enemy with a volley of turret fire. The Huey wavered, then lost height. Bond's pilot attempted to follow, but it was a maneuver meant to trick the Greeks. As soon as they were even with the enemy, someone in the Huey launched another missile.

"Evasive action!" the sergeant shouted.

The Blackhawk swerved awkwardly, but it wasn't enough to avoid the weapon entirely. It skimmed the bottom struts, blowing them off. The helicopter went wildly out of control.

"We're going down!" the sergeant yelled in English.

Bond stepped into the open doorway of the helicopter and aimed the Stinger at Hera's Huey. They were rapidly falling away from the target.

By God, Bond thought. He was going to hit Hera before they crashed if it was the last thing he did.

"Ask the pilot to try and keep the helicopter steady for just a moment!" Bond said to the sergeant. "Then hold on to my belt!"

The helicopter was losing height at a frightening pace. No one was sure if there was land or water below.

The pilot managed to get the Blackhawk back under some sort of control, but the aircraft was still rocking and falling.

"This is the best you're going to get," the sergeant told Bond.

Bond nodded and took a bead on the enemy Huey. He straightened his body and pivoted backward out of the opening, putting his trust in the sergeant to keep him from falling. Bond aimed directly at the Huey's cockpit and fired the missile. The Stinger shot off with a loud *whizzzzz* and a flash of bright light, just clearing the Blackhawk's rotor blades.

The missile hit the Huey dead on target. Bond winced when it exploded into a fireball brighter than the sun on a summer's day. He prayed that the fireproofed briefcase could be recovered.

The Huey plummeted ten thousand feet and crashed into the

sea. Another explosion completely demolished it, sending all of its occupants to a dark and watery grave.

"Welcome to Hades, Hera," Bond said to himself.

The Blackhawk's pilot was having great difficulty keeping his craft in the air. It was inevitable that they would crash into the ocean too. Their only hope was that the pilot could keep the copter level so that the impact wouldn't destroy the ship and everyone in it. One man began to distribute life jackets.

There was a tremendous noise as the Blackhawk hit the water. Everyone inside was flung in different directions, but the aircraft didn't break apart. Water began to pour into the ship, and someone shouted, "Out! Everyone out!"

Bond followed the other men out of the hatch into the cold, dark water. He surfaced and saw that they had all made it, but the Blackhawk was sinking rapidly. The other wreckage was still floating on the water in flames, which provided a surprising amount of illumination. Much of the murky water was well lit.

The life jacket kept Bond afloat, but he was able to dive and swim underneath the Blackhawk. He saw a lot of debris floating down to the bottom of the sea. There were two bodies—guards—just beginning to float back up. Bond surfaced, took a breath, then continued his search for Melina Papas's body. He saw a body in a tattered dress entangled in the struts of the sinking hulk. Bond swam to it and discovered it was one of the other Decada women. Most of her skin had been burned away.

Bond removed his life jacket and tied it to the strut, decreasing his buoyancy. He dived underneath the wreck again, pushed away the metal panels and tried to get inside. The flames were intense, but he forced himself to think of nothing but the metal briefcase. Too many lives were at stake.

He crawled into what was left of the burning hull and found three bodies, all charred and grotesquely mangled. The metal briefcase was handcuffed to the wrist of one. Bond held his breath and put his arms around the warm, wet body. He hauled her out of the wreckage and into the water, picked up his life jacket, and surfaced for air. After putting on the jacket, he draped Melina's body over his shoulder and began to swim away from the floating sepulchre.

He saw some of the Greeks swimming several yards ahead of him.

One of them shot off a flare into the sky, brightly illuminating the entire area. The water was rough and choppy, and Bond had a difficult time keeping afloat. He grabbed a bobbing piece of the aircraft and hung on to it, allowing it to carry him slowly toward the others.

Bond was just beginning to catch his breath when he was startled by the sudden appearance of a revolting, black, burned face. Hera, or what was left of her, broke the surface next to Bond. She looked like a demon from hell. Her red hair was completely gone, replaced by rolls of sliced, viscous flesh. One remaining eye bulged and her mouth was frozen in a silent scream. Sickened, Bond reached out to push the corpse away, but it suddenly came alive. Hera screamed and threw her hands around Bond's neck. The fright caused him to let go of Melina's body.

Bond fought her hard, kicking the mangled creature. She was grappling with all her might to bring him down. He chopped her in the neck with as much force as he could exert, then punched her in the face. The flesh on her cheek felt crusty and wet. She screamed again, and the vise around his neck loosened. Bond broke away, then lunged for her waist. Once he had a good hold on her, he shoved her head underwater and held it there. Hera struggled like a moray eel, but her wounds had taken their toll. She slowly weakened, and finally went limp after a couple of agonizing minutes. Bond let her go, and Hera Volopoulos sank to the bottom of the sea.

He then dived to retrieve Melina Papas again. She hadn't drifted far. He grabbed the body once again and swam with it, and the briefcase, toward the other men.

They bobbed in the water for fifteen minutes before another helicopter arrived to rescue them.

The Decada's headquarters on Anavatos were destroyed. Very little trace of their organization was left. Several burned bodies were recovered from the sea the next morning—three female skeletons and at least ten males. In the final reports filed by the Greek National Intelligence Service and the Greek military and by Bond, it was assumed that all of the members of the Decada had been killed.

The briefcase had indeed remained intact. The National Intelligence Service took possession of it and successfully opened it without releasing the deadly substance inside. It was immediately sent to a biochemistry lab in Athens so that the vaccine could be reproduced in quantity. Within twenty-four hours, hundreds of vials of the vaccine were on their way to the infected cities. One hundred and fifteen people had died in New York, 212 in Tokyo, and 186 in Los Angeles. Athens, London, and Paris had the least number of casualties—less than 60 in each city. It could have been far worse. In a week, the virus would have raged out of control and hundreds would have died, possibly thousands. Although it would be some time before anyone could be sure that the disease was totally contained, the authorities felt confident that they were off to a good start. The virus itself was sent to the Centers for Disease Control in Atlanta for study and breakdown.

Two days later, James Bond and Niki Mirakos lay in the king-sized bed in his suite at the Grande Bretagne in Athens. They had just eaten a basket of fruit and drunk two bottles of ouzo. Her leg was in a cast, but otherwise she was completely naked.

Bond glanced at his watch. "I have to call M."

He slipped out of bed and walked naked into the sitting room. He dialed the number and went through the routine security checks.

"Double-O Seven?" M sounded extremely pleased to hear from him.

"Yes, ma'am."

"You're right on time. I just received your report. Well done."

"Thank you, ma'am."

"Is the Greek agent badly injured?"

"It's not too bad," Bond said. "She had a bit of knee surgery. She'll be fine in a few weeks."

"That's good to hear," she said. "By the way, we all had a little surprise this morning."

"Oh?"

"The Turkish Republic of Northern Cyprus officially thanked the Republic of Cyprus and Greece for their roles in stopping the Decada. It was an unprecedented gesture."

"Amazing."

"Perhaps this will eventually lead to a new era of peace and cooperation between the two sides."

Bond was doubtful, but he said, "Let's hope so."

Then there was a pause which said volumes to Bond. She was dying to hear anything at all about Alfred Hutchinson.

"Ma'am, you'll be happy to know that Alfred Hutchinson was never a member of the Decada," Bond said. "He did once have an illegal and clandestine operation going with Romanos, until his conscience got the better of him. He was trying to do the right thing in the end. I hope that information brings you some comfort."

"Thank you, James," she said.

She rarely called him James during what was, for all intents and purposes, a business talk. Bond thought she was beginning to act like old Sir Miles after all.

"James," she said, "I want to tell you again how much I appreciate what you've done on this case."

"Don't mention it, ma'am."

"Nevertheless, you helped me through this. Thank you."

Bond hung up and went back into the bedroom. He poured some freshly squeezed orange juice for both of them, then propped a pillow up against the wall and sat on the bed. He stretched out his legs, and stared out of the window at the Acropolis in the distance.

After a minute of silence, Niki said, "What is it, James?"

Bond shrugged and shook his head, attempting to smile.

She took his hand and said, "It's probably none of my business, but I think I know what it is."

"Oh?"

"You've become jaded. The mission is over and you're not looking forward to going back to your existence between assignments. I know how you feel, James. It's like withdrawal from a drug. The threat of death hanging over you is what really makes you tick. Without it, you're unhappy. My advice to you is to try and enjoy *life* too."

Bond pulled her close and kissed her. Then he said, "But the world is not enough."

"What?"

"That's the motto on my family crest. 'The World Is Not Enough.' "

She laughed gently. "It fits you perfectly."

"It's a curse, that's what it is."

"James, you're entitled to feel that way. You are not like other men. You are human, but you have done superhuman things. All men know the facts of life, but you know just as much about the facts of death! You have thwarted Death many times. Someone once said that no man's a god. I'm not so sure that's true. Unlike Konstantine Romanos, you *are* a god."

Bond laughed.

She laughed with him. "No, really! In ancient Greece, men would have proclaimed you to be a god. You would have been another Jason or an Agamemnon or even an Alexander the Great. There would be statues of you on display throughout the country and in museums!"

Bond pushed her face into the pillow. They wrestled playfully for a few seconds, then became still and quiet. Bond knew that even though he had thwarted Death many times, he had come to think of him as an old friend. Without Death standing behind him, scythe in hand and breathing down his neck, life was just a dreadful bore.

She pulled him to her gently. He turned and snuggled closer to her, wrapping his leg around her and pressing his loins into her thigh.

"Mmmm," she said, as she pulled his body directly on top of hers. She reached down and held him. "I must add that what you know about the facts of *life* is pretty impressive too!"

Bond became aroused for the third time since they awoke. "I never told you before, but you're one hell of a helicopter pilot, did you know that?" he said.

She grinned mischievously. "It's just a question of knowing how to get it up."

About the Author

Raymond Benson is the author of *The James Bond Bedside Companion*, which was nominated for an Edgar Allan Poe Award for Best Biographical/Critical work and is considered by 007 fans to be a definitive work on the world of James Bond. He is the author of the James Bond adventure *Zero Minus Ten* and the James Bond movie novelization *Tomorrow Never Dies,* based on the screenplay by Bruce Feirstein. Mr. Benson is a director of The Ian Fleming Foundation and served as vice president of the American James Bond 007 Fan Club for several years. He is also the designer and writer of several award-winning interactive software products, and spent over a decade in New York City directing stage productions and composing music. He has taught film theory classes at The New School for Social Research in New York and a course called "Interactive Screenwriting" at Columbia College in Chicago. Mr. Benson is married, has one son, and lives in the Chicago area.